BROTHERBAND

HAVE YOU READ
JOHN FLANAGAN'S

SERIES?

BROTHERBAND

THE OUTCASTS

JOHN FLANAGAN

CORGI YEARLING

BROTHERBAND: THE OUTCASTS
A CORGI YEARLING BOOK 978 0 440 86992 4

Published in Great Britain by Corgi Yearling,
an imprint of Random House Children's Publishers UK
A Penguin Random House Company

Penguin
Random House
UK

Originally published in Australia by Random House Australia (Pty)
The Bodley Head edition published 2011
This Corgi Yearling edition published 2012

3 5 7 9 10 8 6 4

Copyright © John Flanagan, 2014
Cover art copyright © Shane Rebenschied, 2014. Back cover photo by Shutterstock.com
Cover design by Tony Sahara
Heron illustration by David Elliot

The right of John Flanagan to be identified as the author of this work has been
asserted in accordance with the Copyright, Designs and Patents Act 1988.

All rights reserved. No part of this publication may be reproduced,
stored in a retrieval system, or transmitted in any form or by any means,
electronic, mechanical, photocopying, recording or otherwise,
without the prior permission of the publishers.

Penguin Random House is committed to a sustainable future for our business,
our readers and our planet. This book is made from Forest Stewardship
Council® certified paper.

MIX
Paper from
responsible sources
FSC® C018179

Set in 12/15pt Caslon Classico by Midland Typesetters, Australia

Corgi Yearling Books are published by Random House Children's Publishers UK,
61–63 Uxbridge Road, London W5 5SA

www.**randomhousechildrens**.co.uk
www.**randomhouse**.co.uk

Addresses for companies within The Random House Group Limited can be found at:
www.randomhouse.co.uk/offices.htm

THE RANDOM HOUSE GROUP Limited Reg. No. 954009

A CIP catalogue record for this book is available from the British Library.

Printed and bound in Great Britain by Clays Ltd, St Ives plc

Dedicated to our own Brotherband,
Max, Konan, Alex and Henry.

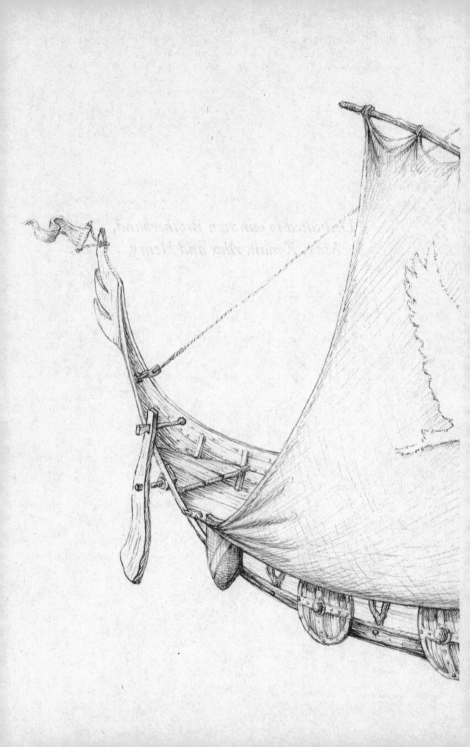

A FEW SAILING TERMS EXPLAINED

Because this book involves sailing ships, I thought it might be useful to explain a few of the nautical terms that are to be found in the story.

Be reassured that I haven't gone overboard (to keep up the nautical allusion) with technical details in the book, and even if you're not familiar with sailing, I'm sure you'll understand what's going on. But a certain amount of sailing terminology is necessary for the story to feel realistic.

So, here we go, in no particular order.

Bow: The front of the ship, also called the **prow**.

Stern: The rear of the ship.

Port and starboard: The left and right sides of the ship, as you're facing the bow. In fact, I'm probably incorrect in using the term 'port'. The early term for port was 'larboard', but I thought we'd all get confused if I used that.

Starboard was a corruption of 'steering board' (or steering side). The steering oar was always placed on the right-hand side of the ship.

Consequently, when a ship came into port it would moor with the left side against the jetty, to avoid damage to the steering oar. One theory says the word derived from the ship's being in port — left side to the jetty. I suspect, however, that it might have come from the fact that the entry port, by which crew and passengers boarded, was also always on the left side.

How do you remember which side is which? Easy. Port and left both have four letters.

Forward: Towards the bow.

Aft: Towards the stern.

Fore and aft rig: A sail plan where the sail is in line with the hull of the ship.

Hull: The body of the ship.

Keel: The spine of the ship.

Steering oar: The blade used to control the ship's direction, mounted on the starboard side of the ship, at the stern.

Tiller: The handle for the steering oar.

Beam: The side of the ship. If the wind is abeam, it is coming from the side, at a right angle to the ship's keel.

Yardarm or yard: A spar (wooden pole) that is hoisted up the mast, carrying the sail.

Masthead: The top of the mast.

Bulwark: The part of the ship's side above the deck.

Gunwale: The upper part of the ship's rail.

Belaying pins: Wooden pins used to fasten rope.

Oarlock or rowlock: The pegs that hold the oar in place.

Telltale: A pennant that indicates the wind's direction.

Tacking: To tack is to change direction from one side to the other, passing through the eye of the wind.

If the wind is from the north and you want to sail north-east, you would perform one tack so that you were heading north-east, and you could continue to sail on that tack for as long as you needed to.

However, if the wind is from the north and you want to sail due north, you would have to do so in a series of short tacks, going back and forth on a zig-zag course, crossing through the wind each time, and slowly making ground to the north. This is a process known as **beating** into the wind.

Wearing: When a ship tacks, it turns *into* the wind to change direction. When it wears, it turns *away* from the wind, travelling in a much larger arc, with the wind in the sail, driving the ship around throughout the manoeuvre. This was a safer way of changing direction for wolfships.

Reach or reaching: When the wind is from the side of the ship, the ship is sailing on a reach, or reaching.

Running: When the wind is from the stern, the ship is running. So would you if the wind was strong enough.

Reef: To gather in part of the sail and bundle it against the yardarm to reduce the sail area. This is done in high winds to protect the sail and mast.

Trim: To adjust the sail to the most efficient angle.

Halyard: A rope used to haul the yard up the mast (haul-yard, get it?).

Stay: A heavy rope that supports the mast. The **back-stay** and **forestay** are heavy ropes running from the top of the mast to the stern and bow (it's pretty obvious which is which).

Sheets and shrouds: A lot of people think these are sails, which is a logical assumption. But in fact, they're ropes. Shrouds are thick ropes that run from the top of the mast to the side of the ship, supporting the mast. Sheets are the ropes used to control or trim the sail — to haul it in and out according to the wind strength and direction. In an emergency, the order might be given to 'let fly the sheets!'. The sheets would be released, letting the sail loose and bringing the ship to a halt. (If *you* were to let fly the sheets, you'd probably fall out of bed.)

Way: The motion of the ship. If a ship is under way, it is moving. If it is making leeway, the wind is blowing it downwind so it loses ground.

Back water: To row a reverse stroke.

So, now you know all you need to know about sailing terms, welcome aboard the world of *Brotherband*!

John Flanagan

PART ONE

THE
PROMISE

PART ONE

THE
PROMISE

CHAPTER ONE

Twelve years prior

Wolfwind emerged from the pre-dawn sea mist like a wraith slowly taking physical form.

With her sail furled and the yardarm lowered to the deck, and propelled by only four of her oars, the wolfship glided slowly towards the beach. The four rowers wielded their oars carefully, raising them only a few centimetres from the water at the end of each stroke so that the noise of drops splashing back into the sea was kept to a minimum. They were Erak's most experienced oarsmen and they were used to the task of approaching an enemy coast stealthily.

And during raiding season, all coasts were enemy coasts.

Such was their skill that the loudest sound was the lap-lap-lap of small ripples along the wooden hull. In the bow, Svengal and two other crew members crouched fully armed, peering ahead to catch sight of the dim line where the water met the beach.

The lack of surf might make their approach easier but a little extra noise would have been welcome, Svengal thought. Plus white water would have made the line of the beach easier to spot in the dimness. Then he saw the beach and held up his hand, fist clenched.

Far astern, at the steering oar, Erak watched his second in command as he revealed five fingers, then four, then three as he measured off the distance to the sand.

'In oars.'

Erak spoke the words in a conversational tone, unlike the bellow he usually employed to pass orders. In the centre section of the wolfship, his bosun, Mikkel, relayed the orders. The four oars lifted out of the water as one, rising quickly to the vertical so that any excess water would fall into the ship and not into the sea, where it would make more noise. A few seconds later, the prow of the ship grated softly against the sand. Erak felt the vibrations of the gentle contact with the shore through the deck beneath his feet.

Svengal and his two companions vaulted over the bow, landing cat-like on the wet sand. Two of them moved up the beach, fanning out to scan the country on either side, ready to give warning of any possible ambush. Svengal took the small beach anchor that another sailor lowered to him. He stepped twenty paces up the beach, strained against the anchor rope to bring it tight and drove the shovel-shaped fluke into the firm sand.

Wolfwind, secured by the bow, slewed a little to one side under the pressure of the gentle breeze.

'Clear left!'

'Clear right!'

The two men who had gone onshore called their reports now. There was no need for further stealth. Svengal checked his own area of responsibility, then added his report to theirs.

'Clear ahead.'

On board, Erak nodded with satisfaction. He hadn't expected any sort of armed reception on the beach but it always paid to make sure. That was why he had been such a successful raider over the years – and why he had lost so few of his crewmen.

'All right,' he said, lifting his shield from the bulwark and hefting it onto his left arm. 'Let's go.'

He quickly strode the length of the wolfship to the bow, where a boarding ladder had been placed over the side. Shoving his heavy battleaxe through the leather sling on his belt, he climbed easily over the bulwark and down to the beach. His crewmen followed, forming up behind him. There was no need for orders. They had all done this before, many times.

Svengal joined him. 'No sign of anyone here, chief,' he reported.

Erak grunted. 'Neither should there be. They should all be busy at Alty Bosky.'

He pronounced the name in his usual way – careless of the finer points of Iberian pronunciation. The town in question was actually Alto Bosque, a relatively unimportant market town some ten kilometres to the south, built on the high, wooded hill from which it derived its name.

The previous day, seven of his crew had taken the skiff and landed there, carrying out a lightning raid on the market before they retreated to the coast. Alto Bosque had no garrison and a rider from the town had been sent to Santa Sebilla, where a small force of militia was maintained. Erak's plan was to draw the garrison away to Alto Bosque while he and his men plundered Santa Sebilla unhindered.

Santa Sebilla was a small town, too. Probably smaller than Alto Bosque. But, over the years, it had gained an enviable reputation for the quality of the jewellery that was designed and crafted here. As time went on, more and more artisans and designers were drawn to Santa Sebilla and it became a centre for fine design and craftsmanship in gold and precious stones.

Erak, like most Skandians, cared little for fine design and craftsmanship. But he cared a lot about gold and he knew there was a disproportionate amount of it in Santa Sebilla — far more than would normally be found in a small town such as this. The community of artists and designers needed generous supplies of the raw materials in which they worked — gold and silver and gemstones. Erak was a fervent believer in the principle of redistribution of wealth, as long as a great amount of it was redistributed in his direction, so he had planned this raid in detail for some weeks.

He checked behind him. The anchor watch of four men were standing by the bow of *Wolfwind*, guarding it while the main party went inland. He nodded, satisfied that everything was ready.

'Send your scouts ahead,' he told Svengal. The second in command gestured to the two men to go ahead of the main raiding party.

The beach rose gradually to a low line of scrubby bushes and trees. The scouts ran to this line, surveyed the country beyond, then beckoned the main party forward. The ground was flat here but, some kilometres inland, a range of low hills rose from the plain. The first rose-coloured rays of the sun were beginning to show about the peaks. They were behind schedule, Erak thought. He had wanted to reach the town before sun-up, while people were still drowsy and longing for their beds, as yet reluctant to accept the challenges of a new day.

'Let's pace it up,' he said tersely and the group settled into a steady jog behind him, moving in two columns. The scouts continued to range some fifty metres in advance of the raiding party. Erak could already see that there was nowhere a substantial party of armed men could remain hidden. Still, it did no harm to be sure.

Waved forward by the scouts, they crested a low rise and there, before them, stood Santa Sebilla.

The buildings were made of clay bricks, finished in whitewash. Later in the day, under the hot Iberian sun, they would glisten and gleam an almost blinding white. In the pre-dawn light they looked dull and grey and mundane. The town had been built with no particular plan in mind, instead growing over the years so that houses and warehouses were placed wherever their owners chose to build them. The result was a chaotic mass of winding alleys, outlying buildings and twisting, formless streets. But Erak ignored the jumble of houses and shops. He was looking for the repository — a large building set to one side of the town, where the gold and jewels were stored.

And there it was. Larger than the other buildings, with a substantial brass-bound wooden door. Normally, Erak knew, there would be a guard in place. But it seemed his diversion had achieved the result he wanted and the local militia were absent. The only possible resistance could come from a small castle set on a cliff a kilometre away from the town itself. There would possibly be armed men there. But the castle was the home of a minor Iberian nobleman and its location here was a mere coincidence. Knowing the snobbish and superior nature of the Iberian nobility, Erak guessed that the castle lord and his people had as little to do with the common tradesmen of Santa Sebilla as possible. They might buy from them, but they wouldn't mix with them or be eager to protect them in an emergency.

They headed for the repository. As they passed a side street, a sleepy townsman emerged, leading a donkey loaded with what seemed to be an impossibly heavy stack of firewood. For a few seconds, head down and still half asleep, the man failed to notice the force of grim-faced, armed sea wolves. Then his eyes snapped open, his jaw followed suit and he froze in place, staring at them. From the corner of his eye, Erak saw two of his men start to detach from the main body. But the firewood seller could do them little harm.

'Leave him,' he ordered and the men dropped back into line.

Galvanised by the sound of Erak's voice, the man dropped the donkey's halter and took off back into the narrow alleyway from which he had emerged. They heard the soft sound of his bare feet flapping on the hard earth as he put as much distance between himself and the raiders as he could.

'Get that door open,' Erak ordered.

Mikkel and Thorn stepped forward. Mikkel, whose preferred weapon was a sword, borrowed an axe from one of the other sea wolves and together, he and Thorn attacked the heavy door. They were Erak's two most reliable warriors, and he nodded appreciatively at the economy of effort with which they reduced the door to matchwood, placing alternate axe strokes precisely where they would do the most good, each building on the damage the other had caused.

The two men were best friends. They always fought together in the shield wall, each trusting the other to protect his back and sides. Yet they were a contrast in body shapes. Mikkel was taller and leaner than the average Skandian. But he was powerful and hard muscled. And he had the reflexes of a cat.

Thorn was slightly shorter than his friend, but much wider in the shoulders and chest. He was one of the most skilled and dangerous warriors Erak had ever seen. Erak often thought that he would hate to come up against Thorn in battle. He'd never seen an opponent who had survived such an encounter. Belying his heavy build, Thorn could also move with blinding speed when he chose.

Erak roused himself from his musing as the door fell in two shattered halves.

'Get the gold,' he ordered and his men surged forward.

It took them half an hour to load the gold and silver into sacks. They took only as much as they could carry and they left easily the same amount behind.

Maybe another time, Erak thought, although he knew no subsequent raid would be as easy or as bloodless as this one. In retrospect, he wished he'd caught hold of the firewood seller's donkey. The little animal could have carried more of the gold back to the ship for them.

The town was awake now and nervous faces peered at them from behind windows and around street corners. But these were not warriors and none were willing to face the fierce-looking men from the north. Erak nodded, satisfied, as the last of his men, each laden with two small but heavy sacks, emerged from the repository. He breathed a small sigh of satisfaction. It had been easy, he thought. Easier than he had expected.

Laden as they were, they couldn't maintain their previous jog as they followed the path through the scrubby undergrowth back to the beach. At least a dozen of the townspeople followed them, as if unwilling to let their gold and jewels simply disappear from sight. But they kept their distance, watching in impotent fury as the sea wolves carried away their booty.

'Thorn, Mikkel, bring up the rear. Let me know if there's any change,' Erak said. It would be all too easy to become complacent about the men shadowing their footsteps, and so miss any new threat that might arise.

The two men nodded and handed their sacks of loot to other crewmembers, then faded to the back of the column.

They marched some twenty metres behind the main party, turning continually to keep the following townspeople in sight. Once, Thorn faked a charge at a couple who he felt had come too close, and they scampered hurriedly back to a safe distance.

'Rabbits,' said Mikkel dismissively.

Thorn grinned and was about to reply when he caught sight of movement behind the straggle of townspeople. His grin faded.

'Looks like we've got some rabbits on horseback,' he said. The two raiders stopped to face the rear.

Trotting towards them, following the rough track through the undergrowth, were five horsemen. The newly risen sun gleamed off their armour and the points of the spears they all carried. They were still some distance behind the raiders but they were coming up fast. The two companions could hear the faint jingle of their horses' harness and their equipment.

Thorn glanced back to the main party of raiders. They were about to enter a narrow defile that led down to the last stretch of open ground to the beach. He let out a piercing whistle and saw Erak stop and look back. The rest of the party continued to move as quickly as they could.

Thorn pointed to the riders. Uncertain whether Erak could see the new enemy, he held up his right hand, with five fingers extended, then brought it down in a clenched fist close by his shoulder — the signal for 'enemy'. He pointed again to the riders.

He saw Erak wave acknowledgement, then point at the entrance to the defile, where the last of his men were just passing through. Thorn and Mikkel both grunted in understanding.

'Good idea,' Mikkel said. 'We'll hold them off at the entrance.'

The high rock walls and narrow space would encumber the horsemen. It would also prevent them flanking and encircling the two sea wolves. They'd be forced into a frontal attack. Normally, that might be a daunting prospect, but these were two experienced and deadly fighters, each secure in his own skills and those of his companion.

They both knew that Erak would not abandon them to this new danger. Once the gold was safely at the ship, he'd send men back to help them. Their job was only to buy time, not to sacrifice themselves so the others could escape. And both men felt confident that they could hold off a few country bumpkin horsemen.

They doubled their pace, covering the ground to the defile. Behind them, they heard a ragged cheer from the townspeople as they saw the raiders seemingly running for their lives ahead of the avenging horsemen, who urged their horses to a gallop, determined to catch these interlopers before they could escape into the narrow gully.

The two warriors had no intention of escaping. Rather, as they reached the defile, Mikkel and Thorn turned and drew their weapons, swinging them experimentally as they faced the approaching riders.

Like most Skandians, Thorn favoured a heavy, single-bladed battleaxe as his principal weapon. Mikkel was armed with a long sword. Both of them wore horned helmets and carried large wooden shields, borne on the left arm, with a heavy centre boss of metal and reinforcing metal strips around the edges. They presented these to the oncoming riders, so that only their heads and legs were visible — as well as the gleaming sword and axe, still moving in small preliminary arcs, catching and reflecting the sunlight as the two warriors stretched their muscles.

It seemed to the horsemen that the shields and swords blocked the defile entrance completely. Expecting the Skandians to run in panic, they were somewhat taken aback now at this show of defiance — and at the confident manner of the two men facing them. They drew rein about thirty metres short of the two men and looked at each other uncertainly, each waiting for one of the others to take the lead.

The two Skandians sensed their uncertainty, and noted the clumsy way they handled their spears and small round shields. There was none of the easy familiarity that could be seen in an experienced fighter.

'I think these boys are still wet behind the ears,' Mikkel said, smiling grimly.

Thorn nodded. 'I doubt they've seen any real fighting.'

They were right. The horsemen, who had come from the castle in response to a messenger who had run all the way from Santa Sebilla, were young and only half trained. They were all from well-to-do families. Their indolent parents had always supplied their every whim: new chain mail, a sword with a gold-chased hilt, a new battlehorse. They viewed their training in the knightly arts as more of a social activity than a serious one. They had never before faced armed and determined warriors like these two and it suddenly occurred to them that what had begun as a lighthearted expedition to send a few ill-bred raiders running in panic had quickly turned into a dangerous confrontation. Someone could die here today. So they hesitated, uncertain what they should do next.

Then one, either braver or more foolhardy than his fellows, shouted a challenge and spurred his horse forward, awkwardly trying to level his spear at the two Skandians.

'Mine, I think,' said Thorn, stepping forward a few paces to accept the charge. Mikkel was content to let him do so. Thorn's long-handled axe was the more effective weapon against a horseman.

Thorn summed up his opponent through slitted eyes. The youth was bouncing around in his saddle like a sack of potatoes, trying to steady his spear under his right arm and keep it pointed at his enemy. It would be ridiculously easy to kill him, Thorn thought. But that might simply rouse the anger of his companions. Better to humiliate him.

Bracing himself, he caught the spearhead on his shield and flicked it easily to one side. Then he slammed the flat of his axe into the shoulder of the charging horse, throwing it off balance. As it stumbled, he drove forward with his shield, hitting the animal again and sending it reeling to one side. The horse struck the rough rock wall beside the defile and lost its footing, crashing onto its side with a terrified neighing. The rider barely had time to clear his feet from the stirrups and avoid being pinned under the fallen horse. He fell awkwardly to one side, his small shield underneath him. He scrabbled desperately at the hilt of his sword, trying to clear the long blade from its scabbard. When it was half drawn, Thorn kicked his arm and hand, finishing the action and sending the bared sword spinning away out of his grasp.

The young rider looked up at Thorn with horrified eyes. He flinched uncontrollably as he saw the terrible war axe arcing up and over. Then it slammed into the hard ground, a few centimetres from his face. The Skandian's eyes, cold and merciless, held his. Then Thorn said one word.

'Run.'

The young Iberian scrambled clumsily to his feet and turned to escape. As he did, he felt a violent impact in his behind as Thorn helped him on his way with his boot. Stumbling and crying in panic, the boy blundered back to where his companions were waiting, their horses moving uneasily from one foot to the other, the riders' fear communicating itself to the animals.

Behind him, the boy heard the two Skandians laughing.

Thorn's instincts had been correct. The apparent ease with which he had dealt with the rider was far more disconcerting than if he had simply killed him. By letting him live, he had shown the utter contempt with which he and his companion regarded these neophyte warriors. Such disregard made the Iberians even more uncertain.

'I think you've made them nervous.' Mikkel grinned at his friend.

Thorn shrugged. 'So they should be. They shouldn't be allowed out with pointy sticks like that. They're more danger to themselves than anyone else.'

'Let's see them off,' said Mikkel. 'They're starting to annoy me.'

Without any warning, the two Skandians brandished their weapons and charged at the small group of horsemen, screaming battle cries as they went.

The shock of it all was too much for the demoralised group of riders. They saw the terrifying warriors charging across open ground at them and each one was convinced that he was the target they were aiming for. One of them wheeled his horse and clapped spurs to its flanks, dropping his spear as his horse lurched suddenly beneath him. His action was infectious. Within seconds, all four horsemen were streaming across the plain in a ragged line, the riderless horse with them, and their dismounted companion stumbling awkwardly behind them, encumbered by his thigh-high riding boots, spurs and flapping, empty scabbard.

Mikkel and Thorn stopped and rested on their weapons, roaring with laughter at the sight.

'I do hope they get home all right,' Mikkel said and Thorn laughed all the louder.

'Are you ladies ready to join us?' It was Svengal, sent back with five men to reinforce the rearguard. 'It seems you don't need any help.'

Still laughing, Thorn and Mikkel sheathed their weapons and walked back to join Svengal and the others at the mouth of the defile.

'You should have seen it, Svengal,' Mikkel began. 'Thorn here simply frightened them away. The sight of his ugly face was too much for them. It even made a horse fall over.'

Svengal let go a short bark of laughter. Hurrying up the defile at the head of the reinforcements, he had seen how Thorn dealt with the charging rider. He was impressed. He knew he could never have pulled that move off. In fact, he couldn't think of anyone other than Thorn who might have managed it.

'Well, you played your part too,' Thorn was saying in reply. 'Although I must admit I *was* magnificent.'

'I'm not sure that's the word I'd —' Mikkel raised his arm to clap his friend on the shoulder when the spear hit him.

It came out of nowhere. Later, thinking over the event, Thorn realised it must have been the spear dropped by the first of the fleeing horsemen. He surmised that one of the following townspeople, overcome with rage and frustration, had retrieved it and hurled it blindly at the Skandians, then run for his life into the scrub and rocks before he could see the result.

The result could not have been worse. The heavy iron head penetrated underneath Mikkel's raised arm, burying itself deep in his upper body. He let go a small cry and fell to his knees, then crumpled sideways. Horrified, Thorn dropped to the ground beside his friend, seeing the pallor of Mikkel's face as the life drained from his body.

'Sword . . .' Mikkel gasped. If a sea wolf died in battle without a weapon in his hand, his soul would wander in the netherworld for eternity. Svengal had already drawn his own sword and thrust it into Mikkel's groping fingers. The stricken man looked up in thanks, then turned his gaze to his best friend.

'Thorn,' he said, the effort of speaking that one word almost too great.

Thorn bent his head close to Mikkel's. 'Hold on, Mikkel. We'll get you to the ship.'

Somehow, the ship meant safety and salvation, as if the simple act of being on board could negate the effects of the terrible, life-sapping wound in Mikkel's side. But Mikkel knew better. He shook his head.

'My wife . . . and the boy . . . look out for them, Thorn.'

Thorn's vision blurred with tears as he gripped his friend's hand, making sure that Mikkel's grip on the sword hilt didn't weaken.

'I will. You have my word.'

Mikkel nodded and seemed to gather his strength for one last effort.

'Won't . . . be easy . . . for him. He'll need . . .'

The pain and the shock were too much. He couldn't finish the sentence. But there was still a last remnant of light in his eyes. Thorn gripped his hand tighter, willing him to finish. He needed to know his friend's last wish, needed to know what he wanted done.

'He'll need what, Mikkel? What will he need?'

Mikkel's lips moved wordlessly. He took in a great, shuddering breath that racked his body. With a final effort, he spoke one word.

'You,' he said, and died.

CHAPTER TWO

Six years later

Karina Mikkelswife found Thorn one winter morning. He was huddled in rags and a moth-eaten old fur, lying semi-comatose in the lee of her eating house. The light snow overnight had powdered his hair and the ratty fur, turning them white. But his face and hands were blue with the piercing cold and his nose ran incessantly.

Thorn had become so drunk the previous night that he had lost his way while heading back to the boatshed where he lived. He had crawled into the shelter of the wall, out of the wind, and lay down, vaguely hoping to die.

Which he probably would have done had Karina not intervened.

She tried to rouse him, calling his name and shaking him by the shoulder. But he slapped her hand away and mumbled incoherently, turning away from her, his eyes still closed, his mind far away.

She shook him again, harder this time, and he cursed her, knocking her hand aside angrily. A steely light gleamed in her eyes.

'Hal!' she called to her ten-year-old son, who was working in the kitchen, cleaning the dishes from the previous night's dinner.

'Yes, Mam?'

'Pump a bucket of water and bring it here. And be quick about it.'

He arrived a few minutes later, holding the bucket out from his body with an extended arm so that the freezing contents wouldn't spill on him. He gaped as he made out the figure slumped against the wall.

'It's crazy old Thorn,' he said as he set the bucket down. 'What's he doing here?'

Karina's eyes narrowed again as she heard the phrase. Obviously, this was how the local boys referred to the decrepit former sea wolf. It's a crying shame, she thought, remembering what an amazing man Thorn had been before he had lost his hand.

The raid when Karina's husband, Mikkel, had lost his life had turned into a succession of disasters. On the return trip, *Wolfwind* had been dismasted in a storm. In the struggle to clear the wreckage and save the ship from sinking, Thorn's right arm had become hopelessly trapped in a tangle of ropes and broken timber and he lost his hand.

Thorn had been devastated by the loss. With only his left hand, he could no longer wield a sword or axe, nor pull an oar. He had no skill as a navigator and, although he'd been a competent helmsman in his time, a steering oar often required two hands in rough weather.

Consequently, there was no useful place he could fill on a wolfship and he had found himself on the beach, with no way of continuing the life he loved. In addition, he had lost his best friend.

He had sunk into a deep depression, looking for comfort in an ale or brandy tankard. There was little comfort in either, but there was oblivion, and strong drink helped him forget his loss, albeit temporarily.

It also soothed the pain that would hit him without warning, searing through the stump of his right arm and seeming to come from the missing hand itself. Thankfully, that was an infrequent occurrence and as time passed it became even more so. But it gave him a further excuse to continue drinking.

His hair and beard grew long and matted and unkempt, and he seemed to go grey long before he should have. He washed infrequently and took no interest or care in his appearance. He degenerated into a staggering wreck of a man, mourning the loss of his right hand — which seemed to have taken his self-respect with it. None of his friends or former shipmates could rouse him from this downward spiral of self-destruction. Even Erak, who had been his skirl, or ship's captain, before becoming Oberjarl of Skandia, couldn't reach or reason with him.

'He's not that old,' Karina said tersely to her son.

Hal raised his eyebrows, peering more closely at the unconscious Thorn. 'Really? He looks about a hundred.'

'Is that so?' she said. To a boy, she knew, anyone over twenty-five appeared positively ancient. She cocked her head to one side, giving in to curiosity — knowing she shouldn't, but doing so anyway.

'And just how old d'you think I am?' she asked.

Hal made a deprecating gesture with his hands and smiled at her.

'Oh, you're nowhere near that old, Mam,' he said reassuringly. 'You wouldn't be more than sixty-something.'

Karina was, in fact, thirty-eight. She was slight compared to the more full-figured Skandian women, but she had strikingly beautiful looks. More than that, she had a calmness and a confidence about her, even when she had first arrived in Hallasholm as a slave, captured on a raid in Araluen. And that's when she had taken the eye of Mikkel Fastblade, one of Skandia's foremost warriors. Mikkel had bought her from the man who had captured her and immediately set her free. Seeing the determination in Mikkel's eyes when he made an offer, Karina's captor promptly added another thirty per cent to the price. Mikkel had paid it without hesitation. Even now, over ten years later, Karina was still considered a beauty in Hallasholm and in the past year alone had refused four would-be suitors.

She regarded her son coldly and he shifted uncomfortably from one foot to another. Something he'd said had offended her, he thought. But he couldn't figure out what it might have been.

Perhaps it was Hal's total lack of tact that sealed Thorn's fate, dispelling any sense of compassion that Karina might have felt for him. She jerked her thumb at the full bucket.

'Let him have it,' she said.

Hal hesitated, looking from Karina to Thorn to the bucket.

'Let him have . . . what exactly?' he asked, wanting to be sure.

Karina put her hands on her hips. Sixty-something indeed, she thought. 'The water. Let him have it . . . in the face.' She leaned down and pulled the collar of Thorn's ragged fur away from his face. As before, he tried to bat her hand away.

'Mam . . .' Hal said, uncertainly. Thorn might be old and dirty and ragged and dishevelled. He might be a wreck who could be seen staggering around the village and his right arm might be missing below the elbow. But for all that, he was a big man, known to have a very bad temper. And perhaps it might not be wise for a small woman in her sixties and her ten-year-old son to throw water on such a person – at least not without an escape route planned.

Karina's foot began to tap rapidly on the snow-covered ground. This was never a good sign, Hal knew. She gestured to the bucket again.

'Throw it.'

Hal shrugged and picked up the full bucket.

'Now,' she said.

And he did.

Thorn came awake with a roar as the first of the water hit him. He sounded rather like an angry bull walrus that Hal had heard the previous summer – although the walrus couldn't match Thorn for volume. Thorn tried to sit up, flailing his arms to gain balance.

Karina noticed that the bucket was still a third full.

'And the rest,' she ordered. Obediently, Hal threw the remaining water at the roaring, flailing figure. When a person roars like a wounded bull walrus, of course, it follows that the person's mouth is wide open. Thorn's certainly was as he received the remaining four litres of water.

The roar changed to a gasping, choking splutter as the water went down his throat. He coughed and retched and lurched to one side, as if fearing a further soaking. But the bucket was empty now and after a few seconds he realised there was no more to come. His eyes opened, bleary and bloodshot. He squinted in the bright morning light that reflected off the snow around them, and made out the two small figures standing over him.

Hal was still holding the empty bucket, although as Thorn's bloodshot gaze fell upon him, he tried to hide it behind his body.

'You threw that on me,' Thorn said accusingly. 'Why did you do that?'

'Because I told him to,' Karina said. There was a tone in her voice that didn't encourage further argument. Instead, Thorn opted for misery, in a pathetic whine intended to melt a hardened heart.

'I could have drowned! I'm soaked to the skin. I'll probably catch my death of cold. How could you be so . . . cruel?' he protested.

But Karina's heart was beyond melting. She was angry — angry beyond belief at the way Thorn had let himself go, had let himself be reduced to this shadow of his former self.

'Get up, Thorn!' she ordered crisply.

He flailed around, trying to find purchase in the slippery snow.

'Throw water on a poor sick freezing man,' he muttered. 'What sort of woman would do that? How could anyone be so heartless? I'm sick. I can't help myself. Now I'll die of the galloping pleurisy, soaked to the skin out here in the snow. Will anyone care? No. Certainly not the witch who threw water all over me and drowned me . . .'

'You're making a lot of noise for a drowning man,' Karina said. Then she gestured to her son. 'Get him on his feet, Hal.'

Hal stepped forward carefully. He still wasn't sure that Thorn was safe to be near. But he got hold of the man's left arm and dragged it across his own shoulders, bending his knees to get power into his attempt to heave the stricken derelict to his feet. As he came close to Thorn and raised his arm, he caught a solid whiff of the man's considerable body odour and turned his face away, trying not to breathe through his nose.

'Whoah!' he exclaimed, fighting the instinct to gag. 'He really reeks, Mam!'

Thorn lurched to his feet, crouched over, swaying uncertainly, holding onto the boy to prevent himself falling again. This had the effect of dragging Hal deeper into the gagging fog that had built up over seven unwashed months. The boy tried to lurch away. Thorn clung to him desperately and the two of them swayed uncertainly back and forth, feet slipping in the snow.

'Oh by Gorlog's claws and nostrils, Mam! He stinks! He really stinks! He's worse than Skarlson's old goat!' Hal complained.

In spite of her anger, Karina couldn't totally suppress a smile. As smells went, Skarlson's old goat was as bad as they came. She went to step forward to help steady the two of them, then thought better of it and kept her distance.

'Don't curse,' she said absently. Gorlog was one of the second rank of Skandian gods, like Ullr the hunter or Loki the liar, although unlike them, Gorlog had no specialised skills. She wasn't sure that invoking his claws and nostrils ranked as a curse but it wasn't suitable language for a ten-year-old.

'Get him into the kitchen.'

Hal led the bulky, one-armed man on a zigzag path to the back door of the eating house. Together, they staggered up the three steps to the door and went inside. Thorn raised his head gratefully as the warmth of the room wrapped around him. There was a fire blazing in the hearth and Hal led him to it, depositing him clumsily in a large, curved-back wooden chair, then backing away hastily.

The warmth of the kitchen might be welcome to Thorn, wet and freezing as he was. But it also had the effect of accentuating the thick miasma that hovered around him.

Karina, entering behind them, blanched and turned her face away for a moment. Then, gathering her resolve, she moved towards the pathetic figure, huddled in her favourite chair.

'You can go, Hal,' she said and the boy scuttled gratefully away into their living quarters behind the dining room. She heard water splashing into a basin and guessed that he was trying to wash the stink away. She stepped closer to Thorn, standing over him, forcing herself to endure the renewed olfactory assault.

'Thorn, you disgust me,' she said. Her voice was low, but it cut like a whip and the old sea wolf actually flinched. For perhaps a second, a brief glimmer of anger showed in his eyes. But almost immediately, it died away as he pulled his protective coat of self-pity back around himself.

'I disgust everyone,' he said. 'What's special about you?'

'I don't care about everyone. I care about me. There was a time when people looked up to you. Now they laugh at you. Even the boys call you crazy old Thorn. It's an affront to see what you're doing to your life.'

Now anger did flare in Thorn. 'What I'm doing? What I'm doing?' He held up the scarred stump of his right arm, pulling the ragged sleeve back from it to bare it. 'Do you think I did this to myself? Do you think I chose to be a cripple?'

'I think you're choosing to destroy your mind and your body and your self-respect, along with your arm,' she told him. 'You're using your arm as an excuse to destroy the rest of you. To destroy your own life!'

'It's my life. I'll destroy it if I want to,' he retorted. 'What right do you have to criticise me?'

'I have the right because you promised Mikkel that you'd stand by me and Hal. You swore you'd see that we were all right. You let us down. And you continue to let us down with every day that you try to destroy yourself!'

Thorn's eyes dropped away from hers.

'You're doing all right,' he muttered. But she laughed harshly at his words.

'No thanks to you. And no thanks to the promise you made. A promise you broke, and continue to break every day!'

'Not my fault,' he said, in a voice so low she could barely hear it. 'Leave me alone, woman. There's nothing I can do for you.'

'You promised,' she said.

He reared his shaggy head up at her, goaded now to full anger. 'I promised when I still had my hand! It wasn't my fault that I lost it!'

'Maybe not. But it was your fault when you let everything else go with it! You're killing yourself, Thorn! You're destroying a good man, a worthwhile man. And to me, that's a crime! I won't stand by any longer and watch while you do it.'

'Haven't you noticed?' he said, sarcasm heavy in his voice. 'I'm not a man any more. I'm a cripple. A useless cripple who's no good for anything, no good to anyone!'

'I don't recall it saying anywhere that a man is measured by how many hands and legs he has. A man is measured by the worth of his spirit, and the strength of his will. Most of all, he's measured by his ability to overcome tragedy in his life.'

'What would you know about tragedy?' he shot back at her. She held his gaze until, once more, his eyes dropped from hers.

'You only lost a hand,' she said finally. 'I lost an entire man. A wonderful man.'

He kept his eyes down, nodding his head in apology. 'I'm sorry,' he said. 'If I could bring him back, I would.'

'Well, you can't. But there is something you can do for me.'

Thorn laughed bitterly, shaking his head at the idea. 'Me? What can I do for anyone?'

And in that second, Karina had a flash of insight. She knew what Thorn needed to hear.

'You can help me. I need you,' she said.

He looked her directly in the eyes then, searching for any sign of dishonesty or falsehood.

'Hal needs you,' she continued. 'He needs a man's influence and guidance. There are things you can tell him that I can't — about being a warrior and about the bond that forms among shipmates.' She paused to let that thought sink in, and saw that it had reached him. 'He's growing up fast and it's not easy for him. He's different from the other boys. He's half Araluan and half Skandian. And life is hard on people who are different. He needs someone to show him how to stand up for himself. I can't do that.' She paused. 'You could.'

'Maybe . . .' Thorn began. She could see he was thinking about it, starting to accept the idea that he might have something useful to do with his life, instead of drinking it away.

'Or you could just continue to feel sorry for yourself and waste your life,' she said.

He didn't respond to that immediately. But after several seconds, he asked, 'How did you know about the promise?'

'You told me,' she said. 'One night when you were drunk.'

He frowned, thinking. 'When was that? I don't remember it.'

She smiled sadly and shook her head. 'I can't remember which one. There were so many, Thorn.'

He nodded. 'That's true.'

Karina could see he was wavering. 'Look, I need help around the place here. The eating house is a good business and it's growing. It's getting to be more than I can handle on my own. I could use help with things like firewood and the heavy work around the place — cleaning and repairs and painting. They're all things you can do with one hand. And you can keep an eye on Hal. Teach him the skills he's going to need as he grows older. You can move in with us. You'd have a warm place to sleep.'

Thorn was shaking his head. 'No. I couldn't live in the house with you. That wouldn't be proper. People would talk. It'd be bad for your reputation.'

She smiled. 'I think I could bear it,' she said. 'But if it bothers you, you could fix up the lean-to at the back of the house. That'd stop people gossiping.'

He thought about it and nodded several times to himself.

'Yes. That'd be all right.'

'I'll pay you, of course,' Karina added. Once again his gaze shot up to meet hers. She could see a sense of pride in his eyes — something that had been missing for years now.

'I don't want charity,' he said.

She laughed at him. 'And you won't get it! I'll make sure you earn every kroner I pay you.'

'Well then . . . maybe this would work out.' Thorn pursed his lips. The idea of working for Karina was an attractive one. And the notion that he might be able to help the boy and guide his steps through early manhood was one that fascinated him. It was not the path he might have chosen for himself, but definitely something that could be worth doing. If he couldn't use the skills he'd learned any more, at least he could teach them to someone else, he thought. That would be a useful thing to do. And above all, Thorn wanted to be useful. He'd spent long enough feeling useless.

'One thing,' Karina added. 'You'll have to stop drinking.'

There was no compromise in her voice. Thorn hesitated. 'Sometimes my arm hurts,' he said.

But Karina was firm. 'I'm sorry to hear that. But I'm sure there were times when you felt lots of pain before you lost the arm. And you dealt with it.'

'That's true,' he admitted.

'Then you'll just have to deal with the pain when it happens — without trying to drink it away.'

He took a deep breath. 'I think I can handle that,' he said, committing himself.

She smiled at him. 'I'm sure you can.'

'So I might get busy looking at that lean-to today. Might as well get it shipshape and then move in. Then you can give me a list of things you need me to do.'

'There is one thing that's top priority,' Karina said, and when he looked at her with a question in his eyes, she continued, in a voice that brooked no argument.

'Have a bath. A long one.'

That had been six years ago — it was now twelve years since the raid that had cost Hal's father his life, and Hal was almost sixteen. In that time, Thorn had become a familiar sight around Karina's inn. He had moved into the lean-to at the back of the main building, although his idea of 'making it shipshape' left a lot to be desired, in Karina's eyes. He patched a few leaks in the roof and several of the larger gaps in the walls. But the lean-to remained a dark and forbidding cavern, strewn with his clothes and belongings. And while his personal hygiene had improved somewhat, it still left a good deal to be desired.

'I'm twelve times cleaner than I used to be,' he announced proudly.

When Karina pointed out that this meant his bathing schedule had gone from once a year to once a month, which was nothing to really boast about, he muttered darkly, 'I don't get all that dirty. Baths are for them as is dirty.'

From time to time, he felt the lure of the brandy keg, particularly on those nights when the pain throbbed in his missing hand. But he fought it and overcame it. He knew that Karina had given him a second chance and he knew that would be a one-time thing only. And as he fell into the routine of working round the inn, he realised that he could not afford to risk going back to his old ways.

The work itself was satisfying – particularly to someone who had come to believe that his days of being useful were over. He cut wood for the fire, wielding the heavy axe with his left hand as if it were no more than a small hatchet. He looked after the ongoing maintenance jobs around the inn and, at the end of each day, he felt the satisfaction of having done a worthwhile job. Of being of value to someone.

Perhaps this kind of menial work wasn't as fulfilling as being a warrior. But it was a long way better than being a drunken, morose wreck.

Best of all, he became part of Hal's life as the boy grew older. He delighted in Hal's enthusiasm and energy. And in his imagination and inventiveness. The boy had an affinity for tools, and a natural ability to work with wood. Thorn had been a capable carpenter himself at one stage. Of course, with a missing hand he was no longer able to carry out the fine detailed work he used to do. But he found that Erak had saved his old kit of tools and he presented them to the boy, then patiently taught him how to use each one — adze, chisels, knives, spoon-drills, planes and small shaping axes. With good tools of his own, and under Thorn's tutelage, Hal's natural ability grew into real skill.

As a result, the old sea wolf became a willing accomplice in Hal's constructions. The boy had become more than a skilled craftsman — he had an inventive streak that, to Thorn, bordered on genius.

'He sees something in his mind, a new way to do something,' Thorn had said on more than one occasion. 'Then he just makes it!'

CHAPTER THREE

'Pass me another bucket, Thorn.'

Hal was perched on a ladder in his mother's kitchen, twisting sideways so that he could tip buckets of water into a large cask. He grunted as he took another full pail from the shabby old former sea wolf and lifted it above his shoulder height. As he did so, he noted with one corner of his mind that Thorn was hoisting the buckets up to him without any sign of effort, even though he had only one hand to work with.

As the water splashed into the half-filled cask, there was an ominous groaning sound.

Thorn frowned. 'What was that?' he said suspiciously.

Hal handed him down the empty bucket and made a dismissive gesture.

'Nothing. Just the cask staves settling into place under the weight.'

'I know how they feel,' said Stig, entering the kitchen with two more buckets that he had filled from the well in the yard outside the kitchen. 'How many more of these will you need?'

Stig was Hal's best friend. As a matter of fact, aside from Thorn, he was Hal's only real friend. The other Skandian boys tended to ostracise Hal, taunting him because of his mixed parentage, and because his mother was a former slave. But they never did so in Stig's hearing. Stig was big and well muscled and was known to have an unpredictable temper. As a result, the others trod warily around him.

There was another ominous creaking sound from the cask.

'You're sure that's the staves settling?' Thorn said.

Hal cast an impatient look at him. 'It was a dry, empty barrel,' he said. 'They always do that. The wood expands, the staves creak against each other.'

'I'll take your word for it,' Thorn said. 'My experience has been more with full barrels in the past.'

'You did your share of emptying them, though,' Stig said. He grinned to make sure Thorn knew he was joking, not criticising. Thorn took the comment philosophically.

'That's true,' he said, shaking his head in regret over some of the excesses of his past.

The cask was Hal's latest brainwave. He had decided to install a running water system in his mam's kitchen. A zigzag pipe ran down from the cask to the kitchen bench. A spigot at the base of the cask would allow water to run out through the pipe and down to the basin.

'You'll never need to fetch water from the well,' he had told his mother, not noticing her dubious expression. 'Thorn can fill the cask for you each morning.'

He had constructed all the components in his workshed and waited for a day when Karina had gone down the coast to a market some ten kilometres away. Then he'd summoned Thorn and Stig and begun to install his new system for her.

After mounting the cask on a bracket he had already set high on the kitchen wall, and attaching the piping, they had begun filling the cask with buckets of water pumped from the well.

Now that the cask was a little over half full, impatience got the better of them.

'Why don't we try it?' Thorn suggested. He was eager to see the new system working.

As if in response to being mentioned, the cask gave another of those ominous creaks that had been worrying Thorn. He glanced at Hal, who shook his head impatiently.

'It's the staves settling,' he said. 'That's all.'

He stepped forward, placing a large basin under the end of the pipe. He pulled on a cord attached to one side of the spigot and turned it. The action was a little stiff and the wooden peg squeaked in protest. They heard the soft gurgle of water running out of the cask. It zigzagged down the piping until a silver stream of liquid splashed out of the lower end and began to fill the basin.

Stig and Thorn applauded and Hal beamed.

'It works!' he said triumphantly. Then, realising that such a reaction might imply that he had feared it might not work, he nodded to himself and said, in a more matter-of-fact tone, 'Yes. Excellent. Well done. Just as I thought.'

The water was nearing the brim of the basin and he reached up casually to tug on a second string that would shut off the spigot.

It stuck. The spigot refused to turn.

Water began to spill over onto the surface of the table. He tugged the string again, harder this time. The spigot remained stuck. Water continued to flow. And now it was slopping off the edge of the table and onto the kitchen floor.

He tugged harder.

There was a creaking sound once more.

Thorn frowned doubtfully. 'Sounds like those staves are still settling.'

In his haste to drill holes into the wall beams, Hal had gone slightly off line with one. As a result, the nail supporting one side of the bracket and the cask had missed the timber wall beam. It was supported only by the weak plaster covering. As the weight in the cask grew, the nail had lost its tenuous hold. The bracket was gradually tilting to the side, causing the groaning noise that they had all heard. It was now held in place by only the weak, crumbling plaster, and Hal's final attempt to switch off the spigot was enough to break it free.

'Look out!' Thorn yelled. He grabbed Hal by the front of his shirt and heaved him bodily over the table, away from the path of the toppling cask. Stig, sitting to one side, let out a shrill yelp of terror and dived headlong under the sturdy table.

With a resounding crash, the cask hit the edge of the table and disintegrated into its component pieces. Staves and iron hoops flew in all directions, and the thirty-odd bucketfuls of water inside the cask were released in one enormous torrent. Under the table, Stig was momentarily flattened by the weight of water falling on him. He let out a gurgling screech.

The pipes and connecting sections followed the cask, crashing onto the table and the flooded kitchen floor, bouncing and clattering as they disassembled themselves.

Hal, held erect by Thorn's iron grip on his collar, watched in horror as his beautiful invention, lovingly built over several evenings, destroyed itself in a matter of seconds. The kitchen was a tangle of barrel staves, hoops, pipe sections, bracket timbers and flooding water. The wall where the bracket had been fastened now displayed a gaping hole where the plaster had been torn loose, exposing the beams beneath it.

One of the iron cask hoops had been set spinning by the fall. It continued to spin unevenly on the floor, going from rim to rim, the 'yang-yang-yang-yang' sound it made the only noise in the ruined kitchen.

Stig's startled face appeared over the far side of the table. His blond hair was plastered down by water. His shirt was totally saturated.

'I think those staves are well and truly settled now,' Thorn said.

And that, of course, was the moment that Karina chose to return from the market.

'You shouldn't encourage him, Thorn,' Karina said, as she kneaded dough for a loaf of bread.

Thorn was on his knees, stacking a supply of cut firewood for the stove. He shook his head, smiling faintly.

'I can't help it,' he said. 'He's so enthusiastic about his ideas. He puts so much energy into them.'

'Too much,' Karina said sternly. 'He starts brother-band training next week. He can't be distracting himself with this sort of nonsense.'

She waved a floury hand around the kitchen. The only evidence of the previous day's chaos was several fresh patches of plaster on the wall above the work table.

Hal had spent most of the previous afternoon mopping up the kitchen, sluicing water out the door with a flat wooden blade fastened to a broom handle, collecting and removing the shattered timber, staves, channels and barrel hoops and re-plastering the huge gouges torn in the wall by the bracket as it collapsed. When the new plaster was thoroughly dry, he would repaint it.

'He won't have the time or energy,' Thorn told her. 'Brotherband training will keep him on the go all day.'

'And a good thing,' Karina muttered, almost to herself.

Thorn straightened up from his crouched position by the woodbox. He pressed the back of his hand into the small of his back and groaned softly.

'I'm getting too old for all this bending and stooping,' he said. Then, as Karina continued to pummel the lump of dough with her fists and the heel of her hand, he added, in an appeasing tone, 'He was only doing it to make your life easier, you know. He wanted to surprise you.'

'He certainly managed that,' Karina said, setting the thoroughly kneaded dough into a bowl, and covering it with a linen cloth. 'I'm just wondering how destroying my kitchen could be seen as making my life easier.'

She poured more flour onto the table, shaping it into a mound and making a well in the centre, preparatory to forming another loaf.

'The idea was good,' Thorn objected mildly. 'It was just a detail that went wrong.'

Karina stopped working and regarded him. 'He always says that when one of his ideas goes wrong.'

'They don't always go wrong,' Thorn said. 'Some of them are surprisingly good. The heating system he designed for your dining room was quite ingenious.'

Karina nodded reluctantly. 'I suppose that's true. I just tend to remember the disasters — particularly when they flood my kitchen.'

She poured a mixture of water and milk into the well and pushed the side in, moving the mixture around with her hands to form a thick dough.

'He's a good boy,' Thorn told her. 'He did a good job cleaning up the mess yesterday. And he worked all night in the eating hall for no payment to make it up to you. His heart's in the right place and there's no malice in him.'

She sighed, beginning to knead. 'I know, Thorn. I just worry about him. Where is he this morning, do you know?'

Thorn opened the oven firebox and fed a few pieces of wood into it. Karina was going to need a good hot oven for the bread, he knew.

'I think he said he and Stig were going down to Bearclaw Creek to work on the boat.'

Karina sighed heavily. 'That boat. That blessed boat. It takes up all his spare time lately. Do you think that's an idea that'll work?'

'I can't see why it shouldn't. I've seen that sort of sail rig before, in the Constant Sea.' He grinned. 'It'll be fine — so long as he gets the details right.'

'The problem with getting the details right on a boat,' said Karina, 'is that if you don't, you tend to drown.'

She attacked the dough with renewed vigour. Thorn watched her dexterous movements for a few seconds then looked thoughtfully at his single hand.

'Can I try that?' he asked.

Karina looked up at him. She knew he was constantly looking for tasks he could accomplish one-handed. She nodded and stepped aside, wiping her hands on her apron. Then she noticed his hand and a frown darkened her face.

'Wash your hands first,' she ordered, then realised she had used the plural form.

Thorn didn't seem to notice. He poured water into the basin, sloshing his hand around, working his fingers open and shut and rubbing them with the stump of his right arm until she nodded. Then he began to pound and turn the dough, hitting it and stretching it with the heel of his hand, then folding it in on itself again with his strong fingers. He was clumsy at first, but he rapidly developed a good rhythm.

Karina prepared another mound of flour, water and yeast and began to work on a third loaf. They continued in silence for several minutes, then Thorn rolled his loaf into a large ball and placed it in a basin. He regarded the end result and nodded in satisfaction at having discovered something else he could do.

'He'll be fine, Karina. You don't have to worry about him,' he said.

She looked up at him. A tendril of hair had fallen in her eyes. She glanced at her dough-covered hands, then blew upwards to get rid of it.

'I'm a mother, Thorn. It's my job to worry. Still, it's good that Stig's with him,' she added. 'At least he has one friend.'

CHAPTER FOUR

People in Hallasholm weren't too surprised at the friendship that had developed between Hal and Stig. After all, the two boys seemed to have a lot in common. Each had lost his father at a relatively early age and entered his teenage years without the guidance of a male parent. So it seemed logical that they should seek each other out. But the beginning of their friendship had nothing to do with logic or common ground.

There were major differences in the boys' situations. Hal's father had died an honourable death, facing enemies on the Iberian coast. Stig's father, by contrast, was not dead. Olaf had simply disappeared some years back. He was an expert warrior, but an inveterate gambler, and he had got himself into serious debt. Faced with the disgrace of being unable to pay his debtors, he had skulked away from Hallasholm one dark night. The wolfship he crewed on had just returned from a raid and the spoils were yet to be divided. Olaf, assigned to be the night guard, absconded with the pick of the plunder — money and jewels for the most part — leaving behind him his furious former shipmates and his wife and son.

And while Hal's mother had been left well provided for after Mikkel died, and had been able to buy a small eating house — which had since become one of the most popular eating houses in Hallasholm thanks to Karina's excellent cooking — Stig's mother was forced to earn a living as a laundrywoman, taking in washing for other families in Hallasholm. It was menial work, and a considerable comedown from her former position as the wife of a warrior. But she was a strong-willed woman who believed there was no dishonour in hard work and she kept her head high. For Stig, however, the shame of his father's crime, and the pain of his desertion, cut deeply.

Soured by his father's actions, he became moody and suspicious, always thinking that the other boys were talking about him, mocking him for his father's weakness. His temper would flare at the slightest provocation, whether intended or accidental, and he was constantly getting into fights, often taking on more than one opponent at a time.

He took a lot of beatings but he doled out a lot of punishment as well. As a result, the other boys in Hallasholm began to steer clear of him. You never knew when an innocent comment might be taken the wrong way.

Of course, as boys will do, some of them tended to make comments that were not so innocent, taunting him from a safe distance and from the security of overwhelming numbers.

In a warrior society like that of the Skandians, boys tended to band together in cliques or groups. Tursgud was the leader of one of these. He was tall, well built, handsome and an excellent athlete. He was also supremely arrogant, and he delighted in taunting loners like Stig and Hal. In Stig's case, he could usually be assured of an enraged response. Stig would charge at him, fists swinging wildly, whereupon Tursgud and his followers would administer a beating. Tursgud never taunted Stig in a one-on-one situation. He always did so when he had three or four of his cronies to back him up.

Hal might have been tempted to seek Stig's friendship, had he not shared in the general wariness about the troubled boy. Besides, Stig diverted some of Tursgud's attention from Hal and he knew that if he took the other boy's side he would be drawing attention to himself. Bitter experience had taught him that this was not a wise thing to do.

And so matters continued, until the day of the lobster trap incident.

It was a crisp autumn day — one of the last when the inhabitants of Hallasholm might expect to enjoy a few hours of clear, bright sunshine. All too soon, the dark, rolling clouds of winter would be upon them, and they would endure months of bitter winds and deep snow.

Hal had taken his fishing pole and set out to see if he could lure a few fat bream onto his hook. He passed through the village on the way to one of his favourite fishing spots.

Several groups of boys were contesting a ball game on the common green, kicking a round, inflated bladder towards goal posts. The rules seemed to be flexible. Occasionally, a boy would pick up the ball and run with it, a signal for others to tackle him and crash him to the ground. Often as not, his own team members would be the first to do so. Hal watched from a distance for a few minutes. He felt the usual twinge of regret that he wasn't included in these games, and that he lacked the confidence to ask if he could join in. Then he heard Tursgud's voice, shouting down the others as he loudly proclaimed his interpretation of the rules. Hal shrugged and continued on.

His fishing spot was to the west of Hallasholm, where the cliffs rose steeply from the ocean and the waves crashed against their bases. It was a small inlet, where the force of the waves was broken by a ring of large rocks a little offshore. A precarious track led down the cliff face to the bottom, where a flat rock gave him a good spot to fish from. The track made it a tricky spot to reach, which was why it was a good fishing spot. Experience had taught him that fish avoided places that were easy to reach.

As he approached along the cliff top, another figure emerged from the rocks some fifty metres ahead of him. After a few seconds, Hal recognised Stig and he frowned. The path down to his fishing spot was well concealed and he had no wish to reveal it to someone else. The location of a prime fishing spot like this was something to be protected and he decided he'd wait until he was sure that Stig had moved on.

He followed, maintaining the distance between them, moving carefully among the rocks to avoid drawing Stig's attention. There was no telling how Stig might react if he realised someone was following him. Hal felt a sense of relief as he saw the other boy go past the point where the track led away down the cliff face. He saw that Stig was heading for the next inlet around the rocky cliff top.

Stig was carrying a long willow pole, around three metres in length, and a large wooden bucket with a tight-fitting lid. He had a coil of rope around his shoulder. He was going poaching, Hal realised.

Hallasholm's professional fishermen had their own special spots, where they set traps for lobsters and crabs. They paid a fee to the Oberjarl to reserve these spots for their exclusive use. No other fisherman would go near them, but it was not uncommon for the boys in the town to slip out and raise the traps, taking any of the succulent shellfish that were inside. Hal had done so himself on several occasions. It was a risky business. If the fishermen caught a boy poaching from their traps, he would be severely beaten. Perhaps it was that element of risk that made the practice popular among the boys.

The inlet Stig was heading for was a spot where a canny old fisherman named Dorak set his traps. It was an exposed spot, but the deep water and jumble of submerged rocks at the base of the cliffs made it a prolific breeding and feeding ground for lobsters. Dorak had several traps set there, each marked by a coloured buoy. He would wait for relatively calm weather, then access the cove by boat. Stig must be planning to climb down the cliff face and use the long pole to reach the closest traps, Hal thought. He'd store the lobsters in the sealed wooden bucket.

Hal watched as the other boy uncoiled the rope, tied it to a low tree stump close to the cliff edge, then dropped it over. With the pole slung over his back and the bucket looped over one arm, Stig seized the rope and began to walk himself backwards down the cliff face.

Hal waited several minutes then moved to the cliff to peer over the edge. Stig was at the base of the cliff, standing on a rock shelf and leaning over the water as he reached for a yellow buoy a few metres out. The willow pole had a hook on the end and Stig tried several times to snag it through the ring on top of the buoy, without success. The pole was long and unwieldy and he had it at maximum reach. And the buoy was surging up and down as the waves passed under it so that he repeatedly missed his mark.

The waves slapped against the rock shelf where Stig crouched, throwing spray high in the air and drenching him. Angrily, he dashed the cold salt water out of his eyes and reached once more for the buoy. The distance was just a little too far. Dorak had been robbed before and he had taken to setting his traps further out from the shore — close enough to be in among the lobsters' feeding ground, but just too far to be reached easily by a boy with a long, hooked pole.

A wave slammed into the rock, then sucked back, revealing a shelf below the spot where Stig was standing. It was a metre or so closer to the buoy, but when the waves came in, it was fully submerged. Hal could see the green shine of weed covering it. It would be slippery, he knew.

But now Stig lowered himself so that he was sitting on the edge of the rock, reaching down with his feet for the ledge below him. A wave came in, hitting the rock with a muffled *whump*. Then it receded, momentarily revealing the submerged ledge. Stig slid his backside off the rock, reaching down with his legs for the treacherous foothold.

'Careful . . .' Hal muttered to himself. He could swim well. His mother, raised among the fenlands of Araluen, had taught him when he was young. But he knew that most Skandians never bothered to learn. It seemed like a paradox when so many of them spent their lives in ships. But, as Thorn had told him, most of them felt that, in the event of a shipwreck, the ability to swim would only prolong the agony. In addition, the year-round cold of the Stormwhite Sea made swimming an unattractive proposition.

Stig's left foot slipped on the weed-covered shelf as the water surged in again, coming up to his waist. He quickly reached behind him and gripped the rough surface of the rock as the water surged out, trying to drag him with it. It was touch and go for a moment, then he recovered his balance and his footing.

Hal realised that he'd been holding his breath. He released it now in a long sigh.

Stig, secure once more, stretched out with the willow pole. The buoy was now within easy reach, but it was still dancing up and down as the waves passed under it. The hook at the end of the pole caught the loop of rope on top of the buoy, but then the buoy sank with a wave and the hook came loose. Again Stig tried, and again he just failed. Another wave struck the shelf, sending spray high into the air, then receded. The next wave was already lifting the buoy higher and, for a moment, as it met the outgoing wave, the buoy was still.

Stig released his grip on the rock behind him and leaned out, both hands now on the pole. He sighted carefully, then passed the hook through the loop of sodden rope. But he was unprepared for the sudden drag as the buoy sank and he teetered precariously for a second or two. Then the incoming wave whumped into the shelf again. Solid water ran over the rock, then cascaded back into the ocean. The force of the outgoing water caught Stig, already off balance, by surprise. With a startled cry, he slipped from the shelf.

On the cliff overhead, Hal watched, horrified, as the other boy fell awkwardly into the surging water. He heard Stig's yell of alarm, cut off abruptly as the water closed over his head. Then Stig reappeared, several metres offshore, as the undertow dragged him away from safety. He thrashed the water, went under, then resurfaced.

Hal realised that the air trapped in Stig's sheepskin vest would keep him afloat for the time being. But it would soon become waterlogged and then it would begin to drag the boy under. There was no time to lose. He leapt to his feet and raced along the cliff edge to the rope. He stripped down to his underwear, retaining his knife belt. Then, as an afterthought, he wrapped his discarded shirt around his hands, seized onto the rope and, facing back towards the cliff, dropped over the edge, fending off with his feet as he fell.

The rope sizzled through his shirt, which began to smoke from the friction. But it protected his hands from being seared as he dropped through the air. In seconds, it seemed, he hit the rocks at the base of the cliff. His knees buckled and he fell awkwardly, bruising his hip. But he was up instantly, running to the spot where Stig had gone in.

He saw Stig's wooden bucket and grabbed it up. The lid was fastened securely, hinged at one side and held with a metal hasp at the other. He looped the rope handle over one arm, ran to the edge and paused. Stig was seven or eight metres away from the rocks, floundering helplessly. Already, the vest was becoming sodden and the trapped air was escaping from it. Hal saw the boy's mouth open wide as he tried to scream, then choked helplessly as a wave slapped him in the face, filling his mouth with sea water. He could see that Stig was close to giving up. He had only seconds to act.

He paused, waiting as a wave ran in, rising before him, about to slam into the rock face. Then he tossed the bucket into the water and went in after it, leaping as far as he could over the incoming wave.

The shock of the icy water closing over his head hit him like the kick of a mule. It was all he could do not to gasp helplessly and swallow water while he was underwater. But he resisted the urge and fought his way back to the surface. He roared aloud then, with the shock and the cold. The bucket was floating close by and he grabbed the rope handle, turning on his back and holding it to his chest, and kicking out with his legs.

The bucket gave him buoyancy and he glanced over his shoulder to spot Stig. There he was! Five or six metres away. His struggles were becoming weaker. The heavy vest was now a death trap and the cold and the mouthfuls of sea water that he'd swallowed joined with it to take him under. His arms thrashed the water still in a desperate, clumsy parody of swimming. But his energy was all but gone.

Hal swam up behind the exhausted boy. It was as well that Stig was so far gone, he thought. If he'd had more energy, he might well have dragged them both under. As it was, he was barely conscious. Hal thrust the bucket at him, pushing it against his chest.

'Hold onto this!' he told him, burbling the words as water slopped into his mouth. 'It'll keep you afloat!'

Instinctively, Stig grabbed at the bucket, wrapping both arms around it. He felt an instant surge of relief as the bucket took his weight and he realised he was no longer sinking. He heard a voice close by his ear.

'Relax! Don't struggle! The bucket will keep you afloat! Just let yourself go limp. Trust me!'

Stig did as he was told. He was aware of something tugging at the shoulders of his sheepskin vest as Hal slashed away at the tops of the armholes with his fishing knife. Then the heavy, sodden garment fell clear and drifted away, sinking slowly, and he felt even lighter in the water.

He opened his mouth to thank his rescuer. A wave promptly slapped him in the face and he swallowed sea water again, panicking as it choked him. He tensed up and began to struggle.

'Shut up! Shut up and relax!' Hal yelled at him, feeling his body tense. And Stig heard him and obeyed again, clasping the bucket firmly to his chest.

Hal studied the rocks where he'd jumped in after Stig. The waves were rising and falling more than a metre, alternately leaving the rocks bare, then flooding up and over them, smashing against them with enormous force and sending spray fountaining high into the air. If he tried to get Stig ashore there, the odds were good that they'd both be slammed into the rock face. There was even a chance that the precious bucket might be shattered. Their best chance would be to swim round to Hal's secret fishing spot, where an offshore hedge of rocks broke the force of the incoming waves. It would mean a swim of over a hundred metres in the rough sea, towing Stig. But there was no other choice. Hal felt a brief flicker of fear as he wondered if his own energy would hold out. One hundred metres wasn't too far to swim in calm water. But the sea was rough and the water was brutally cold and energy-sapping.

'Putting it off won't make it easier,' he said to himself. He seized hold of Stig's collar and began towing him, swimming in a one-armed side stroke, kicking with his legs and stroking with his free arm.

The cold was eating into him as he cleared the point. He wanted above all to stop and rest for a while. They could just drift here, he thought. The empty bucket would support them both. Then he realised in a moment of clarity that, if he stopped, he would never start again. The cold was all-pervasive. He couldn't feel his fingers and toes. It was draining his energy away as his body tried to fight it. He shook his head determinedly and continued stroking, kicking more strongly in an effort to drive warming blood into his legs and feet.

It would be so easy to stop and rest, he thought. So easy to doze off for a few seconds . . .

'No!' he shouted. At least, he tried to shout. The word came out as a garbled grunting sound, cut off by another mouthful of cold sea water. He coughed, spluttered and kept swimming.

Behind him, Stig was a deadweight. It seemed an eternity before they rounded the sheltering hedge of rocks and he could strike out for the flat rock in the cove behind them. With his last strength, he managed to shove Stig up onto the rock, assisted by the gentle surge of a small incoming wave. Then he clambered up after him, dragging himself painfully on his belly and knees over the rough, barnacle-crusted rock, and fell exhausted beside him.

'Don't tell anyone what I was doing,' Stig said anxiously.

It was an hour later. They were squelching their way back to Hallasholm, having recovered their strength — as well as Hal's outer clothes and Stig's rope from the clifftop. Hal's shirt, of course, remained at the base of the cliff and neither of them had the energy to retrieve it.

Hal looked at him quizzically. 'I wasn't planning to,' he said. 'But it's not such a big thing. Everyone poaches lobsters from time to time. I've done it myself.'

'Everyone doesn't have a father who was a thief,' Stig replied heavily. 'I know what they'll say. Like father, like son. Any time I do anything wrong, people can't wait to point out that my father was a thief.'

'But that doesn't mean you are,' Hal said. 'If that were true, people would say I'm a hero like my dad was. But they don't.'

Now it was Stig's turn to study his companion for a few seconds.

'They'll change their tune when I tell them you rescued me,' he said, then added hurriedly, 'We don't have to say anything about the lobster trap, of course. We can just say I was fishing and fell in and you came in after me and . . .'

He stopped. Hal was already shaking his head.

'Let's not talk about it at all,' Hal said. 'If you tell people I saved you, it'll just annoy Tursgud and he'll come after me and make my life a misery. Besides, it was nothing special. Anyone would have done what I did.'

'I wouldn't,' Stig said emphatically. Then he added, with a grin, 'I couldn't have, anyway.'

Eventually, they decided to say nothing at all. But it was noticeable that over the ensuing weeks, the two boys began to spend more time together, and a genuine bond grew between them.

As a result, Stig's wild, erratic behaviour and bouts of temper grew less frequent. The fact that he had a friend and companion who didn't pre-judge him because of his father's misdeeds seemed to mellow him. But his reputation was already established and that tended to stick, even if he did calm down considerably.

Neither boy ever intended to speak about the events at the cliff that day. But of course, their mothers eventually worked the truth out of them.

Mothers always do.

PART TWO

THE
HERON

PART TWO

THE
HERON

CHAPTER FIVE

Bearclaw Creek began as a mere trickle, forcing its way out between a jumble of rocks in the high country above the coast. It joined with a dozen similar rivulets as it wound down the mountains and eventually widened into a respectable body of water as it came closer to the sea.

In the final stretch of its journey, the creek crossed a small meadow a few hundred metres outside the town limits of Hallasholm. At this point, there was evidence of a considerable amount of recent activity. Offcuts of wood and cordage littered the ground. There were work trestles and benches and a tarpaulin shelter had been rigged to provide protection during wet weather. The smell of sawdust and sawn timber permeated the air. A small, ramshackle jetty stood on the bank of the creek close by the work site.

The *Heron* was moored alongside this jetty, her mooring lines creaking gently as they stretched then slackened with the movement of the water.

She was a sleek craft, some fifteen metres long — or about half the length of a standard wolfship. She was pierced on each side for four oars, whereas the newer wolfships could carry ten oars a side. Even moored alongside the small jetty that led out from the bank, she gave the impression of speed.

She was Hal's boat, and the result of an enormous stroke of luck the previous summer.

When he had turned thirteen, he applied for a job at Anders' boatyard. Anders was an irascible, middle-aged man who was generally intolerant of teenage boys. He considered them to be flighty and unreliable. But he saw that Hal was different to the general run of boys in Hallasholm so, with some misgivings, he agreed to give the boy a trial. It didn't take him long to see that Hal was a skilled and meticulous worker. His attention to detail and the precision of his work was impressive in one so young and Anders hired him immediately. Hal took to spending most of his spare time in the boatyard.

Two years after Hal came to work for him, Anders took on a commission from Gunter Moonstalker, a retired sea wolf. Gunter, too old and arthritic now to serve on a wolfship, still yearned for the old days and wanted a boat for cruising. He stipulated a boat that would be similar in lines to a wolfship, but small enough that he and a few friends could handle it. Anders drew up a plan, aided by Hal, who was fascinated by the project. Over the winter months, they worked indoors in the boatyard workshop, carving the prow and stern pieces, splitting logs to form the planks, shaping the frames for the hull and selecting a section of timber for the keel. As the materials were made ready, they were stacked along one side of the boatshed in a steadily growing pile of finished components.

Then, unexpectedly, Gunter Moonstalker died.

Anders was faced with a problem. The boat had been specifically designed to Gunter's requirements. It was too narrow in the beam for a fishing boat and too small to be a trader. It was not a boat that Anders would be able to sell easily and, in the meantime, the frames and planks and spars were taking up valuable room in his workshop.

Hal solved the problem for him.

'I'll buy it,' he said. It had long been his ambition to have a boat of his own and he had saved virtually every kroner Anders had paid him against the prospect of buying one. This seemed like too good a chance to miss. They negotiated a fair price – Anders had already received half the agreed fee from Gunter, after all – and the boat was Hal's. Anders added one stipulation.

'You'll have to move it out,' he said. 'I can't have it taking up room here.'

Hal agreed readily, and he had enlisted Stig and Thorn to help him move the boat to the ramshackle jetty at Bearclaw Creek.

Knowing that when the boat was complete he would need a crew, he had also approached three other boys to help.

Ulf and Wulf were identical twins. Nobody could tell them apart, not even their mother, and that made other boys wary of them. In addition, they traded on the fact that nobody could identify them, often swapping identities at will to confuse people. Hal had always believed that twins had a special bond between them but Ulf and Wulf seemed to be exceptions to this rule. They fought all the time, like cat and dog — or rather, as Thorn once said, like cat and cat.

Ingvar helped as well. He was a massively built boy whose muscles were greatly appreciated when it came to moving the heavier items, such as the bags of river stones that would be used for balance.

Ingvar would have had the makings of a mighty warrior, except for one failing. His eyesight was so poor that he could barely see details past a metre away. The prospect of going into battle beside Ingvar was a daunting one. Once the battle began, there was no way he would be able to distinguish friend from foe. He would be just as likely to decimate his allies as his enemies. But he was a good-natured boy, philosophical about his disability and always willing to help. And when it came to carrying heavy weights over long distances, he had no peer.

As the summer wore on, the boat had taken shape. The twins and Ingvar worked on the project from time to time, although they didn't share the same dedication as Hal and Stig. In Ingvar's case, it was often in response to a summons when there was heavy lifting to be done — when the keel needed to be placed in position on the trestles, for example, or when a plank had to be bent in against its will so that they could fasten it to the bow section.

As the boat progressed, Stig had noticed a subtle change in his friend. Although Hal was usually reticent and avoided drawing attention to himself, when it came to building the boat, he became far more assertive. He knew what he was talking about and he knew what he wanted, and this knowledge gave him the confidence to take control and direct the others in their tasks. He gave clear and understandable directions and would not tolerate shoddy work from them, often insisting that a job be redone so that it was up to his standards.

Now, in the final week of summer, it had become a race against time to get the little craft finished before brotherband training began.

Once that happened, there would be no time for shipbuilding. Hal and Stig and the others would be fully occupied, training in the skills they would need to master if they were to be accepted into the ranks of Skandian warriors and sea wolves. They would work from dawn till dusk, studying and practising weapons craft and battle tactics — although the latter were relatively simple in the Skandian world, usually consisting of a headlong charge in response to the command, 'Let's get 'em!'

They would practise seamanship, ship handling and rowing. They would study the techniques of navigation, both by coastal landmarks and sailing instructions — which they would have to commit to memory — and by the stars. All in all, it would be a busy time.

Which was why Hal and Stig were now working feverishly get the ship ready for its first sea trial. The last major project was the mast and sails.

Hal had devised a new and revolutionary sail plan for his boat. The traditional wolfship had a tall mast. The cross yard, a wooden spar that supported the large square sail, was set at right angles. When the wind was directly astern of the ship, the square sail provided a great deal of power. Even with the wind from the side, it could still drive the ship along, although at a reduced pace.

But the square sail's weakness came when the ship was facing the wind. A wolfship could only tack, or sail into the wind, at a very shallow angle. Past that, the unsupported sides of the sails fluttered and lost shape and power.

Hal had noticed how seabirds, particularly the graceful heron, could glide forward into the wind, and he designed a triangular sail shaped like a bird's wing. Instead of a cross yard, he designed a long, flexible yardarm fastened at the bow of the ship. When this yardarm was hauled up, the front end remained fastened to the deck, so that the yard swivelled up at an angle to the ship's hull. The wind would fill the triangular sail to form a powerful, smooth curve of canvas. A system of ropes could tauten or loosen the sail and the yardarm that supported it, moving them in or out depending on the strength and direction of the wind, so harnessing its power to drive the ship along.

Because the front of the sail was kept rigid by the curving wooden yardarm, it could face much closer to the wind than a traditional square rig without collapsing and losing its shape.

Hal had tested the design on models and estimated that his ship would be able to sail three times closer to the wind than any wolfship.

What made the design even more revolutionary was that he fitted the boat with not one but two sails and yards, one on either side of the mast. If the wind blew from the right-hand side, he would raise the left-hand sail. If the wind was from the left, he would raise the right-hand sail. If the wind was from the stern — the rear of the boat — he could raise both sails at once and let them right out so that they formed a giant letter M.

The two sails could also be connected by a pulley system, so that as one was lowered, it helped raise the other.

In a tribute to the seabird that had inspired his radical sail design, Hal named his ship the *Heron*.

'Do you think it'll work?' Stig asked. He'd never seen a rig like this. In fact, he'd never seen any rig other than the standard wolfship's square sail.

'Of course it'll work. I've already tried it on models and it works perfectly.'

'There's no small detail you've overlooked?' Stig asked.

Hal eyed him balefully. He'd worked late the night before, cutting and shaping the left-hand sail, to be ready for today's sea trial. 'I don't think so,' he said.

'You don't think you'll need reef points on both sails?'

Hal was ready with a crushing reply when he realised that Stig was right. He'd forgotten the reef points, a line of cords set into the sail, about two-thirds of the way up. In heavy weather, they could be tied around the yardarm, gathering the top third of the sail in against the yardarm so that the area exposed to the wind was reduced. He hesitated, looking at the sky.

'I doubt we'll need them today. Weather looks fine.'

He tried to ignore Stig's steady, cynical look. He was grateful when he heard a voice calling a greeting and was able to change the subject.

'Here are the the twins and Ingvar,' he said. 'And just in time,' he added under his breath.

For her first voyage, Hal planned to take the *Heron* down the coast a few kilometres under oars before he hoisted the sail. He had asked the other three boys to come to the meadow at noon to help with the rowing. The three of them and Stig would be sufficient to move the boat at a reasonable speed, while he took the steering oar.

The boys had agreed readily. They were all eager to see the *Heron*'s first voyage under sail and there was an air of expectation about them as they boarded the boat. They looked with interest at the twin yards and sails laid out either side of the mast, then took their places on the rowing benches and looked at Hal.

Hal cast off the bow rope and, as the incoming tide began to swing the front of the boat clear of the jetty, he ran back and released the stern rope as well. The *Heron* was now free and drifting with the tide.

'Oars,' he ordered. 'All together.'

The four rowers lowered their oars into the water and heaved.

The *Heron* glided forward, gathering speed under the impetus of that first, powerful thrust. Hal felt a thrill of anticipation as the steering oar came alive in his hands. He pulled it and the ship obediently swung to starboard. The small waves chuckled under the bow and he could feel the boat responding, feel the faint vibrations through her fabric.

'Heave,' Stig called softly, setting the stroke for the other three. He repeated this three times, until they were all in rhythm, then saved his breath for rowing. The boat carved a smooth path through the sheltered waters of the creek. After several minutes, Hal became aware that he was having to keep a gentle pressure on the steering oar, as the *Heron* tried to veer slightly to port. For a moment, he wondered if there was some fault in the boat. Was the keel not completely straight? Then he smiled as he defined the reason.

'Ingvar,' he called, 'back off a little.'

Ingvar looked up at him apologetically. The young giant's massive arms and shoulders were putting more power into his oar than the other rowers could manage. The added thrust on the right side was causing the faint swing to the left. He reduced his effort, then glanced at Hal, blinking his short-sighted eyes.

'How's that?' he asked.

Hal let go of the steering oar for ten to twenty seconds. The boat was now travelling in a straight line.

'That's fine,' he said and took the steering oar again.

'It was probably Wulf's fault,' Ulf said, from his seat in front of Ingvar. 'He never pulls hard enough.'

'I'll pull hard enough on your stuck-out ears, you bowlegged monkey,' Wulf snapped back. 'How would you like that?'

Hal and Stig exchanged a puzzled grin. It amused them that the twins, identical in every aspect, would constantly abuse each other's physical appearance.

'Try it, you ugly gnome, and I'll wrap this oar around your thick skull,' Ulf replied willingly.

Hal smiled and took a deep breath of the salt air. The sun was shining. The sea was calm. There was a steady wind and Ulf and Wulf were bickering.

All in all, you couldn't ask for much more.

CHAPTER SIX

There was a small swell running and *Heron* lifted to the first of the waves as they emerged from the mouth of the creek. Hal rode the movement easily, his feet set apart for balance. To their right, he could see the town of Hallasholm — a tidy sprawl of pine-log buildings and thatched roofs. Smoke rose from chimneys and he could smell the fresh scent of pine smoke overlaid on the salt breeze.

The mole, a protective rock wall that ran round the harbour, shielding the boats from heavy weather and winter storms, blocked the sight of the two or three dozen wolfships and smaller craft that were moored there. But Hal could see the small forest of bare poles formed by their masts.

Hal nudged the steering oar gently and swung onto a diagonal course away from the coast, heading to the left, away from the town. *Heron* rose and fell smoothly under his feet as the swell rolled under her keel. The other boys had settled into a smooth rowing rhythm — one they could maintain for hours if necessary — and he exulted in the feeling of being under way, at the helm of his own ship.

Stig glanced up at him from his rowing bench.

'How does she handle?' he asked.

Hal grinned back at him. 'Like a bird.'

Gradually, the town dropped behind them, until it was little more than a blur on the horizon, appearing when the ship rose on the crest of a wave, then disappearing as she dipped into the trough. Far enough, Hal thought. He was eager to see how she handled under sail.

'Stig, Ingvar,' he said quietly. 'Stand by to raise the left-hand sail.'

The boys had been awaiting the order for the past five minutes. They ran their oars inboard, stowed them along the centre line, and moved forward to the short, heavy mast. Hal checked the telltale, the long pennant streaming from the high sternpost that told him the wind's direction. It was coming from ahead, over their right-hand side at an angle of about sixty degrees.

He hesitated. This was the moment when he would discover if his idea worked. For a second or two, he was filled with uncertainty. What if the sail simply shivered in the wind and the boat wallowed without any driving force? He knew his friends wouldn't laugh at him if this were the case. But word would get out and others would.

Then his lips formed a grim line. It would work, he told himself. The idea was sound.

'Haul away,' he ordered.

Stig and Ingvar heaved on the ropes that sent the slim yardarm rising smoothly up the mast, taking the sail with it. Instantly, the sail billowed out, flapping in the wind.

'Ulf and Wulf, trim the sail.'

The sail hardened into a smooth swelling curve. As the wind pressed into the taut sail, *Heron*'s bow began to swing to the left, under the pressure. Now was the moment, Hal thought. He heaved on the steering oar, forcing the bow to the right, back towards the wind.

Obediently, the boat responded, swinging back until they were heading across the wind, then up into it. Then further upwind still. Hal felt a huge surge of relief. Vaguely, he could hear the other boys cheering.

They had never seen a ship sail at such an angle to the wind before. Hal estimated that they were heading at about forty-five degrees into the wind. He shook his head in delight. A well-built wolfship couldn't manage much more than fifteen degrees. He heaved the steering oar further over and *Heron* responded, moving closer still to the wind.

Eventually, as the angle became too steep, the big, tri-angular sail began to flutter and lose shape. He eased the rudder and, as the bow swung back, the wind hardened the sail and began to power the boat once more.

'She's flying!'

He hadn't noticed Stig's approach. He looked now into his friend's delighted face and a huge smile broke over his own.

'No small details overlooked,' he said and Stig pounded his shoulder with delight.

'None indeed! She's fantastic! She'll sail rings around the best wolfship!'

Hal looked down at the other boys. They were staring up in wonder at the sail, realising they were seeing something new. Something exciting. Something unique.

They had known that Hal had designed a new sail, but they had never really queried the details, nor realised how much more efficient it would be.

At forty degrees to the wind, *Heron* flew. The deck vibrated under Hal's feet. It was one of the most exciting moments of his life. The wood felt alive. He eased the steering oar, letting the bow drop off once more so the wind was blowing more from their beam.

'Haul in,' he said and Stig and Ulf jumped to the ropes. As they hauled in on the sail, tightening it, the boat accelerated. She also began to lean under the pressure of the wind, so that water ran in over the downwind rail. No sense in swamping her, Hal thought.

'Ease off,' he ordered. They loosened the ropes a little and the boat came more upright.

He let go a long whoop of delight and the other boys, startled for a moment, joined in. He couldn't wait to tell Thorn about this. Couldn't wait to show it to him. His only regret was, with brotherband training about to start, he would have little time to experiment and practise with the new boat.

He glanced ahead. *Heron* swooped down a wave and sliced into the trough, sending silver spray feathering back on either side of the bow, cascading over them. They barely noticed. He could see a long headland in the distance, jutting out from the coast and barring their path. They'd have to go about to clear it. He decided they might as well do it now, while they had plenty of time and sea room in hand.

'Get ready to go about,' he said, pointing to his right — the starboard side.

Stig looked at him, saw the determined set to his jaw. 'You're going to tack her?'

Hal nodded. 'Why not? We'll drop the port sail when she comes up into the eye of the wind, then raise the starboard one as she comes round. It'll be easy.'

Stig looked doubtful. Tacking meant turning the ship into the wind, until the sail came around and filled on the opposite side of the ship. It was a manoeuvre that wolfship captains avoided whenever possible. Tacking a square sail put immense pressure on the mast, yard and rigging, and ships had been driven astern and even dismasted in the manoeuvre.

It made more sense to wear the ship — to sail it round through three-quarters of a circle, with the wind behind it, until it was facing the opposite tack. But Hal's triangular fore and aft rig would come through the the eye of the wind much more easily. And at no time would it present a huge square mass of sail, with all the potential risk that it entailed, to the headwind.

'Come on,' Hal told Stig, nodding towards the still distant headland. 'That lump of rock isn't getting any further away, you know.'

As it turned out, the tack went smoothly and uneventfully. Hal let the ship gather speed for a few minutes, then swung her up into the wind. As the wind came dead ahead, the sail flapped and lost its shape. But the *Heron*'s momentum kept her turning. On Hal's command, Stig and Ingvar began to haul down the left-hand sail. It was linked by a pulley arrangement to its partner, so as it came down, the right-hand sail slid smoothly up the mast. By the time *Heron*'s bow had crossed through the wind, the new sail had filled and the ship was powering along on its new course.

Hal grinned as Stig rejoined him. The ship had swung through a ninety-degree angle to the right and was now surging along, slicing through successive waves. She would clear the headland easily, he saw. He realised that he'd been tensed up during the tacking manoeuvre and he forced himself to relax, loosening the iron grip he had kept on the steering oar. He twitched it experimentally, watching the ship respond. Behind them, the wake described a series of sudden curves.

'She's beautiful,' he breathed. And she was. Fast, agile and responsive, she was everything he had hoped she might be. His grin widened even further.

'Now let's see how fast we can take her back to Hallasholm.'

CHAPTER SEVEN

It was standard practice that a lookout was maintained at Hallasholm harbour, to keep an eye out for strange ships.

A wooden tower stood at the landward end of the mole, currently manned by a junior sailor who had recently been assigned to his first wolfship. The job of lookout was a boring and often fruitless task and, as such, it was usually assigned to junior crew members. As the older sailors said, there was very little for a lookout to do and most junior sailors were extremely capable of doing very little.

There was a practical side to the arrangement, of course. Younger sailors had younger eyes and were likely to see a strange ship sooner than their older comrades.

On this day, the lookout saw a very strange ship indeed.

Her hull looked like a wolfship, only smaller — perhaps slightly more than half the size of a normal wolfship. And she was coming up fast, very fast. She seemed to be skimming the sea like a low-flying seabird. He could see the regular flashes of white spray at her bow as she cut through the low waves — catching up to each one, slicing her way through, then chasing down the next in line.

But what really took his attention was the sail. He had never seen a sail like this one. It was a large, swelling triangle.

'Ship!' he called to a small group of sailors below, who were loading stores into a wolfship moored alongside the mole. They looked up at him, then looked out to sea, following the direction of his pointing arm. But they were too low to see the newcomer.

'What is she?' the first mate of the wolfship called up to him. Even from a distance, his annoyance with the lookout was obvious in his voice. Lookouts were supposed to report the type and number of ships approaching, not simply yell 'Ship!' like a frightened maiden aunt finding a burglar in her parlour.

'Is it one of Arndak's trading fleet?' the first mate added. Each year, around this time, a small flotilla of trading ships brought back goods from Sonderland and the south coast of the Stormwhite. The ships carried wool and fleeces and cooking oil and salted meats — goods that would help the people of Hallasholm get through the winter. They had been expected now for some days.

'No. She's not a trader. She's a . . .' The lookout stopped and admitted, in a puzzled tone, 'I'm not sure what she is.'

Muttering dire insults about the mental deficiencies of young sailors, the mate crossed the mole and ran nimbly up the wooden ladder to the observation platform. The tower vibrated to his heavy tread and the lookout moved to one side to make room for him as he emerged onto the platform.

The mate looked, frowned, looked harder.

'Well, I'll be . . .' he began, then stopped. The ship was coming about. The strange sail suddenly fluttered loose and was hauled down. As it slid down, another identical sail rose up the mast on the opposite side. It bellied out for a few seconds then, as the crew — he could see now there were only a few of them — hauled in the sheets, it formed into a perfect, hardened curve. The ship, which had slowed fractionally during the manoeuvre, now accelerated forward.

'Well, I'll be . . .' he began again, then realised that he had no idea what he would be. He leaned over the railing to where his crew were looking up at him. As tends to happen when a person looks upwards, they had allowed their mouths to gape open.

'Stop gawping at me like hungry seagulls and someone go fetch the Oberjarl,' he yelled. Obediently, most of the mouths closed and one of the sailors headed off at a run for the Oberjarl's hall.

'What is she, Klaud?' called one of the sailors.

The mate shrugged. 'Some strange kind of ship. She has a weird-looking pointy sail,' he added.

That set them all talking. None of them had ever heard of such a sail. They weren't even sure what he meant.

'You want us to sound the alarm?' another called and he shook his head.

'She's only small. No more than half a dozen men on board. But keep your axes handy just in case.' He touched the hilt of his knife, reassuring himself that it was riding on his hip in its scabbard. No sense in facing strangers without a weapon of some sort.

He turned his attention back to the ship. She was closer now. He pursed his lips in surprise as he realised how quickly she was closing the distance to the harbour. And she was arrowing for the narrow harbour entrance. His skilled eyes gauged angles, distances and leeway for a few seconds, projecting her path over the intervening distance. He realised that if she held her current course, she would slide straight through the middle of the narrow harbour mouth. He nodded his approval of the unknown helmsman.

'Knows what he's doing,' he remarked to the lookout, who glanced at him, uncomprehending. Klaud realised that the young man had no appreciation of the skill that was being displayed. He shook his head wearily.

'Forget it,' he said.

On board *Heron* Hal had just made the same mental projection of course and angles. He smiled to himself, satisfied with his ship and his own judgement. Stig had rejoined him on the steering platform once the sail was reset on the new tack.

'You're not taking her back to the creek?' he asked, although it was obvious that Hal had no intention of doing so.

'I think we've earned the right to show off a little, don't you?' Hal said.

Stig raised his eyebrows. 'I don't see the rest of us showing off too much. But then, you seem to be doing enough for everyone.' He leaned across Hal to look past the bow towards the harbour. 'I guess we'd better get the oars ready.'

But Hal shook his head. 'No oars. I'm sailing her in.'

That definitely caught Stig's attention. He looked back at his friend.

'Talk about showing off,' he said.

'I think I've earned the right,' Hal told him and Stig shook his head.

'Well, I'd better get the fenders rigged for when you sail headlong into the wharf. Try not to hit the Oberjarl's ship. You do know she's moored directly opposite the harbour mouth, don't you? Or is that another of those "small details" you sometimes overlook?'

'Of course I know that,' Hal replied. In fact, he *had* overlooked that small but rather important fact. 'Don't worry. I won't be hitting anything,' he muttered. Then, realising that his friend might have a point, and that the harbour was a rather restricted space, he called to Ulf and Wulf.

'Let the sail out a little, boys.'

'I'll do it,' Ulf said. Or perhaps it was Wulf.

'Get out of the way. I'll do it,' his brother, Wulf (or Ulf) snapped. They glared at each other.

'JUST DO IT!' Hal yelled and they both jumped to the ropes, letting the sail out so that their speed reduced. As the wind pressure eased, Hal felt the bow of the ship come a little to the right. He adjusted the tiller to compensate.

He wished he had the nerve to sail full speed into the harbour but Stig was right. If he misjudged, it could be very embarrassing. For a moment, he had a ghastly mental picture of *Heron* with her bow buried deep into the splintered flank of the Oberjarl's wolfship, and he shuddered at the thought. *Wolfwind* was Erak's pride and joy. Once, when a visiting wolfship had accidentally scraped her paintwork coming alongside, Erak had chased her terrified skirl around the harbour with his battleaxe.

A more sedate speed might be wiser, he thought.

'Ease that sail a little more,' he ordered. He ignored Stig's knowing snigger. He checked his course again, and nudged the steering oar until he was satisfied they would pass through the harbour mouth with room to spare.

Not a lot of room, mind you. But room.

On the wharf, Erak had made the same assessment of the strange ship's course. Word had spread quickly around the waterfront about the approaching ship and a considerable crowd was gathered now to see it.

'He looks as if he plans to sail straight through the harbour mouth,' he said, his voice deceptively calm. 'And he's heading right for my ship.'

'That's the way I see it,' Klaud agreed. Erak turned to the young lookout who had first sighted the strange ship.

'You. What's your name?'

The young man was pleased to be singled out by the Oberjarl and half expected to be praised for being first to sight the unusual ship that was now heading for them.

He stepped forward and bowed slightly, bobbing his head to the Oberjarl.

'It's Helligulf, Oberjarl,' he said.

Erak looked at him in some surprise. 'Helligulf?' he repeated. He was continually baffled by the trendy, exotic names parents were giving their sons these days. 'What sort of name is that?'

'My mam made it up, Oberjarl,' Helligulf explained, with some pride.

Erak shook his head slightly. 'Why?'

Helligulf, sensing that the legendary warrior was less than impressed by his mam's creativity, shrugged his shoulders uncertainly.

'Ummm . . . I'm not sure, Oberjarl.'

'Well, while you're figuring it out, step aboard *Wolfwind* and fetch me my battleaxe.'

As the younger man hurried to do his bidding, Erak said grimly to Klaud, 'Never hurts to be ready.'

Klaud hid a grin. He'd been present on the previous occasion when Erak had pursued the offending ship's skirl with his axe. It had taken three men to restrain the furious Oberjarl.

Erak shaded his eyes now and peered at the fast-approaching ship.

'He's got a helmsman's eye,' he said, in reluctant admiration of the unknown skipper's judgement of the line he needed to maintain. 'Anyone know who it is?'

'It's young Hal,' a voice said behind him. Erak turned and saw a ragged, unkempt figure standing close by. Thorn, he recognised. Then he made the connection.

'Mikkel's son?' he said. 'That Hal?'

Thorn nodded. 'The same. That's his ship. He designed her and built her himself.'

Which was stretching the truth slightly. After all, Anders had quite a hand in the hull design, even if the sail plan had been Hal's doing. There was pride in Thorn's eyes as he watched the trim little ship bearing down on the harbour mouth. The sail idea had obviously worked, he thought, which must be why Hal had brought her back to the harbour to show her off.

He just hoped the boy had the skill to stop her in time when he made it through the harbour mouth.

'He's just short of his sixteenth birthday, chief,' Thorn told him. As a former member of Erak's crew, he was privileged to call him 'chief' rather than his formal title of Oberjarl. He thought it might be wise to mention Hal's youth to Erak. It might make the Oberjarl more forgiving in case of any accidents. Helligulf chose that moment to return with Erak's battleaxe. The Oberjarl took it and hefted it, feeling its familiar weight and balance.

'He'll be just short of his head if he takes even a splinter out of my ship,' he said grimly.

Thorn shook his own head confidently. 'There's no risk of that, chief.'

He hoped he was right.

CHAPTER EIGHT

The harbour entrance was flying towards them, drawing closer and closer. Hal stood by the steering oar, every muscle tensed, eyes slitted in concentration as he gauged the remaining distance. He noticed the sizeable crowd on the harbour mole watching and his mouth went dry with nervousness.

'When I order it,' he called to his crew, 'drop that sail and get to your oars. Run them out ready as soon as we go through the entrance.'

His tension communicated itself to the others as they moved to the halyards and sheets. Stig tried reasoning with his friend one more time.

'Hal, wouldn't it be wiser to lower the sail out here and row her in?' he suggested. Hal's eyes were still riveted on the harbour entrance.

'Probably,' he said. But his tone of voice told Stig that he had no intention of doing so. The bigger boy shrugged and turned to the others.

'Be ready to move quickly.' He glanced at Ingvar. 'Try not to fall over, Ingvar.'

Ingvar smiled, taking no offence. 'Do my best, Stig,' he promised.

Hal crouched at the steering oar, his hands alternately gripping and releasing on the oak handle. While the palms of his hands were damp with nervous perspiration, his mouth was dry. As the entrance loomed closer, he judged the moment was right.

'Let go the ropes! Down sail! Do it! Do it! Do it!'

There was no real need for those final instructions. The other boys were every bit as tense as he was. But he couldn't restrain himself.

The sail flapped and thundered as Ingvar and Stig cast loose the sheets – the restraining ropes that controlled it – and the harnessed force of the wind was suddenly released. At the same moment, Ulf and Wulf began hauling down the yardarm. Ingvar and Stig scrambled to help them, roughly gathering in the flapping sail and stuffing it under the yardarm. Time to stow it neatly later, thought Stig.

'Oars! Oars!' shouted Hal. Even without the sail, they still had plenty of momentum and the edge of the mole seemed to shoot by him. He heard the clatter of wood on wood as the crew ran out the oars. Ahead of him, *Wolfwind* loomed closer and closer. He thrust savagely on the steering oar and *Heron*'s bow began to swing. He had time to note that when the boat wasn't heeled under the sail's pressure, the rudder turned her more quickly. But he still wasn't sure if it was turning fast enough.

On shore, a glitter of sunlight on bright metal caught his eye. He glanced quickly towards it and his heart leaped into his throat as he realised it was the battleaxe in the Oberjarl's hand.

'Row starboard oars!' he yelled. 'Heave! Do it! Do it! Do it!'

Wulf and Ingvar were on the starboard oars. They set their feet against the footrests and heaved mightily, straining every muscle of their arms and backs so that they rose off their seats with the effort.

It was enough. *Heron*'s bow, under the extra turning thrust of the oars, swung clear of *Wolfwind*. Hal let go a huge breath, and realised he'd been holding it ever since he'd yelled those last orders to the rowers. As *Heron* curved around, she began to wash off speed in the turn and, as a result, the bow came round more rapidly.

Finally, she rounded up into the wind, completing a vast circle and facing back the way she had come. She rocked gently on the wake of her own passage, riding the water like a resting seabird.

Dimly, Hal could hear a smattering of applause from the wharf. He slumped against the tiller as Stig joined him.

'Well,' his friend said, 'that *was* exciting.'

Hal glanced at the rapidly dissipating circle of white water *Heron* had left behind her.

'Exciting? It was never in doubt,' he said, with a confidence he certainly hadn't been feeling some minutes before.

Stig gave a short laugh. 'Never in doubt? Then what was all that shrieking you were doing? *Do it! Do it! Do it!*' he mimicked, in a pretty fair approximation. Hal thought it would be best not to comment.

'Let's take her in to the beach,' he said.

Stig feigned surprise. 'The beach? You don't want to moor alongside *Wolfwind*?'

Finally, Hal cast aside his air of nonchalance. 'No, I most decidedly do not!' he said, with heartfelt sincerity.

Stig grinned at him, then scrambled back to his oar. 'Did you notice that Erak had his battleaxe?' he called.

Hal nodded wearily in reply. 'Why do you think I was doing all that shrieking?'

In addition to the wharf, where three or four wolfships could moor to load supplies, the harbour mole protected a stretch of sand and pebble beach, where other ships were run ashore. Hal took *Heron* in under oars and ran her prow up onto the sand, feeling the slight grating sensation under his feet as he did so.

She talks to me, he thought to himself.

In a way, it was true. He could sense the ship's reactions to outside forces through the vibrations under the soles of his feet. He was attuned to her so that she was almost an extension of his body. He shook his head at the fanciful notion. She was a ship. She was an inanimate assemblage of planks and spars and cordage. She had no life of her own, he told himself.

But deep inside, a tiny voice told him he was wrong.

The crowd on the wharf had made their way to the beach to inspect this strange new craft and to see who had been sailing her. Many of them were seamen and they had all admired the skill shown by her helmsman and crew as she shot into the harbour, rounded to neatly and came to a stop. The more skilled among them had also noted how the ship had made her approach to the narrow harbour mouth with virtually no corrections in course. Her skipper had set course from half a kilometre out to sea and held to it, bringing the ship straight in on one tack through the narrow harbour entrance. That required either enormous luck or the sort of instinctive ability to judge angles and distances that could never be taught.

None of them, of course, were aware of the heart-stopping terror that her helmsman had felt when he had seen the Oberjarl's ship looming up across his bows.

Now, as the crowd streamed along the beach to inspect the *Heron* at close quarters, Hal could hear the surprised exclamations as they identified the crew.

'It's Hal Mikkelson — the Araluan boy,' he heard someone say and he sighed quietly. He knew that in spite of his Skandian father, he would always be known as an Araluan. Perhaps, he thought, that was why he had decided to stage such a flamboyant display. He knew Skandians placed a high value on seamanship and ship handling and saw them as particularly Skandian abilities. Perhaps, without realising it, he had wanted to be accepted as an equal.

Other voices added their surprised comments.

'There's that Ingvar boy. My, but he's a big one.'

'But clumsy,' another added, as Ingvar tried to vault lightly over the side, caught his foot on the rail and ended up sprawling on the wet sand at the water's edge.

'There are those awful twins, too. I wonder what they're fighting about now.'

Ulf and Wulf, true to their nature, were shoving and mouthing insults at each other as each tried to be first ashore.

'And look, it's Stig Olafson. They're all just boys.'

'So who was at the helm?'

Hal secured the steering oar with a looped cord and went forward, dropping over the side onto the beach.

He glanced eagerly around the gathering crowd and for a moment his heart sank as he could see no sign of Thorn. Then he grinned as he saw the tattered, untidy figure sitting on an upturned skiff, a little away from the general press. Thorn wasn't fond of crowds, he knew. He'd spent too many years as an outcast, often finding himself the butt of cruel jokes, to make him feel comfortable among large numbers of people.

Hal waved and Thorn responded with a discreet nod of his head.

The crowd parted as the Oberjarl thrust his way through. Hal noted, with a sense of relief, that he no longer had his axe in his hand.

Erak looked around the group of five boys, standing close together. Like some of the others, he had half expected to see an older person among them.

'Who's the skirl?' he asked, although after Thorn's earlier comments, he already had a good idea. His eyes lit on Hal and the boy looked down, scuffing his feet in the sand. Suddenly, in spite of his fierce desire to be accepted, he felt reluctant to admit to it. It seemed excessively boastful.

He felt a hand drop on his shoulder and looked up to see Stig beside him, grinning at Erak.

'It was Hal, Oberjarl. He's a master helmsman.'

Stig had no qualms about claiming credit for Hal. Hal had earned their respect, and Stig was going to see he got it.

Erak studied Hal closely. Over the years, he'd kept a watchful eye on the boy and his mother. Hal's father had been a crewman on board *Wolfwind*, and a good skirl had an obligation to look after his crew and their families.

'So it was you. It was very prettily done. Are you really as skilful as your friend says? Or are you lucky?'

Hal met his gaze. He remembered the heart-stopping terror he'd felt when he'd seen the battleaxe in Erak's hand.

'A bit of both, I think, Oberjarl,' he said. And Erak nodded, recognising the truth in the statement.

'Nothing wrong with being lucky. What's this crazy sail plan you've got there?'

He was walking down to the ship now. Someone had placed a boarding ramp against the rail and he climbed up, studying the twin yardarms and the bundled-up sails. Hal and Stig joined him. Others clustered round the bow of the beached ship, straining to see.

'It's my design, Oberjarl. It's based on a bird's wing,' Hal said.

Erak frowned. He shoved one of the yardarms with his toe.

'Why? What's the point? I mean, it's pretty, but why do you want a sail like a bird's wing?'

'She'll point higher into the wind than a square sail,' Hal said.

Erak looked doubtful. 'So you say.'

'She'll point three times as high as a wolfship,' Stig interjected indignantly. 'She'll sail rings around a wolfship!'

Erak turned slowly to regard him. There was a long silence and Stig's face began to redden.

'Who are you? His lawyer?' Erak asked.

Stig cleared his throat nervously. The Oberjarl was not a man to annoy. But still, he had no right to denigrate *Heron*'s performance. He hadn't seen what Stig and the others had seen.

'I'm his first mate,' he said firmly. From the crowd below, they heard a cackle of laughter.

'Good for you, boy! A first mate should always stick up for his skirl!'

'Shut up, Svengal,' Erak said, without looking. Svengal had been his first mate for more years than they could remember. He was now the skirl of *Wolfwind*, except for those times when Erak decided he wanted to go to sea again. On those occasions, Svengal reverted cheerfully to his old position.

The Oberjarl measured Stig carefully. He liked what he saw. The boy was tall, well built and ready to meet the Oberjarl's eye, even if he was tending to go a little red in the face as he did so. Svengal was right, he thought. A good first mate should stand by his skirl. And if this boy was ready to stand by the half-Araluan boy, that fact spoke well of Hal. This pair would merit watching, he thought, making a mental note to make sure they were assigned to the same brotherband the following week.

Still, there was one point he was not prepared to let pass. He gestured at the bundled sail once more.

'You say she'll sail rings around a wolfship?'

Stig nodded determinedly. 'That's right.'

'Do you include *my* wolfship in that assessment?' Erak asked.

Stig hesitated. He glanced sidelong at Hal and saw the minuscule shake of his head, the warning look in his eye.

'Ah . . . of course not, Oberjarl.'

Erak nodded, satisfied. 'Thought as much.' He nudged the yardarm with his toe again.

'Looks flimsy,' he said, then turned and stepped easily down the boarding ramp, moving nimbly in spite of his bulk.

When Erak was safely out of earshot, Stig turned to his friend. 'Of course, she'll sail rings around *Wolfwind*,' he said.

'Then why didn't you tell him that?' Hal asked, grinning.

'I like my head where it is.'

CHAPTER NINE

Gradually, the crowd began to drift away, their curiosity over the new ship and her crew satisfied. Ingvar and the twins said their goodbyes. Hal had decided to leave the ship beached overnight. They would return it to the creek the following day. He and Stig rigged anchors to hold *Heron* fast when the tide rose. A few people lingered, asking questions about the boat and its sail plan. Thorn sat on the upturned skiff watching them, some metres away. He had a satisfied smile on his face.

The two boys went back aboard the ship and furled the sail properly, binding it neatly to the yardarm. They stacked the oars neatly fore and aft, either side of the mast, and tidied up the boat.

'That was amazing,' Stig said.

Hal grinned happily. 'It was better than that,' he said. Then he frowned. 'Although I wish Erak hadn't said that — about it being flimsy.'

Stig shook his head, discounting the comment.

'He was just saving face,' he said. 'He's a traditionalist. When a new idea comes along, he'll always look to find something wrong with it — even if it's not true.'

They climbed back down to the beach and stopped in surprise. There were two girls standing by the ramp, waiting for them. Hal's breath came a little faster as he recognised Lotte Ilafsdotir.

She was the same age as he, with a neat, slim figure and blonde hair that had just a hint of red in it. There were a few freckles dusted on her face but they made her look even prettier in his eyes. Hal had admired Lotte for years — as had every red-blooded young male in Hallas-holm. Several times, he had summoned up the courage to strike up a conversation with her. She had been polite, but distant, leaving him in no doubt that there was no chance she would ever be interested in him. Which, of course, only made him more desperately interested in her.

She smiled at him now, her eyes appraising him and, apparently, finding him worthy of interest for the first time.

'Hello, Hal,' she said.

He took a deep breath. 'Lotte. How are you?' he said, trying to make sure his voice didn't crack. His throat felt dry all of a sudden.

Lotte's companion, taller than she and dark haired, smiled at Stig.

'Hé, Stig,' she said, smiling. Nina was every bit as beautiful as her friend Lotte. But Lotte had that inde-finable something extra. At least, that was true so far as most boys were concerned. Stig, however, had always worshipped the ground Nina walked on. Now he flushed and went red to the roots of his hair.

'Hé, Nina,' he said thickly. Then, turning to Hal, he blurted, 'Well, I'd better be going. See you tomorrow.'

He turned to leave but, to his surprise, Nina, after a quick conspiratorial glance at Lotte, fell in step with him.

'I'll come with you,' she said.

'Oh . . . um . . . all right. Fine,' Stig said. He wished he could think of something to say. Something gallant or romantic. He recalled that Nina had suffered a bout of stomach flu a week earlier.

'So, I guess you're not chucking up any more?'

She smiled at him. 'No. That's all over.'

Stig ground his teeth in frustration. Another romantic quip like that, he thought sarcastically, and she'd be putty in his hands.

Hal and Lotte watched them go, smiling. Lotte laughed quietly.

'He's a silver-tongued devil, that one,' Hal said, and was rewarded by another gurgling laugh. Lotte had a delightful laugh, he thought. He liked hearing it. He tried to think of another amusing comment to make but, for the life of him, he couldn't. He realised that he was staring at her, his mouth gaping slightly open. He closed it suddenly, making an audible 'clop!' noise. Lotte seemed not to notice. She stepped closer to the *Heron* and ran a hand over the smooth planks of the bow.

'Is this really your ship?' she said, eyes wide.

Hal nodded. 'Yes. The others helped me build it. But she's mine all right.'

'She's beautiful,' Lotte said, turning to admire the sleek lines.

I was just thinking the same thing, he thought, looking at Lotte. He wondered if he should say it aloud, then decided it was just too corny. Someone else might get away with it. Not him.

'Would you take me out in her sometime?' Lotte asked, her head tilted prettily to one side.

Hal licked his lips. They had suddenly gone dry again. Lotte was talking to him! She was actually asking him if she could go out on his ship one day! But before he could answer, he felt a violent shove on the back of his shoulder and went staggering, throwing up his hands just in time to save himself from crashing into *Heron*'s bow.

'Who do you think you are, you Araluan weasel?' said a harsh, angry voice.

Hal turned to find himself facing Tursgud. Big, muscular, handsome. And angry. His face was flushed and his eyes were dangerously narrowed. He was flanked by two of his regular companions, both big and athletic like himself.

'Tursgud!' Lotte said, alarmed at the sudden assault. 'What are you doing?'

Tursgud glanced quickly at her, then ignored her. He advanced a pace on Hal, standing just too close, intentionally invading Hal's personal space.

'Think you can go sneaking behind my back and making eyes at my girl, do you?' he challenged.

Lotte bridled angrily. 'Your girl? I'm not your girl! I'm not anybody's girl!'

Again, Tursgud ignored her. Hal faced him warily, tensed and ready for another attack.

'I'm not aware she's your girl, Tursgud,' he said.

'I'm not!' Lotte put in. But Tursgud continued to ignore her, his eyes blazing at Hal.

'Why don't you just stay away from where you're not wanted and play with your silly little boat with its silly little sail,' he said. He shoved Hal again, sending him back a pace or two.

'Or go back to that greasy slophouse where your mother tries to poison her customers.'

That was too much. Hal's temper boiled over at the insult to his mother and he reacted without thinking. He thrust forward and shoved both hands into Tursgud's chest, sending the bigger boy stumbling and falling in the soft sand. One of his companions reached down to help him but he slapped the proffered hand away angrily as he leapt to his feet.

'Right! That's it, weasel!' he yelled. He grabbed Hal's shirt front in his left hand and drew back his right, fist clenched.

And found he was unable to move it forward again.

He turned, startled, to see Thorn's unshaven face a few centimetres from his. He hadn't heard the old beggar approaching. He looked with surprise to where his right wrist was locked securely in Thorn's left hand.

'Let go of me!' he shouted. He tried to wrench his arm free, but Thorn's grip was like iron.

'Why don't you shut up?' the shabby odd-job man suggested. He glanced at Lotte, who was watching in astonishment, her mouth sagging open. She'd never seen anyone confront Tursgud in this way. Even adults were often wary around him.

'Miss, it might be a good idea if you left,' Thorn said gently. 'Things could get ugly here.'

Lotte glanced at Hal and he nodded. Without further word, she fled up the beach, looking back once when she reached the esplanade, then disappearing in the direction of her parents' home. To tell the truth, she was frightened of Thorn. Most of her life, she had known him as a dirty, dishevelled, bad-tempered drunk. When she was younger, she and the other children used to throw sticks at him and call him names, then flee in delighted terror when he roared and shambled after them, lurching drunkenly as they fled, light footed as deer.

'You'd better let me go, you old wreck,' Tursgud said. His voice was strained as he fought not to show how painful Thorn's grip was becoming. 'My father is the Maktig!'

The Maktig was the Mighty One, the title Skandians bestowed each year on their champion of all warriors. Thorn smiled. His teeth were rimmed with green.

'Just as well I'm not squeezing *his* wrist, isn't it?' he said, and as Tursgud released his grip on Hal's shirt front and drew back his left fist, he continued, with a grim note in his voice, 'Throw that punch, boy, and I'll break your wrist.'

And, incredibly, he increased the pressure of that already devastating grip, squeezing and rolling his fingers so that the bones in Tursgud's wrist were crushed painfully together. Tursgud caught his breath in a gasp of agony and felt his knees buckle slightly. His eyes were very close to Thorn's and for a second he could see a light of suppressed violence there.

Then the light died and Thorn smiled at him, releasing his wrist and shoving him away so that he fell to his knees in the sand.

'Now get out of here,' Thorn said quietly.

Tursgud scrambled to his feet, nursing his bruised wrist. He half ran up the beach, followed by his surprised comrades. They had never seen him bested like this — and to have it done by a one-armed former drunk made it all the more disconcerting. When he was a safe distance away, Tursgud turned and spat his hatred back at Thorn.

'You dirty old cripple!' he screamed. 'You'll pay for this!'

Then he turned and ran, followed by his comrades.

'You're going to have to watch out for that one,' Thorn said.

Hal shook his head wearily. 'Why is he always so horrible? Why does he always want to pick a fight? I've never done anything to him! Why does he hate me?'

Thorn regarded him seriously for a few seconds.

'Because he fears you,' he replied.

CHAPTER TEN

Hal spent the night pondering Thorn's words to him. Why would Tursgud be afraid of him? It didn't make sense. Tursgud was much bigger and stronger than Hal, and much more popular. He had a wide circle of friends who sought his company eagerly. Hal, on the other hand, was something of an outcast among the other young people in Hallasholm. With the exception of Stig, of course.

So why should Tursgud fear him? Hal had tried to quiz Thorn about it as they walked back to the eating house for the evening meal service but the old sea wolf had brushed his questions aside.

'You'll figure it out,' he said enigmatically.

Hal was still wondering about it the next morning, as he weatherproofed *Heron* for the duration of his brother-band training. The other boys had joined him at first light to help bring the neat little ship back to the creek, mooring her securely to the jetty. Then Stig, the twins and Ingvar had made their farewells. They all had family commitments on this last day before their training was due to begin.

He carried the sails, yardarms and other loose fittings ashore, unshipping the steering oar and storing them out of the weather under the canvas shelter that they'd rigged when they were building the ship. Then he cut a long sapling, trimmed it of smaller branches and ran it lengthwise down the ship, supported either end by two X-shaped frames. He secured another tarpaulin over the sapling, tying it down tightly every few metres of its length so that it formed a tent-shaped cover over the hull. That should keep the worst of the rain out of her, he thought.

'You'll have to bail her out every so often,' said a voice behind him. He turned and saw Thorn watching him. He had no idea how long he had been there — probably long enough to avoid helping him carry the gear ashore, he thought. It continued to surprise him how Thorn could move so quietly when he chose. In times past, he had blundered and stumbled noisily about Hallasholm, careering into buildings and people, knocking things over.

Hal was tempted to ask him once more about what he had said the previous day. But he decided against it. If Thorn hadn't wanted to expand on the statement then, there was little chance that he'd do so now. Instead, Hal pointed to the long bundle Thorn was carrying under his right arm. It looked like a seaman's kitbag — a cylindrical canvas sack about a metre and a half long. It was obviously packed full of something.

'What have you got there?' he asked.

Thorn glanced down at it. 'It's for you.'

Then he set the bag down without further explanation. Hal found that vaguely annoying. 'It's for you' didn't really answer his question. But he knew that Thorn wouldn't be prompted to explain until he was good and ready.

'Are you just about finished there?' Thorn asked.

Hal studied him curiously. Thorn boasted about the fact that he bathed and shaved once a month. Even if I don't need it, he'd say. Yet he always seemed to be in exactly the same grubby, unshaven condition from one day to the next. Surely, Hal thought, there must be some days when he looked clean and tidy and shaven?

'Stared at me long enough?' Thorn said brusquely. 'Think you'll know me next time you see me?'

'Oh, sorry! Yes,' Hal said. He shook his head to dismiss the thought.

'Good. Now if you've finished fiddling with your boat, come over here. I've got something I want to run through with you.'

Mystified, Hal followed him to a level patch of ground, clear of wood chips, timber offcuts and shavings. Thorn turned to face him, studying him for a few seconds, then nodded, seeming to be satisfied with what he saw.

'All right, shape up to me,' he commanded.

Hal frowned at him. 'Shape up to you?'

Thorn nodded impatiently. 'Yes! Shape up as if you're going to hit me!'

'Why would I want to hit you?'

'Why would you want to hit me?' Thorn repeated quietly, shaking his head and looking to the sky as if seeking an answer there. 'Let me put it this way,' he continued, bringing his gaze back to Hal. 'Do you want to learn to fight or not?'

'Well, yes,' Hal said awkwardly. 'But . . .'

He stopped, realising that he didn't want to voice the thought that had sprung to his mind. Thorn moved closer, his head tilted to one side, and fixed a fierce glare on the boy.

'But maybe you think a broken-down tramp like me can't show you anything about fighting?' he asked, an ominous note in his voice.

Hal backed away a little, spreading his hands in a placatory gesture.

'No! No! Of course not!' he said. But the embarrassed tone was enough to tell Thorn that, yes, that was exactly what he had been thinking.

Hal wanted to learn how to fight. But he wasn't sure that Thorn was the person he would pick to show him. For a start, Thorn only had one hand. And secondly, for years he'd been a figure of pity. Hal was fond of Thorn, certainly. But that was more because Thorn had been an enthusiastic supporter of Hal's ideas in recent years, and always willing to help with his schemes. As a result, he saw Thorn more as a somewhat down-on-his-luck admirer than as any kind of mentor.

'Maybe you think that I was always a hopeless cripple? That I was always like this?' Thorn brandished the scarred stump of his right arm. Hal could see now that he had offended his friend and he felt genuinely sorry for it. But still . . .

'Of course not,' he began. Thorn didn't let him continue.

'You do know that I served in Erak's crew before this happened!' He held up the truncated right arm again, shaking it in front of Hal's startled face. 'You *do* know that, don't you?'

'Of course I do,' Hal protested. He couldn't prevent the unworthy thought *but that was a long time ago* sliding into his mind. Thorn seemed to read the thought and his eyes narrowed.

'All right. I can see I'll have to show you.' He stepped back to give Hal room and raised his left fist and the fore-shortened stump of his right arm in a defensive posture. 'Take a swing at me.'

'Thorn, I don't want to hit you,' Hal said awkwardly.

Thorn gave a short bark of laughter. 'Don't worry. You're not going to!'

'Look, can't we just forget this?' Hal pleaded.

'No, we can't. Now take a swing.'

'You're not going to be happy until I do, are you?' Hal said and Thorn nodded, saying nothing. 'All right then . . .'

Hal took a half-hearted swing at the shabby figure before him. Surprisingly, his fist whistled through empty air. He hadn't really seen Thorn move. Perhaps he had swayed slightly to one side, but Hal couldn't be sure.

'Gorlog's nostrils!' Thorn said, his voice full of scorn. 'If that's the best you can do it's as well I stopped Tursgud killing you yesterday.'

Hal felt the blood rising to his face. He didn't want to hit the disabled old man. But the taunt about Tursgud aroused his anger.

'Would you feel more at home if you tried to slap me?' Thorn sneered, and Hal's anger burst free, like water cascading through a breach in a dam. He took a wild roundhouse swing at Thorn.

And missed. Again, Thorn's jaw simply didn't seem to be in the same space as Hal's fist. Yet again, he'd seen no violent movement. Maybe Thorn had leaned back slightly. Just centimetres, no more.

He frowned and stared at his opponent.

Thorn sneered at him. 'You just don't get any better, do you?'

Hal's last vestige of self-control snapped and he leapt at him, swinging with his left hand this time. That should catch him by surprise, he thought.

His fist hit a brick wall, stopping dead in the air. He had a moment to realise that Thorn had caught it in his own left hand. In the same moment, there was a blur of movement in front of his face and he found himself looking at the scarred stump of Thorn's right arm. It had seemed to come out of nowhere and stopped a few millimetres short of his face.

Thorn released his hand and stepped back. The anger and sarcasm seemed to have gone now.

'All right, let's talk about this for a few minutes,' he said.

Hal shook his head, mystified. This wasn't the Thorn he had come to know. This Thorn was confident and capable, not the shabby odd-job man Hal was accustomed to.

'The majority of people, when they want to hit you, will do as you just did: swing a big roundhouse punch,' Thorn said. 'Punches like that have a lot of power behind them. But the problem is, they're easy to see coming. So they're easy to block and dodge. Even you could probably do it.'

'Oh, thank you so much,' Hal said.

Thorn raised his eyebrows. 'No need to get snippy, boy. Not after the display you just put on. The point I'm trying to make is that a straight punch, like the one I just threw at you —' he indicated his right arm — 'is a lot harder to dodge. It's harder to see it coming and it gets to the target faster because it travels a shorter distance.'

Hal frowned thoughtfully. Thorn was explaining this in a way he understood — appealing to his analytical nature.

'I see,' he said slowly.

Thorn glanced keenly at him and gave a satisfied nod. 'On top of that, a straight punch can carry a lot of force behind it, as long as you put your shoulder and weight into it. Step into it as you punch. Try it. Hit my hand.'

He held up his left hand, palm out, to Hal. The boy drew back his right fist and Thorn stopped him.

'Use your left,' he said.

Hal looked at him, puzzled. 'But I'm right-handed,' he explained.

'Most people are. So Tursgud will expect you to favour your right. Use your left and you'll catch him by surprise — the way you just tried to do with me. Your instincts were good, but the execution was pretty dreadful. Don't take a big swing, just jab him first with your left — a straight punch. Then use a hooking right hand. Now try it.'

Hal threw a tentative straight jab at Thorn's big, calloused palm.

'Get your weight behind it!' Thorn barked. 'Use your shoulder!'

Hal tried again and felt a far more satisfying smack of contact as he hit Thorn's hand.

'Now step in!'

This time he felt there was even more force behind the punch.

'Again!'

He hit again. Thorn's commands came faster and faster as he ordered him to repeat the blow. Hal could feel the impact of each punch travelling up his arm, jolting against his shoulder. But he also noticed that, as he improved the technique, he had begun to drive Thorn's hand back. On the fifth attempt, the old sea wolf actually staggered back a half pace. He grinned fiercely at Hal.

'Imagine if that had been Tursgud's jaw!' he said.

Hal nodded, grinning at the idea. It created a very satisfying mental picture, he thought.

'Now, I want you to try something else. Hit with the left, then follow through immediately with your right. Keep coming in. Hook it across and finish him off.'

'Finish him off? With just two punches?' Hal said sceptically. But Thorn nodded.

'Just try it. Right hand a little higher. You keep it up there in case he's inconsiderate enough to take a swing at you. Then hit straight with the left and immediately hook right. Go!'

Smack! Smack! The two punches hit Thorn's palm within a few seconds of each other, rocking his left arm back. He smiled.

'That's the way! Straight left, then bring the right across. If you hit him in the nose with the left, his eyes will tear up and he won't see the right coming.'

Hal nodded. His hands were tingling from the repeated contact with Thorn's work-hardened palm. Thorn pointed to the sack that he'd brought with him.

'Now you just need to practise. That sack is stuffed full of old wool, bits of canvas and sailcloth. Hang it in your shelter there and practise hitting it whenever you get the chance. Get those two punches working for you.'

'I still think I may need more than two punches to finish off Tursgud,' Hal said.

Thorn pursed his lips thoughtfully. 'Funny thing is, the majority of fights are won or lost in the first few punches. Most people don't go round expecting to be attacked. So the aggressor has all the advantage. He hits first and, because he's going forward, there's maximum power behind his punches. Try something else. Hit my hand again, but step back as you do it.'

He held up his hand and again Hal threw a punch. But as instructed, he stepped back. He could feel the weakened result.

'If someone attacks us, our instinct is to back away. And once you start going backwards, it's hard to stop. Your attacker will just keep piling in, throwing punch after punch and driving you back. So go against your instinct and move forward if you're attacked. Take it to him. Get in close and those straight punches will start working for you. And you'll get some force behind your punches.'

Hal thought about what the old man had said and he nodded to himself. It was a natural reaction, when someone started throwing punches, to back away. And he could see that if he did that, an attacker would have all the advantage on his side. It was good advice, he thought. Then he frowned, wondering.

'Why did you bother to show me this today, Thorn?' Hal asked.

The older man shrugged. 'You're starting brotherband training tomorrow and you'd better know how to stand up for yourself. I was watching Tursgud yesterday. He'll try to dominate you, Hal, because he fears you.'

'You said that before. Why would Tursgud be afraid of me?'

Thorn shook his head. 'I said he fears you. He's not afraid of you personally. He fears what you are. He can sense that you're a leader. And that's a challenge to him. He wants to be the one that the others look to. Sooner or later, it's going to come to a head between the two of you. And you'd better be ready for it.'

Hal looked doubtful. He didn't see himself as a leader and he still couldn't see that Tursgud's animosity was born from any kind of fear. But he didn't doubt that sooner or later they would clash again. In the light of that fact, it was probably a good idea to practise the technique Thorn had just taught him. He picked up the sack and carried it into the work shelter where he'd stowed the fittings from *Heron*. He hung the sack from one of the beams and punched it thoughtfully. It was heavy and it resisted the punch.

'Do you really think I'll be able to beat him?' Hal asked.

Thorn pursed his lips again and hesitated.

'Maybe. Maybe not. But you'll hurt him enough to convince him to leave you alone.'

CHAPTER ELEVEN

At sea: south of the Sonderland Coast

A rose-coloured glow was beginning to seep across the eastern horizon, like ink spreading in a pool of water, Arndak thought. He looked around in the strengthening dawn light. The other three small ships of his trading fleet were all in sight, although they had scattered somewhat during the dark hours. The sea was calm and the wind was moderate.

He looked back to the east. The sun was beginning to show itself above the horizon now, a blindingly bright arc of light that was rapidly growing bigger. To the west, the sea was still in comparative darkness.

Forward, towards the bow of the ship, he could see members of the crew stirring from their sleep. He decided they'd been resting long enough.

'Lower the sail!' he ordered. 'Shake out those reefs then send it up again.'

During the dark hours of the night, they had travelled with the big square sail reefed — with part of it bundled up and tied to the yardarm to reduce its area. Now, with daylight, they could take full advantage of the wind. He heard the creaking of ropes as the crew lowered the large yardarm and sail and set to work untying the reefing cords. With the sail lowered, the ship gradually lost speed and wallowed in the small waves. He saw the others in the fleet were doing the same thing, then glanced forward and noticed his nephew, Ernak, standing with nothing to do.

'Up the mast and take a look around, boy!' he called, and the twelve-year-old turned and began to shinny up the bare pole like a squirrel going up a tree. He reached the small cross bar that served as a lookout position and scanned the ocean on all sides.

'All clear, Uncle!' his young voice piped. Then he hesitated and peered towards the west again — where the new light was just beginning to reach. 'No . . . wait . . . there's something . . .'

Arndak's heart rate quickened. He resisted the urge to question Ernak. He was a good boy and he'd give a full report when he was more certain of his facts. He'd seen something. Odds were that it was another ship. It could be totally harmless. On the other hand . . .

He clasped and unclasped his grip on the steering oar. 'Stay up there while we hoist the sail again,' he called. Then, turning to the sailors who had been loosening the reefs, he called, 'Get a move on!'

His first mate waved acknowledgement. He and three others began heaving on ropes, and the yardarm, with the square sail attached, began climbing the mast again. The fabric bellied out in the wind, then steadied and firmed as the crew hauled in on the restraining ropes and brought it under control. The ship began to surge forward through the water once more.

'It's a ship, Uncle!' Ernak called. 'A big one! She's got her sail hoisted and she's rowing as well.'

So she's in a hurry, Arndak thought to himself. He could think of only one reason for that. He looked at the other ships in his fleet. They were all smaller and slower than *Spraydancer*, his ship. Reluctantly, he called an order to his mate.

'Ease the sail a little. Let the others catch up.' He felt *Spraydancer*'s speed lessen and grimaced. With an unknown ship chasing them, he hated to reduce speed. But he wouldn't abandon the other ships of his fleet. He took a battered brass horn from a rack beside the steering oar, raised it to his lips and blew three loud blasts on it — the signal for the other ships to close up.

'She's gaining on us, Uncle!'

Of course she is, Arnak thought. He lashed the steering oar in place and leapt nimbly onto the bulwark beside the steering oar, steadying himself on one of the stays that secured the mast, and scanned the sea to the west.

As *Spraydancer* rose on the crest of a wave, he caught a momentary glimpse of a dark rectangle showing above the distant horizon. On the next wave, the rectangle was larger, and he thought he could make out a dark shape below it. The stranger was coming up fast.

We can't outrun her, he thought. We'll have to outfight her. He dropped nimbly back to the deck and reached for his shield and war axe, left handy by the steering oar.

'Weapons, men,' he called. The crew hurried to retrieve their shields, which were stowed along the outer bulwarks of the ship, and their axes, swords and spears. The clatter of weaponry was reassuring. Arndak glanced at his other ships and saw that their crews were also arming themselves. He nodded in satisfaction. His ships were laden with valuable goods — oil, wool fleeces and brandy. Plus there was a supply of iron for weapon making. And finally, there was the cash chest on board *Spraydancer*, holding the money he had earned selling trade goods to the Sonderlanders.

He wasn't giving any of that up without a fight.

'She's a big ship, Uncle!' That was Ernak again, keeping him informed. He smiled grimly. The boy had learned well while he had sailed with his uncle.

'Ten oars a side, maybe,' Ernak continued. 'Could be more.'

That was bad news. Ten oars a side meant twenty men. Plus there'd be a relief rowing crew so they'd be facing thirty or forty. He had six men on *Spraydancer*, not counting Ernak. The other ships carried four or five men each. They were badly outnumbered.

'She's closing fast!'

He looked astern. He could see the other ship from deck level now as *Spraydancer* rose on successive waves. Fast and heavily manned. In Arndak's eyes, that meant only one thing. She was a pirate.

He hesitated. Perhaps their best chance would be to abandon the other three ships and concentrate all his men aboard *Spraydancer*. But he was loath to give up their cargoes to the pirate. And his hesitation proved to be his undoing. Even as he reached for the horn to signal his ships again, the pirate ship came into full view and he could see she was bearing down on the furthest ship in his fleet, little *Rainbow*. The newcomer was a black-hulled ship, and he could see that Ernak's estimate had been accurate. She had ten oars a side, beating regularly and driving her forward at high speed. As she lifted on a low swell, he saw something else that made his heart sink. At the base of the bow, she carried a ram — a protruding iron-shod beam that could smash into an enemy's timbers and sink her in minutes.

The pirate ship's port side oars came upright as she ran alongside *Rainbow*. The two ships crunched together. The pirate's captain had chosen not to ram but a wave of men poured over the bulwarks, boarding the little trading ship and overwhelming her crew. He could hear the sounds of battle, axes and swords clashing against each other and hammering on oaken shields. He heard men shouting, heard the defiant war cries of the *Rainbow*'s crew. Then, in minutes, there was silence. The pirates cut the ropes holding *Rainbow*'s sail aloft and, as it crashed to the deck, they hurried to reboard their own ship, leaving the trader drifting helplessly, her crew murdered in a few brief seconds.

Now the pirate ship swept purposefully towards *Sealion*, the next of the fleet in line.

'He'll pick us off one by one,' Arndak said softly to himself. 'Down sail! Out oars!' he bellowed. He heaved on the steering oar, bringing the ship's bow around. His only chance would be to join up with *Golden Sun*, the nearest ship to him. There were five men aboard her. If he combined their crews, they might have a chance . . .

But as *Spraydancer* swung round into the wind and her crew began to heave on the oars, he saw that his decision had come too late. The black ship barely paused beside *Sealion*, sending a dozen men aboard to overwhelm her four crewmen. Once they were aboard, the pirate set course for *Golden Sun*, and after a few minutes, Arndak could see she was going to win the race. He realised his nephew was still perched on the lookout spot and yelled at him to come down. The boy slid down to the deck, grabbed up a spear and ran back to join his uncle.

'What will we do, Uncle?' he asked.

'The only thing we can, boy. We'll fight them. But you'd better stay back here.'

'I'm not afraid of them,' Ernak said resolutely.

Arndak smiled grimly at him. 'I know you're not. But stay clear of the fight. Your mother would never forgive me if you got knocked on the head.'

He saw the rebellious look in the boy's eyes and his brows came together in a scowl. No longer the uncle, he was now the ship's skirl.

'Do as I say,' he snapped.

There was fighting on board *Golden Sun* now, and the pirates who had captured the *Sealion* had begun rowing to rejoin their own ship.

'In oars,' Arndak ordered. No sense in having the crew wear themselves out. 'Form up on me.'

His crewmen gathered their weapons again and moved back to join him, forming a defensive line near the ship's stern.

His eyes narrowed as he followed the progress of the fight on board *Golden Sun*. The clash of weapons had died away and there was a series of splashes alongside. He realised that the pirates were throwing the crew's bodies overboard.

'Scum,' he muttered. Those crewmen had been his companions and friends for years. He tested the weight of his axe. 'I'll see a few of you go down before I let you take this ship.' He looked along the line of grim faces beside him.

'It's been a pleasure sailing with you, men. There's nothing left for it now but to make it hard on these swine. Let's take as many of them with us as we can.'

There was a roar of assent from his men and he smiled. They had seen that there would be no quarter given. There would be no surrender. Perhaps that was a mistake on the part of the pirate captain. With no hope of surrender, his men would fight even harder.

And seven Skandians could be a truly formidable force.

The pirates had scrambled back aboard their own ship now and it swung away from the smaller trading ship. The oars came out again and the black ship sliced through the water towards *Spraydancer*. The captured *Sealion* was a little way off, her oars thrashing the water to foam as the pirates onboard raced to catch up.

Arndak saw the pirate's bow angle slightly away from his own as the ship came on. He wasn't going to ram, then. He probably suspected that there was a cash chest somewhere on board the lead ship and he didn't want to lose it. Instead, the pirate aimed to meet *Spraydancer* bow to bow, at an oblique angle.

'Let him come,' Arndak said grimly.

CHAPTER TWELVE

There was a grinding crash as the pirate ship ran alongside. *Spraydancer* lurched violently under the impact but the crew, long accustomed to sudden movement underfoot, kept their balance easily. Then, with a chorus of yells and screams, the pirates leapt over the port bow in a swarm.

Several of them lost their footing as they hit the decks of the Skandian trader. But they recovered quickly and moved aft, their comrades pressing from behind.

And found themselves facing a shield wall of seven grim-faced Skandian warriors.

They hesitated then, shoving back against the mounting pressure from behind, eyeing the massive axes in their enemies' hands. For a moment, the two forces eyed each other, then Arndak bellowed the time-honoured Skandian battle command.

'Let's get 'em!'

The seven Skandian warriors surged forward. As they went, they instinctively formed a wedge shape, with

Arndak at the point and three men either side. They smashed into the disorganised pirates, their heavy oaken shields used as weapons of offence, slamming into the pirates and hurling them to either side.

Then the deadly Skandian axes went to work, rising and falling, smashing through thin armour, beating down their opponents' weapons by sheer force, cutting, hacking, biting into flesh and bone.

The first rank of the pirates fell before that massive onslaught. The deck ran red with their blood and the Skandians trod them underfoot as they surged forward, driving the rest of the boarding party back towards the bows.

For a moment, it seemed that they might succeed in forcing the pirates back onto their own ship. But the numbers against them were too great. A spear slammed into the warrior on Arndak's left and he fell back with a strangled cry. Then a pirate slid forward on hands and knees, under the massive oaken shields, and stabbed upwards into the thigh of another Skandian. He fell with a cry of pain and, in a moment, the Skandian wedge was disrupted.

Arndak fought on grimly, protected by his shield and the whistling arc carved by his massive war axe. Any who ventured inside it were cut down, tossed aside like rag dolls. But in spite of it all, he was wounded several times. In the heat of the moment, he felt no pain. He continued to hack and slash at the hated enemy. He saw another of his men go down, tripped by a spear shaft thrust between his feet, and a pack of pirates swarmed over him. Snarling with rage, he aimed an overhead blow at a pirate in front of him. The terrified man saw death descending on him and tried to parry the axe with his sword.

He might as well have used a piece of straw. The axe smashed the blade in half, then cut deep into the man's shoulder. Arndak heaved to free his weapon and finally jerked it loose. The sudden release caused him to stagger back several paces. At the same time, the attacking pirates stepped back as well, surrounding the bleeding, heavy-breathing figure, but unwilling to come within reach of that terrible axe.

Arndak shook his head and looked around. His comrades were all down — either dead or dying. He was alone.

But he wasn't finished, and the dead and maimed pirates on the deck of his ship were testimony to the fact that he was still a dangerous enemy. He brandished the axe aloft and yelled an inarticulate challenge at the pirates. Vaguely, he sensed he was on the edge of madness — the berserker's rage that sometimes overtook Skandian warriors at the height of a battle.

The pirates took another involuntary step backwards. Then their ranks parted and a slim, tall figure stepped forward.

He was olive skinned, with long, black hair that hung in ringlets. The face was handsome, and he was smiling. But there was an unmistakable gleam of malice in his eyes. He had a round metal shield and a long, curved sword, held carelessly, point down. Studying him, Arndak sensed that both shield and sword could spring into action in the flicker of an eye. This was a warrior — and a very dangerous one.

'Skandian,' the pirate said, 'my name is Zavac, captain of the *Raven*.'

He jerked his head towards the black ship alongside *Spraydancer*'s bow.

'Leader of this band of murdering scum, more like it,' Arndak said, with the utmost contempt. Zavac seemed unmoved by the insult.

'As you wish,' he said. 'In any case . . .'

'In any case, you're going to be the next one to die here,' Arndak told him. 'And I'll be delighted to send you to the netherworld.'

Zavac's smile widened. 'I'd expect no less of such a brave fighter,' he said. 'But before you dispatch me, I suggest you look behind you.'

Arndak gave a hollow laugh. 'Do you think I'll fall for an old trick like that?' he said scornfully. 'I didn't come down in the last shower of rain, you know . . .'

His voice was cut off by a shrill cry of pain from behind him and his heart sank. He turned and saw his nephew, Ernak, held fast by a pirate. During the brief, bloody fight, the *Sealion* had come up astern of *Spraydancer* and several pirates had boarded. Now one of them held Ernak firmly in his grasp, a curved knife thrust against the skin of his throat. A small trickle of blood ran down from where the blade touched the boy's skin. That must have caused Ernak's unwitting cry of pain, Arndak thought dully.

'Now drop your weapons,' Zavac said smoothly. For a moment, the Skandian debated whether he had time to strike down the pirate and rescue his nephew. But he realised it was hopeless.

'The boy will die,' Zavac said softly, divining his thoughts. Arndak emitted a long groan and released his grip on the axe. It fell heavily to the deck.

'And the shield,' prompted Zavac.

He let the shield drop from his arm. It struck the deck and rolled into the rowing benches.

'Now tie them both up,' Zavac said to his crew.

Half a dozen of the pirates leapt upon Arndak, forcing his hands behind him, lashing them with leather cords, then dragging him to the stern. They kicked his feet from under him and secured him to one of the frames that formed the hull shape. His nephew was similarly restrained.

Zavac watched, then pulled a small stool close to them and sat on it. He tossed an order over his shoulder to his men.

'Search the ship. He'll have a cash chest somewhere on board.'

His men hurried away to do his bidding. Arndak, his eyes fixed on the pirate leader, heard the sound of axes smashing into wood as the pirates tore up the deck planking in search of the cash chest. After a few minutes, there was a cry of triumph.

'Bring it here,' Zavac called, without looking.

Two of his men lugged the heavy chest to him and let it fall to the deck. He threw back the lid and smiled at the pile of gold and silver inside.

'Very nice,' he said. 'A good day's work.'

'It was months of work for me and my men,' Arndak told him bitterly and Zavac turned that humourless smile on him once more.

'Yes. But they're all dead, aren't they?'

'And I soon will be,' Arndak told him. He said it without any sign of fear. He had accepted his fate. 'But spare the boy, I beg you.' He had no hope that the pirate would agree, but he had to make the attempt, for his sister's sake. Surprisingly, Zavac nodded his head thoughtfully.

'You know, that might be possible. But I'd want something from you in return.'

'Name it,' Arndak said.

The pirate leaned forward on his stool, bringing his face closer to the skirl.

'I've heard rumours of a fabulous treasure in your home port of Hallasholm,' he said softly.

Arndak caught his breath. He could only be referring to one thing — the Andomal.

The Andomal was Hallasholm's most treasured, and valuable, artefact. Nobody was really sure how the Andomal had come to exist. It had been hauled up in a fishing net several hundred years before. It appeared to be a giant piece of amber, some twenty-five centimetres in diameter. It had been worn into an almost perfect globe by the action of the ocean over many decades.

Its sheer size alone made it valuable. But embedded deep inside it was a blackened, wizened claw of some kind of giant lizard — popular legend had it that it was a dragon's foot. That was what made the Andomal priceless. It was unique and awe-inspiring. There was nothing else like it in the known world.

The uncertainty about its origin led to its name. In the old tongue, Andomal meant 'Thing'.

Zavac, watching keenly, saw Arndak's fleeting reaction.

'I see you know what I'm talking about,' he said. But, as Arndak refused to say anything, the pirate looked at the boy beside him. 'It's a strange treasure that's worth more than a boy's life,' he said.

Ernak glared at him, then turned to his uncle.

'Don't tell him, Uncle,' he said fiercely and Zavac's smiled widened.

'Uncle?' he said. 'This boy is your nephew? And you have it in your power to save him. Tell me about this treasure and I swear I'll take him with us. And I'll set him ashore safely somewhere on the Skandian coast.'

Arndak's thoughts were racing. The Andomal was a great treasure. The shrine that held it was set at the top of a steep hill above the town, and it was securely guarded day and night by a rotating honour guard of six warriors, men specially chosen for their courage and prowess in battle. Only the finest warriors could aspire to guard the Andomal.

There was only one path leading up to the shrine and it was easily defensible. A large alarm bell was in place. If the shrine was under attack, its defenders could rouse the entire town in seconds. Arndak turned his scornful gaze on the pirates who had invaded his vessel. If he and his crew could hold them at bay as long as they had done, they would have little chance against six hand-picked warriors in a perfectly constructed defensive position. He took a deep breath.

'It's called the Andomal . . .' he began.

He saw the light of greed in Zavac's eyes when he finished telling him. Of course, he left out the details of how the Andomal was protected, although he knew the pirate would expect something of the kind. He merely said that it was guarded day and night.

Zavac sat back. He had unconsciously leaned further and further forward as Arndak told him about the Andomal.

'Yes,' he said slowly. 'That sounds like a great treasure indeed. It must be priceless.'

'The Skandian Oberjarl would pay anything to have it returned if it were stolen,' Arndak said. He had no qualms about encouraging Zavac to steal the treasure. *You'll never get near it*, he thought. *And with any luck, one of the guards will take your thieving head off.*

Zavac stood abruptly and called to his men.

'Get this chest on board the *Raven*,' he ordered. 'Then sink this ship. We'll burn the others. No sense leaving any evidence behind.'

Two of his men seized the chest and began to lug it forward. Others leapt down into the rowing benches and began to smash holes in the hull, below the water line.

Zavac looked down quizzically at the skirl and his nephew.

'It's been nice talking to you,' he said. 'Although I'm sure you didn't tell me quite everything.'

He turned on his heel and Arndak called out to stop him.

'Wait! Take the boy with you! You gave me your word!'

Zavac turned back to him. There was no sign of the smile now. 'So I did. But we all know that the word of a pirate is worth nothing.'

Then he turned and left the *Spraydancer*, leaping nimbly across to his own ship.

'Be brave,' Arndak told his nephew as the ship began to settle. He was proud of the boy. He held his chin high and endured the fear as he waited to die, without complaint or whimpering.

As the water closed over them, it occurred to Arndak that there was one night in the year when the Andomal was not so securely guarded.

But it was too late to do anything about it.

PART THREE

THE
BROTHERBANDS

CHAPTER THIRTEEN

Twenty-eight boys assembled outside the town in a small field set aside as a training ground. They were the boys who were turning sixteen that year and it was an unusually large number. In an average year, there might be sixteen to twenty boys selected into their brotherbands.

The brotherbands were a unique Skandian concept, born of the fact that Skandians were traditionally sea-farers. Many years ago, they had created a training system where boys were placed in small groups to practise and learn together. Each group was called a brotherband. Its members would bond as a team while they learned tactics, weapon skills, seamanship, ship handling and navigation.

The brotherbands replicated the concept of a ship's crew, where shipmates had to work together and to trust their companions, sometimes with their lives. Quite often, boys who trained in a brotherband together would be recruited into the same ship's crew, and would serve and work and relax together for the rest of their lives. Brotherbands formed bonds and lifelong friendships.

And they taught their members the value of combining their varying skills to best advantage.

Since a successful ship's crew required a captain, or skirl, to command it, the brotherband system also developed another vital skill: leadership. Natural leaders tended to come to the fore in the bands. They were the boys with that little extra, that indefinable quality that caused the others to look to them for ideas and direction. Sometimes, at the beginning of their training, a band would elect its most popular member as leader. But popularity wasn't always the most important part of leadership and, quite often, before the training period was over, that leader would have been replaced by someone else — someone who had shown that he had the necessary confidence and ability to command.

Hal and Stig arrived at the assembly ground together. They were early and there were only a half dozen or so other boys already there. Most of them greeted Stig, and some nodded vaguely to Hal. He looked around nervously. Tursgud, with his band of followers, hadn't arrived yet. Knowing Tursgud, he'd swagger up at the last possible minute, Hal thought. He rubbed his knuckles absentmindedly. After dinner with his mam the previous night, he'd headed back to the shelter where he'd hung Thorn's sack. He'd hammered away at it for several hours, working to perfect the sequence of punches that Thorn had shown him, doing them over and over again in sequence so that they became instinctive. Finally, shoulders aching and knuckles reddened by the rough canvas, he'd called it a night, trudged back up the hill to his mam's house, and fallen into bed, exhausted.

'Hope we're picked in the same band,' Stig said eagerly. Hal nodded, although he doubted that it would happen. With twenty-eight boys, he suspected there would be three bands formed today. He knew that each brotherband needed at least eight members in order to be able to row the ships they would be training on.

Stig was shifting eagerly from one foot to the other, looking around at the other boys as they gradually drifted into the assembly area, waving and responding to their greetings. He was filled with nervous energy and anticipation. Brotherband selection was a big day in any boy's life and he was looking forward to it. He didn't see that Hal would have any problem being picked. Hal was smart and intelligent and inventive, he thought — and a good friend. But then, Stig was an optimist.

Hal, on the other hand, faced the day with a certain sense of resignation. Stig was big and athletic and, perhaps most important, a Skandian. Any brotherband would welcome him as a member, despite his hot temper. Whereas Hal knew he would be one of the last to be chosen. It would be embarrassing to stand waiting, while other boys' names were called and they moved to join their bands.

And he knew that any band who did choose him would do so reluctantly, probably resenting the fact that they had to do so. He wouldn't be surprised, he thought gloomily, if his was the last name to be called. And then he could look forward to three months of being mocked, insulted, ordered around and given the most boring and menial tasks to carry out.

'What's Erak doing here?' Stig said, breaking through his gloomy thoughts.

Hal looked up. This was a surprise. Normally, the Oberjarl took no part in the selection of the brotherbands. From time to time he might visit the training ground and check on progress. But the first day was usually something that didn't concern him.

Yet here he came, striding alongside Sigurd, the former ship's skirl who had been given the overall responsibility for training the brotherbands. Sigurd had a reputation as a hard taskmaster and a strict disciplinarian. Boys coming under his control usually did so with a distinct sense of nervousness. He was short-tempered and had no patience for those who were lazy or foolish. Yet most agreed that he was fair and didn't play favourites.

Sigurd and Erak were deep in conversation as they made their way through the gaggle of expectant boys to the small platform set on one side of the training ground. The boys drifted along behind them, as if drawn by some invisible force, gradually forming a loose half circle in front of the two men, three ranks deep.

And now, of course, Tursgud and three of his close companions swaggered in, thrusting their way through to the front row, regardless of the occasional angry glances they drew. Hal, in the back row, noticed that Erak looked up and nodded a greeting to Tursgud. The boy nodded back confidently, standing with his legs braced apart, hands thrust into his belt.

Tursgud's father was the Maktig, of course. As his son, Hal supposed Tursgud was allowed a certain familiarity with Erak. Tursgud made no bones about the fact that he intended to follow in his father's footsteps and become the Maktig one day. And there was every likelihood that he would.

Still, as Stig had observed on more than one occasion, perhaps he could wait till he *was* the Maktig before he started putting on airs.

Erak said a few more quiet words to Sigurd, then stepped back, leaving the platform to the grizzled old seafarer. On an impulse, Hal turned round and studied the trees a hundred metres away. Brotherband selection was a more or less private event and spectators were discouraged. But some sixth sense told him they were being watched. Sure enough, standing under a clump of half-grown conifers, he could see the ragged figure of Thorn. He'd had a suspicion that the man might show up to watch.

His attention was drawn back to the front as Sigurd cleared his throat noisily.

'All right! All right! Settle down and pay attention!' he called.

There was really no need for either instruction. The twenty-eight boys had been waiting since he arrived for proceedings to commence. He already had their attention and they were already settled down. But the half circle of boys unconsciously shuffled closer to the platform where Sigurd was standing.

'Everybody here?' he looked up, casting his gaze around them. A few boys looked at those on either side of them, as if to make sure that they were, in fact, present.

'Sing out if you're not here,' he commanded and a nervous laugh ran through the group. They thought it might be a good idea to laugh at any joke Sigurd might crack. They were all in awe of him and nervous of the fact that for the next few months they would be subject to his discipline. People in authority, they knew, liked it when their jokes were appreciated, even if the jokes were a little feeble.

'All right, let's get under way,' Sigurd said crisply, after studying them for a few seconds.

Hal was surprised. He had half expected that some kind of roll might be called, to determine if anyone was missing. He didn't realise that Sigurd, in the past few seconds, had quickly done a head count and ascertained that the correct number of nervous boys was standing in front of him. Sigurd had been doing this job for years. He could do a head count like that in seconds.

'Today,' Sigurd began, 'you're going to be selected into your brotherbands.' He paused, then added, 'That's in case any of you thought this was the Hallasholm Ladies' Needlework Society. If so, you may leave now.'

Again, a nervous ripple of laughter went through the assembled boys.

'First thing we do is select brotherband leaders. Any nominations?'

Predictably, one of Tursgud's followers, standing on his right side, called out Tursgud's name. Sigurd nodded. Like everyone else, he wasn't surprised.

'Tursgud. Seconder?' he demanded.

'Second!' the person standing on the other side of Tursgud called out.

Sigurd had a board with several sheets of parchment clipped to it in his left hand. He made a note on it and glanced up at Tursgud.

'All right. Proposed and seconded. Congratulations, Tursgud.'

Tursgud shrugged. The matter had never been in doubt, after all. Congratulations seemed unnecessary.

'Anyone else?' Sigurd looked around the group.

'Rollond!' called a voice. A few heads craned to see who had called out, but most of those present weren't surprised at the nomination. Rollond was a popular figure among the age group. He was the son of a successful and well-known wolfship captain. He was an excellent athlete and had quite a reputation as a wrestler. Unlike Tursgud, however, he had no pretensions about his own importance. He'd make a good brotherband skirl, Hal thought. He found himself hoping that Rollond might select him for his band. He and Rollond were by no means friends, but at least there was no animosity between them.

'Second!' he called, before Sigurd had time to ask for a seconder. A few people looked around, surprised that he had spoken. Rollond, who was at the end of the second rank, turned to see who had seconded his nomination. He hadn't recognised the voice and he'd expected the call to come from one of his close friends. He frowned, then nodded acknowledgement as he realised it had been Hal.

'All right. Rollond. Who else?' Sigurd looked around the group of boys but there was a reluctance among them now. Everyone knew that any further captain elected would be competing with Rollond and Tursgud – and their respective groups of friends. The brotherbands competed against each other through the training period and there was a lot of prestige involved in being part of the winning band. On the other hand, there was a lot of embarrassment about being the losers. It was a stigma that could cling to you for years to come. Most of the boys present would rather be a member of a winning band — with Tursgud or Rollond as the captain — than captain of their own losing one. Inevitably, the group's failure would be attributed to its leader.

Sigurd cast his glance over them impatiently. 'Come on. With these numbers, we really need three teams. Anyone else?'

But there was no reply. Then, impulsively, Stig put his hand up. 'Hal!' he yelled.

Beside him, Hal closed his eyes and cursed silently.

CHAPTER FOURTEEN

Sigurd turned to see who had spoken. Stig was obscured by the boys in front of him and he leaned to one side.

'Hal!' he repeated. Some of the other boys sniggered. Stig's face began to redden.

'Shut up!' Hal whispered ferociously to his friend. He didn't need this sort of embarrassment. He didn't want any attention drawn to him, today of all days.

'Hal who?' Sigurd asked, genuinely puzzled. The sniggering now swelled into laughter.

Stig's face grew redder. 'Hal Mikkelson!' he shouted defiantly.

From his position in the front rank, Tursgud turned to face him, shaking his head in disbelief and mock pity.

'You can't be serious,' he said. 'You're not seriously proposing "Hal Who" as a team skirl, are you?'

The laughter grew more widespread and Stig's neck and face grew even redder as his anger approached boiling point. He glared at the boys around him.

'What's the big joke?' he demanded.

'I'd say "Hal Who" is the joke, wouldn't you?' Tursgud said, in an intentionally audible aside to one of his friends.

Hal, eyes down, unwilling to meet anyone's gaze, jabbed his elbow into Stig's ribs.

'Shut up!' he pleaded. 'Just let it go and shut up!'

But Stig wouldn't be silenced. He was incensed for his friend, and also enraged that people were laughing at him. His hands bunched into fists and he glared around the circle of grinning faces.

'Go on!' he threatened. 'Keep laughing and I'll bash your heads in!'

It was a mistake. Taken individually, most of those present would have been wary about raising Stig's anger. He would make a formidable opponent. But he hadn't challenged an individual. He'd challenged the group, and they reacted as a group.

'Ooooooooh!' they all chorused mockingly. Stig swung from side to side, like a tormented bear. As his gaze lit on those boys near him, they quickly composed themselves and hid their grins. He lunged towards one who was a little slow wiping the grin from his face.

'Right!' he yelled, drawing back his fist. 'Laugh this off!'

'THAT'S ENOUGH!'

Sigurd's voice, trained over the years to carry orders to his crew above the roar of a Stormwhite gale, brought Stig up short. He stopped, fist still poised, looking uncertainly at the furious instructor.

'What the blue blithering blazes do you think this is? We're not in barnskole here! We're not a bunch of squabbling children! This is brotherband! This is where you're supposed to learn to act like men! Like men! Understand?'

Stig hung his head. His face was still red, but now it was with shame more than anger. Slowly, he lowered the raised fist.

'Sorry, sir,' he muttered.

Beside him, Hal hissed at him. 'For pity's sake, Stig!'

'One more outburst like that,' Sigurd warned him, 'and you'll be kicked out on your ear! And I'll be happy to do the kicking! Do you understand?'

'Yes, sir,' Stig said in a low voice. He was totally mortified — and terrified at the prospect of being expelled from brotherband training.

'I CAN'T HEAR YOU!' Sigurd bellowed, so loud that the boys nearest him involuntarily stepped back a pace.

'Yes, sir! Sorry, sir!' Stig said in a louder tone, his eyes still cast down in shame.

Sigurd regarded him for several seconds, then glanced down at his sheet of notes.

'All right. We have a nomination for Hal Mikkelson as our third skirl. Anyone care to second?'

'Are you kidding?' It was Tursgud who spoke, and he followed the question with a short laugh. Again, a few around him sniggered, cutting themselves off quickly as Sigurd's angry gaze swept over them. Tursgud, however, remained defiant, smiling at the instructor.

'You find it amusing, do you?' Sigurd challenged.

Tursgud shrugged, unfazed by the question. 'It just doesn't make sense, sir,' he said. 'He's the son of a slave. He's not even Skandian. He's Araluan.'

A few others, emboldened by his stance, muttered agreement.

Sigurd glared at them. 'Karina Mikkelswife is a free woman,' he told them in a cold voice. 'And her late husband was a Skandian. He was also a good friend of mine. Bear that in mind when you talk about her. And her son.' He glanced back at his notes and a voice, clearly audible, came from the crowd.

'The mongrel.'

Sigurd's eyes snapped back up, glaring in the direction from which the unidentified voice had come.

'Who said that?' he demanded. But there was no reply and long seconds passed as he glared at the boys in front of him. Then, realising he was getting nowhere, he said once more, 'Hal Mikkelson has been nominated. Is there a second?'

As if there will be after all that, Hal thought bitterly. He looked at his friend, tight lipped. He knew Stig had meant well. But Hal wished he'd kept his big mouth shut. He had no wish to be the leader of a brotherband. Aside from that one brief moment of glory when he brought the *Heron* into harbour, he spent most of his time avoiding drawing attention to himself.

Sigurd's question met with an ongoing silence. Finally, he accepted the inevitable. He struck a line through Hal's name on his notes.

'All right. Other nominations. Anyone?'

Silence. Nobody was willing to draw attention to themselves. Sigurd tapped his foot impatiently as he looked from one face to another. Many of them, he noticed, wouldn't meet his gaze. Tursgud did, of course, but he was an arrogant piece of work. And Rollond held his gaze too. Sigurd noted with interest that Hal was one of the few others who did.

'Come on,' he prompted. 'We need another skirl. You can nominate yourself if you want to.'

But nobody was willing to risk it. He looked around and shrugged at Erak. The Oberjarl stepped forward.

'All right,' he said to Sigurd, 'we'll start with the two skirls we've got and see how we're doing by the time we're down to the last nine or ten.'

Sigurd nodded agreement. Anything to break this impasse. Not for the first time, he found himself wondering why he'd ever let himself be talked into doing this job.

'We'll do it that way then,' he said. 'Tursgud. You're over there.' He indicated a spot to his left. 'Rollond, over here.'

The two selected brotherband skirls moved forward and took up their positions. Sigurd produced a five-kroner coin.

'We'll toss for first pick, then take it turn and turn about. You call it, Rollond,' he said. He'd heard enough from Tursgud for a while, he thought, as he spun the coin in the air, then caught it, slapping it down on the back of his left fist.

'Axes or bones?' he asked Rollond. The tall boy shrugged slightly. There wasn't any great advantage in going first. He would make his first choices from his immediate circle of friends, and he knew Tursgud would do the same.

'Bones,' he said.

Sigurd uncovered the coin and glanced briefly at it. 'It's axes,' he said. 'Your first pick then, Tursgud.'

Tursgud grinned, stepped forward a pace and nodded at one of his friends.

'Knut,' he said. 'Come and join the winning band.'

'Just the names. Never mind the blather,' Sigurd said. His curt tone hinted at the fact that Tursgud had said enough for one day. Tursgud glanced at him, surprised. He wasn't used to being corrected in public.

'Dell,' Rollond said crisply and one of his friends grinned and stepped forward to join him.

And so it began. At first, the selections were fast, as the two young skirls chose their own close circle of friends. But, as the line beside each of them grew, the choices became more considered. Tursgud had selected eight men and Rollond seven, when Rollond looked around the diminishing group of boys in front of him. He went to call a name, then changed his mind.

'Stig.'

Stig, who had been looking down at his shoes, still embarrassed by the earlier confrontation with Sigurd, jerked his head up. He reddened and hesitated, looking at Tursgud. Instinctively, he knew that if Rollond chose him, Tursgud would choose Hal, just to split them up and get his revenge on them.

Stig hesitated. Rollond frowned at him and gestured to him.

'Come on,' he said impatiently.

But still Stig stood his ground. 'It's just . . . I sort of want to be with Hal,' he said, indicating his friend beside him. 'Are you going to choose him too?'

Rollond shrugged. He wasn't having someone else dictate his choices for him.

'I don't know. I might. Or I might not. But I have chosen you, so get up here.'

Stig shifted his feet nervously. He was racked with uncertainty. But there was one avenue open to him.

'I pass,' he said. The rules of brotherband selection allowed each boy one refusal. There was a low murmur among the group. People rarely passed, even if they did have the right to do so.

'You idiot,' Hal muttered at him. Stig's jaw was set in a stubborn line. He didn't know how to solve the quandary of being separated from Hal but at least he'd postponed it. Rollond considered him for a few seconds. He was annoyed at Stig's refusal. Stig was definitely the best choice out of those who were left. He made eye contact with Stig now and shook his head briefly. The message was clear: *I won't call on you again.*

'Still your pick,' Sigurd prompted Rollond. The boy looked briefly at the remaining choices.

'Anton,' he said. Anton, who had been dreading being picked in Tursgud's group, smiled with relief and hurried to join Rollond before he could change his mind.

'Go ahead, Tursgud,' Sigurd ordered.

Tursgud hesitated a second, then a broad grin crept over his face. Hal, watching him, knew what he was going to say.

'I pick "Hal Who",' he said. His close friends, grouped around him, grinned and nudged each other. They could see months ahead of them when they could torment and bully Hal.

'No! That's not happening!'

Erak's voice boomed across the field. He stepped forward to join Sigurd again and pointed a finger at the surprised Tursgud.

'This is brotherband selection, not an excuse for you to indulge your petty disputes!' he said. 'There's bad blood between you and Hal. You're not going to use your position as skirl to get revenge. That's not what the brotherband system is about.'

Tursgud threw his hands wide and looked around, feigning surprise.

'That was never my intention!' he said indignantly. 'And I resent you implying it!'

Erak stepped closer to him. Tursgud was big and muscular. Yet Erak dwarfed him.

'Don't try playing pattycake with me, sonny. I resent you thinking I'm too stupid to see what you have in mind.'

Tursgud was furious. He was definitely not accustomed to being treated this way.

'My father . . .' he began, but Erak cut him off.

'Yes, yes. We're all aware that he's the Maktig. Gorlog's breath, you've told us often enough! Now shut up about it and get on and choose.'

Their eyes locked for a few seconds. Then Tursgud's eyes dropped.

'All right,' he said bitterly, and Erak turned away to resume his former position. 'I choose . . .'

Erak turned back suddenly. 'Not Stig either! Same reason.'

Tursgud paused, mouth open. Erak had forestalled his

plan. He had been about to call Stig's name. Now Rollond stepped forward.

'Then we have a problem, Oberjarl,' he said angrily. 'Because I'm not choosing Stig again. He's already turned me down and I don't want him.'

Erak took a deep breath. He was very obviously losing patience.

'Your objection is noted,' he said, in very precise tones. 'Now get on with it! You!' He jerked a thumb at Tursgud. 'Choose!'

So the selections went on as Rollond and Tursgud chose their final brotherband members. Hal looked around at the dwindling group of those who were not chosen. As he'd half expected, Ulf and Wulf were still unchosen, and their angry scowls made it a good bet that they would remain that way. Ingvar had spent the selection process smiling hopefully and looking myopically around as others were chosen ahead of him. With each choice, he remained hopeful.

Stefan and Jesper had also not been chosen.

Stefan was a clown. That could have made him popular, but he usually used his dagger-sharp wit to make fun of others. Although, now that Hal thought about it, he realised that Stefan never chose anybody weaker than himself as the butt of his jokes. He seemed to delight in puncturing the egos of those who had too high an opinion of themselves — Tursgud was a favourite target, as was the Oberjarl's Hilfmann, Borsa, another person who had a firm belief in his own importance in the world.

In addition to his quick wit, Stefan was an expert mimic. He could impersonate anyone in Hallasholm, usually to their detriment. If you weren't looking, you would never be sure whether it was Stefan or the actual person who was talking.

Jesper was a thief. He never wanted to keep anything. He simply couldn't resist the challenge of picking someone's pocket or helping himself to their purse without their noticing. On one occasion, he had actually removed a silver bracelet from a blacksmith's wrist while he had been talking to the man. Hal had seen him do it and couldn't believe his eyes. Of course, the moment he had the bracelet, Jesper had held it up triumphantly to return it, a broad smile on his face. The blacksmith didn't see the joke and Jesper had to use another of his natural skills — his ability to run like the wind — to escape a dreadful fate.

That left Hal and Stig, and an eighth boy, Edvin. Hal didn't know him too well. He was a quiet boy who kept to himself. He was one of those people who was average at just about everything. He had average skills and athletic ability. He wasn't good at sports. Nor was he bad. He liked reading and he had been quick to pick up the basic mathematics they had all been taught as youngsters in barnskole. But he was the type of person who would always be overlooked on occasions like this. Hal, Stig and the others might be intentionally ignored. With Edvin it was different. People just forgot he was there.

Rollond had just chosen his ninth recruit. Now he and Tursgud looked expectantly at Erak. They had assessed the remaining eight boys and there were none among them that they wanted in their bands.

Erak considered the situation. He ran his eye over the small gaggle of boys who remained unchosen. He could have guessed who most of them would be before the selections began.

'Very well,' he said. 'You each have ten members. And there are eight left over. Those eight will become the third brotherband selected here today. We'll say they were selected by default,' he added with a small smile.

'They'll be at a disadvantage. There aren't as many of them,' Sigurd put in.

Erak shrugged. 'We'll either have two nines and one ten or two tens and one eight,' he replied. 'So someone will always be disadvantaged. And I can't see anyone from the selected groups volunteering to change over to even up the numbers.'

There was an instant murmur of agreement from the two bands. Nobody wished to be switched now into what was obviously the weakest brotherband of the three.

'I suppose you're right,' Sigurd agreed. Then he looked at the slightly bewildered group of leftovers. They remained where they had been originally standing. Aside from the twins and Stig and Hal, they were scattered, separated by the empty spaces where the twenty chosen boys had been standing.

'All right, move together. You're the third brotherband. Start acting like one.'

'You can't do that!' It was Tursgud, of course, his voice cracking with anger as he shouted at Erak. 'They weren't selected, so they can't be a brotherband! Send them home! You can't do this!'

He looked around, seeking support from the others, but there was none forthcoming. Erak beckoned him forward.

Tursgud approached the massive Oberjarl warily. Erak smiled at him. It wasn't a friendly smile.

'Actually, I can do it,' he said, 'even though my daddy isn't the Maktig. Because *I'm* the Oberjarl. Understand?'

Tursgud dropped his eyes. 'Yes,' he muttered.

'Yes, what?' Erak said, very softly. Tursgud looked up again and saw a very dangerous light in the Oberjarl's eyes.

'Yes, Oberjarl,' he amended.

Erak nodded, satisfied. He made a gesture for Sigurd to take over once more.

'Very well,' the instructor said. 'Now that we have that settled, you can choose the symbols for your bands. Skirl Rollond, what do you choose to call yourselves?'

'The Wolves,' Rollond replied instantly. Each brother-band assumed an animal totem as their symbol. They would have a banner emblazoned with their choice and it would fly outside their barracks, and they would be known by that name for the training period. Rollond and Tursgud had chosen well in advance, of course, knowing they would be team skirls.

'Tursgud?' Sigurd asked.

Tursgud seemed to have recovered his confidence. He looked up and announced in a firm voice, 'Sharks.'

'Very well.' Sigurd looked at the remaining boys, now standing together in a loose group. Without knowing why, he assumed Hal would be their spokesman.

'Do you have a choice?' he asked, directing the question at him.

Hal hesitated. He'd never thought this would be a possibility so he had no answer ready. He looked at Stig, and at the others, saw their faces were equally blank. Sigurd chewed impatiently on the ends of his moustache.

'Well, I suppose you don't have to decide right away. You can talk it over and tell me later this —'

'Herons!' Ingvar interrupted him and everyone turned to look at him in surprise. There was a beaming smile on his face and he nodded at his new brothers. 'Herons,' he repeated, then added, 'Like Hal's boat.'

The others exchanged glances. Stefan and Edvin seemed noncommittal. But the other five all began to smile and nod agreement.

Sigurd hesitated. Usually, teams selected fierce, warlike names. 'Are you sure?'

Hal paused, then, seeing confirmation on the faces of his companions, he replied. 'Why not? We'll be the Herons.'

Tursgud, predictably, snorted in derision. 'Herons? Herons aren't too dangerous. Unless you're a fish!' His friends laughed. Surprisingly, it was Edvin who replied.

'And of course, that's just what a shark is. A big, dumb fish.'

The other Herons erupted in laughter, watching Tursgud flush with anger. Even a few of Rollond's Wolves joined in. And in that moment, Hal knew that they were, in fact, a brotherband.

CHAPTER FIFTEEN

First order of business was for the brotherbands to construct their living quarters. Three cleared areas had been selected for the purpose, and each band was taken to a different clearing, where a pile of building material was waiting for them.

Gort, the assistant instructor who led the Herons to their living area, pointed to the pile of materials.

'Everything you need is there,' he said. 'You just have to work out how to put it together. You've got the rest of today and tomorrow to do it. If I were you, I'd get some kind of shelter in place before evening. It's going to rain tonight and this is where you'll be sleeping, ready or not.'

He turned to go, then remembered something and turned back to them.

'Oh, and Sigurd said you'd better formally select a skirl,' he said, then he made his way off through the trees. The Herons looked around at each other.

'Well . . . I suppose Hal was already nominated . . .' Stefan began. And Ulf (or was it Wulf?) backed him up.

'That's right. And he's our best helmsman. So, since he'll be in control during the sailing contests, it makes sense if he's in charge the rest of the time.'

There was a murmur of agreement. Even those who hadn't sailed with Hal had heard about his entry into the harbour two days ago. Surprisingly, even Wulf, or Ulf, agreed with his twin. That in itself was a rarity.

The only person who seemed to be against the idea was Hal himself.

'You don't want me as your leader,' he said. 'Choose someone else.'

Stig grinned at him. 'Who?' he said. 'Not me, that's for sure. I'd keep losing my temper. Look around you. Can you see anyone else suited for the job? You're smart. You're a thinker. That's what we're going to need for a leader. Particularly since we're a few men short.'

Again, there was a murmur of ageement from the others. But Hal shook his head reluctantly.

'Don't rush into this,' Hal objected. 'Tursgud hates me. You all know that. If you elect me as leader, he'll hate you as well.'

Jesper made a disparaging gesture. 'So what? He hates us anyway.'

'That's true,' Ingvar put in, in his deliberate, almost ponderous way. 'The only person Tursgud likes is Tursgud.'

There was a small ripple of amusement.

Hal couldn't help smiling at his big companion. 'That's very wisely put, Ingvar.'

Ingvar nodded seriously in reply. 'People often don't notice, but I'm a very wise person at times,' he said, then spoiled the effect by adding, 'When I'm not falling over my own feet.'

'All right,' Edvin said, 'are we all agreed? Hal is our skirl?'

There was a moment of hesitation, then seven heads nodded and seven voices gave assent. Hal shook his head. He couldn't help feeling that he'd been manipulated into this position.

'Don't say I didn't warn you,' he said.

'What do we do with this lot?' Stig asked, prodding the pile of lumber, rope and canvas with one boot. The materials were piled higgledy-piggledy: long pieces, heavy pieces, short pieces and light pieces, logs and planks were mixed haphazardly, with canvas and rope tossed among them or under them. Nobody said anything. After a few moments, Hal became aware that the others were looking at him.

'What?' he asked. 'What are you looking at me for?'

'You're the skirl,' Edvin said. 'Take charge.'

Hal took a deep breath. He studied the building materials for a few seconds.

'When we're building a boat,' he said finally, 'we sort out the materials. We put similar pieces together so we can see what we've got.'

'I can see what we've got,' Stig said. 'We've got a mess.'

'So what do you want us to do, Hal?' Edvin prompted him. Hal hesitated, then took the plunge. If he didn't take charge, they'd be finished before they even started.

'Start sorting,' he said, jerking a thumb at the wood and canvas. 'Put similar pieces together so we can see what we've got. Then we can work out the best way to use it.'

They went to work and, within half an hour, they had the materials sorted into neat piles. Hal strode along the line of beams, fingering his chin thoughtfully. Now that he had a specific problem to deal with, he felt more confident about issuing orders.

'All right,' he said, after pondering for some minutes. 'These eight beams will be our basic floor plan. Four long and four shorter. We'll lay them out in a rectangle. That'll be the shape of our barracks.'

'Don't we just need four?' Stefan asked, indicating a rectangle on the ground.

'Four on the ground, to form the floor,' Edvin told him. 'And four above it to form the ceiling. You've got to think in three dimensions.'

'Oh . . . yeah,' Stefan said, nodding.

Hal looked appraisingly at Edvin. He caught on fast, he thought.

'These four shorter poles will be the corner posts,' he continued. 'And we'll build roof frames from the lighter timber there.'

'What are these planks?' Stig asked. 'Are they for the roof?'

Hal appraised the timber he was referring to. His work in the boatyard had given him the ability to quickly size up a stack of timber and assess the approximate area it would cover. He shook his head.

'Not enough of them for that,' he said. 'They'll barely cover half the area we're setting up.'

He dismissed the problem for the moment.

'We'll worry about that later. Let's get these top and bottom frames together. We'll notch each beam so that it fits into the others. Ulf, Jesper and I will work on the bottom frame. Wulf, Stefan and Edvin, you do the top. Stig and Ingvar, get busy digging post holes for the corner posts.'

They started work. Hal and his two companions selected a level spot where the barracks would be built and placed their four beams – roughly trimmed pine trunks – in position, forming a rectangle approximately four metres by five. They began notching the beams where they intersected, cutting halfway through each so that when one was placed at right angles on top of the other, the notches lined up and the logs slotted together. Then they hammered hardwood spikes into the joints to hold them tightly.

Edvin, Stefan and Wulf mirrored their actions on the top frame. The little clearing echoed to the ringing crack of axes on wood and hammers on nails, counterpointed by the dull thudding of Stig's and Ingvar's crowbars as they drove them into the soft ground to form the post holes.

Unnoticed among the trees, Erak and Sigurd watched the busy, efficient scene. They had already observed progress at the other two sites – or rather, the lack of it.

'Look at that,' Erak said. 'He's got them organised. He's started them building. The other two groups are still stumbling around, wondering which end of a hammer is which.'

Sigurd shook his head. 'Who'd have thought it?'

Erak looked sidelong at him. 'I did,' he said. Then he relented, because it hadn't been his own thought entirely. 'Or rather, Thorn did. He told me that boy had something special about him. He's a thinker and a planner — and that's what we need.'

'Thorn?' Sigurd said, surprised. 'The drunk?' He remembered seeing Thorn stumbling around Hallasholm going from one tavern to another. It occurred to him that he hadn't seen him doing so for some time.

'He's off the drink,' Erak said.

'People like him are never really off it,' Sigurd replied.

Erak pursed his lips. 'Maybe he is. I hope so. In any event, he was right about the Araluan boy.' He scratched his beard thoughtfully. 'Let's get back and see how Tursgud's bunch are managing.'

It was late afternoon. The Heron team had the basic structure for their barracks completed. The four floor frames and their matching roof beams were in place, the latter supported at their four corners by poles sunk into the post holes Stig and Ingvar had dug. They stood back to inspect their work. Hal nodded, satisfied. As the structure grew, so did his confidence. He was actually beginning to enjoy the feeling of directing the other boys in their tasks, he realised.

'We'll build A-frames for the roof,' he said, 'and stretch canvas over them. Then we can cover the canvas with pine branches. That should keep it pretty waterproof.'

'What about the walls?' Jesper asked. 'There doesn't seem to be enough timber for them.'

'More canvas. We've got plenty of that. In effect, we're building a big, timber-framed tent.'

Stig glanced towards the east, where a mass of cloud had gathered and was roiling towards them, its shape changing constantly as it was driven by the winds.

'We'd better get a move on with the roof,' he said. 'It'll be raining in an hour.'

Hal followed his line of sight and saw that he was correct, saw too that there would be no time to build the sort of structure he had in mind

'We'll have to rig something temporary,' he said. He thought for a moment, then the image of the *Heron* sprang to mind, with the tarpaulin rigged along its hull to keep rain out. 'We'll set up a ridge pole and stretch canvas over it. The rain will pool in it, but most of it should run off. Just don't anybody touch it where the canvas sags.'

If that happened, he knew, the water would immediately run through the canvas, flooding the interior.

'Stig, Ingvar, Edvin and I will take care of the roof,' he said. 'Ulf and Wulf, dig a drainage trench around the outside to keep the groundwater running away.' He glanced around, wondering if he'd left anything out, and suddenly realised the purpose of the planks Stig had asked about earlier. He pointed to them now.

'They're floorboards,' he said. 'Jesper and Stefan: start nailing them to a couple of beams so they're off the ground.'

'You said they won't cover the entire area,' Stefan pointed out.

Hal nodded. 'I know. But they'll make a raised sleeping platform big enough to keep us off the ground.'

Stefan nodded. 'Good thinking,' he said. 'That must be why we made you the boss.'

'I thought it was my good looks and sparkling personality,' Hal said.

Ingvar, who had been listening, shook his head very deliberately. 'No. That was definitely not the reason,' he said.

Stefan and Stig grinned. Hal bowed slightly in Ingvar's direction.

'Thanks for pointing that out, Ingvar.' He noticed that Ulf and Wulf had selected two shovels. The tools were identical but that didn't stop them quarrelling over the selection. Ulf wanted the one Wulf had, and vice versa. Hal walked over to them and said, very quietly, 'Why don't you just swap?'

That stopped the argument in its tracks. The two twins looked at him, startled, then at each other. Then, with very bad grace, Ulf snatched the shovel from Wulf's hand and thrust the other shovel at him. Wulf took it, glared at it suspiciously, then nodded with very bad grace.

'Start at the back,' Hal ordered them. 'Dig the trench about a metre from the tent. And work in opposite directions so you meet up again at the front.' He glanced at Stig and said in a lower voice, 'That should keep them apart for at least an hour.'

Stig grinned. 'And that's the real reason we elected you leader. Nobody else can handle those two.'

In fact, it was just over forty minutes when the work was finished. Jesper and Stefan had completed the sleeping platform and joined the others in stretching the canvas over the ridgepole and around the sides. There was only enough to cover three sides of the structure, so they left the front open. They could fill it in later with logs or pine branches, Hal thought.

The rain was starting to fall as they finished their work. A few minutes later, Ulf and Wulf met at the front of the building and the bickering began once more. Sighing, Hal went to see what was the trouble this time. The others grinned and followed him.

'What's the problem?' he said. Ulf, or perhaps it was Wulf, pointed contemptuously at his brother's trench.

'Ulf's trench is too shallow. Mine is much deeper. It'll hold more water,' he said.

Hal made a mental note that it was Wulf speaking, not Ulf. Or perhaps not. The twins had been known to swap identities in the past, just to confuse people. They seemed to enjoy that almost as much as arguing with each other.

'But mine is wider than his,' Ulf replied.

'Yours should be deeper,' said the other. Hal gave up trying to differentiate between them. He'd taken his eyes off them as he studied the two trenches and he suspected they might have changed places.

'Yours should be wider,' one brother insisted vehemently.

'Deeper is better.'

'Only if you're a numbskull.'

'Numbskull yourself! Want me to numb your skull with this shovel?'

'Want to try it?'

'You dare me to?'

'You want me to?'

'Go ahead.'

'No. You go ahead!'

'No. You go —'

'Oh for pity's sake, will you SHUT UP!' Hal could stand it no longer. The two brothers stopped in surprise. He shoved his way between them, pointed at one and said, 'You! Which is your trench?'

'The good one,' the twin replied. Then, seeing a very dangerous light in Hal's eye, he added, 'The deep one.'

'And why is a deep trench better?' Hal asked.

The twin shrugged and smiled at such an easy question. ''Cause it'll hold more water.'

His tone implied that Hal should have known that. It was obvious, after all. His brother sniffed in contempt. Hal rounded on him.

'What's so good about a wider trench?' he demanded.

The second twin mirrored his brother's shrug. They even move the same way, Hal thought.

'Because if it's wider, it'll hold more water,' the twin said.

'So,' said Hal, forcing himself to be calm, 'a deeper one holds more water . . .' He looked to Twin Number One for confirmation. Twin Number One nodded.

'And a wider one will hold more water?' This time, he sought agreement from Number Two. Another nod. Finally, Hal abandoned the enforced calm.

'You blasted, blithering idiots, one's wider, one's deeper — so they'll both hold THE SAME AMOUNT!'

The two brothers stood, quite taken aback. They frowned, their lips moving in silence as they considered what Hal had said.

'That's right,' said one. 'I didn't think of that.'

'Neither did I,' said the other. Then he added quickly, 'Although I'm sure I would have.'

'I would have too!' his brother insisted immediately.

'Oh, you say so now —'

'STOP!' Hal yelled at them. 'STOP! STOP! STOP!' Once more, they fell silent. He pointed at the nearest twin.

'You! What's your name?'

'Why it's Wulf, of course. Everyone knows that.'

Hal glared at him balefully. He kept his eyes fixed on Wulf, in case he and his brother decided to switch places once more, and called to Stig.

'Stig, fetch me a short piece of rope, would you?'

'You going to tie him up?' Stig asked, grinning.

'Why not hang him?' Ulf said.

Hal, his eyes still fixed on Wulf, snapped his fingers at Stig. 'Get me the rope. Light cord. Half a metre or less.'

When Stig obliged, Hal stepped forward and knotted the rope around Wulf's wrist, cutting off the excess with his knife.

'There. Now we all know who's who,' he said. 'Wulf has a *wope* on his *wist*.'

'That's a little childish, isn't it?' Edvin asked.

Hal glared at him. 'Can you think of a better way of remembering?'

Stig's grin was wider than ever now. 'Don't you mean "wemembering"?'

'No. I don't,' Hal said, very deliberately, then he asked Edvin again. 'Well, can you?'

'Um . . . as a matter of fact, I can't,' Edvin admitted.

'Good. Then until you can, keep your criticism to yourself.'

Edvin made a conciliatory gesture.

'So now,' Hal continued, 'I'm going to get out of the rain.' He shook his head at the twins once more. 'It's probably going to be a long night. At least it'll be a dry one.'

He went into the tent. The others followed until only the twins were left outside in the rain. It was still light, but it was getting heavier with each passing minute. Slowly, trickles of water began to flow down the two trenches, meeting at the front where the twins had dug a release trench.

Wulf looked after Hal and grinned at his brother.

'He's quite smart, isn't he?' he said.

Ulf nodded. 'He is indeed. A real thinker. Not as smart as us, though.'

'No,' said Wulf. He unknotted the cord around his wrist and tied it on his brother's wrist instead.

CHAPTER SIXTEEN

The following morning, the Herons were roused from their blankets by Gort, who was banging a hardwood stick on an old barrel hoop, just inside the entrance of the tent. The clanging note of the iron hoop rang in their ears as they rolled out of their blankets, alarmed by the sudden cacophony.

'Out of bed! Come on! On your feet! Ten minutes to wash and dress! Then get yourselves to the training ground!'

The boys, still befuddled with sleep, searched blearily for shoes and breeches, reluctant to leave the warmth of their bedding. Gort glanced around the interior of their tent, impressed.

'This is pretty good,' he said. 'You slept a lot drier than the other teams.'

'It leaked a bit,' Hal told him, pointing to a few places where the rain had forced its way through the canvas. 'But we'll sort that out this morning.'

Gort was shaking his head. 'No you won't. You've got other things to do this morning. Now get a move on if you don't want to miss breakfast.'

Edvin was frowning at the instructor as he balanced on one leg, pulling on his breeches.

'But you said we had yesterday and today to build our quarters,' he protested.

Gort smiled at him. 'Did I? I must have been lying.' Then the smile disappeared. 'NOW GET MOVING!'

Startled, Edvin and the others hurried to the creek to wash, then finish dressing. Then, still under Gort's command, they double-timed to the training ground where they had assembled for team selection the previous day. There was now a large open-sided tent set up as a dining area, with three trestle tables and benches — one for each of the three brotherbands. The Herons were the first to arrive and helped themselves to the fresh bread, hot bacon and fried eggs, tea and coffee.

The hot food and drink revived their spirits considerably and they watched cheerfully as the other bands straggled in, damp and stiff from sleeping on the wet ground. The new arrivals glared balefully at the Herons, who smiled back at them and raised coffee mugs in a mock salute.

Tursgud was one of the last to arrive. He looked to be in a bad temper, and was rubbing at a stiff spot in his back.

'Hey there, Tursgud!' Stefan greeted him. 'Look who's here before you? Hal Who and Hal Who's Herons, that's who!'

The other Herons laughed, and even one or two of the Wolf brotherband chuckled at Stefan's play on words. Tursgud pointed a threatening finger at Stefan.

'Keep it up, joker!' he said. 'I'll settle your bacon one of these days!'

Which was an unfortunate expression to choose, because, as Tursgud reached the serving table, he found that the bacon was finished, the early arrivals having taken it all. He scowled around the tent, then ordered two of his team to share their bacon with him. Reluctantly, they complied.

Watching this byplay, Hal frowned thoughtfully. That sort of bullying wouldn't do a lot for the Sharks' team spirit, he thought. Tursgud might have been better to wait. Surely one of his team would have offered to share with him. He was unpopular with the members of the Heron brotherband, because he'd spent years bullying them and making fun of them. But his own followers seemed to like him well enough.

Or did they, Hal wondered.

Stefan, meanwhile, was patting his stomach contentedly.

'Mmmm, my bacon has settled quite nicely, I think,' he said to nobody in particular. The others laughed and Tursgud shot him a malevolent glance from the next table.

Hal leaned forward, seeing Stefan was casting around for another witticism at Tursgud's expense.

'Let it go, Stefan,' he said quietly.

Stefan looked at him in surprise. Of all of them, Hal had the most reason to dislike Tursgud. In fact, Stefan was throwing these verbal barbs at the bigger boy on Hal's behalf. He admired the half-Araluan boy. He had been impressed by the leadership and decisiveness Hal had shown the previous day — not to mention the way he had dealt with Ulf and Wulf. He felt the Herons had done well to have him for a leader.

'We've got a long three months ahead of us,' Hal explained. 'No sense in poking the shark unnecessarily.'

'No,' Stig agreed, then smiled. 'After all, we'll find plenty of necessary ways to poke him.'

Sigurd, seeing that the Herons were first to finish their breakfast and had cleared their plates and cutlery, dropping them into a copper cauldron filled with hot water, beckoned them to gather around him.

'Hal, I believe you've been officially elected skirl. Is that right?'

Hal nodded. Sigurd looked at the rest of the band.

'Good choice,' he said, to Hal's surprise. Hal had no idea that Erak and Sigurd had watched him supervising the building of their barracks tent the day before. But he didn't have further time to reflect on it. Sigurd handed him a bundle of parchment sheets.

'These are the tasks you'll be ordered to undertake over the next two months,' he said. 'They're not in order. You'll only know on the day what task you have to perform, so you have to be constantly ready for any one of them. Teams must compete in every event. Any team that doesn't is disqualified from the overall competition. Clear?'

The boys nodded. There was no more joking now. Stig and Edvin, standing close to Hal, craned over his shoulder, trying to read the list of tests they would be set. Sigurd claimed their attention again.

'You can read them later!' he snapped. 'There's no set schedule for these tests. We might ask you to do one tomorrow, or next week. Or the week after. We might ask you to do tasks two days running, then nothing for several weeks. In between, we'll be assessing your skills and teaching you more of them. You might care to know, however, that you've already had your first test.'

He paused and it was Hal who asked the obvious question, although he thought he knew the answer.

'What was that, Sigurd?'

'Getting your living quarters organised,' the instructor told them. 'You've got points on the board for that. You did the best job of the three bands.'

The Herons murmured with pleasure.

Stig glanced at his friend. 'Good work, Hal.'

Hal shrugged. 'Long way to go yet, Stig.'

Sigurd noted the exchange. Erak could be right about this boy, he thought. Erak was usually right. He cleared his throat and got their attention once more.

'Head back and tidy your living quarters. Then get your kit together. We'll be assessing your skills today so be back here with any weapons you already have in twenty minutes.'

The band hurriedly filed out of the mess tent. As they left, Hal could hear Sigurd addressing the other groups, who were cramming the last of their breakfast into their mouths.

'Hurry up. You've got two minutes left. Then come to me for your list of assessments. And by the way, do yourselves a favour and take a look at the quarters the Herons have built. You'd be wise to copy their design. They've already won assessment points for it.'

That'll put a smile on Tursgud's face, Hal thought. He made a mental note to talk to Stefan and ask him to put a rein on his tongue. The boy's constant needling of Tursgud could only make life more difficult.

When their living quarters were spick and span, with bedding rolled and personal equipment and clothing neatly stacked in each sleeping space, Hal made a quick inspection. He found Ingvar's bedding was unevenly rolled, so that it spilled out one end like a half-cooked sausage. His personal items were stacked any which way. He beckoned to Edvin.

'Can you give Ingvar a hand? Show him how to roll the bedding evenly and get his kit into shape.' Edvin nodded and Hal called to Ingvar. 'Ingvar! This won't do! It looks like a dog's breakfast. Pay attention to Edvin and get this tidied up.'

'Yes, skirl,' Ingvar said sheepishly. He lumbered over and bent his head as Edvin showed him how to fold his bedding instead of bundling it into an unmanageable roll. Similarly, Edvin stacked his personal items, with the largest on the bottom, explaining to Ingvar that this was the most efficient way to do it. Hal watched as Ingvar listened, nodding his head from time to time. Like a lot of big people, he did tend to be clumsy, and his poor eyesight added to the problem. But Hal had noticed that Ingvar had a good heart. Another boy might have resented being told what to do by someone almost half his size. But Ingvar actually seemed to appreciate the fact that Edvin wasn't criticising him so much as helping him.

Edvin let him study the job he'd done, then unrolled the bedding and gestured to it.

'Now you try it again,' he said. 'And don't try to roll it so tightly.'

This time, Ingvar made a better job of it. The result wasn't as neat and symmetrical as Edvin's, but it was a big improvement. Edvin caught Hal's eye and raised his eyebrows in a question.

Hal nodded briefly. 'That'll do.'

Edvin slapped Ingvar on his massive shoulder. 'Nice work,' he said. 'I'll check you again tomorrow, to make sure you've got the hang of it.'

'Thanks, Edvin,' the young giant said. He was beaming with satisfaction. It occurred to Hal that nobody had ever praised Ingvar in the past. All he had ever received was criticism. Hal filed that thought away.

'You heard Sigurd,' he called to the others. 'If anyone has personal weapons, collect them and bring them along. Then form up here in two files.'

Stefan hesitated. 'Is that really necessary?' he asked.

'Possibly not,' Hal said. 'But we're a brotherband. That means we're a team. It's time we started acting as a team. All right?'

'All right,' Stefan replied.

Hal watched him for a few seconds. He still wasn't totally at ease giving orders. But Stefan seemed to accept his reasoning. With a faint sense of relief, Hal entered the tent and retrieved his crossbow from beside his folded bedroll.

The crossbow had been a present from Thorn the previous year. The one-armed sailor, like all sea wolves, had a cache of money, jewels, weapons and assorted items that he had 'liberated', as the saying was, in his career as a raider. Mind you, his stash wasn't as large as it used to be. In his lost years, Thorn had begun selling his plunder for ridiculously low prices in order to buy ale and brandy. Erak had eventually stepped in and confiscated what was left, ensuring that Thorn didn't lose it all.

Thorn had taken the crossbow during a raid in Gallica many years ago. He had given it to Hal for his fifteenth birthday. The boy had been delighted. His mother was less so, but no mother was ever enthusiastic when someone gave her son a weapon capable of shooting a missile over two hundred metres.

At first delighted, Hal quickly saw a few faults in the crossbow's basic design and went to work to correct them. The body of the weapon, for example, was a piece of timber in one straight line. That made it difficult to line up. The shooter's eyeline was always slightly above the line the bolt would take. He kept the trigger mechanism and discarded the stock, replacing it with one of his own design, shaped so that the shoulder piece sloped down from the body of the bow, bringing the aiming line up level with his eye. He carved the butt of the new stock in a curve so that it nestled firmly into his shoulder. Then he worked on the triggering mechanism as well. It was roughly formed and stiff. He filed it and oiled it so that the action was smooth and the release easy.

Then, after trying the weapon out, he added one more important modification.

At first, he had been nervous about showing the changes to Thorn. He worried that the shabby odd-job man might be insulted by the fact that Hal wasn't satisfied with the crossbow as it stood. But Thorn had been delighted, patting him on the shoulder.

'Trust you to come up with a way to improve it!' he'd said. 'I might have known.'

The other boys were ready now. They had a variety of weapons they had brought. They all wore saxe knives, the long, heavy knives that could be used as a weapon as well as for everyday tasks. In addition, Jesper had a small hunting bow, although it was a low-powered, short-range weapon compared to the crossbow. The twins had throwing spears and Stig had an axe. It had belonged to his father as a boy. It wasn't a full-sized war axe — such a weapon would be too heavy, even for Stig's muscles — but it was a substantial weapon nonetheless. Stefan and Edvin had no weapons of their own.

Ingvar's family didn't have the money to buy him a weapon. Instead, he had fashioned a huge club from a branch of oak. It was a simple weapon but with Ingvar's massive strength behind it, it would be devastating. Hal put out a hand to look at it.

'May I see?' he said and Ingvar handed it over. Hal was deceived by the ease with which Ingvar handled the weapon and he nearly dropped it when he felt the enormous weight. But he recovered, and swung it with two hands. For such a simple weapon, it was surprisingly well balanced, he thought. He handed it back.

'All right, form up in two ranks. Stig, call the step. Double time to the training ground.'

This time, nobody asked whether it was really necessary. Hal took the front left-hand rank, with Jesper by his side. The others formed up behind them, with Stig at the rear, calling the step. They jogged through the trees to the training ground.

They had lost a little time when Edvin was showing Ingvar how to fold his kit and the other bands were already there. They looked up at the compact group of boys as they jogged in step onto the training ground, coming to a halt together as Stig called the order. It looked impressive. Tursgud sneered but Rollond was slightly annoyed that he hadn't thought to bring his team here like that. They had simply ambled to the training field like a mob of cattle, in no fixed formation.

'In future,' he told his second in command, 'that's how we do it too.'

CHAPTER SEVENTEEN

There were three assistant instructors working under Sigurd. Their names were Gort, Jarst and Viggo and each of them was responsible for one of the brotherbands. Gort was assigned to the Herons and he approached them now, eyeing them off as they stood in their two ranks, facing him.

'Very pretty,' he said, with a note of sarcasm in his voice. 'But there are no marks for being pretty, if that's what you had in mind.' He glanced at Hal. 'Was that what you had in mind?'

'No, sir,' Hal answered, standing to attention. 'We just thought it would be better if we all arrived together.'

'Hmmmphh,' Gort muttered. In fact, he and the other instructors had been impressed with the Herons' disciplined arrival. But he wasn't going to let them know that. He glanced along the line of them now, looking at the motley collection of weapons they carried.

'We'll be assigning you weapons for training purposes, of course,' he told them. 'But let's see what you've got already.'

He walked down the line, studying the weapons, and stopped when he saw Jesper's bow. He held out a hand and Jesper passed it to him. Gort flexed the bow several times, then grunted.

'All right for hunting small game,' he said. 'Not much use in a battle. There's no power there.'

He passed the bow back and moved on, stopping again when he noticed the huge club that Ingvar had grounded beside him.

'Good grief,' he exclaimed. 'That's nearly a tree! Let's see what you can do with it.'

Ingvar peered at him, blinking rapidly, not sure what was expected of him.

'Sir?' he asked.

Gort beckoned him impatiently. 'Step forward and let's see you swing that thing. If you can,' he added, doubtfully.

Ingvar nodded and blinked several times. He stepped forward, stumbling over his own feet and lurching awkwardly until Ulf caught his elbow and steadied him. He smiled apologetically at Gort, who raised his eyes to heaven. Thankfully, the expression was lost on Ingvar, who could see only a vague blur where the instructor was standing.

'Well, come on then!' Gort snapped.

Ingvar blinked in his direction. 'Sir?'

'Let's have you! Take a swing!'

Now in fairness to Ingvar, the command 'Take a swing' could be interpreted as 'Take a swing at me'.

Ingvar wasn't totally sure, so he hesitated still, peering at the blurred figure in front of him. He didn't know if Gort was ready to defend himself.

For Gort's part, he simply meant to see if Ingvar could wield the club with any dexterity, although he doubted that was possible, given its sheer size and obvious weight. As the boy hesitated, he prompted him again.

'Come on! We don't have all —'

He was going to say 'all day', but he suddenly realised that the tree-trunk-sized club was whistling through the air at blinding speed, and in the next half-second would knock his head clean off his shoulders. With a startled yelp, he dropped flat on the still-wet ground, feeling the wind of the massive weapon as it passed over his skull, missing him by a few centimetres.

'Lorgan's dripping, blood-red fangs, boy!' he bellowed, invoking a highly unpleasant Skandian demigod. He scrambled to his feet, brushing mud and wet grass from his jacket. 'Drop that club!' he roared, as Ingvar swayed uncertainly, not sure whether to try another swing.

Obediently, Ingvar let the huge piece of timber fall to the turf. The dull thud it made sent a shiver of fear up Gort's spine. The fear translated to anger.

'You idiot! Are you trying to kill me?'

'No, sir,' Ingvar began. 'But you said "take a swing".'

'Not at me! Why would I want you to take a swing at me?' Gort's voice was shrill. He was well aware that the other Herons were struggling to keep the grins off their faces.

Hal stepped forward apologetically. 'I don't think he meant to hit you, sir.'

'Well, actually . . . Ow!' Ingvar was silenced by a painful jab of Wulf's elbow in the ribs. Gort looked at him suspiciously and Hal hurried on, reclaiming the instructor's attention.

'He's very short-sighted, sir. He can't see much past a metre away. Everything gets blurry.'

'That's right, sir.' Stig joined in. 'His depth perception is pretty terrible. He probably thought you were much further away than you actually were.'

'No, I . . . Oww!' Ingvar began and was again silenced by Wulf's elbow.

Stig turned to him and said, with heavy emphasis on his words, 'That's what you thought, Ingvar, wasn't it? You thought he was further away. *Didn't you?*'

'Oh . . . ahh . . . well, possibly I did. Yes. I'd say that's just what I thought, now you mention it.'

Then Hal chimed in again. 'His eyesight really is dreadful, sir. Ask anyone!' He appealed to the other boys in the group and they all added their voices in a chorus of agreement.

'Blind as a bat, sir!'

'Can barely see beyond his nose!'

'Can barely see his nose!'

Gort was beginning to feel like a stag being attacked by dogs on several sides at once.

Ingvar looked at his band brothers, an aggrieved expression on his face. 'Oh, come on! I'm not that bad!' he said. But again, Wulf hit him in the ribs with his elbow. 'Owwww!'

'Yes you are. Shut up!'

Ingvar rubbed his now bruised ribs and frowned in the direction of his tormentor.

'Cut it out! That hurts! Who is that, anyway?' He knew it was one of the twins, but he didn't know which one.

Wulf saw the annoyed light in Ingvar's eyes and thought quickly. 'It's Ulf.'

'I'll settle with you later then,' Ingvar promised.

By now, hearing the chorus of excuses, Gort had decided that Ingvar hadn't intentionally tried to behead him. He waved a dismissive hand at the huge young man.

'All right. Pick up your club and get back in line. And next time you decide to swing it, make sure I'm at least ten metres away.'

'Yes, sir,' said Ingvar, vastly chastened by the event.

Gort watched Ingvar warily as he retrieved his club, then resumed his place in the ranks. The instructor seemed to relax.

'All right, what else have we got?' His eyes lit on the spears in the twins' hands. 'You any good with those stickers? Can you throw them? And I don't mean at me!' he added hurriedly.

'Actually,' Ulf said, 'we're pretty mediocre.'

'He's mediocre,' Wulf put in. 'I'm sort of . . . ordinary.'

'That's the same thing!' Ulf retorted angrily.

Wulf rounded on him. 'It's not! Mediocre is second rate. Ordinary is . . . ordinary.'

'Like there's a difference!' Ulf began. But Hal stepped in quickly.

'Shut it! Shut it now! Both of you!'

The twins fell silent, mouthing silent insults at each other. Hal turned to Gort, his hands spread in apology.

'Sorry, sir. They argue a lot.'

'So they do,' Gort said. 'Gorlog help you if they're always like that.'

Hal nodded morosely. 'They usually are,' he admitted.

Gort turned back to the twins. 'All right, without further discussion, let's see if you can hit those targets over there.'

He indicated a pair of roughly man-shaped targets about thirty metres away. The twins looked in the direction he was pointing.

'Which one?' asked Ulf.

Gort shrugged. 'I don't really care. Just pick one each and take a throw.'

'Then I'll take the —' Wulf began.

But Hal, seeing the potential for another mindless squabble, quickly intervened. 'Wulf! You take the one on the right! Ulf, take the left one!'

Even Gort was impressed with the sudden steel in his voice, and the unmistakable tone of command. The twins looked at him, then shrugged.

'Okay,' they said in unison. And, moving in perfect unison, they both drew back their arms, balanced, stepped forward and, in perfect unison, cast.

And, in perfect unison, they missed.

Gort studied them for several seconds. 'You'll need to work on that,' he said. They hurried off to retrieve the spears and Gort moved on to Stig. He examined his axe, felt its weight and heft and nodded appreciatively.

'Pretty good,' he said. 'Show me a few moves. And remember the rules. If you decapitate the instructor, the team loses points.'

And the instructor loses his head, Hal thought. But Stig merely grinned at Gort.

He took the axe, dropped into a crouch, then began miming strokes at an imaginary enemy, moving forward as he did so, swinging overhead and side arm, single handed and double handed. He even mimed a few parries of imaginary counterstrokes. After a minute or two, Gort called a halt.

'Not bad,' he said. 'But your timing is a little off and you're not getting your full weight into the strokes. You can't let the axe do all the work.'

Stig looked downcast at the criticism, but Gort clapped him cheerfully on the shoulder.

'You can't expect to know it all right away,' he said. 'That's why we're here to train you. You've got the basic ability to be a good warrior. You just need to learn a bit of technique. Give me a couple of months and I'll turn you into the most feared axeman this side of the Constant Sea.'

Stig cheered up at that. The idea of being a feared axeman appealed to him — although he would have liked to be feared on the other side of the Constant Sea, too.

Gort then turned his attention to the crossbow slung over Hal's shoulder. The weapon interested him but he saw it more as a novelty. Aside from spears and the occasional javelin, the Skandians didn't really go in for missile weapons.

'Where did you get your hands on this?' he asked. Hal shrugged the weapon off his shoulder and held it out for the instructor's inspection.

'Thorn gave it to me,' he said and Gort nodded thoughtfully.

'Aaah, yes. Thorn. The old drunk,' he said, more to himself than to Hal. But Hal bristled at the slur on his friend.

'He hasn't had a drink in years!' he said angrily. 'He's a friend of mine. Maybe he was a drunk once, but he's over it.'

Gort looked up at him. Their gazes locked and held. Gort's unspoken message was clear. That was no way to speak to an instructor. Hal flushed and dropped his gaze.

'Sorry, sir,' he mumbled.

Gort nodded several times. The boy had learned his lesson, he thought. He continued, in a gentler tone. 'Loyalty to a friend is a good thing, skirl. But if he is your friend, you should know this: a drunk is never completely "over it". The risk is always there that he'll start drinking again when things get tough. You simply can never depend on him.'

You don't know him like I do, Hal thought angrily. He was about to voice the thought when he realised that he would never convince Gort. And chances were, if he argued with him, he would cost his team demerit points. He swallowed his anger.

'Yes, sir,' he said. 'I'll try to remember that.'

'Good,' said the instructor. 'Now let's take a look at this crossbow of yours.'

Gort took the bow and turned it over, examining it. It was unlike any crossbow he'd ever seen. And even though Skandians didn't use them, they had faced them often enough.

'I thought you Araluans were born with a longbow in your hands?' he mused.

Hal kept his temper in check. He disliked being forced into a mould: *You're Araluan. Therefore you must shoot a longbow.*

'I was born here,' he pointed out. 'There aren't a lot of longbows around these parts.'

'Still, it's your national weapon, isn't it?' Gort continued.

Hal refrained from saying, 'I'm Skandian, not just Araluan.' He knew people would always see the side of him that was different, never the side that was the same.

Gort noted his silence but had no idea what caused it. 'Never felt the urge to try a longbow?'

Hal shook his head. Since the attempted invasion by the Temujai, there had been a company of Araluan archers stationed in Hallasholm as part of the treaty negotiated between the two countries. Ever conscious of the fact that he was already regarded as an outsider, Hal had made it a point not to mix with them. But he had singled out one of the platoon commanders one day and asked him about the longbow. The answer had been depressing.

'You need to train with it from a very early age,' he explained to Gort now. 'Shooting a longbow is an instinctive thing. You have to attune yourself to the bow and more or less sense where your arrow's going to go when you're shooting. It takes years to develop any skill.'

'And this is different?' Gort asked.

Hal nodded. 'It's a lot easier to point and aim. There are certain shooting disciplines you have to practise, but it's a lot simpler than the longbow. It's slower to shoot, of course, because it takes time to load.'

Gort was admiring the workmanship on the polished wooden stock. It was simple and unadorned, but beautifully crafted and finished.

'Never seen one like this,' he mused. 'Where did Thorn get it?'

'He was on a raid in Gallica, I believe,' Hal told him.

Gort frowned thoughtfully. 'Doesn't look Gallican,' he said. He knew that the Galls usually made their crossbows with a simple, straight-line butt. This one was altogether more impressive.

'I made a few improvements,' Hal said and Gort looked at him, eyebrows raised.

'Oh, you did, did you? The Galls have been making them for hundreds of years, but you thought you could improve on their design?'

'That's right,' Hal said. He was still a little riled by Gort's earlier comments about him being Araluan. 'And I did,' he added.

The instructor sensed the boy's hostility. He handed him the bow and gestured towards the targets nearby. 'Well then, let's see how successful you were,' he invited.

Hal placed the crossbow on the ground and put his foot in the metal stirrup at the front. Using both hands, he hauled back on the heavy cord until he felt it click over the retaining claw. Then he took a quarrel from his quiver and placed it in the slot, against the cocked cord.

The two targets were barely thirty metres away — an easy shot. He aimed, almost casually, drew in a breath and held it, then squeezed his hand around the trigger lever.

The string released with a solid THUNK! The crossbow bucked in his grip and the quarrel, the short, heavy arrow, streaked across the thirty-metre distance, burying its head in the soft wood of the target.

Gort pushed out his bottom lip, surprised and impressed. 'That's pretty good.'

Hal shrugged. 'It's pretty short range,' he pointed out.

Something in his voice told Gort that he hadn't set a particularly difficult test. He looked around. There was an old shield propped up on the other side of the training field. It would be used later in the week for axe and knife throwing lessons.

'Let's see you hit that,' he said.

Hal reloaded, then stared thoughtfully at the shield, his lips moving silently as he estimated the range. Somewhere between seventy and eighty metres, he guessed. He raised the crossbow and flipped up the graduated rear sight that he had added to it. This had been his final, and best, modification.

'Hold on!' said Gort. 'What's that?'

'It's just an extra idea of mine,' Hal explained. 'Lining up the bow is easy. You're looking straight down the line of the shot, after all. Where it gets hard is estimating how much the quarrel will drop over a distance.' He touched the rear sight with his forefinger, indicating the etched lines he had placed there. 'This gives me reference points for sixty, eighty and one hundred metres. I line up the correct one with the sight at the front . . .' He indicated the small pin set at the front of the crossbow. '. . . and I know how far above the target to hold my aim. See?'

Gort saw that the crossbow was angled upwards as Hal settled the foresight on a point between the sixty- and eighty-metre marks.

Hal relaxed, lowering the bow, and looked sidelong at Gort.

'A longbow shooter has to estimate that. It takes years of experience. I've pre-measured these marks, so I know exactly how much elevation to give the quarrel for any given distance. As long as I hold steady when I shoot, the quarrel will be on target.'

Gort gestured for him to continue. Hal raised the bow again. Breathed in, exhaled, then took a half breath. He lined the sight up, setting the pin just above the eighty-metre mark again, and released.

Again, the crossbow gave out its ugly THUNK! as the quarrel streaked away.

And slammed into the bottom half of the shield, a little offline to the right. The shield spun sideways under the impact, torn loose from its supports. It rolled a few metres, then fell on its side, wobbling round and round for a few seconds until it finally settled. The watching Herons let out a low cheer.

'Needed a bit more elevation,' said Hal, pursing his lips.

Gort raised his eyebrows. 'All the same. It's impressive.' He gestured for the other Herons to gather round him and they moved into a loose half circle.

'All right,' he said. 'We'll issue you with your other weapons today. Some of you will be better suited to the sword, I think.' He nodded at Hal and Edvin. They were the two with the lightest builds.

'Stig, you keep your axe. It's a good weight and balance for you. Jesper, Stefan and you twins, it'll be axes for you too.' He looked at the twins. 'Forget about the spears.

You can use 'em as tent poles if you like. Lose the bow as well,' he said to Jesper. 'Use it for hunting if you want, but that's it. Hal, the crossbow is a good weapon. But you'll have to practise that by yourself. There's no one here who can teach you how to use it.'

Hal nodded. 'Understood,' he said. He felt a small sense of relief. He had half expected to be told not to waste his time with the crossbow.

'All right,' Gort said, clapping his hands together. 'The armourers have set up a tent. It's over there, at the end of the training ground. Let's get over there and get you some weapons. Then you have the rest of the day to make final improvements to your quarters, and go over the list of tests we have in store for you.'

With a mental jolt, Hal remembered the list they had been given that morning. He had barely had time to do more than glance at it before cramming it under his folded bedding and double-timing to the training ground. Things were beginning to move fast, he realised. Then he noticed that Gort and the others were already striding across the field to the armourers' tent.

'You coming, or did you want me to fetch your sword for you?' the instructor called back to him.

Slinging the crossbow over his shoulder again, Hal set off at a jog to catch up to them.

That afternoon, after they had eaten lunch in the mess tent, the Herons sat around their camp site, examining the weapons they had been issued.

They were plain, utilitarian items, without unnecessary embellishment. And they weren't new. Most of them had notches or dents in their handles and the blades were speckled with light rust and needed an edge put on them. But the boys handled them with something approaching reverence. These were more than just weapons. These were symbols of the fact that they were on their way to becoming men. To becoming warriors. They were real weapons, not the play weapons that they had used as boys.

Hal's sword was plain steel. The blade was straight and double-edged, with the hilt wrapped in leather, and a brass crosspiece and pommel. The leather, he noted, was stained by a previous owner's perspiration. The scabbard was leather, boiled so that it was hardened into the necessary shape, and reinforced at the base and top with brass.

He held the sword up, testing the feel. It was heavy, and the weight dragged the blade down. Within thirty seconds, his wrist was beginning to feel the strain. But perhaps that was how a sword was supposed to feel. If you were swinging a sword at someone, you'd probably want some weight behind it, he thought.

He laid the sword aside. He'd sharpen and oil the blade later but, for the moment, he wanted to go over the list of tests and assessments that would be set for them. He became conscious of someone standing in front of him and looked up to see Stig.

'You were talking about thatching the roof with pine branches,' his friend reminded him. Hal screwed up his mouth thoughtfully, then shook his head.

'The canvas seems to be doing the job for now,' he said. 'Maybe you and Jesper could put some more roof frames under the canvas to stop the rain from pooling so much.'

Stig nodded, studying the canvas. There were A-shaped frames at either end and in the middle of the ridgepole. But when it rained, the water did pool between them and the canvas sagged.

'I'll get onto it,' he said and walked away, calling for Jesper to join him.

Hal glanced around and saw Ingvar studying the twins, a slight frown creasing his forehead. That might mean he was thinking. Or it could be that he was simply trying to focus his vision more clearly.

'You all right, Ingvar?' he called out. 'Something on your mind?'

Ingvar looked at him and smiled benignly, shaking his head.

'Just watching the twins, skirl,' he said. Then he turned his attention back to them. They, of course, were squabbling quietly. They had been issued with identical axes, but now Ulf wanted Wulf's and Wulf wanted Ulf's.

Or vice versa — which amounted to the same thing, really. Hal smiled as he had the thought.

'Something funny in the tests?' Edvin was sitting close by, watching him. Hal realised he had been staring unseeing at the list of assessments when he had smiled at the convoluted situation with Ulf and Wulf.

'Not really,' he said. 'Just wool-gathering.'

'Mind if I see?' Edvin said, holding out his hand. Hal shrugged and passed him the list. Edvin flicked through the sheets, reading aloud as he went.

'Hmmm . . . navigation and seamanship exercise. Day. What do we use for a ship?'

The normal practice was for each band to be assigned a ship – similar to a wolfship but somewhat smaller. Each one could accommodate up to six rowers a side.

'I was thinking of asking permission for us to use the *Heron* – my ship,' Hal said.

Edvin considered the idea and nodded agreement. 'Not a bad idea. She'll be lighter than the other ships, and we'll only have seven rowers, while the Sharks and Wolves will have eight or nine each. Although I guess we'll have to cut our number down to six, otherwise we'll be unbalanced.'

Hal shook his head. 'Not when one of them is Ingvar,' he pointed out and Edvin gave a small grunt of appreciation.

'Hadn't thought of that.' He glanced at the list again. 'Wrestling. Individual test.'

'Stig,' they both said at the same time. They looked at each other and smiled.

'Can he beat Rollond and Tursgud?' Edvin asked. They were the obvious choices for the other two teams.

Hal shook his head doubtfully. 'He might. If he can control his temper long enough. He tends to get wild and that's his undoing.'

'Strength test,' Edvin continued, looking back to the list. 'What do you think that could be?'

'Last year, it was a tug-of-war, I believe. Can't see why they'd do it differently this year.'

'Not terribly fair if we're two men short,' Edvin commented.

'Nothing we can do about that. Pity it's not an individual event. We could nominate Ingvar.'

Edvin studied the list. 'No. The individual ones are listed as individual. Look: wrestling, individual. Foot race, individual.' He paused, turning to a new sheet. 'Night attack,' he read. 'That must be a team event. Wonder what that is?'

'I guess we'll find out,' Hal said. He sounded distracted and Edvin looked up at him to see he was watching Ingvar again.

'Something on your mind?' Edvin said.

Hal shrugged. 'Have you noticed that for the past half hour, Ingvar hasn't taken his eyes off the twins?'

'I hadn't. But I see what you mean. I wonder what he's thinking?'

'With Ingvar, who knows?' Hal replied. 'What else is on the list?' He forced himself to look away from Ingvar but no more than a few seconds passed before he glanced back again.

'Mountain race,' Edvin read. 'No details of that. And obstacle course. That sounds like fun.' His voice left no doubt that he didn't think it sounded like fun at all. 'That's about it.' He realised that Hal was distracted once more, watching the hulking silent form opposite.

'You'll get a crick in your neck if you keep watching him,' he said.

Hal sighed in frustration. 'He's got something on his mind. I know it. I just wish I knew what it was.'

That evening, they found out.

CHAPTER EIGHTEEN

The Herons sat around in their tent, cleaning their new weapons. Hal inspected them as each boy finished. He knew their instructors would be examining them the next day. Most of the axes and swords passed muster, but he pointed to the blade of Jesper's axe.

'There's still a notch there in the edge. You should grind that away. And there's still some rust as well, where the head joins the handle.' Hal had already noticed that Jesper tended to slacken off after a while when the work got too hard. Jesper looked more closely at the axe blade, frowning at the spots Hal had pointed out.

'It's fine,' he said. 'It's just a speck of rust. You can hardly see it.'

Hal hesitated, then, keeping his voice friendly, he tried again.

'Maybe you should look at it again. All right?'

Jesper shrugged. 'Yes. Yes. Anything for a peaceful life. I'll get onto it later, all right?'

Hal stood awkwardly for a few seconds. He wasn't comfortable issuing orders but he supposed he'd have to get used to it. He just wished that Jesper would be a bit more co-operative. As he turned away he made a mental note to check Jesper's axe again before lights out.

That was when Ingvar made his move. He stood up and lumbered across to where the twins were working on their axes. They looked up at him, surprised. Ingvar didn't usually initiate conversations.

'What is it?' Wulf asked.

Ingvar rubbed his side. 'My ribs still hurt,' he said. There was a strange note in his voice that made the other boys set aside whatever they were doing and pay attention.

Ulf frowned at the massive boy. 'Your ribs? What's that got to do with us?'

Ingvar peered at him, blinking rapidly. 'One of you kept hitting me in the ribs this morning. Remember? And I said "Who's doing that?" and whoever it was said "It's Ulf".'

Wulf suddenly grinned as understanding dawned. He'd elbowed Ingvar in the ribs when Gort was questioning him. And then he'd claimed to be his brother. Now, sensing that Ingvar was looking for retribution, he congratulated himself on his quick thinking.

'That's right!' he said brightly. 'It was Ulf!'

'What are you talking about?' Ulf asked. 'I did not.'

'Definitely Ulf,' Wulf insisted. 'He's the one you want.'

Ingvar could see the two blurry shapes in front of him. He wasn't sure which one was speaking at any time and he wasn't sure who was who. But he knew there was one way of telling. His hand shot out and fastened on the arm of the twin nearest him, who happened to be Wulf. It took Wulf by surprise. As Gort had discovered that morning, Ingvar could move with surprising speed when the mood took him.

He dragged Wulf upright, ignoring his indignant cries. Then he ran his other hand down his arm, finding the bare wrist. He smiled. It was not a pretty sight.

'You're Ulf,' he said.

Wulf struggled to break his grip. 'No!' he said. 'No! I'm Wulf. That's Ulf there! Not me! I'm Wulf!' Desperately, he pointed to his brother. But Ulf shrugged his shoulders and grinned evilly at his twin.

'Me?' He said. 'I'm certainly not Ulf. I'm Wulf!'

'You liar!' Wulf shouted at him. He was beginning to panic now. Ingvar's grip was becoming quite painful. 'I tell you, I'm Wulf.'

'No, you're not,' Ingvar told him. 'Remember what Hal said? *Wulf has the wope on his wist.*'

Too late, Wulf realised his mistake.

'We swapped!' he screeched. 'I gave the rope to Ulf. We did it to trick Hal!'

'Oh, did you now?' Hal said, beginning to smile.

'No,' Ingvar insisted again. '*Wulf has the wope on his wist.* That's what Hal said. And I don't feel any *wope* on this *wist.*'

'Tell him!' Wulf appealed to his brother. 'Tell him before . . . Whuuuuummmmphhhh! Aaaah!'

These final sounds were forced from him as Ingvar suddenly jerked him forward and wrapped him in a bear hug, lifting his feet off the ground and crushing the air from his lungs with his immensely powerful arms.

Wulf could feel his ribs buckling under the dreadful pressure of Ingvar's arms. He was being bent backwards as the huge boy leaned his upper body forward, all the while maintaining the pressure of the bear hug, with his hands locked together in the small of Wulf's back. Wulf's vision swam and he thought hazily that a real bear could hardly be more powerful, or more painful.

He tried to plead for mercy but there was no air in his lungs and he could only manage a small, gasping cry. 'Ah-ah-ah-ah-ah!'

Then Ingvar increased the pressure and Wulf couldn't even make that noise. His feet kicked helplessly in the air.

'That's enough, Ingvar,' Hal said quietly.

The others had risen and gathered in a circle around Ingvar and Wulf. Most of them were smiling broadly. Ulf, in particular. Ingvar lessened the pressure slightly and they all heard the droning wheeze as Wulf dragged air into his tortured lungs.

'You think so, Hal?' Ingvar asked mildly.

Hal nodded. 'I think so. Put him down.'

'All right,' Ingvar said suddenly, and released his grip. Wulf crumpled to the ground like an empty grain sack, folding up on himself as he collapsed. He gasped gratefully for air and wondered if his ribs were still intact.

'He shouldn't have elbowed me,' Ingvar said mildly, peering around at them.

Hal couldn't resist a grin. 'Well, I'm certainly not going to argue with you about that,' he said. Then added: 'Or anything else for that matter.' He stooped and knelt beside the gasping, groaning Wulf.

'Did you really swap that rope with your brother?' he said. 'Just to trick me?'

Wulf nodded. He wasn't in the mood or any condition to deny anything. 'Yes . . .' he groaned. 'It was a joke. Just a joke.'

Hal prodded him in the ribs and Wulf doubled up under the touch.

'Does that hurt?' Hal asked.

Wulf nodded several times. 'Yes. It does. It really hurts.'

Hal smiled. 'Good. It serves you right.' He stood up and looked at Ingvar. 'Ingvar, from now on, you're our master at arms. You'll be responsible for discipline.'

Ingvar beamed, then thought about what Hal had said. 'What . . . do I have to do exactly?'

'If anyone annoys me, you squash him,' Hal told him and Ingvar nodded happily.

'Yes. I can do that.'

Just then, the horn sounded from the training area, signalling two minutes to lights out. There was a general scramble to undress and get into bed. As he extinguished the lantern and rolled into his blankets, Hal remembered that he hadn't re-checked Jesper's axe. He shrugged and yawned.

I'll do it in the morning, he thought.

Their training began in earnest the following day.

Breakfast was a hurried meal. They were given half an hour to eat, return to their quarters, make beds, fold blankets and clean up their area, then head back to the training ground with their weapons. It was now that they learned a little more about the scoring methods they would be subject to during their training.

The assessment tasks carried the most points, of course. The team doing best in each task could receive a maximum of one hundred points — less if the instructors decided so. The team coming second received twenty points. There were no points for the losers.

As they had already learned, points would also be awarded for good performance in their day-to-day training. The Herons had already earned some points for the construction of their living quarters. But now they found out about demerits, or negative points. Points could be deducted for sloppy work, inattention to the instructors, arriving late for meals or a training session or, as the Herons found out to their chagrin, for poor presentation of their weapons.

Sigurd called a snap inspection of weapons as soon as the teams arrived back at the training ground after stowing their kit. He walked quickly along the lines of boys as they held their weapons ready for his examination. He seemed to be barely glancing at the axes and swords as he passed. But as he reached Jesper, he paused for a second, and glared at the boy. Jesper's reddening face told him all he needed to know. The boy was aware that his weapon wasn't up to standard. Sigurd flicked a forefinger against the axe head.

'Rust,' he said briefly. 'And there's still a nick in the edge.' He glanced round, caught Hal's anxious eye. 'Twenty demerit points to the Herons. That wipes out the points you won yesterday for your camp site,' he said. He moved on down the line, nodding brief approval at the other weapons as he inspected them, then walked briskly away to inspect the other teams.

The moment he left, a chorus of bickering broke out among the other Herons as they gathered around Jesper.

'Nice work, Jesper,' said Stig.

'Yeah. Now you've dropped us all in it, right and proper,' Stefan told him.

'Why should we all lose points because you're too lazy to look after your kit?' Ulf put in.

Jesper flushed angrily. 'Don't blame me! I didn't know Sigurd was going to be so fussy. It's only a speck of rust, after all.'

'Well, if we don't blame you, who do we blame?' Ingvar demanded. There was an ugly silence for a few seconds as they all glared at each other. Finally, Hal spoke.

'Me,' he said. 'I'm to blame.'

He was standing a little apart from them and they all turned in surprise to look at him.

'You?' Stig said. 'What are you talking about?'

'You elected me as skirl. It's my responsibility,' Hal said. His breath was coming quickly and he felt his heart beating more rapidly than normal. He realised he'd reached a defining point. All his life, he'd avoided drawing attention to himself, avoided the conflict that it would bring. Now, he decided, it was time for that to end.

Stig made a dismissive gesture. 'Well, yes, we elected you skirl, but that was just . . .' He paused, seeing Hal's cold look.

'That was just what?' Hal demanded. 'A joke? A game? A bit of fun to annoy Tursgud?'

'No. Of course not,' Stig said uncertainly. The others made corroborating noises.

'You elected me as skirl. I'm taking that seriously, even if you aren't,' Hal said. 'In future, if I give an order, I want it carried out.' He turned to Jesper. 'I told you to clean that axe and you didn't do it. If you disobey an order again, I'll punish you.'

'You'll what?' Jesper said incredulously.

'I'll punish you. I'll put you on fatigues. You'll do extra work. You can empty the slop buckets and dig out the drainage trenches — anything I tell you to, in fact.' He looked around the rest of the group, seeing their surprised faces. 'Does anyone have a problem with that?' he demanded.

No one would meet his eye. They looked at the ground and shuffled their feet.

'This isn't a game!' he told them. 'This is brotherband training. It's our future. If you want me as skirl, you have to agree to obey my orders — not just the ones you like or the ones you agree with, but all of them. Otherwise, pick someone else.'

He paused, giving them a few seconds to let his words sink in.

'Well?' he said. 'What's it to be?' He was surprised when Jesper was the first one to speak.

'All right,' he said. 'You're the skirl.'

There was a muttered chorus of agreement from the others.

'Good,' Hal said. 'Just remember, we're a team. We're all rewarded together and we're all punished together.'

Again, they mumbled their consent. He looked around the ring of faces, searching for any sign of rebellion or disagreement and seeing none. Finally, for the first time in several minutes, he relaxed, letting out a long sigh of air. He was surprised to find that his hands were shaking with tension and he hurriedly thrust them into his pockets to conceal the fact.

'Now let's get on with it,' he said.

Out of the corner of his eye, he had seen Gort approaching. The instructor had the look of a man who was about to make them suffer.

For the next hour, they were put through a gruelling session of physical exercise.

Jogging round the perimeter of the training area, then breaking into a sprint for fifty metres, then jogging some more. Then sprinting. Then jogging, with no let up until their breath came in heaving gasps and their sides were sore.

Then, on a signal from Gort's whistle (and how they grew to hate that whistle!), they would drop to the ground and perform twenty slow push-ups.

Slow push-ups were the worst. By the twelfth, most of them were trembling in the arms as they raised their bodies from the ground, then slowly, slowly, lowered them down again.

As the count hit twenty, there was no time to relax. They were on their feet again and running to the spot where a long, roughly trimmed young tree trunk was waiting for them.

They would work with this. Lifting it high above their heads, then lowering it slowly onto the right shoulder.

Then up again, slowly once more. Then down on to the left shoulder. They would repeat this pattern ten times, then raise the log high again and turn to face in the opposite direction, their hands clawing onto the rough bark surface, forced to change their grip as they turned, scrabbling to keep control of the heavy, unwieldy piece of timber.

Stefan, seeing the other two groups already exercising with their logs, quickly positioned himself behind Ingvar in the line. As the bigger boy hoisted the log high above his head, Stefan could barely continue touching it with his fingertips. In effect, Ingvar was doing the work for both of them. Gort, however, had trained hundreds of boys in his time and was alert to this trick.

'You!' he called, pointing to Ingvar. 'Move to the end of the line. Don't lift the log higher than the rest of them.'

Ingvar complied, standing at the rear of the line and hoisting the log with his elbows bent.

Gort smiled at Stefan. 'Nice try,' he said. 'Ten demerits.'

There was a mumble of anger from the other boys. Except for Jesper, who was standing behind Stefan. He looked around, made sure Gort wasn't looking, and kicked Stefan in the seat of the pants. When Stefan turned angrily, Jesper grimaced at him.

'That's one from the team,' he said.

They worked with the log until their arms ached and their knees were trembling with fatigue. They kept in time to a series of short, shrill blasts from Gort's detested whistle. Finally, a long blast signalled that the exercise was over.

'That's it!' Gort said. 'Put the log down.'

Thankfully, they tossed the log to one side, sending it thudding onto the grass. A piercing shriek from the whistle startled them.

'Put it down, I said. Not chuck it away! Now pick it up again!'

Wearily they stooped and worked their fingers under the rough wood, trying to get purchase. Exhausted as they were, it was much harder to lift the log off the ground than it had been before. But they managed it, bringing it up to waist height.

'Now, shoulder height!' Gort ordered and they raised the log to their right shoulders.

'Left shoulder!' he ordered, emphasising the command with a whistle blast. They complied, groaning as they lifted the log above their heads and brought it down on the other shoulder. Somehow, the effort seemed much harder since they had stopped, thinking the exercise session was over.

'Right shoulder!' *Peeeep!* Again, they obeyed. 'Waist height!' *Peeeep!*

They lowered the log to waist height, changing their grip as they did.

'Now lower it slowly. Sloooowly!'

Peeeeeeeeeeeeeeeeeeeeeeeeeeeeeeep!

They obeyed the long, drawn-out whistle blast, slowly lowering the log until it hovered a few centimetres above the ground.

'And down!' *Peep!*

This time, they made sure they lowered the log the last few centimetres before releasing it. Inevitably, one or two of them caught their fingers underneath and swore quietly. Then they straightened, rubbing their sore backs, rolling their shoulders to ease aching muscles.

'Right! Collect your weapons. Double-time to the weapons area.'

And so the pattern of their days was set. Hard physical exercise, followed by equally hard work, training with their weapons.

Hal would stand before a pine post wrapped with tattered, frayed old rope. In addition to his sword, he had been issued with a heavy wooden shield. Sword drill consisted of a sequence of pretend attacking and defensive moves. He would swing the heavy sword overhand to thud against the frayed, tattered rope padding, then raise the heavy shield to protect himself from an imagined counterstroke. Then swing the sword again, this time in a sidestroke, to hit the rope-padded pole. Again, raise the shield. Then spin to hit the pole backhanded. Then raise the shield. Then strike overhand again and begin the entire sequence once more.

It was dull and repetitive and hard work. The others around him performed similar actions with their axes and a few swords. The weapons area was filled with the dull thud of blades striking rope-padded pine. Occasionally, a richer note would ring out as an axe or sword blade struck bare wood, where the padding had finally been chopped away.

And all the time, the tempo was set by the continuing, and infuriating, *peep-peep-peep!* of their instructors' whistles.

By the end of the session, Hal's right wrist and arm would be aching from swinging the heavy, unbalanced sword, and the continual impact with the training post.

And his left shoulder and biceps would be on fire from the weight of the massive shield. Most of the others felt the same. Although some, notably Tursgud, Stig and Rollond, seemed to take the gruelling weapon drills in their stride.

Ingvar, of course, slammed his heavy club into the target pole over and over, without any visible effort, although his fellow students learned not to walk too close to him when he was doing it. His peripheral vision was as bad as his normal vision.

They would break for twenty minutes for lunch, slumping gratefully on the benches with their bowls of rich stew and thick bread. The food was good and nourishing and there was plenty of it. Their instructors knew the importance of keeping their energy levels up. But the brief lunch break was just enough for their hard-working muscles to cool and stiffen, so that they would ache dully for the rest of the day and into the night.

In the afternoons, they would study the theory of seamanship, ship handling and navigation. These were the sessions Hal enjoyed most, particularly the navigation.

He looked forward to the third week, when they would switch from theory to practical work, on board ship. He had already spoken to Sigurd about using the *Heron* in their exercise. The instructor had relayed the request to Erak, who had agreed — albeit reluctantly. He still had misgivings about the little ship's revolutionary new sail plan, but he accepted that with fewer rowers, the Herons would be disadvantaged in a larger ship.

Sigurd was also interested to see Hal's growing confidence as the leader of his brotherband — and the growing respect that his teammates showed him. Very little went unnoticed by the chief instructor and he sensed that, after the incident with the rusty axe, Hal had drawn a line in the sand with his companions.

The day's instruction ended in the late afternoon, at which point the boys were free to return to their quarters and rest, go over notes they had taken during the various classes, or practise techniques they had been shown that day. Hal, even though he was exhausted and his arms ached, made a point of returning to the shelter where the *Heron* was moored, and working on the punching bag Thorn had given him. The others, particularly Stig, wondered what he was up to. But they were too tired to try to find out.

After half an hour's hard work, Hal would return to the camp site in time to clean up for the evening meal. Then the three groups would return to their respective quarters to wait for the lights-out signal. Most of them never heard it. They were usually fast asleep long before the horn sounded its mournful note through the forest.

CHAPTER NINETEEN

Thorn sat with his back against a tree, watching the brotherbands at weapons drill.

To be accurate, he wasn't watching all of them. His attention was focused on Hal as he swung the heavy sword at the practice post. His movements were tired and clumsy, Thorn thought, and he frowned. Hal wasn't built heavily, like Stig or Tursgud. But he was well balanced and athletic and he normally had excellent hand-eye co-ordination. He should be performing better.

Thorn grunted in displeasure as he watched the sword rebound awkwardly from a strike against the post, nearly falling from Hal's grip. Then the shield came up in defence.

'Too slow. Too slow,' Thorn muttered to himself.

He looked around for the instructor, Gort. The man seemed unaware of Hal's problems. He was pacing down the line of boys standing at their practice poles, blowing time with that annoying whistle of his. As long as they moved in time, he seemed content.

Thorn realised that it was early days yet. It was only the third day of full training, after all, and part of the reason for the drills was to develop and harden the boys' muscles. But still . . .

'If he learns bad technique to begin with, he'll never get over it.'

He looked back to the boy again, noting his flat-footed stance and the clumsy stroking method.

He's teaching him to use it like an axe, Thorn thought. Then he shrugged. Most of the Skandians were axemen. Gort, with his build, would almost certainly be one. He had obviously never learned any of the subtler techniques that could be employed with a sword. His method was to simply batter, batter, batter at an enemy's defence until it collapsed under his assault. These drills would increase strength and, as far as Gort was concerned, sheer strength was the key to victory.

'You wouldn't last five minutes on a real battle-field,' Thorn said in Hal's direction. Hal was the sort of opponent other warriors sought out. He looked ill at ease and ill prepared. He'd be an easy victim for an experienced fighter. It was that thought that decided Thorn. He heaved himself to his feet and started across the field to where the boys were training.

He knew better than to approach Hal directly. Gort was in charge of the Heron brotherband and he wouldn't appreciate Thorn interrupting without so much as a by-your-leave. So the old seafarer stopped about twenty metres short of the group of boys, staying behind them, out of their line of vision, and waited to catch Gort's eye.

But his presence didn't go unnoticed by other eyes. Across the field, training with the Sharks, Tursgud saw him. His pride still rankled when he thought of how Thorn had gripped his wrist that day by the harbour and forced him to back down.

'What's the dirty old drunk doing here?' he said.

One of his companions glanced around. 'Maybe he's looking for a job as a target,' he sneered.

Tursgud swung his axe viciously at the pole, aiming for a spot where the rope had frayed away. The blade sank into the exposed wood with a vicious *thunk!* and he had to wrench it free.

'Send him over here,' he said. 'I'll get rid of his other hand for him!'

The Sharks around him laughed unpleasantly. Jarst, their instructor, was at the far end of the line, correcting a boy's technique. He glanced up angrily, frowned as he saw Thorn across the field, then snapped at the sniggering boys.

'Shut up and get back to work!'

Tursgud looked around at his cronies, miming fear. They stifled their laughter and went back to their drill.

Thorn had been standing for some minutes when Gort finally decided to take notice of him. He had seen the bearded, unkempt figure almost as soon as he arrived. But he had ignored him, hoping he would become bored and go away. Friends and relatives were discouraged from watching brotherband training sessions. And they were certainly not welcome to interrupt. Finally, however, Gort decided that it was pointless and rather stupid to pretend he hadn't seen Thorn. If the other man had waved, or called out or whistled, he would have felt justified in telling him to leave. But Thorn merely stood, patiently and quietly. Gort walked over to him.

'What do you want?' he asked unpleasantly.

Thorn gestured with his thumb to a spot some metres away.

'Can we move over there?' he asked. 'I don't want to disturb your class.'

'You already have,' Gort told him but Thorn shook his head.

'No. I haven't,' he said in a mild tone. 'I've stood here quietly and not many have noticed me. But if you don't lower your voice, they all will.'

Gort was irritated to realise that Thorn was right. He impatiently led the way to a spot a little away from the practising boys.

'Come on then,' he said. And turning around, he was surprised to find that Thorn was right behind him. He hadn't heard the other man moving.

Thorn smiled apologetically at him. No sense in antagonising the man, he thought.

'So what do you want?' Gort repeated.

Thorn intentionally kept his tone neutral and non-confrontational, although Gort's ill-tempered attitude was beginning to annoy him.

'The boy Hal,' he said. 'That sword is too heavy for him. And the shield is way too big.'

Gort shrugged. 'He gets what he's issued,' he said shortly. 'We don't have a big selection of swords for him to choose from.'

'Some of the other boys have good weapons,' Thorn pointed out.

'Some of the other boys have parents who can afford to buy them decent equipment,' Gort replied.

He looked the shabbily dressed, unshaven man up and down. 'If you want to, you can buy him a decent sword,' he said sarcastically.

'I don't know about buying one. But I can certainly get one for him,' Thorn said. If he'd noted the sarcasm in Gort's last remark, he didn't show it.

'Oh really, and where would you find a sword?' Gort moved closer, thumbs thrust into his belt. He expected Thorn to step back and was surprised when he didn't.

'Erak's store room,' Thorn said. And Gort's eyes opened a little wider.

'The Oberjarl's store room?' he asked incredulously.

Thorn nodded. 'There's only one Erak I know and I believe he is the Oberjarl.'

Gort was confused. He found it hard to believe that this ragged, rather dirty beggar would have access to Erak's store room. But the man had spoken confidently enough. It might be wise to find out more about him before he refused outright.

While he was thinking, Thorn continued. 'Another thing. Why have you got him training with a sword?'

'Obviously, because he's not big enough to swing an axe properly.'

Thorn nodded as if that was the answer he expected. 'Then where's the sense in giving him a shield that's the size of a cartwheel?'

Gort opened his mouth to reply, but realised that the man had a valid point. He hesitated. To be honest, he hadn't given the matter of a shield any thought. Finally, feeling he was being put on the defensive and not enjoying it, he challenged Thorn.

'I suppose you can get him a better one of those as well? From Erak's store room?' But if he expected to win the point or for Thorn to back down, he was disappointed.

'I think I could lay my hands on a better shield too,' Thorn said.

Which put Gort in a quandary. If a friend or family member could provide equipment for one of the trainees, he had no right to refuse them. But still, he didn't like to appear to back down in front of this strangely disquieting one-armed man. He temporised.

'I'll have to clear it with Sigurd,' he said. 'Come and see us at the end of the lunch break and I'll tell you then.'

'That's fair enough,' Thorn said. 'I'll see you then.'

And he turned and walked away, leaving the burly instructor staring after him, shaking his head uncertainly.

Gort mentioned Thorn's suggestion to the chief instructor while the boys were rushing through their lunch. He scoffed at the fact that Thorn claimed to have access to the Oberjarl's store room and was surprised at Sigurd's reaction.

'Do you know who he is?' Sigurd asked.

Gort shrugged. 'He's just an old drunk, isn't he?'

Sigurd nodded several times. 'That's what I thought until a few days ago,' he said. 'I was talking to the Oberjarl about him. He's got quite a story.'

Gort was intrigued. Like most Skandians, he loved a saga. He made a gesture for Sigurd to keep talking.

'So tell me,' he said. But Sigurd was already rising from his bench, seeing the first of the students getting ready to leave the meal tent.

'No time now,' he said. 'I've got a navigation class. Ask me another time. It's an amazing tale.'

Gort, his curiosity frustrated, knew there was no point in pressing Sigurd further at this point. Instead, he called out after his rapidly retreating back, 'So what about this sword and shield? What do I tell him?'

Sigurd glanced back at him as he left the tent. 'Tell him to go ahead.'

And Gort was left to wonder about the mystery behind the strange, one-armed old sea wolf.

CHAPTER TWENTY

Lessons were finished for the day and Hal, as was his habit, made his way to the inlet where the *Heron* was moored. He was surprised to find Thorn waiting there for him.

The older man had brought a small loaf of fresh bread and some sliced cold beef from Karina's kitchen. He handed it to the boy and watched with a smile as he wolfed it down. There was a flask of cold buttermilk as well and Hal drained half of it then sat back with a sigh of satisfaction.

'Hungry then?' Thorn asked him, still smiling. Hal nodded emphatically. He'd gulped the food so quickly that for a moment he couldn't speak. Thorn continued. 'Don't they feed you up there?'

'Yes. The food isn't bad at all,' Hal said, finally finding his voice. 'But they work us hard too. And they don't have fresh bread like my mam bakes.'

'Actually, I made that loaf,' Thorn told him, with a

certain amount of pride in his voice. 'Although I'm surprised you could taste it, it went down so fast.'

'You made it?' Hal said, surprised.

'I have hidden depths. Been working on the punch bag?' He nodded towards the shelter, where Hal had hung the sack filled with wool and canvas scraps.

'Every day,' Hal told him. He held up his hands and Thorn could see how the knuckles were reddened and chafed from his repeated onslaughts on the bag.

'Good. Let's see how you're doing.' Thorn led the way to the shelter and watched as Hal took a stance in front of the bag. He pursed his lips with satisfaction as he saw how the boy stayed on his toes, moving lightly, keeping his balance. Then Hal's fists shot out in a rapid salvo of blows.

Smack! Smack! Smack! He drove his left straight at the bag, three rapid shots that set it swinging. Then he danced in and unleashed a ripping right hook that jerked the heavy bag off to the side. He repeated the sequence almost immediately.

'Keep your shoulder behind it,' Thorn said quietly. After a few punches, he noted that Hal would occasionally use his arms only, instead of getting any body weight and shoulder behind the punch. 'Remember, most fights are won with one or two punches. Make sure they count.'

'Better,' he said, as the boy set his teeth and stepped into his punches, feeling the extra power that drove the bag back until it jerked fiercely against its retaining rope. Thorn let Hal throw a few more punches. He was doing well, he thought.

'All right. That's enough.'

Hal straightened and stepped back, wiping beads of perspiration from his forehead. He looked at Thorn hopefully, and grinned as the one-armed man delivered his verdict.

'That's good. You're doing well. Just keep that right hand up a little more when you're throwing the left. And keep your chin tucked in, instead of hanging it out there as a target.'

'I'll remember that,' Hal said.

Thorn knew he would. The boy took instruction well, he thought.

'How's the training going?' he asked.

Hal grimaced. 'It's hard work,' he said. 'I'm enjoying the navigation classes. We're working on the theoretical stuff at the moment.'

There were two sides to navigation. One was theoretical, or anecdotal. It required the voyager to memorise various sets of conditions, water depths, tidal flows, prevailing currents and the differing types of seabeds found in different areas. For example, if a skirl found his ship in ten fathoms of water on a sloping shale seabed at high tide, with a prevailing north wind and a current that set north-west, he would have a fair idea that he was off the south-eastern coast of Sonderland. The records had been collected by Skandian seafarers for different parts of the world over several centuries. They were a jealously guarded secret, made known only to Skandian navigators.

The other side was the practical side, where the boys learned to tell their position by gauging the altitude of various stars and the sun, and by use of a sun compass, which they were also taught how to construct.

Thorn shook his head. Only a select few could manage

the intricacies of navigation. That's why skilled navigators were so highly regarded by the Skandians.

'Could never keep all that stuff in my mind,' he admitted. Hal grinned at him. 'How about the weapons classes?'

Hal sighed. 'More hard work. I don't feel I'm doing so well there. I feel like I'm clumsy and too slow.'

'You are,' Thorn told him and the boy looked up, surprised.

'You've been watching?' he asked.

Thorn didn't reply. It was obvious that he had been.

'How do you find that sword they've given you?' he asked, instead.

Hal shrugged. 'It's kind of heavy. But I guess I'll get used to it,' he said hopefully.

Thorn regarded him carefully for a few seconds. 'No reason why you should,' he said. 'It looks as if it's badly balanced. And the shield is way too heavy. It's an axeman's shield.'

'Nothing I can do about it,' Hal said resignedly.

Thorn snorted in derision. 'Maybe you can't. But I can. Come on.'

He turned abruptly and headed for the path that would take them into Hallasholm. Hal was caught by surprise and had to hurry to catch up.

'Where are we going?' he asked. But instead of answering the question, Thorn branched off on another subject. It seemed to be a habit of his, Hal thought.

'The trouble is,' Thorn said, 'you're being trained by axemen, and they're training you to use a sword like an axe — just swinging hard and battering your enemy.

That's a part of fighting with a sword, of course. But there's another part, and that's using the point. You've got to be ready to take advantage of any momentary gap in your enemy's defence and lunge through it. Eight centimetres of the point will drop an enemy just as quickly as half a metre of edge.'

'Like the punches you've shown me?' Hal said and Thorn looked at him, pleased that he'd made the connection.

'Exactly,' he said. 'And, like the straight punch, a lunging sword blade is harder to avoid than a wild swipe. Axemen just batter away at each other and, in the end, the person who hits hardest will win.'

'So the bigger man will always win in the end?' Hal asked.

'Not necessarily,' Thorn told him. 'There's some technique involved, of course. A smaller man can sometimes develop more power by better timing and by getting more weight behind the stroke. Again, like your punching practice.'

Hal nodded, frowning thoughtfully. Once again, he found himself wondering how Thorn knew so much about these things. But he'd learned not to ask. The reply was most likely to be a slightly bitter comment along the lines of, 'I wasn't always like this, you know,' with the right arm stump brandished as he said the words 'like this'.

They'd reached the outskirts of the town now. Hal tried another question.

'Where did you say we were going?' he asked, hoping that phrasing it like that might elicit an answer. Thorn scowled at several children who he thought were staring at his stump.

'I didn't,' he said briefly. He snarled at the children, who scattered, giggling, then he strode out faster. Hal had to half run for a few paces to catch up. He shrugged philosophically. He'd find out where they were heading soon enough. One thing he knew, there was no point in asking Thorn over and over. If he didn't want to say, he wouldn't.

So Hal was considerably surprised when they stopped outside the Oberjarl's Great Hall. This was where Erak consulted with his council of jarls, staged official feasts, heard and judged disputes and issued official edicts. His private quarters were behind the huge public hall and Thorn led the way there now. A few sentries stood around the Great Hall, keeping an eye on the constant stream of people who filed in to deliver requests for the Oberjarl. Erak wasn't present but the visitors left the written requests with his Hilfmann, who was seated at a cluttered desk at the front of the hall. The sentries glanced at Thorn and Hal without too much curiosity. The Hilfmann glanced up once, nodded to Thorn and then went back to work. Hal had the feeling that Thorn was a regular visitor here.

They went through a side door at the far end of the hall, opposite the plain pinewood chair that served as the Oberjarl's throne. Hal found himself hurrying along behind Thorn through a low-ceilinged, timber-lined gallery. There were locked doors on either side. These, he knew, led into the living quarters of some of the more senior jarls. Many of them chose to live here, rather than maintaining their own households.

The gallery came to an end and they were facing a large double door, built of oak and reinforced with iron strips. Thorn gestured to it casually.

'Erak's quarters,' he said. Then he pointed to a smaller door on the right-hand side of the gallery.

'This is the one we want. It's his store room.' He produced a large iron key from inside his tattered jacket and inserted it in the lock.

'Um . . . Thorn? Should we be doing this?' Hal asked anxiously. He realised this was where Erak kept all his treasures — the booty and plunder he had hoarded from his time as a sea wolf raider and the share from other raids that he was paid as Oberjarl. Thorn stopped and looked sidelong at him.

'You scared of the Oberjarl, boy?' he asked.

Hal considered the question for a few seconds, then replied. 'Yes. I am, actually.'

Thorn emitted a short bark of laughter. 'Good! So you should be! He's a terrible man when he's angry!'

Which didn't do a lot to calm Hal's nervousness about breaking in to Erak's treasure room. But Thorn had the door unlocked and was swinging it open, gesturing for Hal to go first. Hal hesitated, then stepped through.

And stopped. It was a large, unfurnished room and it was packed to overflowing with treasure. Jewels, gold, silver, chests of coins. Armour. Weapons. Statues. Artworks. In the centre of the room was an enormous chandelier, made from hundreds of pieces of faceted glass. It hung from the ceiling but the ceiling was so low that most of the chandelier was draped on the ground.

Thorn saw Hal looking at it and sniggered.

'Ridiculous, isn't it? It was Ragnak's, before Erak became Oberjarl and claimed it. He thinks it's very artistic. Come on.'

They threaded their way through the heaped treasures. Some of it, Hal saw, was nearly priceless. Other pieces, like the chandelier and several ridiculous statues of nymphs and small winged creatures that looked like babies with tiny wings, were simply gaudy and probably worthless.

'I had no idea Erak was so rich,' he said quietly.

Thorn looked over his shoulder at him. 'Or had such bad taste.' Erak's treasure room seemed to amuse him mightily. 'Look at that,' he added.

The object he was referring to was a marble statue of a little boy, standing naked on the edge of a wide marble basin, in a rather suggestive pose.

'It's a fountain,' he explained. 'Erak stole it on a raid in Toscana. The boy's supposed to pee into the bowl. But Erak's never managed to get it to work. Bit of a sore point with him, as a matter of fact.'

'It is pretty ghastly,' Hal agreed. Thorn was bending over a large chest against the back wall of the room, fumbling with the clasp. 'Should you be doing that?' Hal asked.

'This is my stuff,' Thorn told him, rummaging in the chest. 'Erak took it to look after it for me when I was . . . you know . . . sick.'

Hal nodded. He and his mother had an agreement that they would refer to the time when Thorn was a drunk as the time when he was sick. Thorn had picked up on it as well. He didn't like to think about how low he had sunk in that period.

'Aah! Here it is!' the scruffy old sea wolf said triumphantly, dragging a long object wrapped in oilskin from the chest. Several necklaces and a bag of silver coins spilled out at the same time but he ignored them. Quickly, he unwrapped it and handed it to Hal.

'It's your father's sword,' he said.

Hal took it in both hands, holding it out in front of him to study it. It was a plain, utilitarian weapon. The hilt was bound in fine wire and there was a brass pommel and crosspiece. The blade was hidden in a leather and brass scabbard attached to a wide leather belt. He tested the weight of the sword, lifting it up and down a few times.

'It feels just as heavy as the other one,' he said.

'A sword has to have some weight,' Thorn told him. 'Otherwise you might as well hit your opponent with a feather. The secret is in how that weight's balanced. Take it out of the scabbard.'

Hal drew the sword with a faint scraping sound of metal on leather. Then, as he held it aloft by the hilt, his eyes opened in surprise.

The weight of the sword seemed to drop away, somehow. It felt light and agile and easy to move back and forth. There was a faint sense of mass in the tip of the blade, but the sword didn't weigh heavily on his wrist the way his other sword did, dragging it down and making him work to keep the point up. The weight was balanced beautifully between the hilt and the point. He felt as if he could wield this sword all day without tiring.

'This was my father's?' he said, turning the blade in his hands to look at it. The blued steel was unadorned except for the channels down the blade on either side. They served two purposes, he knew. They stiffened the blade, and also allowed blood to escape, so that the sword could be withdrawn from a wound more easily.

'He knew a good sword when he saw one,' Thorn agreed. 'That one will do you quite well.'

'I should think so,' Hal said quietly. He couldn't take his eyes off the weapon, picturing his father brandishing it as he charged ashore on a raid. Unthinkingly, he suddenly flourished it above his head, as he imagined his father might have done.

Thorn stepped back hastily as the blade flashed past his nose. He stumbled on a pile of furs and only just stopped himself from falling.

'Be careful with that!' he barked and Hal flushed, lowering the sword carefully, then replacing it in the scabbard.

'Sorry,' he mumbled. Thorn glared at him as he recovered his equanimity.

'So you should be. It's a sword, not a fairy wand, you know.' He looked around the dimly lit store room. 'Now where has Erak kept his . . .'

He got no further. The door to the gallery opened to admit Erak. The Oberjarl peered round suspiciously, then his expression cleared as he recognised Thorn and his companion.

'Oh, it's you, Thorn. And the Master Mariner, I see. How are you, young Hal?'

'Well enough, thank you, Oberjarl.'

'Is that Mikkel's sword?' Erak asked, squinting his eyes to see the sword in Hal's hand more closely.

'Yes. They gave the boy a great unbalanced lump of iron. Thought he might as well have this,' Thorn said.

He was poking around the far wall, shifting items aside to see what was behind them.

'Good choice,' Erak said. He looked at Hal. 'It's an excellent sword, that one.'

Hal nodded. 'It certainly feels better than the one they issued me with.'

Erak grunted. 'Anything would. Those issue weapons are pretty dreadful. And good swords are hard to come by. Thorn!' he said, distracted by the other man's rifling through his belongings. 'Are you looking for something in particular, or just planning on robbing me blind?'

'You had three or four Gallican shields,' Thorn replied. 'Thought you might contribute one to the boy. They've issued him with the wheel off an oxcart.'

'Behind that stuffed bear,' Erak told him, pointing.

Thorn looked behind the huge stuffed bear, which had been in Erak's storehouse for some years and looked rather the worse for wear − or, rather, moths. There was a clatter of metal as he dragged a shield into view, several others falling to the floor as he did so. He left them where they lay and handed the shield to Hal. It was a wood frame, covered with a curved metal sheet and painted deep blue, with a white diagonal stripe. The top edge was a straight line. The sides started out straight but halfway down they formed into a curve so that they joined in a point at the bottom. Hal slipped his arm through the leather loop and gripped the handhold, testing the feel.

'That's a lot lighter,' he said appreciatively.

'The Galls make good shields,' Erak told him. 'Mind you, it's a bit light to block an axe stroke directly. Try to deflect the axe as much as you can.'

'How do I do that?' Hal asked. Surprisingly, Erak looked to Thorn and it was he who answered.

'Don't present the shield straight on to the stroke. Slant it so the axe glances off. In a pinch you can block it. But don't do it too often.' He frowned at Hal. 'Didn't hear you thank the Oberjarl for giving you the shield,' he said.

'Oh! Yes, thank you, Oberjarl,' Hal said.

Erak grinned. 'I don't recall I had much choice. Thorn ordered me to hand it over, didn't he?'

Thorn snorted and muttered disdainfully and Hal smiled in return.

'Well, thanks anyway. And thanks to you, Thorn, for the sword.'

Thorn shrugged the thanks aside and motioned towards the door.

'It was yours by rights, anyway,' he said. 'Now come on. Time you were getting back to barracks.'

Erak held up a hand. 'If you don't mind, Thorn, I'd like a word in private with Hal. Could you wait outside for a few minutes?'

'What do you want to talk about?' Thorn asked.

Erak looked at Hal, his head inclined to one side. 'Hal, do you understand the phrase "a word in private"?' he asked. Hal nodded and the Oberjarl continued. 'Later on, can you explain it to Thorn?'

'Oh all right!' Thorn said, his curiosity frustrated. 'I'm going. Don't be too long.'

CHAPTER TWENTY-ONE

Erak waited until the door closed behind Thorn. He looked around, saw a wooden chest with a padded top, and sat down, motioning for Hal to find a seat for himself among all the clutter. When the boy was seated, on a small stool carved in the shape of an elephant, the Oberjarl regarded him for several long moments.

Hal realised that Erak wasn't quite sure how to begin. We could sit here in silence until this elephant comes to life, he thought.

'So, Oberjarl?' he prompted.

Erak started as he realised he'd been sitting staring at the boy.

'I just wanted to say thank you,' he said and Hal frowned, puzzled by his words.

'Thank me?' he said. 'For what?'

'For what you've done for Thorn,' the Oberjarl replied.

'What I've done? I've done nothing. He's doing things for me.' Hal pointed to the sword and the shield, leaning against a statue of a whiskery Teutlandt king. 'I've done nothing.'

But Erak was shaking his head. 'You've done a lot more than you know. You've given him a focus for living. You mean a great deal to him.'

'Well, we're friends, I know that, but . . .'

'It's more than that, Hal,' Erak interrupted him. 'He's proud of you. He sees so much potential in you and he wants you to succeed. You've dragged him out of that well of self-pity and depression he dug for himself after he lost his hand. That was nearly the end of him, you know.'

'I can imagine,' Hal said thoughtfully. 'It must have been a terrible thing to face up to.'

'Worse than you can imagine.' Erak paused once more and Hal sensed he was trying to decide whether to continue any further. Then he nodded slightly to himself as he came to a decision.

'How much do you know about Thorn?' he asked.

Hal thought, then shrugged. 'Well, not a lot, really. He was a friend of my father. He was a member of your crew. But then he became a bit of a drunk after he lost his hand —'

'That's putting it mildly,' Erak interjected and Hal continued.

'Yes. Then my mam gave him a bit of a talking to and he straightened himself out . . .'

'That she did,' Erak said, smiling. Hal looked up.

'When my mam gives you a talking to, you tend to listen,' he said, with heartfelt sincerity. He'd been on the receiving end of more than one in his life.

'Since then, he's helped around Mam's eating house, doing odd jobs and chores. But . . .' He paused, trying to frame his thoughts into words. Lately, he'd been seeing hints of a different side to Thorn.

'But what?' Erak prompted.

Hal frowned. 'He seems to know a lot about fighting, and weapons and so on.' He indicated the sword and shield beside him.

'He should,' Erak told him. 'He was the Maktig.'

'Thorn?' Hal's eyebrows shot up in surprise. 'Thorn was the Maktig?'

The Maktig, or the Mighty One, was the highest pinnacle of achievement a Skandian could aim for — the champion warrior of all Skandia. To be the Maktig, a warrior had to possess superlative strength, agility, speed and endurance. He had to excel with all weapons — axe, sword, spear and saxe knife. And with no weapons. He had to beat all comers in a gruelling annual challenge for the position. The Maktig was revered and respected throughout the country. The Maktig was a larger-than-life figure — a hero worthy of the great sagas.

The Maktig was definitely not a tattered, shabby, tangle-bearded tramp sleeping in a grubby, evil-smelling lean-to.

'Gorlog and Orlog!' Hal muttered. Orlog was Gorlog's lesser known brother, only invoked in moments of great stress or surprise. 'Thorn was the Maktig?' He still couldn't believe it.

'Three years running,' Erak told him.

'WHAT?' Hal's voice cracked. So far as he knew, nobody had ever been Maktig for more than one year. It simply couldn't be done.

'Nobody else has ever achieved that,' Erak told him, confirming his thought, at least in part. 'The second year, the man he beat was his best friend, Mikkel. Your father. Mikkel was good, but his axe skills weren't quite up to scratch.' He nodded towards the sword. 'He was a swordsman. But Thorn was immensely strong and skilful with all weapons. And he was fast. So very fast. Fast and powerful and deadly. I doubt there'll ever be another to achieve what he did.'

He let Hal absorb this amazing news for some seconds. Then he continued, with a sad note in his voice.

'That's why it hit him so hard when he lost that hand. When someone's raised up so high, they have a long way to fall. In one stroke, Thorn lost his ability, his status, his sense of worth and his career. He went from being a man everyone looked up to, to a man everyone pitied. What made it even worse was that, when Mikkel was dying, he asked Thorn to protect you and your mother. Thorn couldn't see how a one-armed man could do that. He felt he'd let down his friend. And you, and your mam.'

'No wonder he started drinking,' Hal said, almost to himself. He looked around the treasure room, his gaze lighting on the trunk at the back that belonged to Thorn.

'He was lucky you were a friend — and you kept him from squandering all his treasure,' he said.

Erak pursed his lips uncomfortably. 'I owed him that.'

'Because you were his skirl?' Hal asked. In the few days he had spent as a brotherband skirl, he had begun to realise that in a crew, loyalty travelled both ways. A skirl had to be loyal to his crew, just as they had to be loyal to him.

'Partly,' Erak agreed. 'But mainly because I was the one who cut off his hand.'

The terrible words were said almost casually and, for a moment or two, Hal didn't realise their import. Then his jaw dropped.

'You?' he gasped. 'But . . . I thought he lost it in battle? I just assumed that . . .' He paused. He didn't really know what he'd assumed.

'It was the voyage when your father died. We were caught in an early storm off Cape Shelter on the way home. Just blew up out of nowhere. Before I knew it, we were taken aback and dismasted. There was a tangle of wreckage over the side, dragging us down. Thorn was the first one to get there and start cutting it loose. He reached over the side to clear a piece of mast and his right hand became tangled in the mess of ropes. Then we got it cut free before we realised he was caught up in it. The mast was going over the side and he was going with it. I only had seconds to act.'

'You cut off his hand?' Hal said, horrified at the decision the Oberjarl had been faced with.

Erak nodded. His expression was bleak.

'I had to choose. Let him lose his hand or his life. Later, he told me he wished I'd let him go over the side with the mast.' He shook his head at the memory.

'I don't think I'd have the courage to do what you did,' Hal said. Erak shrugged.

'It wasn't so brave,' he said. 'It wasn't my hand. Anyway,' he gathered himself, shaking off the memory of that terrible day, 'that's why I'm so glad to see Thorn with an interest in life. He can see you have abilities far beyond his, and he wants to help you.'

'My abilities? But he was the Maktig! What can I do?'

'You're a thinker. A planner. And you're rapidly becoming a leader from what Sigurd tells me. Look, I can go out into the street and find at least a hundred men who are good axemen. But leaders? Thinkers? They don't come along too often and Thorn knows it. He sees it in you.' He smiled. 'We had a little bantam rooster of a fellow through here a few years back who helped us see off the Temujai. He was a leader and a planner.'

'That was the Ranger, wasn't it? From Araluen?'

'That's the one. I actually got to like him, in spite of myself. Thing is, we need people like him. And you,' he added.

Hal shook his head thoughtfully. 'I'd never thought of myself that way.'

'Well, start doing so,' Erak told him. 'On top of everything else, you're a fine helmsman. Very few men could have brought that ship in the way you did the other day. That's a skill that can't be taught.'

Hal grinned. 'My knees were like jelly while I was doing it,' he said. 'I was terrified I'd ram *Wolfwind*.'

'And you should have been,' Erak agreed. 'I didn't say you were smart, just skilful.'

Hal grinned. 'Point taken,' he said. Then he became serious. 'Thanks for telling me about Thorn, Erak.'

'That's all right. I felt it was time you knew. But don't tell Thorn you know. He doesn't like to be reminded of what he once was. It hurts too much to remember.'

'How could people have forgotten that he was the Maktig?' Hal asked, but Erak merely pulled a face.

'It was a long time ago, almost twenty years — before you were born. People age and other people forget. And after all, Thorn hasn't exactly behaved in a way that would make them want to remember, has he? People don't like it when they think their idols have let them down.'

'I guess that's true,' Hal said. 'Thanks for telling me. I won't let on to Thorn that you did.' He paused, then said, 'I suppose I'd better be going or I'll miss the dinner call at camp.'

Erak waved a hand towards the door. Hal collected the sword and shield and picked his way through the jumbled treasures.

'How do you like my fountain?' Erak called after him.

Hal looked again at the naked little boy posed on the edge of the marble bowl.

'It's very . . . artistic,' he said.

Erak screwed up his face thoughtfully. 'I can't get it to work. Maybe you could look at it sometime? I hear you're good with things like that.'

'Maybe,' Hal said doubtfully, reaching for the door handle. Time he got out of here, he thought. But as he opened the door, Erak had one last thing to say.

'Hal,' he called. 'Thorn has big expectations of you. Don't let him down.'

Outside, he found Thorn waiting, kicking idly at the dust in the street. Several small children were standing at a safe distance, staring at him. They had never seen such a ragged, untidy figure in their lives. He looked up as Hal emerged from the Great Hall, glaring at him suspiciously.

'So what was all the talking about?' he demanded.

Hal shrugged. 'Nothing much. He asked how the training was going.'

Thorn's suspicions were somewhat assuaged, but not completely. He thrust his face closer to Hal's. 'Did he say anything about me?'

Hal assumed an innocent, blank look. As a teenager, used to being questioned by adults, it was something he could do almost without conscious effort.

'You? No. He didn't say anything about you.'

Thorn looked hard at him for a few more seconds. Hal maintained the look of blank innocence. Finally, the old sea wolf turned away, satisfied.

'Just as well,' he muttered.

CHAPTER TWENTY-TWO

The next day, they were given their first major assessment task.

They assembled after breakfast at the training ground, as they did every day. They went automatically to their separate areas, prepared for two hours of gruelling physical training, followed by weapons drill. But today, the routine changed.

The three brotherband instructors, and the head instructor, Sigurd, strode out of the mess tent in a group and made their way to the centre of the training ground. Twenty-eight pairs of eyes followed them curiously, wondering what was about to come. They didn't have long to wait.

At a nod from Sigurd, Gort produced that much-hated whistle from his jerkin and blew a piercing blast on it. Not that there was any need to draw their attention. Everyone present was already watching.

'Right!' Sigurd yelled, in a wind-quelling bellow. 'Assemble here, everyone! In your bands.'

As the boys started to straggle across the field from three different directions, he added, 'AT THE DOUBLE!'

That got them moving. By now, they knew that the last person to arrive after that command was liable to incur a penalty for his team. That unfortunate person was one of Rollond's group. He slipped on a patch of wet grass and fell, twisting his ankle. Hal saw him fall and breathed a silent prayer of thanks. Until that happened, Ingvar had been the prime candidate to be last.

Sigurd glared at the late-arriving Wolf as he limped in to join the group.

'Fifteen demerits,' he snapped. A few of the Wolves muttered in annoyance, glaring at their straggling teammate, although it certainly wasn't the poor boy's fault.

'Shut up!' Rollond barked, and earned an approving glance from Sigurd.

'Just as well you spoke up, skirl. I was about to. And that would have meant more demerits.'

The offending boys hung their heads, not wishing to meet Sigurd's, or Rollond's, eyes. Sigurd paused just long enough to make sure the message had registered with them, then went on briskly.

'Today's your first assessment.'

There was a murmur of interest from the three bands, quickly silenced as he glanced up angrily at them.

'It's the mountain run,' he said, and that caused another buzz of interest, equally quickly silenced by another glare from Sigurd.

He's enjoying this, Hal thought. He loves getting us talking, then shutting us up.

Sigurd held out his hand and Viggo thrust a handful of parchment sheets into them. Sigurd held them up for the assembled boys to see.

'You'll be racing on Boarshead Mountain. There are three routes up the mountain. At the end of each one is a tent. In the tents are three figures. A wolf, a shark and a —' he hesitated, then his lip curled in disdain '— a birdy.'

The Herons shifted uncomfortably. The other teams laughed quietly. This time, Sigurd made no effort to silence them.

'The contest is simple,' he continued, as he handed the maps of each route to the three team skirls. 'Each route is the same length and difficulty as the others. You run up and fetch the figure, then run back. We time you.' He indicated three water clocks on a table outside the mess tent. 'Fastest time wins the points. One hundred of them. Second gets twenty. Last . . . gets nothing.' He paused, and looked directly at Hal and his group.

'Any questions? No? Then get back to your normal training areas, study the maps and think about who's going to be doing the running. I'll be round to ask you in a few minutes.'

Tursgud laughed. 'No question. I'll run for the Sharks.'

Sigurd regarded him keenly. 'Is that so? Well, once you decide, there's no changing. So be sure you choose correctly. Now get going!'

As they double-timed to their training area, Hal felt a flood of panic rising in his chest. He had no idea who would be the best choice to run for them. Ulf and Wulf were both fast. And Jesper had shown a good turn of pace in their daily sprint and long-distance training sessions. But speed wasn't all this would take. Boarshead Mountain was steep and rough. Whoever ran it would need strength and endurance as well as speed. He realised that Stig had moved up to jog alongside him.

'I'll run it,' his friend said, as if he was reading Hal's thoughts. Hal glanced at him. Stig could well be the best choice for this. He was certainly the closest they had to Tursgud and Rollond.

They reached their training area and the boys gathered in a loose half circle around him. He felt their eyes on him, waiting for him to make his decision. He cursed himself. This was his crew, his team. He should have taken the trouble to learn their abilities better. Stig was probably the best choice, he thought. But he wasn't sure. Then he shook his head. You're the leader. Make a decision and stick to it, he told himself.

'Stig,' he began, 'I think maybe you —'

But he got no further. Edvin interrupted him.

'Hal, we all have to run. This is a team event,' he said. All eyes turned to him and he continued. 'Remember when we went through the assessments, we noticed that the individual tests were listed that way: "Wrestling, individual. Foot race, individual. Navigation, individual." But for the mountain race, it just said, "Mountain race". That means it's a team event.'

Hal frowned as he tried to recall the list. 'I think you're right,' he said slowly. 'And if you are, that's why they've put this one first. If we'd already done a few others, we'd be more familiar with the wording. We'd be more likely to realise that it's not just a test of speed and endurance . . .'

'It's a test of our intelligence — our ability to read and interpret instructions,' Edvin said. He and Hal looked at each other and nodded agreement. 'Remember what he said to Tursgud just now?' Edvin continued. *Be sure you choose correctly.* Not *be sure you choose the best person.'*

Hal chewed his lip thoughtfully. He was convinced that Edvin was right. But what if he was mistaken? They would come last in the assessment — and they'd make a laughing stock of themselves.

The other boys had looked on in silence as Hal and Edvin discussed the wording of the assessment. Now Ulf chimed in.

'Better hurry up and decide. Here comes Sigurd,' he said.

They all turned and saw the burly figure of the instructor striding towards them, flanked by his three assistants. Hal came to a decision.

'We'll all run,' he said. He saw the doubtful looks on most of the faces around him. Only Edvin and Stig seemed to believe he had made the right choice. Ingvar seemed oblivious to the whole thing. But then, he usually did. Ingvar seemed to live in his own private world — possibly a result of his extremely poor sight.

There was no time for further discussion. Sigurd was upon them now, and the other three instructors were close behind him.

'Form up,' Hal ordered and the boys quickly moved into a ragged line, facing Sigurd. For a second, Hal considered ordering them to straighten the line, then discarded the notion. Skandians weren't big on close order drill, he thought.

Hal stepped to the front of the line, positioning himself in the middle as Sigurd stopped before them.

'Very well, skirl,' Sigurd said. 'Who's running for your team — for the birdies?'

Hal set his mouth in a straight line, refusing to show any reaction to the jibe. He took a deep breath, then committed himself — and his team.

'We're all running, sir. We'll do it as a team.'

Sigurd's gaze snapped up, surprised. He said nothing for a few moments, then he asked carefully, 'Are you sure? I'll give you a chance to reconsider.'

That tipped the scales for Hal. Sigurd was not the type to give him a chance to reconsider. It simply wasn't consistent that he should suddenly give them a second chance at anything. He's trying to trick me, Hal thought.

'No, sir. Put us all down as the runners.'

Sigurd shook his head as he made a notation on the sheet he was carrying.

'Your funeral,' he muttered. 'Right, get yourselves over to the starting point.'

Hal formed the Herons into two files and they double-timed across to the start point by the mess tent. The other bands were already assembled there. Rollond and Tursgud stood a little apart from their crews, stretching in preparation for the run.

'Very well,' Sigurd told them. 'Here are the runners. For the Wolves, Rollond. For the Sharks, Tursgud.' He paused and all eyes turned on the remaining group, which was what he had intended. 'And the Herons tell me they all intend to run the course.'

There was a shout of laughter from the other boys.

'Good idea,' Tursgud called out, grinning broadly. 'That way at least one of them might finish.' There was more laughter, which Sigurd allowed to run its course before speaking again.

'That won't happen. Everyone who starts must finish.' He looked at Rollond. 'You're first to start, get to the start line.'

Rollond took one more look at the map, then crammed it into his jacket. He nodded to Sigurd to show he was ready. Sigurd, in turn, nodded to Gort.

The whistle shrilled and Rollond took off, running like a stag, light footed and long striding, for the trees at the bottom of the mountain. His teammates cheered him on until he disappeared into the trees fringing the field. At the mess tent, Jarst removed the pin from the first of the water clocks. Water began dripping slowly down into the bottom receptacle.

The scene was repeated for Tursgud. He jogged lightly from one foot to the other as he waited for the start signal, exuding confidence. Then he was away, with the Sharks' cheers to urge him on.

Then, finally, it was the Herons' turn.

'Very well, birdies. One last chance to reconsider?' Sigurd looked at Hal. But Hal set his jaw and shook his head. 'No? Very well. No flying, birdies, that would be cheating and you know . . .'

He must have signalled to Gort with his hand behind his back, because he was still in mid-sentence when the start whistle sounded. Caught off guard, Hal hesitated for a second. Then, cursing, he took off at a run.

'Come on!' he shouted to the others and they streamed after him, the laughter of the other bands loud in their ears.

The climb was brutal. The path they were set on was narrow and steep and winding. In places, it disappeared completely, leaving them to negotiate shale-laden collapses and steep rock walls. When the trail resumed, the trees and undergrowth had grown in to crowd it, so that whoever was leading had to force a way through. Hal organised a roster where he, Stig, Jesper and Stefan alternated as the leader – who had the hardest job. Poor Ingvar fell several times in the first fifty metres of the climb. Eventually, Hal assigned the twins to him to keep him on his feet. They each took him by a hand and dragged him up the steep path.

Even so, he fell repeatedly, often bringing the twins down with him. After a while, Hal and Edvin replaced them.

Eventually, Hal noticed that the trees were thinning. He could see more and more of the sky around them and feel the wind more keenly. At ground level, it had been a gentle breeze. Here, it cut through their sweat-dampened clothing like a chill knife.

'We made it!'

It was Stig, whose turn it was to take the lead. The others straggled up beside him, Hal and Edvin arriving last of all, leading the lumbering Ingvar. A small two-man tent was pitched in the lee of some rocks. Stig indicated it to Hal.

Hal realised, with a mild sense of surprise, that they had all waited for him to look inside the tent. He gestured to Stefan.

'Get the bird,' he said, his breath coming raggedly. He simply didn't have the energy to stoop and crawl into the tent. He thought that if he did, he might well just lie down inside and not come out.

Stefan went down on hands and knees and crawled into the tent. A few seconds later, his grinning face emerged, and he held up a carved bird figure for them to see.

'Got it!' he said, scrambling to his feet. He held it out to Hal, who took it and examined it. There was nothing extraordinary about it. It was a rough carving of a seabird.

He looked around, took a deep breath and shoved the figurine inside his jacket.

'All right,' he said wearily. 'Let's go back down. Ulf, Wulf, you take Ingvar for a while.'

He had thought the downward route might be easier. But he was sadly mistaken. They plunged down, trying to keep their balance in the steeper parts, falling and sliding on the frequent patches of shale and loose scree. Going downhill worked a completely different set of muscles and, before long, their calves and ankles ached unbearably and they were cut and scratched in a dozen places where they had fallen. After several hundred metres, Hal learned it was best if Ingvar went first, with his two acolytes. That way, when the huge boy fell, he didn't bring down those of his teammates who were ahead of him. And in any event, they had to keep to Ingvar's speed, as they all had to arrive back together.

Eventually, weary, bruised, scratched, with wrenched muscles and turned ankles, they blundered out onto level ground again, and saw the training area several hundred metres away. Although he had expected it, Hal's heart sank as he made out the figures of Tursgud and Rollond by the finish line. He had hoped that they might have somehow beaten one of them.

'Couldn't one of them have fallen and broken a leg?' he muttered savagely as he led the Herons at a weary jog towards the finish line.

'What?' said Stig, jogging beside him.

Hal shook his head irritably. There was an ironic cheer from the other two groups, and a few catcalls as the Herons staggered wearily to the line. Hal glanced at the scoreboard where the times had been scrawled in charcoal.

Rollond: 42 minutes.

Tursgud: 47 minutes.

Jarst, who was attending the water clocks, pushed in the stopper as the last of the Herons — Ingvar, naturally — crossed the line. Hal noticed angrily that the timekeeper had exhausted one water clock and had begun to use a second. Jarst studied the level expended on the second bowl and called out.

'Herons, one hour twelve minutes.'

The Wolves and the Sharks laughed — the Wolves loudest of all because they had the winning time.

Sigurd, his face neutral, stepped forward to confirm the performances.

'Fastest time was Rollond. Second was Tursgud. Slowest were the Heron team.'

The Wolves began whooping and pounding each other on the back in celebration of their win. Two of them hoisted the grinning Rollond on their shoulders and began to parade him round the training area. The Sharks were more subdued. But still, Hal thought, he would have been glad of the twenty points for second place. He glanced at Edvin, who shrugged wearily and hung his head.

'Sorry,' Edvin muttered. 'My fault.'

Hal was tempted to agree, but he knew that wouldn't be fair. The decision had been his. Edvin had only done his best to advise him.

He opened his mouth to say so when Sigurd's bellow interrupted him.

'SHUT UP! SHUT UP AND PUT THAT MAN DOWN!'

He was pointing to the boys chairing Rollond on their shoulders. His face was red with anger. Gradually, the cheering and yelling died away. The boys he was pointing to, embarrassed and confused, set Rollond back down on the grass. He started towards Sigurd, a puzzled frown on his face.

'I'm sorry, sir, is there something wrong?'

'Yes, there's something wrong,' Sigurd replied. He slapped the sheet of assessments with the back of his hand.

'This assessment was a group exercise. Rollond and Tursgud are disqualified. The Herons win. One hundred points. There's no second place getter since both other teams were disqualified.'

He nodded to Hal and his team, turned on his heel and strode away. Hal heard a howl of triumph from his crew, felt an enormous impact on his shoulder as a massive hand sent him staggering several paces.

'Thank you, Ingvar,' he said. He didn't even have to look.

CHAPTER TWENTY-THREE

From then on, the assessments came when the teams least expected them. Four days after the mountain run, they had only just begun their physical conditioning session when Sigurd strode onto the training ground, sounded a horn and summoned them.

'Assessment!' he announced. 'Foot race! Ten minutes!'

The race track had been laid out the night before, while they slept. It was marked by flags on slender willow poles and led from the training ground down the hill, through the town of Hallasholm, around the harbour and back uphill to the training ground.

'Select your runners,' Sigurd ordered. He looked meaningfully at Rollond and Tursgud. 'This one's an individual test.'

Tursgud scowled at the Herons. 'I'll run for my team,' he said briefly.

Hal had known he would. He guessed that Tursgud's ego wouldn't allow him to nominate anyone else for any of the individual tests. He had to excel at everything. Hal looked at Rollond, saw the tall boy hesitate and knew he wanted to confront Tursgud directly. But he shook his head, as if dispelling the thought, and pointed to one of his team, a lean, long-legged boy who had shown a remarkable turn of speed during the daily training exercises.

'Henjak,' he said. The boy grinned and started shaking his arms and legs to loosen up the muscles.

'I'll run,' said a voice close to Hal. It was Stig. But Hal held up his hand in a negative gesture. He had decided he wasn't going to be caught unprepared again. He knew there was a foot race in the list of assessments and he'd been studying the relative speeds of his team members during the daily sprints and distance runs. Stig was fast. But Jesper was faster.

Possibly it was his background as an incorrigible thief that had helped him develop such speed, Hal thought, with a wry smile.

'I'm choosing Jesper,' he said to his friend, in a quiet tone. He didn't want to embarrass Stig in front of the others. He saw his friend's face flush with sudden anger.

'I can beat Tursgud,' he said.

'You might be able to. But the question is, can you beat Henjak?'

As well as assessing his own team's performance, Hal had tried, as far as possible, to keep tabs on the two opposing brotherbands to see who their fastest runners were. He knew little about Henjak, admittedly. But he'd seen how fast Rollond was. If he thought Henjak was the better choice to represent the Wolves, Henjak must be very fast indeed.

For a few seconds, Stig glared at him. There's that temper of his, Hal thought. Then his friend abruptly turned on his heel and walked away, throwing an angry, 'Fine then,' over his shoulder.

'Come on, skirl! We don't have all day!' Sigurd was waiting impatiently for his decision.

Hal looked up and said, 'Jesper will run for the Herons.'

He saw the look of surprise on Jesper's face, instantly replaced by wariness. Jesper had seen Stig talking to Hal and had assumed that Stig would be the runner. Now the reason for the angry reaction was clear. Jesper hoped that his selection wouldn't put him in Stig's bad books. The big boy would be a dangerous enemy to make.

Hal nodded reassuringly to him and Jesper shrugged his shoulders, then made his way to the start line. Tursgud and Henjak were already waiting for him. Henjak smiled and leaned over to shake hands. Tursgud ignored both his opponents. Henjak, still smiling, rolled his eyes at Jesper, jerking his head towards the Sharks' leader.

He looks confident, Jesper thought. He's not scared of Tursgud. He thinks he'll beat him easily. He's the big threat.

He squared his shoulders. Hal had shown faith in him, he thought. He determined to repay his leader by beating this gangly, friendly, confident boy. And beating him thoroughly.

'All right, runners,' Sigurd said. 'On the start line . . . GO!'

There was no preparation. No countdown. Just the sudden, explosive order.

Jesper was a thief. He was used to taking off on a fraction of a second's notice and he shot away like a startled hare, gaining a five-metre advantage over the other two, who wasted time looking to Sigurd for confirmation that the race had actually started. Then they both bolted in pursuit of Jesper's fast-disappearing form.

The remaining boys all started yelling encouragement as the three runners, with Jesper still in the lead and Tursgud and Henjak in hot pursuit, left the training area and started on the downhill path to the town. The three brotherbands streamed across the field to keep the runners in sight.

Hal went to move with the rest of the group but a hand on his shoulder stopped him. It was Stig, and he could tell his friend was still angry.

'Some friend you are,' Stig said bitterly.

Hal shook his head in frustration. 'Stig, just because I didn't select you doesn't mean we're not friends. I tried to choose the best person for the task.'

'Jesper?' Stig said, disbelief evident in his voice.

'Yes. Jesper.'

'I beat him when we ran yesterday,' Stig said.

Hal nodded acknowledgement of the fact. 'Yes. I saw that. But I don't believe he was running full out yesterday. And he's beaten you every other time.'

Stig paused uncertainly. He obviously hadn't considered that fact.

'Well, he'd better win this time,' he said.

Hal spread his hands in a conciliatory gesture. 'Stig, I didn't do this to annoy you. I'm the team leader. I have to do what I think is best. I told you, you have to go along with all my orders, not just the ones you agree with.'

He saw the anger slowly draining from Stig's face as his friend thought about what he had said. Eventually, and a little grudgingly, he replied. 'I guess so. Let's hope you're right.'

'Come on,' Hal said, clapping him on the shoulder. 'Let's go watch them race.'

They joined the others. The training area was a large meadow set on high ground, overlooking the town of Hallasholm. The race course curved down the hill, hidden in places by the trees, then entered the town itself. It followed a loop through the town, obscured from their view for the most part, then reappeared at a point where it wound back up the hill.

The yelling and cheering that had followed the runners down the hill died away as the observers lost sight of them.

'Where are they?' Hal asked the nearest person to him. Then, realising it was Ingvar, who was looking in entirely the wrong direction, he muttered, 'Never mind.' He jogged Edvin with his elbow instead and repeated the question.

'Behind the trees,' Edvin told him, pointing to a large stand of trees just above the town. Almost as soon as he spoke, the yelling began again as the runners emerged into view. The three boys were bunched in a tight group. It was impossible to tell who was in the lead, if anyone was. They sprinted, as if joined together, into the outskirts of the town. Then they were lost to sight again. Faintly, the sound of cheering could be heard from the town. The people of Hallasholm must have been aware that the race would be run today, Hal thought. They had probably seen the course being marked out the previous day.

Anxiously, the members of the three brotherbands scanned the town, looking for some sight of the racers. Occasionally, there would be a brief flash of movement between buildings, but they could never be sure who was winning. One thing they could see was that one of the runners had opened a gap between himself and the other two. Someone from the Sharks started to yell in triumph, then abruptly fell silent as he realised he wasn't sure that it had been Tursgud he'd seen in the lead.

Then Henjak emerged from the town, running like a hare towards the track that led uphill to the training area. The Wolves went wild with delight, screaming encouragement to their man. The Sharks and the Herons remained silent, anxiously straining to see the first sight of the next runner. Then Jesper and Tursgud emerged from the town, running neck and neck. First one would surge away a few paces, then the other would reel him in and go past. Then the first would make up the gap between them and they'd be neck and neck once more.

'Come on, Jesper!' a voice bellowed close to Hal's ear. He jumped in surprise, then realised it was Stig urging their runner on. He grinned at him. Typical Stig, he thought. A few moments of flaring bad temper, then everything was back to normal again.

The other Herons followed his example, yelling encouragement to Jesper. The Wolves and Sharks were shouting as well, the Wolves loudest of all, as Henjak increased his lead over the other two, then went out of sight in a large dip in the ground that hid him from those watching above.

'I think Henjak is gaining,' Stefan said.

Stig glanced sidelong at him. 'It's not over yet,' he said. 'Jesper can still catch him.'

'Even second would be good,' Ulf said, earning himself a glare from Stig.

'Blast second! He can still win! Come on, Jesper!'

Ingvar plucked at Hal's sleeve. 'What's happening, Hal? Are we winning?' he asked anxiously.

Quickly, Hal brought him up to date on the progress of the race. Ingvar nodded as he took it in, then, without warning, roared, 'COME ON, JESPER!'

Hal jumped in fright at the sudden, deafening noise. That large frame and huge chest could produce a prodigious volume of noise.

'Warn me if you're going to do that again, will you?' he demanded.

Ingvar shrugged apologetically. 'Sorry, Hal.' Then he added, 'I'm going to do it again now.'

'Be my guest,' Hal said, just before Ingvar let rip with another thundering roar.

'COME ON, JESPER! RUN! RUN!'

Surreptitiously, Hal moved a pace or two away from him.

Without warning, Henjak seemed to float into sight over the top of the rise just below them, a hundred and fifty metres from the finish line. The cheers from the Wolves grew even louder, while the other two bands fell silent. Jesper and Tursgud were now hidden from sight below the rise Henjak had just topped.

'Well, so much for "he can still win",' Wulf said. Stig scowled at him.

'Second will be all right,' Stefan said.

The tension was palpable. Henjak was coasting towards the finish line, spurred on by the shouts and cheers of his fellow Wolves. He was far ahead of the other two and the only question now was who would come in second – Tursgud or Jesper. The Sharks and the Herons waited in unbearable silence to see who would be leading when they came over the rise.

'There they are!'

Nobody knew who shouted it. Suddenly, Tursgud and Jesper appeared over the crest of the grassy rise, their arms and legs pumping, feet pounding the turf, with not a centimetre between them.

The yelling redoubled as they came on. One hundred metres to go and they were still neck and neck. Seventy metres. Fifty metres.

And then, Tursgud, centimetre by centimetre, began to forge ahead of Jesper.

Seemingly in the background, Hal registered that the Wolves' cheering had redoubled in volume as Henjak crossed the line. They gathered round their triumphant runner, slapping him on the back and shouting congratulations. Henjak accepted the praise with a grin. He barely seemed to be breathing heavily. The Herons and the Sharks continued to urge their respective runners on.

'Jesper!'

'Tursgud!'

'Jesper!'

'Tursgud!'

The shouts alternated, overlapped, alternated again as the runners came closer. Hal's heart sank as he saw that Tursgud was now a metre ahead of the Herons' runner.

Tursgud might be arrogant, overbearing and unlikeable, he thought. But he had to admit that the big Skandian boy was a true competitor. He had a real winner's spirit, one that refused to lie down and give up.

They crossed the finish line with Tursgud a metre and a half in the lead. At the last instant, Jesper tried to hurl himself over the line first, but to no avail. He fell forward in the attempt and rolled over, lying on his back, gasping for breath.

Tursgud, once he was across the line, slowed, staggered and stopped with his hands on his knees, bent over, heaving in huge, ragged gasps of air. Henjak walked across to him and held out his hand. Tursgud shook it perfunctorily, then turned away, to be surrounded by his supporters and teammates.

Hal started towards Jesper, who still lay prone on the ground, one arm over his eyes. But Stig beat him to it. He leaned down and helped Jesper to his feet, supporting him with one arm round his shoulder.

'You did your best,' Stig told the dejected boy.

Jesper shook his head. 'It wasn't good enough,' he said miserably. 'You should have run.'

Stig looked up and gave Hal a wan smile.

'I wouldn't have done any better,' he said.

Hal nodded acknowledgement to his friend. He couldn't tell if Stig really believed it or not, but he was glad he'd said it.

Sigurd was totalling the points on the scoresheet that he kept. This time, there was no need to announce them. Everyone had seen the result. He finished what he was doing and looked up at the three brotherbands. They were standing in separate groups, either praising or consoling their respective runners.

'Attention!' he shouted and they all turned instantly to face him. 'Lunch will be an hour early today.'

He waited while the mumble of appreciation died down. Boys, he thought. Tell them they could eat early and they'd forget all their troubles. Then he continued.

'You runners had better get some rest. The team strength test will be held this afternoon.'

CHAPTER TWENTY-FOUR

While the boys hurried through their lunch — although with the prospect of another assessment, some of them found they had lost their appetite — Gort, Viggo and Jarst prepared the field for the strength test.

It was a simple enough task. They painted a white line on the grass and laid out a thick rope, about fifteen metres long, across it, at right angles to the line.

The three brotherbands emerged from the mess tent and made their way to the competition ground. Sigurd waited till they had assembled then took a position in front of them.

'The team strength test is simple enough,' he said. 'It's a tug-of-war. One team grabs one end of that rope there. Another team grabs the other. Then, on the word, each team tries to pull the other across that white line. If one person from either team is dragged across the line — even so much as a toenail — the test is over. Each team will face both other teams and the one with the winning score gets the hundred points. Next best gets twenty. If there's a tie, then the two tied teams will re-compete for first and second. Clear?'

The group nodded and a few voices mumbled that yes, it was clear, sir, very clear. Sigurd's face suffused with anger.

'I SAID, IS THAT CLEAR?' he roared. This time, all twenty-eight boys answered crisply.

'Yes, sir! Clear, sir!'

'Very well,' he growled, scowling around at them. 'I'll draw the names of the competing teams from this helmet.'

He reached into the old, battered helmet that he had been holding by his side and drew two slips of parchment from it.

'First match-up,' he announced, 'Sharks and Wolves.'

There was a mutter among the assembled boys. Hal felt a slight sense of relief. He was glad he'd be able to watch a contest before the Herons had to compete. Tursgud and Rollond had briefed their teams during lunch over the positions they would take. The two most important were the head of the line and the tail, or anchor. Each team chose its biggest, heaviest boy for the anchor position. And Tursgud and Rollond both took the first place in line.

Jesper moved to stand next to Hal as they watched the preparations.

'It's not fair,' he said. 'There are ten of them and only eight of us.'

Hal nodded. 'We've known that all along. But I'll see what I can do.'

He strode quickly to where Sigurd was watching the two brotherbands assemble along the rope. The instructor looked up, frowning. Hal was undaunted by that. Looking bad-tempered was Sigurd's natural state, he had discovered.

'What do you want?' the instructor demanded.

Hal pointed to his group, standing to one side. 'I was wondering, sir, since there are only eight of us, would the other teams consent to matching us with their eight best men?'

'It's up to the other skirls,' Sigurd told him. Then he raised his voice and addressed them. 'Wolves, Sharks, Hal has asked if your teams are willing to select only your eight best men when you compete with the Herons.'

Hal knew what Tursgud's reply would be. But he was watching Rollond. He could see that the Wolves' leader considered this a fair request. But Rollond hesitated, waiting to see what Tursgud said.

'Not a chance!' snapped the leader of the Sharks. 'They knew they'd be short-handed when we started training. It's not my fault nobody wanted them.'

He turned away, dismissing the Herons and their request. Hal made eye contact with Rollond. He sensed that the tall boy had been about to accede to the request. But now he knew the Sharks had refused, and so were almost certain of at least one win, he had to refuse as well. He couldn't give Tursgud that much of an advantage. He shrugged an apology to Hal, then answered Sigurd.

'No, sir. I'm sorry, but we'll compete with all our men,' he said.

Sigurd nodded. He had expected as much. He turned to Hal.

'There's your answer,' he said. But Hal wasn't quite ready to give up.

'So we'll be disadvantaged in all the team events? Is that what you're saying?'

Sigurd looked around, making sure nobody was within earshot, then lowered his voice anyway. 'I suppose so. Unless you can find some way to compensate for the difference.'

'Compensate? How would we do that?'

The instructor shrugged his heavy shoulders. 'Use your ingenuity. I'm told you have plenty of it. See if you can't find a way to even things up. Know what I mean?' He rubbed his forefinger alongside his nose in a meaningful gesture.

Hal frowned. 'Are you saying we should look for a way to cheat?'

Sigurd shook his head. 'No. I'm saying *use your ingenuity*. Look, we're training you for battle here. Let's say one day you find yourself outnumbered by an enemy. If you can find a way to make them think you have more men that you really have, is that cheating?'

'I suppose not,' Hal said slowly, not sure where the instructor was going with this. Sigurd nodded at him, and tapped his nose in that conspiratorial gesture once again.

'Let me put it this way: it's only cheating if you're caught doing it. Otherwise, it's good tactics.'

'I understand,' Hal said. 'At least, I think I do. Maybe I'd better get back to my team.'

'Maybe you'd better.'

Hal turned and walked back to where the Herons were gathered. Jesper cocked his head in a question.

'What did he say?'

'He said to use our ingenuity,' Hal told him.

Stig frowned. 'What's that mean?'

'I think it means cheat, but don't get caught doing it,' Hal said. He heard a small snort of amusement from Jesper, but when he tried to make eye contact with him, Jesper moved away, looking anywhere but in Hal's direction.

Hal turned his attention back to the contest. The two anchors had wrapped the rope around their waists. The other boys in the teams were spread along the rope, testing their footing, kicking holes in the turf to make footholds for themselves. They all had their eyes glued on Sigurd. After the way he had started the foot race, they weren't going to be caught napping.

'I'll give the start,' Sigurd said. 'Viggo and Jarst will watch the two teams to make sure there's no cheating . . .'

He paused and Hal wondered idly how you would cheat in a tug-of-war. He shrugged the thought away as Sigurd continued.

'Gort will watch the centre line. If so much as a toe crosses it, he'll signal the end of the contest.'

He gestured to Gort to demonstrate. The instructor produced that whistle from his pocket and blew a shrill blast on it. Several Herons groaned softly.

'When you hear that whistle,' Sigurd told them, 'that's the end of the contest.'

'When I hear that whistle,' Stefan said in a lowered voice, 'it's the end of my sanity.'

The Herons laughed, earning themselves a glare from Sigurd. Quickly, they wiped all traces of amusement from their faces.

'Very well . . .' said Sigurd. He looked left and right, satisfied himself that both teams were ready, then shouted: 'Go!'

The two teams threw themselves back against the rope and it came up instantly, bar-taut. The watching Heron band leaned forward, not sure whether to barrack or not. They all hoped Rollond's team would win because they disliked Tursgud. But they weren't sure how that would affect the final score.

The Wolves' team began to lose ground as the Sharks heaved mightily on the rope. The Wolves inched closer to that white line, leaning back, eyes shut with the strain, groaning in pain and effort as they tried to arrest their slow movement towards defeat.

With one metre to go, they managed it. Rollond summoned all his strength and heaved suddenly and mightily on the rope. The Sharks' slow backward movement was arrested. The two teams strained and heaved and neither moved a centimetre. But the Sharks had expended a lot of their energy in that first desperate lunge backwards, to drag the other team so close to the centre line. Now they had nothing in reserve. The Wolves poured on the pressure and the Sharks moved forward a metre, then another, gaining momentum as they went.

Tursgud screamed abuse and curses at his team, as he struggled to stop himself being dragged over the white line.

'He's wasting breath,' Stig said quietly in Hal's ear.

Hal nodded. 'He never learns, does he?'

'NOW!' Rollond yelled. It was obviously something they had planned in advance. At his call, all the Wolves summoned one last desperate surge of strength against the rope, with their anchor man hurling himself backwards until his back was almost touching the ground.

And that did it.

The one concerted, co-ordinated heave overcame the individual scrabbling and scrambling of the Sharks, and Tursgud was dragged bodily over the centre line.

PEEEEEEEP!

Gort's whistle sounded the end of the test and all the contestants let go of the rope simultaneously, allowing themselves to sprawl on the grass. In the Wolves' case, they were laughing and joking. The Sharks were sullen and ill-tempered.

Sigurd strode forward.

'Good work, Wolves,' he said briskly, then reached into the helmet again and withdrew a slip of paper. He only needed one because it was obvious that the Herons would be competing in the next bout. 'Fifteen minutes to recover. Then it's Wolves and Herons.'

'Good luck to us,' Ulf said sarcastically. They had all seen how the Wolves had overcome the full-strength Sharks' team. They knew that eight of them had little chance against the ten Wolves.

And so it proved. The contest lasted barely fifteen seconds before Stig, who was in the lead for the Herons, was dragged over the centre line.

The watching Sharks cheered ironically when they saw how easily the eight Herons were defeated. They might not win this assessment. But now they knew they were a certainty for second place.

'Fifteen minutes!' Sigurd told the dejected Herons. 'Then you face the Sharks.'

'And good luck to us,' said Wulf this time.

His brother looked at him angrily. 'I said that first,' he snapped.

Wulf thrust his chest out, facing him. 'And I said it second! Want to do something about it?'

'Do you?'

'Oh, stop it, for pity's sake!' Hal told them. They both looked at him in surprise and he realised that half the time, they had no idea that they were actually squabbling. It was just an automatic reflex.

'This is no time for us to be fighting amongst ourselves,' Hal told them. 'We've got to figure a way to beat Tursgud.'

Stig laughed sarcastically. 'Let me know what it is.'

'What's Jesper up to?' Edvin said suddenly. They followed his gaze and saw Jesper had approached Gort. He laid his hand on the instructor's arm to get his attention and said something to him. Gort shook his hand off and gestured angrily back to where Jesper's teammates were waiting. Jesper shrugged and sauntered back to join them.

'What was that about?' Hal asked.

'Oh, I was asking our esteemed instructor if he had any last-minute advice that might help us. But he told me to get to blazes back to my team.'

'I'm not surprised,' Hal said. 'What were you thinking?'

Jesper looked round to make sure nobody was watching, then grinned evilly.

'I was using my ingenuity. I thought we might find a use for this,' he said, and held up Gort's silver whistle. 'I picked his pocket when I put my other hand on his arm.'

Quickly, the boys huddled around him to shield the whistle from view. Hal's mind raced, then a smile spread over his face.

'All right, here's what we do. Jesper, keep the whistle concealed in your hand. Get behind me in the line. When we start to slide towards the centre mark, wait till we get close, then blow the whistle. I'll tell you when.' He looked around the circle of eager faces. 'As soon as we hear that, we all stand up as if it's over,' he continued. 'Let go the rope, groan and moan as if we've lost. The Sharks will do the same thing. Except they'll be patting themselves on the back. We all do that,' he repeated, then looked at Ingvar. 'Except Ingvar. You'll be our anchor, Ingvar. As soon as you hear the whistle, turn and run, pulling as if the three gods of the Vallas are after you.'

Ingvar frowned, then smiled and nodded.

Hal saw that a few of his team hadn't quite understood the result he was aiming for.

'Their anchor will be tied to the rope, so he can't let go. But Ingvar is twice his size and much stronger. He'll be able to heave him over the line and we'll win.' He glanced back at Jesper. 'As soon as we're done, get rid of the whistle.'

He paused, seeing the grins breaking out among the others.

'Everyone clear?' he asked. They all nodded.

'Clear!' they responded.

'Ingvar?' he asked.

Ingvar nodded ponderously. 'Don't worry, Hal. I'm short-sighted, not stupid. I've got it.'

'Then let's go,' Hal said, seeing Sigurd moving towards them to summon them to the final contest.

They moved in a group to take up their positions on the rope. Stig was first in line, with Hal behind him. Then Jesper. Stefan and the twins were behind him, then Edvin and, finally, Ingvar was at the end. The massively built boy wrapped the rope around his waist.

On the other side of the centre mark, his counterpart did the same, and the nine other Sharks took hold of the rope, with Tursgud in the lead position, facing Stig.

'Ready to lose, birdies?' he said sarcastically.

Stig went to reply, but Hal, close behind him, said in a low, urgent voice, 'Ignore it!'

Stig nodded, pushing the sudden burst of anger down with a giant effort. Instead, he smiled at Tursgud. Strangely, he thought, that seemed to annoy the other boy more than a snappy reply. He filed that away for future reference.

Sigurd stepped forward, looking left and right. Gort crouched, eyes riveted on the white mark, his hand hovering near his pocket.

Don't reach for the whistle yet, Hal pleaded silently. Gort's hand played with the edge of his pocket and Hal held his breath. But before the instructor could reach further, Sigurd's command boomed out.

'GO!'

Again, the rope came up taut with a loud snap. Dust and dirt flew from it as the strands tightened suddenly. The two teams heaved, neither moving as they felt each other's strength and power. Then inexorably, the Herons began to slide forward. No amount of bracing their heels into the turf, no amount of leaning back against the rope, no amount of snarling with the muscle-wrenching effort, could stop their slow slide towards defeat.

Stig's feet teetered forward in tiny steps, getting closer and closer to the line. Out of the corner of his eye, Hal saw Gort leaning forward, his hand went into his pocket, and he frowned, searching.

'Now!' Hal gasped.

Jesper, leaning forward over the rope so that Viggo couldn't see what he was doing, put the whistle to his lips.

PEEEEEEP!

At the piercing sound, seventeen boys relaxed, releasing the rope. The Sharks cheered, convinced they had won. The Herons threw their arms up in despair. Several of them fell to the ground. Jesper, overcome with exhaustion, lurched away from the rope and cannoned awkwardly into Gort, who angrily shoved him aside.

And the eighteenth boy, Ingvar, turned and ran like a charging bull, pulling on the rope with all his strength, thrusting with his powerful legs and heaving with the muscles of his massive arms and shoulders and chest.

The Sharks' anchorman, caught by surprise, was propelled past his cheering comrades at a run. As he tried to release the rope around his waist, he tripped and fell and was dragged, sliding on his back, over the line.

Pandemonium.

The Herons were cheering Ingvar, jeering at Tursgud and his team. Tursgud's face was black with fury.

Sirgurd strode among them and bellowed for silence. Gradually, the hubbub died away.

'Gort!' the chief instructor demanded. 'Why did you blow the whistle?'

Gort shook his head, puzzled. 'I didn't. I was reaching for it but I couldn't find it.' He patted his pockets, searching for it, then frowned. 'Wait . . . here it is. I must have put it in the wrong pocket.'

Hal looked at Jesper, who lowered one eyelid in a slow, conspiratorial wink.

'Well, who blew the whistle?' Gort demanded. He was rewarded with a circle of blank looks. 'Viggo! What did you see?'

Viggo shrugged, grinning. 'I didn't see anyone with a whistle, chief. I did see the Sharks' last man being pulled across the line. I guess that means the Herons won.'

'WHAT?' It was Tursgud, his voice cracking with anger and indignation. 'They cheated!' He thrust an accusing finger at Hal and his team, who grinned back at him.

Sigurd slapped his hand down. 'And tell me exactly, how did they manage to do that?'

'They . . . they . . .' Tursgud stammered, then his eyes bored in on Hal as he realised how they had done it. 'They must have had a whistle of their own.'

Instantly, Hal stepped forward, matching Tursgud's indignation. He snapped an order to his team.

'All right, Herons. Turn out your pockets. Now!'

And a shower of small items hit the ground. Pieces of string. A comb. Several coins, a carved wooden figure, a piece of amber, and a smooth, white river rock that Wulf was very fond of.

But no whistle. Hal looked at Sigurd and spread his hands.

'They've hidden it somewhere!' Tursgud insisted.

But Sigurd shook his head. 'It's a silver bosun's whistle, boy. They don't grow on trees, you know. How do you think Hal's team got their hands on one?'

'I don't know. But I . . . maybe they . . . well, I don't know but they must have . . .'

Edvin stepped forward, holding one hand in the air, forefinger raised, rather like a student in barneskole.

'Instructor?' he said hesitantly.

Sigurd turned to him. 'What is it?' he demanded.

Edvin was almost apologetic as he continued. 'It's just . . . I saw a couple of jackdaws a little while back. They're always mimicking sounds, you know?'

Sigurd nodded. That was true. 'I know. What about it?'

'Well . . .' Edvin hesitated, glancing nervously at Gort. 'It's just that Gort *does* blow his whistle an awful lot,' he said, then hurriedly added to Gort, 'Sorry, sir.'

Gort harrumphed. It was true, and everyone knew it.

Sigurd came to a decision. 'Very well, that's the only explanation that makes sense. It was a jackdaw. So the result is, a win to the Herons . . .'

'No!' Tursgud began.

But Sigurd rolled on over him. 'That's two wins to the Wolves, one to the Herons. Nil to the Sharks. That's the way we'll mark it.'

'No! It's not fair! I want a re-match! I protest!' Tursgud was almost screaming in fury. Little flecks of white showed at the corners of his mouth. Sigurd turned slowly and looked at him.

'You protest?' he said, his voice ominously calm.

Tursgud got himself under control and nodded. 'Yes. I protest!'

Tursgud was about to say more, but Sigurd stepped forward, standing with his face a few centimetres from the boy's.

'Well, get this straight. You *don't* protest. You obey! Understood?'

'But my father is the . . .' Tursgud began then, seeing a very nasty light in Sigurd's eyes, he backed away. 'Yes, sir.'

'The result stands,' Sigurd said, then he pushed through the crowd of boys. As he passed Hal, he said in a low tone, 'Don't know how you did it. Don't want to know. But well done.'

CHAPTER TWENTY-FIVE

If Hal expected that to be the end of the matter, he was sadly mistaken.

There was no more training after the strength test and the three teams were allowed to return to their living quarters to clean or mend their kit. The Herons set about their long-delayed task of thatching the barracks roof with pine branches. The canvas cover had been sufficient so far. But they knew that, as the weather grew colder, the rainstorms would become heavier, and eventually they would be facing snowstorms as well.

In addition, Hal knew that the extra layer of branches would keep the barracks warmer during the cold nights to come.

They cut a large supply of pine boughs, carrying them back to the camp site, then trimming them and passing them up to Edvin and Stefan. They were the lightest of the group, and so better suited to moving around on the roof. Ingvar had offered to help them. Hal had seen the others turning away to hide their smiles and he managed to keep a straight face as he thanked Ingvar, but suggested his strength might be better suited to carrying the large bundles of pine boughs in from the forest.

He had a mental image of Ingvar blundering around on the flimsy canvas roof, eventually coming crashing through, bringing a hail of torn canvas and shattered frames with him.

They had almost completed the job when Tursgud and his brotherband strode into the clearing.

The Herons were ill prepared for a confrontation. Two of their number were poised on the top of the roof, where the support structure was flimsy, to say the least. Ulf and Wulf were halfway up ladders, laden with pine boughs that they were passing up to Edvin and Stefan. Stig, Hal and Jesper were trimming the pine boughs so that they were evenly shaped, and Ingvar was in the forest gathering branches.

The Sharks team, by contrast, were in one concerted group. And they outnumbered the Herons ten to seven. They quickly surrounded Hal, Stig and Jesper, cutting Hal off from his other teammates.

'I want a word with you,' Tursgud said angrily.

Hal felt Stig bristling with anger beside him and he laid a hand on his forearm.

'Steady,' he told Stig in a quiet voice. He held Tursgud's gaze with his own. 'Say what you have to say and leave.'

Tursgud gave a short bark of angry laughter. 'Yes. You'd like that, wouldn't you? Well, we're not leaving. You cheated us out of second place and you're going to pay for it.'

Ulf and Wulf scrambled down from their ladders, and found themselves confronted by two of Tursgud's larger companions, who detached themselves from the group surrounding Hal, Stig and Jesper.

Another of the Sharks darted forward and kicked the two ladders away from the wall, leaving Edvin and Stefan stranded on the roof.

'You cheated us,' Tursgud said angrily.

Again, Hal felt Stig ready to step forward and he increased the pressure of his grip on the other boy's arm. There was nothing to be gained by Stig losing his temper here, he thought. They were badly outnumbered. Tursgud had planned this carefully. Hal had no doubt that the Sharks team had waited in the treeline, watching them at work. Then they had picked the moment when the Herons were spread out and vulnerable.

'And exactly how did we do that, Tursgud?' Hal said.

The big boy shook his head angrily. 'Don't bandy words with me, *Hal Who*,' he said, contempt in his voice as he used the disparaging term. 'You cheated us and we all know it.'

'I prefer to say we out-thought you,' Hal said carefully.

'And that wasn't too hard,' Stefan put in, from his perch on the roof.

Tursgud threw an angry glance his way and Hal wished his teammate would learn when to keep his mouth shut. Tursgud turned back to Hal.

'However you put it,' Tursgud said, 'you've earned yourself a beating. And I'm going to give it to you.'

This time Stig, his anger throughly roused, broke free of Hal's restraining grip and stepped forward to confront Tursgud.

'Why don't you try giving me a beating, you overblown bully!' he challenged.

Tursgud eyed him contemptuously. 'Fighting Hal's battles for him, are you, Stig?' he said. Then he sneered at Hal. 'And how about you? Happy to hide behind your friend, are you?'

Hal felt his own anger stir then. He knew that he couldn't let Stig take this fight for him. He had to confront Tursgud himself. He remembered Thorn's words: *He fears you. Sooner or later, it'll come to a head between the two of you.*

'It's all right, Stig,' he said. 'This is my fight.'

Stig looked quickly round at him. 'You're always saying that we're a team, Hal. That we should pick the best man for the job. Well, I'm picking myself for this one. I've been waiting to settle Tursgud's hash for him. I'll fight you,' he said, addressing the last words to Tursgud.

Tursgud smiled at him. 'But I don't want to fight you, Stig. You're rather stupid and annoying, it's true, but I can put up with that. Your Araluan friend, however, is a liar and a cheat. I hear most Araluans are like that. We don't want his sort in Hallasholm.'

'Too bad. Because if you plan to fight Hal, you'll have to go through me first,' said Stig. His face was flaming with anger now and he stepped closer to Tursgud until he stood chest to chest with him. The Sharks' skirl looked at him with bored amusement.

- 267 -

'Oh well, if you insist,' he said, then snapped his fingers.

It was obviously a prearranged signal, Hal thought. Anyone who knew Stig would have known he would choose to confront Tursgud and the Sharks hadn't come here without making plans. Two of them leapt forward, one of them dropping a noose of rope over Stig's shoulders and pulling tight, pinning his arms to his body. Stig yelled angrily but the two Sharks rapidly looped the rope around him several more times, in spite of his struggles. Then one of them kicked his feet from under him and sent him sprawling. Stig cursed at them as they held him down, but to no avail.

Wulf started forward to help him. But the large boy facing him stepped to block him and shoved him back. Ulf shoved him in turn.

'Leave my brother alone!' he shouted. Then the other Shark stepped to block Ulf as well.

The situation was poised to boil over any second, Hal saw. The atmosphere was as taut as a fiddle string. Man for man, the Sharks were generally bigger and stronger than his team. They had been the first boys picked, after all. Now Stig was helpless, Edvin and Stefan were stranded on the roof, and Ulf and Wulf were both facing opponents who were much bigger than they were. That left him and Jesper.

And Ingvar, of course. The massive boy had just emerged from the forest with a load of pine branches. He peered around like a confused bear. He could see shapes, and he realised there were more people in the camp site than when he'd left.

'Hal?' he said. 'What's going on?'

'Take it easy, Ingvar,' Hal said. If Ingvar started throwing punches, he was just as likely to flatten his own friends as the enemy. Once again, he realised how carefully Tursgud had planned this confrontation.

He stepped forward, stopping a metre short of Tursgud, seeing the triumph in the bigger boy's eyes as he realised he'd manoeuvred Hal into accepting the fight.

Most fights are won in the first one or two punches, Thorn had told him.

'All right,' he said reluctantly, 'I'll fight you if that's what you want.'

And without further notice, he sent two lightning left jabs into Tursgud's face, feeling the other boy's nose crunch under the impact of the second, then stepped forward and hooked savagely with his right at the big boy's jaw, hoping to end it there and then.

Unfortunately, his first two punches were too successful, and Tursgud was reeling back in surprise and pain so that Hal's vicious right hook barely grazed his jaw, instead of making the crushing contact he had hoped for.

The watching boys, Herons and Sharks alike, howled like animals as the fight started and they hurried to form a circle round the two opponents. Several of the Sharks caught Tursgud as he staggered back and steadied him, then shoved him forward once more.

He came at Hal like a raging bull, swinging left and right in huge, arcing blows. Hal ducked under one, blocked a second with his own left hand and jabbed now with his right, hitting Tursgud once more.

He was conscious of the other boys screaming encouragement and hate. He followed up the jab and walked into a shattering right hand from Tursgud. At the last moment, he remembered Thorn's advice to keep his chin tucked in. If the blow had caught him on the jaw, the fight would have ended there and then. As it was, it exploded against his cheekbone under the eye, feeling like a sledge-hammer blow. He staggered back, felt hands stop him from falling and shove him forward again.

Tursgud was waiting for him. He joined both hands together and swung them at Hal's head. Hal, still dizzy from that last massive blow, saw it coming and swayed back. He felt the wind of Tursgud's joined hands as they rushed past, millimetres from his face. Then he realised that Tursgud would be off balance in his follow-through and he leapt forward, sending that left hand darting out like a snake once more.

Smack! Smack! Two good hits, one of them above Tursgud's eye. Blood ran from a cut where Hal's fist had caught the flesh against the bony ridge of Tursgud's eyebrow. He hooked right again but Tursgud had learned that trick and blocked the blow with his own right.

Tursgud snarled and lunged forward. The blow to the cheek had cause Hal's eye to swell and close. Hal saw that big left fist begin to swing in a huge arc again. He ducked, but his depth perception was hazy and he couldn't avoid the blow completely. It caught the top of his head and sent him reeling again. He crashed into two of the specta-tors. As before, he felt their hands on him as they held him up, preparing to shove him back into the fight. But this time Tursgud yelled at them.

'Hold him!'

Hal had fallen against two of the watching Sharks. Now he felt their arms lock on his, holding him helpless as Tursgud advanced, measuring the distance between them, his right hand drawing back.

Hal jerked sideways, trying to avoid the blow, lowering his head. He was only partially successful and he grunted in pain as Tursgud's fist hit him. He tried to crouch.

'Hold him up!'

It was Tursgud's voice. But it seemed to come from a long way away. Hal's ears were ringing and he realised that consciousness was slipping away from him. A hand grasped his hair and pulled his head up, sending tears flowing from his eyes with the pain. He opened his good eye and, through a blur of tears, saw Tursgud drawing back that right hand again, slowly and methodically, taking his time to make sure the blow connected.

At the last moment, he lurched sideways again, feeling the fist scrape painfully along the side of his face, tearing at his ear, so that blood started to trickle down from a torn earlobe.

'Hold him, blast you!'

Now the grip on Hal's arms tightened. Once more his head was dragged up by the hair and once more Tursgud, a blurred figure now, was measuring him for the final punch.

This must be how Ingvar sees things, Hal thought. He could hear the spectators screaming still. The Herons were screaming abuse at Tursgud's cowardly attack but, outnumbered as they were, there was nothing they could do. The Sharks were screaming in a savage, animal hatred, urging their leader on.

'Kill him! Kill him!'

He could make out the individual voices. Stig was screaming in frustrated rage. Hal knew it was him but Stig was beyond words. Stefan was yelling abuse at Tursgud.

'You coward! Fight fair!'

'Kill him! Kill him!' That was one of the Sharks. He didn't know who.

'Hal? Are you all right?' That was Ingvar and Hal, in spite of the situation, or perhaps because of it, smiled groggily, his bruised, cut lips flaring with pain.

No, I'm definitely not all right, Ingvar, he thought. He wondered groggily why people invariably asked that question when it was obvious that you were injured. I'm not all right and he's going to hit me again. Any second now.

And then a tall figure suddenly interposed itself between him and Tursgud, seeming to come from nowhere and ramming his shoulder heavily into the leader of the Sharks, sending him sprawling before he could throw that final punch.

'That's enough, you coward!'

Rollond, Hal thought. What's he doing here?

'Get away from him!' Rollond said. Hal felt the boys holding him shoved away, their hands torn free, felt other hands coming to support him.

'Hal? Are you okay?' It was Jesper.

Hal turned and looked groggily at his teammate. 'No. I'm definitely not. What the blazes is Rollond doing here?'

He shook his head to clear his vision. Tursgud, his face streaming blood, his nose at an odd angle, lurched clumsily to his feet.

'Stay out of this, Rollond. This isn't your fight!'

But there was a wariness in his tone as he realised that Rollond wasn't alone. His nine brotherband members were with him and suddenly the numbers were very much against Tursgud.

'It isn't any sort of fight,' Rollond said, contempt in his voice. 'It's a cowardly attack. I should have expected you'd try something like this.'

Tursgud jabbed a finger at the semi-conscious Hal, now supported by Jesper and Ulf. Or was it Wulf, Hal thought groggily. He didn't really care.

'I'm teaching this Araluan scum a long-delayed lesson!' Tursgud snarled.

Rollond took a long moment to study Tursgud's bleeding, broken nose before he answered. When he did, it was with a contemptuous bark of laughter.

'And how are you doing that? By hammering his fist with your nose?'

The Wolf brotherband members laughed. Some of the Herons joined in. But in the main, they were too incensed at Tursgud's treatment of their leader. Two of the Wolves had untied Stig and he scrambled to his feet now, his face flushed with anger. He lunged towards Tursgud.

'You coward! I'll show you!' he began, but Rollond blocked his way.

'Leave it, Stig,' Rollond said in a reasonable voice. 'We've had enough fighting for one day.' He leaned close and added quietly, 'And you should never fight when you're angry.'

'But . . .' Stig began.

'Stig! I nee' you,' Hal called. His voice was thick and he couldn't form words clearly with his swollen and cut lips. Stig turned at his friend's voice and hurried to support him, his face working as his fury at Tursgud competed with concern for his friend.

'I'm sorry, Hal! They tricked me! I couldn't do anything!' Tears were flowing down his cheeks as he studied his friend's battered face. Hal put a hand on his shoulder.

'Le' i' go,' he said. 'Rollon' ish ri'.'

'But ...' Stig turned again to where Tursgud half crouched, sizing up Rollond, realising the fight was over.

'Le' i' go,' Hal repeated.

Stig's shoulders sank as the tension went out of him. 'All right. If you say.'

Hal couldn't say more. It was too painful to speak. He patted Stig's shoulder, tried to smile and winced.

'Now get out of here, you cowardly scum!' Rollond said to Tursgud and his band. 'Try this again and you'll have two brotherbands to contend with.'

Now that the excitement of the fight had gone, some of the Sharks were beginning to look ashamed – of their leader and their own behaviour. They turned and began to walk away, heads down. Tursgud, with one last glare in Hal's direction, turned and followed them.

Stig had lowered Hal to the grass and was supporting his shoulders so he could sit up. Hal looked owlishly around him. He was still dizzy and his eye was almost completely closed. Rollond came over and dropped to one knee beside him.

'Sorry we took so long to get here. One of my boys saw Tursgud and his crew sneaking through the woods towards your camp. I thought he'd be up to no good. So I got the rest of the crew together and got here as fast as we could.'

'Thanks. It wasn't looking good,' said Stig. And Hal nodded and waved a hand to indicate that Stig was speaking for him. Rollond shook his head, looking at Hal with something like admiration.

'You certainly made a mess of Tursgud's looks,' he said. 'His nose is bent way out of shape. That's going to hurt when they fix it.'

Hal nodded again, then, with an enormous, heartfelt effort, he said: 'Good.'

Rollond grinned. 'I doubt he'll try anything like that again,' he said. 'But if he does, we'll be watching for it.' He touched Hal's swollen eye with a gentle forefinger. 'Better get some cold water onto that.'

Then he stood and beckoned to his team.

'Come on, boys. Let's go home.'

CHAPTER TWENTY-SIX

The following day, Hal was sore and sorry for himself. His cut lip and torn ear throbbed painfully and the bruise under his left eye, in spite of Stig's and Edvin's ministrations with cloths soaked in icy cold water, had swollen to a huge purple bulge that forced the eye closed.

His knuckles were scraped raw too. But somehow, they didn't seem to hurt as much when he remembered the feel of their solid, crunching impact on Tursgud's nose. There was a certain satisfaction in the memory.

As they formed up for weapons practice after the morning's physical jerks, Sigurd scowled at Hal's battered face.

'What happened to you?' he asked.

'Walked into a tree, sir,' Hal replied. Sigurd rubbed his chin thoughtfully.

'Looks like the same tree Tursgud walked into,' he said. 'Those branches must have been thrashing around in the wind.'

'Yes, sir,' Hal replied, looking straight ahead and making no eye contact with the chief instructor.

'Don't let it happen again,' Sigurd said.

There was no mistaking the definite tone of command in his voice. Sigurd expected that there would be a few fights among each batch of trainees. Often they cleared the air. But he wouldn't tolerate continuing violence or enmity among the boys. That sort of thing undermined the entire spirit of the brotherband concept. The bands should compete with each other, but not hate or fear the other teams. In the future, they would have to work with them and even fight alongside them.

'Yes, sir,' Hal replied. Sigurd grunted, then walked on, nodding to Gort to commence weapon training.

After several weeks of practising against the drill posts, the boys had graduated to mock combat with wooden weapons, weighted and balanced to simulate their real weapons. Their muscles, after weeks of running, exercising and repeating the set drills against the rope-padded posts, were hardened and toned. The morning exercise sessions no longer left them groaning and panting for breath. They were fit and toughened, and it showed in the speed and power of the blows they struck against each other in the one-on-one practice duels.

Hal had developed into an above average swordsman by this stage. His highly developed spatial awareness — the ability to see and instantly assess angles and speeds that made him a natural helmsman — stood him in good stead here too. He could see a blow coming and instinctively know how much movement he would need to evade it.

As a warrior, Stig was far and away the Herons' best performer. His natural athleticism and strength made him an expert axeman. Plus he had speed, and excellent hand-eye co-ordination, which a lot of bigger boys lacked. Wulf and Ulf were also quite proficient.

The others were competent — although 'competent' in a country that valued weapons skills as highly as the Skandians did would translate to 'highly skilled and dangerous' in most other countries.

Ingvar, of course, was merely dangerous to everyone around him, friend or foe.

Hal was practising strike and counter-strike with Ulf. They wore padded jackets, heavy leather gauntlets and thickly padded leather helmets as they struck, blocked, deflected and, in Hal's case, thrust at each other.

Each crunching impact of weapon on shield, whether given or received, set Hal's injuries throbbing painfully. Plus, with one eye closed, he was having difficulty anticipating some of Ulf's strokes and had only managed to block several at the very last moment. He held up a hand to signal a pause, took off his helmet and wiped the sweat from his forehead, wincing as he accidentally brushed against the swollen black eye. He glanced around, saw none of the instructors watching and moved closer to Ulf.

'Can we hold back a little?' he asked. 'My head is throbbing every time I hit your shield or you hit mine.'

Ulf nodded apologetically. He had been feeling bad that he had been so effectively checkmated in the confrontation the day before. He felt that he and his twin could have done more to help Hal. Although exactly what they might have done, he had no real idea.

'Of course, Hal. Sorry. I wasn't thinking.'

'And take it easy from this side,' Hal said, pointing to his swollen left eye. 'I can hardly see a thing.'

Ulf signalled his understanding. Hal re-donned his helmet and they shaped up again.

Ulf swung his axe in an overhand strike, pulling the blow at the last instant so that it landed on Hal's slanted shield with a minimal impact. Hal replied in turn, sweeping his sword in a low sideways arc, then stopping the blow just before Ulf caught it on his shield. Ulf's follow-up axe stroke was a backhand, so that Hal could see it more clearly. Once again, the force was reduced. Hal prepared to thrust under Ulf's shield when a huge voice bellowed behind them.

'WHAT IN THE NAME OF THE GREAT BLUE WHALE ARE YOU LADIES UP TO?'

They sprang apart, standing to attention. Sigurd had approached them unnoticed, attracted by the reduced noise of their weapons on their shields. Around them, they could hear the ringing cracks of wood on wood. Hal realised where they'd gone wrong.

Sigurd stood with his nose centimetres from Ulf's, bending over the thoroughly frightened boy.

'Are you taking it easy because your poor friend has a big sore eye?' he demanded.

Ulf glanced nervously towards Hal, then his eyes clicked back to the front as Sigurd thundered, 'LOOK AT ME!'

'Ummmm . . .' Ulf began uncertainly. Hal was conscious that the other pairs drilling close to them had stopped to watch. So was Sigurd. He swung round on them.

'GET BACK TO IT OR I'LL DRILL WITH YOU MYSELF!' he threatened. Nobody wanted that. Sigurd was an expert with the axe and everyone knew that any opponent he practised with would end up bruised and battered. Instantly, wooden axes began to crack against wooden shields again. Sigurd turned his gaze back to Ulf, who had managed to back away a pace while the instructor's attention was distracted.

'I DIDN'T HEAR YOUR ANSWER!' he thundered.

Hal stepped forward. 'Sir, I ordered him to back off,' he said. 'My eye was throbbing.'

Sigurd looked at him with some concern. 'Throbbing, you say? How dreadful.'

Somehow, Hal didn't think his concern was genuine. He judged it might be best not to say anything further. Sigurd held out his hand to Ulf, flicking his fingers impatiently.

'Axe,' he said. Ulf handed it to him. Sigurd tested its weight and balance for a few seconds, then looked at Hal once more.

'Did it throb when he did *this*?' he asked, bringing the axe round in a sidelong, smashing arc into Hal's shield. Hal winced at the force of the blow.

'Yes, sir,' he said.

'How about this!'

This time it was on overhead strike, delivered with lightning speed and crushing force. The impact made Hal's knees buckle.

'Yes, sir,' he gasped.

'How about THIS! And THIS! And THIS!'

Three sledgehammer blows, delivered with blinding speed, from three different angles, slammed into the shield and made Hal stagger.

'Yes, sir!' Hal said, as Sigurd paused, looking at him with his head to one side, waiting for his answer. When he heard it, the instructor smiled evilly.

'Well, that's good to hear,' he said. He tossed the axe to Ulf, who caught it awkwardly. 'Keep going,' he said. 'If you slack off again like that, you'll lose twenty points. Ten for slacking off and ten for taking me for a fool.'

'Yes, sir!' both boys replied. They looked at each other, rolling their eyes in relief as Sigurd walked away.

After a few strides, he turned back and they hastily rearranged their faces.

'You might be interested to know,' he said, 'that Tursgud just tried to pull the same trick. Didn't do him any good, either.'

As Sigurd turned away again, Hal was sure he was smiling.

CHAPTER TWENTY-SEVEN

The black ship limped into Hallasholm harbour in the middle of the afternoon.

She was a warship and, under normal circumstances, she would not have been permitted into the harbour. But she was badly damaged, with her mast gone and replaced by a smaller, lighter spar — probably a spare crossyard. Consequently, she was travelling under a heavily shortened sail, showing barely half the normal sail area. As she passed the mole, her crew could be seen bailing, and bucketfuls of silver water showered over her sides into the harbour.

Obviously, there was no chance of a lightning hit and run raid from this ship.

She was the size of a large wolfship, mounting ten oars a side. But her prow, unlike the graceful upward curve of a wolfship's bow, was a severe vertical line. As she rose sluggishly on the waves, the outline of a heavy ram — a protruding, ironshod baulk of timber — was visible at her bow, below the waterline.

Her captain, after receiving permission from the harbour master, ran her ashore on the shingle beach. Her exhausted crew slumped over their benches, finally able to rest from the ceaseless labour of bailing water out of her.

The captain stepped ashore and was escorted by the commander of the harbour watch and two of his men to speak with the Oberjarl.

Erak studied the stranger before him. He was a tall man, well built, but not as bulky as the average Skandian. His hair was long and black and hung in ringlets down either side of his face. He was clean-shaven, with a swarthy complexion and high cheekbones. He had a long, straight nose and dark eyes. He was smiling, but there was a superior air to the smile, Erak thought.

'My name is Zavac,' the stranger said. 'I'm captain of the ship *Raven*.'

Erak glanced sidelong at Borsa, his Hilfmann. 'Seems everyone's naming their ships after birds these days,' he said dryly. He was pleased to see the smile fade from Zavac's face, to be replaced by a slight frown of incomprehension. Erak waved a hand dismissively.

'Never mind. It's a private joke. What can we do for you? I hear your ship is damaged.'

Zavac didn't answer immediately. He looked around the Great Hall, taking in its unsophisticated decor and character. The Great Hall was a timber structure, lined with pine planks. It was warm and comfortable, but low-ceilinged and simple. A log fire blazed at the head of the large room, behind Erak's official chair. Even the chair was unadorned pine, worn smooth and polished to a honey gold by decades of use.

'I assume I'm speaking to the Jarl of this village?' Zavac said, the haughtiness back in his tone.

Erak regarded him, unblinking, for several seconds. Then he yawned. Borsa stepped forward, his tone showing his annoyance.

'You're speaking to the Oberjarl of Skandia,' he said. 'And if you don't lose that superior tone, he's liable to send you and your boat back to sea so you can both sink together.'

Zavac bowed, sweeping his right hand across his body in a graceful gesture, then looked up again.

'My apologies, Oberjarl,' he said smoothly. 'I had no idea where we are. We were caught in a storm days ago and were blown miles off course until I lost all sense of direction. We were dismasted and the broken mast stove in several planks below the waterline before we could cut her free.'

'Sounds nasty,' Erak said.

Zavac nodded. 'We were in a bad way. I couldn't believe our luck when we saw the smoke from the fires in your town. I assume, since you're the Oberjarl, that this is Hallasholm?'

You're lying, Erak thought. You know this is Hallasholm. Why are you lying?

'Where are you from?' Erak asked.

Zavac waved a vague hand towards the south-east. 'From Magyara,' he said. 'East of Teutlandt. Do you know it?'

'I know where it is,' Erak said evenly. 'Never visited.'

'We're traders from Magyara. We sailed from our home port three weeks ago, heading for Cape Shelter.

We were hoping to trade with the settlements along the Sonderland Coast and —'

'What's your cargo?' Erak said suddenly and the captain hesitated. He wasn't prepared for that question.

'Oh ... er ... wine and ... cheeses,' he said. 'The Sonderlanders love our cheeses. We were planning to trade for onyx stones and mother-of-pearl shell.' His eyes flicked away from Erak's momentarily, then returned to meet the Oberjarl's unwavering gaze.

'Of course, we had to throw our trade goods overboard when we realised we were in danger of sinking,' Zavac said.

The statement had the feeling of an afterthought to it, as if Zavac suddenly realised that Erak might ask to see his 'trade goods'.

'Pity,' Erak said. 'We could have used some wine here.'

Zavac smiled apologetically and spread his hands in a deprecating gesture. Erak said nothing, allowing the silence to grow to an uncomfortable length. Finally, he shifted in his chair and spoke again.

'So, I imagine you'll want repair facilities for your ship, timber and cordage, and accommodation for your men?'

Zavac nodded. 'We'll pay well for it,' he said. 'You won't lose by helping us.'

Erak fingered his chin. He didn't trust this Magyaran. But the ship was certainly unseaworthy and no Skandian could send it back to sea again in its current condition. There was an unwritten law of the sea about such things. Finally, he nodded.

'Very well. Work out the details and port payments with Borsa,' he said, and waved a hand dismissively. As Zavac turned to go, Erak held up a hand to stop him.

'One thing,' he said. 'Tell your men to keep their noses clean while they're in Hallasholm. I don't want any trouble.'

Zavac nodded and smiled. 'I understand. This is a quiet town and you don't want the peace disturbed.'

Erak smiled back, but it was like a smile on the face of a shark. 'No. This is a very violent town and if your men cause trouble, my people will break their heads for them. I don't want to be paying any blood money for damage done to your crew. Understand?'

Zavac's smiled faded. He looked for some sign that the Oberjarl was joking, but saw none. He nodded again, slowly this time.

'I understand,' he said, and followed Borsa out of the Great Hall.

Erak waited until the door closed behind them, then turned and called over his shoulder.

'What do you think, Svengal?'

Svengal, his long-time second in command aboard *Wolfwind* and now her skirl, emerged from behind a curtain, where he had been concealed.

'If he's a peaceful trader, I'm my old Auntie Winfredia,' he said.

Erak raised an eyebrow. 'Do you have an old Auntie Winfredia?'

Svengal waved a hand. 'Figure of speech, chief. Figure of speech. He's a pirate, I'd stake my life on it.'

'I agree,' Erak said, with a grimace of distaste. 'Most Magyarans are pirates.'

'I wouldn't put it past them to have sabotaged their own ship so they could get into Hallasholm harbour,' Svengal added. 'It'd be a typical Magyaran trick. Come into town, repair the ship, then rob us blind and run for it.'

Historically, Skandians had been raiders, landing ashore near towns or villages and attacking to steal any valuables they could find. They called it 'liberating' the goods. More often than not, the inhabitants fled at the first sign of a raiding party. Sometimes they fought. And sometimes they won, driving the raiders off. But in Erak's and Svengal's eyes, that was a fair encounter. If the raiders won the fight, there were no reprisals against the defenders because they had the temerity to try to defend their property.

Piracy was a different matter altogether. Pirates — and Erak was right, many Magyarans indulged in the practice — preyed on lone ships at sea. Ships that were smaller than their own and usually only lightly armed. When the ship was captured and her cargo taken, the normal practice was to sink the ship and kill the crew, so that no trace of the pirates' activity would ever be found.

'Keep an eye on him while he's here,' Erak said. 'Any sign of funny business, let me know.'

'Consider it done,' Svengal said. A grin touched the corners of his mouth. 'Do you want me to disguise myself while I'm doing it?'

Erak frowned at him. 'Disguise yourself? As who?'

'I could do myself up as my old Aunt Winfredia,' Svengal said. 'They'd never suspect a thing.'

Erak regarded him stonily. When he had been a simple ship's skirl, he thought, Svengal had never showed him this sort of disrespect. Then he shook his head, remembering. Yes, he had, he thought.

'Get out of here,' he said.

'On my way, chief. And if you see an old woman hobbling around town, be nice to her. She's probably me.'

'Are you still here?' Erak asked. But this time, there was no answer.

CHAPTER TWENTY-EIGHT

Training was finished for the day and the boys were waiting to be dismissed so they could return to their quarters and rest. Sigurd, however, chose to spring a most unwelcome surprise on them.

'Team assessment!' he thundered as he strode onto the training ground. The boys looked at one another with dismay. It had been a long day. They had been practising rowing most of the afternoon. It was hard, gruelling work and their muscles ached. The news became worse with Sigurd's next words.

'Obstacle course! Team assessment! Ten minutes! Get your kit together!'

There were audible groans from all corners of the training field. The obstacle course was a seven-kilometre track laid out around the training area, through thick woods and up and down the lower slopes of the surrounding mountains. As well as being a muscle-wrenching run, it pitted the runners against a series of natural — and, in some cases, highly unnatural — obstacles. There was a steep rock slope to descend, two streams to ford and a pit full of thick, gluey mud to negotiate. This was accomplished by swinging on a rope across the disgusting barrier. There was also a wooden wall, more than two metres high, that each runner had to climb, scramble or jump over as best he could.

At one point, a heavy rope net was staked out, with fifty centimetres clearance between it and the ground, and the runners had to crawl on their bellies beneath it for fifteen metres.

To make things a little more interesting, in Sigurd's words, all these feats had to be accomplished carrying weapons and shields.

'That's the way it'll be if you're in a battle,' he'd told them. 'You may as well get used to it.'

So the Herons swung, climbed, ran, crawled, slid and waded along the course. The event was another time trial and Hal was confident that they were making reasonable time. The more capable and athletic runners, like Stig, Jesper and the twins, helped those less able to negotiate the course. But the final obstacle was their undoing. It was a thick pole, six metres long, set three metres above another muddy pit. At least, the boys all hoped fervently that the substance in the pit was mud. There were dark mutterings that it was something even more unpleasant — and the rancid smell from the pit did little to dispel such rumours. Edvin muttered that he'd heard the town's pigsties seemed to be remarkably clean in recent days.

Seven of the eight Heron teammates managed to negotiate the log — with differing degrees of difficulty.

Stig and Hal ran it easily. Jesper was equally light-footed. That was befitting of someone with Jesper's light-fingered habits, Hal thought. The twins moved at a more sedate pace, all the while throwing insults at each other. Stefan edged along sideways, crouched nearly double, his tongue sticking out between his teeth as he went, mumbling encouragement to himself. Edvin, after a near disaster, when he only managed to save himself from the pit by a last-minute grab at the log, and an undignified scramble back onto it, eventually sat and straddled the pole, inching his way along it to safety.

But the log was Ingvar's downfall – literally.

He clambered onto its smooth, rounded surface like a great, clumsy bear. He crouched fearfully. He was barefoot and his toes were visibly curling in an instinctive action, as if his feet were trying to grip the log. He rose to full height, arms outstretched, wavering dangerously.

'Come on, Ingvar!' the team yelled.

He took one wobbling, uncertain step. His arms wind-milled. He crouched again on hands and knees, peering hopelessly around him.

'How far off the ground am I?' he called.

Hal hesitated, then, knowing that Ingvar couldn't see very well, he replied, 'Barely twenty centimetres!' He figured that if Ingvar didn't think there was a two-metre drop below him, he would manage the log more easily. But Ingvar wasn't fooled. He remembered he had climbed a lot further than twenty centimetres to get onto the log.

'I know that's a lie!' he shouted, clutching the log desperately. 'I can't manage this. I'm sorry.'

'Do it the way Edvin did it!' Stig yelled.

Ingvar frowned. Of course, he hadn't seen Edvin inching his way across the log.

'How was that?' he called back, his voice quavering.

'Straddle it and slide along on your behind!' Edvin yelled. Ingvar thought about that and nodded slowly.

'That might work,' he said. He carefully sat down, dropped his legs either side of the pole, gripped it in front of him with both hands and began to inch along. Instantly, he began to yell with pain.

'Ow! Ow! Ow! Ow-ow-ow!' he bleated, stopping a third of the way across.

'What's up now?' Hal asked him, looking round towards the track that led to the finish line in frustration. Ingvar's hesitation was costing them time, he knew. And that was something they didn't have.

'Splinters, Hal. Splinters. I can't go any further like this,' Ingvar called piteously and Hal's shoulders drooped. He looked at Stig.

'We're going to have to guide him across,' he said. Stig took a pace back in horror, looking at the evil, glutinous mass in the pit.

'Are you kidding? If he falls, he'll take us with him.'

'We've got to, Stig. It's the only way. And every team member has to complete every obstacle.'

As it turned out, Stig's words were prophetic. Ingvar did fall, and he did take them with him. And he did so three times before they squelched, stinking and covered in muck, off the far side of the pole.

As they reached the far side, it was noticeable that their teammates edged away to give them plenty of free space.

'Thanks, fellows,' said Ingvar.

Hal gestured wearily with a dripping, filth-covered hand. 'You'd do the same for us,' he said.

Ingvar looked down at himself, then at his two helpers. His sight wasn't too good but there was nothing wrong with his sense of smell.

'No,' he said deliberately. 'No, I wouldn't.'

They squished their way to the finish line, where they were greeted by howls of laughter from the other teams. Even Tursgud's sense of humour, which had been noticeably absent since his fight with Hal, seemed restored.

'Looks like Hal Who fell in the poo,' he called, causing a fresh burst of hilarity. Hal, seething as he was, had to admit to himself it was a pretty good sally. He squelched up to Sigurd, who backed away, grinning.

'Herons reporting in, sir. How did we do?'

Sigurd looked at him, his head to one side. 'You're kidding, of course,' he said.

Hal shrugged. 'I guess we came last then?'

Sigurd made a note on one of his many sheets of parchment.

'You came so last,' he said, 'you'll probably still be last in *next* year's training programme.'

Two days later, Hal brought the *Heron* into the harbour. The three teams had just finished a trial navigation exercise and *Heron* had finished well ahead of the other two boats. She was faster in just about all conditions, except under oars and running with the wind dead astern. He was pleased with the way his crew were settling down.

They were familiar now with the ship's unusual rig and even Gort, who was sceptical at first, seemed to be impressed by *Heron*'s ability to sail closer to the wind than the two square-rigged ships. Although, at this stage, Hal hadn't demonstrated her full capabilities in that regard. No sense in letting Rollond and Tursgud know what they were up against.

As they ran the *Heron* onto the beach, Hal pointed to the long, black ship beached further down the strand. He'd noticed her earlier when they had left the harbour, but he'd been too busy to ask about her then.

'Whose is that?' he asked Gort.

The instructor grimaced distastefully. 'She's Magyaran. She was dismasted in a storm. Erak is letting her crew do repairs,' he said. His expression left no doubt what he thought of Magyarans and their ships. Hal opened his mouth to ask more but he was interrupted by Sigurd, who was striding along the walkway at the top of the beach.

'Assessment!' he bellowed. 'Wrestling! At the Common Green! Fifteen minutes!'

There was a flurry of activity as the brotherbands hurried to stow yards, sails and masts and make their ships fast. Then they doubled to the Common Green, a large, grassy field in the centre of Hallasholm, where the town's inhabitants were each entitled to graze two animals.

The wrestling ring had been marked out — a chalked circle four metres in diameter. Unlike most of their tests, this one was open to the public and had attracted a crowd of spectators. Skandians enjoyed physical contests and wrestling was a favourite. Hal was sure there would be bets being laid. He saw Thorn sitting off to one side and waved to him. The ragged figure rose and sauntered across.

'Hear you had fun with the obstacle course,' Thorn said.

Hal shook his head and forced a smile. The failure at the pit still rankled. But he guessed it was funny to an outsider.

'We didn't do so well,' he said.

Thorn indicated the chalked circle. 'Maybe you'll do better today. Is Stig wrestling for you?'

'Who else?' Hal replied. Stig was by far their best contestant in this sort of event.

Thorn nodded. 'Make sure he keeps his temper and he should do all right,' he said. 'Good luck.'

He shambled away and sat on an old tree stump. Hal noticed that the other spectators tended to stay clear of him. He smiled ruefully. He'd experienced that himself the other day after the episode with the pit.

Sigurd took a position beside the chalked ring. As he had done before, he drew the first two contestants from the battered old helmet.

'Wolves and Herons!' he announced. 'Five minutes!'

The Herons moved in a group to the circle and crowded round Stig, who took a seat on a low stool, breathing deeply. He had stripped his shirt off, and was dressed only in short breeches that reached to the knees. Stefan stood behind him, kneading the muscles of his shoulders and neck to loosen them.

Hal glanced at Jesper.

'Go see who's fighting for the Wolves,' he said. The other boy nodded and darted away. Hal crouched on one knee before Stig, speaking in a low, urgent voice.

'Remember, take your time,' he said. 'Don't let him rush you into a mistake. And above all —'

'I know, I know,' Stig said irritably. 'Don't lose my temper, right?'

Hal put the irritability down to nervous tension. He pretended not to notice it.

'You'll be fine,' he said soothingly. He looked up as Jesper returned, pushing through the circle of boys around Stig.

'It's Bjorn,' Jesper said. One of the Herons groaned. Bjorn was big and powerful. And he was fast.

'Come on,' said Hal, 'we knew it would be him. He's good. But I think you're better, Stig. Just remember —'

'I know! I heard you the first five times! Don't lose my temper!' Stig's face was red and Hal's heart sank.

You already have, he thought. But he said nothing.

'Thirty seconds!' Sigurd called.

Stig rose from the stool, shaking free of Stefan's massage, and stalked to the edge of the circle. On the far side, Bjorn took his place. Hal assessed him carefully. In spite of his assurance to Stig, he knew it was going to be a close thing. Bjorn was a little heavier. But Stig might be faster. And he was better balanced. That was important in these matches. The rules were simple. If a contestant could throw or force his opponent out of the ring, he won. If a wrestler could pin his opponent helplessly for a period of five seconds, that was another win.

Finally, there were certain holds that were dangerous or extremely painful. If a wrestler managed to catch his opponent in one of them, the judges would intervene if necessary and declare him the winner.

There was no two out of three. It was a straightforward contest. If you won once, you won.

'Ready, Wolves?' Sigurd asked.

'Ready.' Bjorn was casual and confident.

'Ready, Herons?'

'Ready.' Stig's voice was thick with tension. Hal frowned. Not the best way to start a match, he thought.

'Judges?' That was Sigurd again and Hal had to smile as he saw Gort, who was the referee for the bout, reach into his pocket to make sure his whistle was there. As he did so, he glared quickly in the directions of the Herons.

'Ready,' Gort called, and the other two instructors, who would be watching for foul play, repeated his call.

'Then . . . BEGIN!'

Sigurd's command rang across the Common Green, echoing faintly from the houses facing the field, and the fight was on.

CHAPTER TWENTY-NINE

The two contestants moved forward, and began circling each other. Each one was studying the other's stance and fighting posture, looking for some possible weakness that could be exploited. Bjorn was relaxed and moved easily. Hal could tell that Stig was tense, moving a little stiffly, every muscle ready to respond to an attack.

He feinted towards Bjorn and Bjorn stepped back smoothly, then feinted a move in his turn. Stig sprang back like a startled deer and Bjorn laughed.

The skin on the back of Stig's neck grew red.

'Stay calm, Stig,' Hal muttered to himself. The other Herons crowded around him, intent on the contest. So far, there was no shouting or cheering from either side.

Then Bjorn broke the silence. He straightened from his fighting crouch and waved a hand in front of his face, as if fanning a bad odour away.

'Whew! Is there something dead around here?' he asked the circle of spectators. 'Something smells terrible!'

There was a ripple of amusement from the Sharks and Wolves, and from the score of townspeople assembled to watch the bout. Bjorn grinned at them, then appealed, with mock seriousness, to Sigurd.

'Has this boy had a bath since the obstacle course, sir?' he asked.

Stig's face grew redder with anger. Above all else, he hated to be laughed at.

Sigurd replied curtly. 'Get on with it, Bjorn. Cut the chatter and save your breath.'

But Bjorn was unrepentant. He continued to grin as he seemingly ignored his opponent and appealed to the chief instructor. 'Hard to take a breath out here, sir. I really must complain. This is unfair tactics.'

Hal could tell that his friend was about to snap. Stig's temper was being held in control by a thread.

'Stay calm, Stig!' he called warningly. Instantly, Bjorn's grin switched to him.

'Oh, is his name Stig? I thought it was *Stink*,' he said and more laughter erupted from the spectators.

With a bellow of inarticulate rage, Stig charged.

Which was what Bjorn had been hoping all along. In spite of the fact that he appeared to be talking to Sigurd and then Hal, he had been watching his opponent like a hawk and was ready to meet his wild, undisciplined charge. Hal groaned as Bjorn grabbed Stig's wildly flailing arms and backed up a few steps, using Stig's momentum against him.

Then he raised his right foot and placed it in Stig's belly. At the same time, he fell smoothly back onto the grass, then straightened the leg, adding his left leg to the thrust as he rolled backwards onto the grass.

It was a perfectly timed and executed stomach-throw. Stig, held momentarily by the arms, sailed high in the air, describing a giant arc above Bjorn. Then, at exactly the right moment, Bjorn released his grip on Stig's wrists. The Herons' representative flew for several metres, landing heavily on his back with an ugly thud that drove the air from his lungs.

Before he could recover, Bjorn was on his feet and had seized Stig's right foot. With all his strength, he swung the prone body of his opponent through an arc, sliding him on the damp, slippery grass and propelling him towards the chalk line, two metres away.

Stig tried to stop the movement but he was winded and helpless. He slid over the chalk line, out of the ring. Gort's silver whistle blew a piercing blast and the bout was over.

There was an arbitrary rest period of forty minutes before Bjorn was due to fight the Sharks' representative — Tursgud, of course. Bjorn offered to forego the rest, saying he wasn't tired at all after his first bout. Sigurd dismissed the suggestion angrily. As they waited, the Heron team clustered round Stig, trying desperately to raise his spirits. He was sitting dejectedly on the ground, his elbows on his knees and his head in his hands. Hal tried to talk to him but Stig merely shook his head, refusing to acknowledge his friend's presence.

A hand dropped onto Hal's shoulder and he turned, finding himself looking into Thorn's bearded face. Thorn jerked his head to one side, signalling Hal to make room for him, then dropped on one knee in front of Stig.

'Stig,' he said. 'Stig. Look at me. Look at me *now.*'

His voice was soft but there was an unmistakable air of command in it. Stig raised his eyes to meet Thorn's steady gaze.

'You can beat Tursgud,' Thorn said.

Stig's eyes showed his disbelief. His rapid defeat at Bjorn's hands had shattered his confidence. The contest had barely begun before it was over.

'How do you propose I do it?' he said sarcastically. Thorn said nothing for a few seconds, simply held eye contact with the boy. Stig flushed. Then Thorn continued.

'Bjorn didn't beat you. You beat yourself. You let him goad you into losing your temper —'

'Don't start that, Thorn! You sound like Hal! *Don't lose your temper. Stay calm,*' he said, mimicking Hal's attempts to calm him down.

'Hal's right,' Thorn said, still speaking softly, still showing no emotion. 'D'you think Tursgud isn't going to try to goad you the same way? And it'll be easier for him because you hate him. You need to fight smart, Stig. Laugh at him. Make *him* mad instead. Don't fall for his tricks. You can beat him if you do that, believe me.'

But Stig's temper got the better of him once more. Deep down, he knew Thorn was right. But his anger made him hear Thorn's advice as criticism, not support. He lashed out — not physically, but verbally.

'Believe you?' he said scathingly. 'Tell me, Thorn, since you seem to know so much, why should I take advice from a one-armed old drunk?'

Thorn recoiled as if Stig had struck him. The blood drained from his face and for a moment Hal thought he was going to hit Stig. Then, abruptly, Thorn stood and walked away, shoving through the shocked members of the Heron team. Outraged, Hal grabbed Stig by the shirt front and dragged him to his feet. The Skandian boy was a head taller than him, but Hal confronted him chest to chest, his eyes blazing with fury.

'Gorlog blast you, Stig! How could you say that?' he demanded. 'He's trying to help us and you say a thing like that?'

Stig looked around at the circle of faces that surrounded him. He saw nothing there but condemnation. He tried to bluster his way out of the situation. The second he had said the words to Thorn, he knew he was in the wrong, that he had caused deep hurt to a man who had only ever shown him friendship. But he couldn't admit it.

'Well, really, Hal! What does he know about fighting? I know he's your friend, but why should I take advice from him? Really? You know what he's like. He's a broken-down old tramp.'

Hal looked around at the team surrounding them.

'Give us some privacy,' he ordered. 'Now.'

There was no mistaking the authority in his voice. The other Herons avoided his gaze and shuffled away. When he judged they were out of earshot, Hal released Stig's shirt.

'I'll tell you what he knows about fighting,' he said in a quiet voice. 'Who do you think taught me to punch so that I broke Tursgud's nose? Thorn did. Who do you think told me to keep going forward and not to back off?

Thorn did. And do you know how he knows this stuff? Because he was the Maktig — three years in a row.'

Stig's jaw dropped and he involuntarily looked around to see where Thorn might be.

'Thorn?' he said. 'Thorn was the Mak—'

Hal silenced him before he could finish the sentence.

'Shut up! He doesn't want people to remember. I probably shouldn't have told you, so for pity's sake don't let on to him that I did. But think of this, Stig, you've just been given advice by the greatest warrior Skandia has ever known. If you don't follow it, you're a fool. And you're a traitor to our team.'

Stig was shaking his head in anguish. 'Hal, I'm sorry. I didn't know . . . well, how could I know? It's almost unbelievable. No, it *is* unbelievable. Thorn was the —'

'I told you to shut up about it!' Hal cut him off and Stig nodded miserably.

'I've got to find him and apologise,' he said, but Hal was already shaking his head before he could finish.

'Time for that later. Let him cool off for a while. The best way you can show him you're sorry is to beat Tursgud. Show Thorn you've listened to him. Keep your temper under control and fight smart, the way he said to.'

'How do I do that?' Stig said miserably. 'I can't help it. I always lose my temper when people make fun of me.'

Hal grabbed him by the shoulders and shook him violently. 'Do as Thorn said. Make Tursgud mad! Laugh at *him* when he tries to provoke you.'

'But . . . how?'

Hal thought desperately for a few moments, then inspiration struck him. 'When you start to get mad, take a deep breath, and picture Tursgud the way he looked when the Sharks lost the tug of war. Remember how furious he was?'

Stig nodded, grinning faintly at the memory. 'He certainly did look angry,' he admitted.

Hal continued, warming to the theme. 'Then use that picture. And remember how shocked he looked when I broke his nose that afternoon? That's the look you want to put on his face again today,' he added. He could see that he was getting through to Stig.

'One more thing,' he added carefully. 'You know he'll talk about your mother doing laundry.'

Since Stig's father had deserted them, his mother had supported herself and her son by taking in laundry. It was menial work, but there was nothing shameful about it. Yet for some reason, Stig was embarrassed by it. In past encounters, Tursgud had used the fact as a goad, making out that Stig's mother was a drudge, and little better than a slave. Even now, Hal saw Stig's face darken as he mentioned it. He shook Stig's shoulders again.

'Be ready for it! Think of something even more insulting to say back.'

Stig spread his hands helplessly. He wasn't too quick with his tongue and he knew it.

'Like what?' he said. 'His mother never took in laundry. What can I say?'

Hal pursed his lips thoughtfully, then a light dawned in his eyes.

'You know, I think I might have just the thing for you,' he said.

CHAPTER THIRTY

J arst was sounding the bell for the beginning of the next bout — Tursgud and Bjorn. Hurriedly, the Heron team made their way back to the circle to watch the contest.

This bout took considerably longer than the one-sided fight between Bjorn and Stig. The two boys circled warily once more. But this time, Bjorn held his silence. There was no point trying to bait Tursgud and he knew he couldn't afford to let his own attention be distracted. Tursgud was a dangerous opponent.

They closed, each grappling for a hold on the other, grunting and straining as the contest became a test of strength and power. Each one countered the other's attempts to throw him off balance, or to trip or sweep a leg.

On one occasion, Bjorn grappled Tursgud around the waist and tried to lift him, preparatory to a hip throw. But Tursgud managed to break loose, throwing his body to the side and staggering away as he momentarily lost balance.

He came perilously close to the chalk line, but managed to stay inside the circle. Next time Bjorn tried for a similar hold, Tursgud countered by suddenly raising his shoulder under the other boy's chin. Bjorn's head snapped back and he staggered away.

Technically, it was an illegal manoeuvre. But it was difficult to prove that it had been intentional.

Viggo darted forward and stepped between the two wrestlers before Tursgud had a chance to follow up on his advantage. The referee let Bjorn have time to recover, warned Tursgud about any repeat actions, then signalled for the bout to start again.

The end, when it came, came suddenly. Tursgud feinted for a left foot kick to Bjorn's solar plexus. When the Wolves' wrestler countered with a sweeping right arm to knock the kick aside, Tursgud leapt forward, grabbed the arm and threw Bjorn in a cross-body throw.

However, instead of releasing Bjorn's wrist as he went down, Tursgud held on and went with him. Bjorn landed flat on his back, with Tursgud kneeling, facing him on his right side. Before Bjorn could react, Tursgud dragged his opponent's right arm over his leg so that his thigh was beneath Bjorn's elbow, then locked the hand and wrist under his right ankle. On one side, Bjorn's own weight was bearing down on it. On the other, his hand was locked under Tursgud's leg. When Bjorn tried to roll towards Tursgud to release himself, Tursgud simply leaned away, raising his thigh under Bjorn's trapped elbow, putting enormous strain on the joint. The pain was unbearable. Bjorn grunted, tried to rise again. Tursgud leaned away – further this time.

'I'll break it,' he warned. Bjorn looked up at him, eyes slitted in pain. He could tell that Tursgud meant what he said. He would break the elbow if Bjorn didn't submit. But Bjorn refused to do so. He shut his eyes, prepared for the sudden shattering pain, when Gort's whistle blasted out.

'That's enough! You've won. Now release him.'

Tursgud smiled down at Bjorn as the other boy opened his eyes in relief. Then he gave a final, sudden lurch to his left — not enough to break the elbow, but enough to send a lightning bolt of pain through his opponent's arm. Then, and only then, did he release the hold.

Standing in silence, Hal and Stig watched Tursgud swagger back to his cheering team, while Rollond and another member of the Wolves helped Bjorn to his feet. The defeated wrestler cradled his injured arm in his left hand. That last heave from Tursgud had strained tendons and muscles in Bjorn's shoulder.

'You're going to have to watch that he doesn't get that hold on you,' Hal said.

Stig nodded thoughtfully. 'Mind you,' he said, 'if you can react quickly enough, there's a way to break it, and that could put you in a good position.'

'Or you could break your elbow,' Hal said.

Stig considered the statement.

'Yes. That's another possibility,' he admitted.

'Begin!' Sigurd shouted and Tursgud and Stig advanced warily towards each other. Stopping two metres apart, they began to circle, hands held out like claws, knees bent as they shuffled sideways, maintaining their balance. Each boy was intent on watching the other's eyes. That was where they'd see the first sign of a sudden attack.

Tursgud fanned his hand in front of his face, mimicking Bjorn's successful tactic in his contest with Stig. He smiled.

'Phew! Bjorn was right! Something does stink out here!'

Several of the Sharks team laughed. But this time, Stig was expecting the taunt and was ready for it. He smiled back at Tursgud.

'Surprised you can smell anything with your nose plastered all over your face,' he said in a friendly tone. Tursgud's face flushed with sudden anger. On the sidelines, Bjorn laughed aloud.

'Nice one, Stig!' he called and Tursgud glared quickly in his direction.

'How did it happen again?' Stig asked, as they continued to circle each other, occasionally feinting an attack, dancing back and forward as each countered the other's feints. 'I believe some scrawny Araluan boy rearranged it for you.'

On the sidelines, Hal smiled. For once, he didn't mind being referred to as an Araluan. He knew it would enrage Tursgud.

Now the Herons and the Wolves both laughed and Tursgud charged forward in a rage, his hands grappling for Stig's throat. At the last moment, Stig brought his right arm up so that his forearm jolted into Tursgud's jaw, sending the Sharks' leader backwards. It was a legal move, but only just.

'No more of that, Stig!' Viggo warned from the sidelines. Stig nodded.

'Sorry,' he said. But he wasn't. Not one bit.

Tursgud shook his head to clear it and backed up a few paces. His eyes narrowed as he studied his opponent. This wasn't like Stig, he thought. Stig could be relied on to lose his temper and go wild when he was ridiculed, not reply with interest. Then he smiled to himself. Of course, Bjorn had used the same taunt. The Herons must have known that Tursgud would repeat it, so Stig was ready. But there was a tried and true method to raise his anger and Tursgud fell back on it now.

'Is your mam still doing other people's dirty washing?' he asked. But to his surprise, Stig simply smiled again.

'No. She said the sight of your dad's underwear put her right off it. Said he must have worn it till it fell off all by itself.'

The laughter really rang out now. Not just from the other brotherbands, but from the spectators gathered around the ring. Tursgud's temper snapped and he charged, as Stig had hoped he would.

The Sharks' leader wasn't the most original of thinkers. He'd tried the same old taunts and they'd failed, because Stig was expecting them. Now, as Stig also expected, he tried for the same hold that had defeated Bjorn. He grabbed Stig's left arm and pivoted to throw him over his hip to the ground. It was a clumsy attempt and Stig could have prevented it, but instead, he went with it. But as they hit the ground, with Tursgud about to attempt to pin his arm over his knee, Stig quickly twisted to his right, ending on his side, so that his left arm slipped free before Tursgud could lock off the hold.

This placed him behind Tursgud, as he had planned. Quickly, he locked his left arm across Tursgud's throat, anchoring it to the inside elbow of his bent right arm. Then he locked his right hand behind his opponent's head. Too late, Tursgud tried to draw his chin down to prevent the choke hold, but Stig's left arm was solidly in position across his throat, and his right hand was forcing Tursgud's head forward against it.

Before Tursgud could prevent him, Stig wrapped his legs around the other boy's body. No matter how Tursgud plunged and rolled and bucked, Stig clung to him, all the while increasing the pressure on his throat, cutting off the air to his lungs. Tursgud plucked helplessly at Stig's arm. But Stig's forearm was like a steel bar, choking him. He tried to call out but the only sound he could make was a strangled grunt. He was becoming weaker as he tried for oxygen and got none. His hands flailed helplessly and still Stig hung on grimly.

'Enough!' Sigurd yelled and Gort reinforced the command with a piercing blast on his whistle.

Stig released the pressure and rolled away, coming slowly to his feet, grinning at Hal. Tursgud lay for a few moments, gasping and choking as he drew air into his deprived lungs. Hal noted that it was some time before two of the Sharks stepped forward to help him to his feet. Interesting, he thought.

As the other Heron members gathered round, chorusing their congratulations to Stig, Hal slapped his friend on the shoulder.

'Good work,' he said. 'See how much better you perform when you keep your temper?'

Stig grinned and shook his head ruefully. 'I've got you and Thorn to thank for that good advice. And thanks for the crack about Tursgud's father and his underpants. That really did the trick.' He glanced around. 'Speaking of Thorn, where is he? I've got some humble pie to eat.'

But before Hal could answer, Sigurd stepped forward with a most welcome, and unexpected, announcement.

'All right! Listen here, you lot!'

The three groups all turned and moved to stand around him. He looked around the ring of young faces watching him, all of them wondering what surprise he was about to spring on them.

'Today's event was a draw. Each team had one win apiece, so there's no need to award points. You've been working hard for the past weeks and you've all done well. It's the end of the week and now you've got two days off. Go home, relax, spend the weekend with your families and tell your girlfriends lies about how terrific you are. Next week . . .'

He stopped as the twenty-eight boys let out a cheer at the news. Then he held his hands up for silence.

'Next week we're getting into seamanship and ship handling. It's going to be tough, so make sure you're rested.'

With that he turned and walked away, flanked by the other three instructors. As he passed close by, Hal heard him saying to Viggo: 'Let them think it's a holiday for them. It's us who need the break.'

Hal turned to say something to Stig but he wasn't there. Hal looked around and saw him hurrying across the

Green, to where a ragged figure was sitting under a small clump of trees. Hal had a sudden premonition and began to hurry after his friend. He called out but Stig was too far away to hear above the babble of conversation from the other boys and the spectators from the town. He started to run, shoving his way through the milling crowd.

Thorn looked up as the muscular youth approached him. His expression was neutral. He was neither welcoming nor dismissive. Stig stopped in front of him, hands on hips, and shook his head awkwardly, trying to find the right words. Finally, he decided simplicity might be best.

'Thorn, I'm so very sorry. I should never have said that to you. It was my stupid temper speaking, not me. I want to thank you for your advice and help. I was stupid and arrogant and a pig and I apologise to you most sincerely.'

Thorn regarded him for a few seconds. There was a lot of good in Stig, he knew. His downfall had always been that short temper of his. But he could tell that the boy was sincere in his apology.

Maybe he'll learn a lesson from this, he thought. He rose, smiling, and held out his left hand to shake hands with the boy. Stig ducked his head gratefully and seized Thorn's hand with his own.

'I guess I did some stupid, arrogant things when I was sixteen,' Thorn said. He found it hard to resist an apology that came so obviously from the heart. Someone, a long time ago, had given him the advice: *It takes a big man to apologise.* Perhaps it had been his own father. He wasn't sure. But it had been a belief he had taken with him through the years.

'So we're all right?' Stig said anxiously.

Thorn nodded. 'We're fine, Stig.'

Stig heaved a huge sigh of relief. 'Well, praise Gorlog for that! Hal tore me off a terrible strip after you left. I've got to say, the two of you have taught me a real lesson.'

'If you've learned from it, that's a good thing,' Thorn told him. 'Just don't forget it.'

Stig was grinning widely now. As Thorn had reflected, he was a good-hearted boy and he hated to be in conflict with anyone — except perhaps Tursgud. But now his sense of relief made his tongue run away with him.

'I'll remember,' he said heartily. 'After all, it's not everyone who gets advice from a former Maktig, is it?'

Thorn's head snapped up. The blood drained from his cheeks until he was white-faced with fury.

'What?' he demanded, his voice cutting like a whip. '*What* did you say?'

Stig stepped back a pace, confused and uncertain now. Hal chose that moment to come pounding up to them, in time to hear his next words.

'Hal said you were the Maktig. Three times, he said.'

'Stig! Shut up!' Hal yelled. But of course, it was too late. Thorn turned on him, his left hand extended, a finger pointing at Hal like a spear.

'I might have known it was you!' he snarled. 'Who invited you to poke around in my past life?' he shouted. 'I suppose it was that bigmouth, Erak. And now you've told Stig. Who else did you tell, curse it? Who else have you been blabbing to?'

Hal moved his hands helplessly. 'Just Stig. Nobody else. And I told him not to say anything about it,' he added, casting an anguished look at his friend.

Thorn snorted in white-hot fury. 'Well, *that* worked, didn't it?' he spat at them. He looked from one to the other, seething. Hal made another ineffectual gesture, taking a half pace forward.

'Thorn, I didn't mean to —'

'Shut up! Your blasted mouth has done enough damage for one day. Just shut up! Shut up and stay away from me!'

And with that, Thorn turned on his heel and stalked away, fury written in every line of his body.

CHAPTER THIRTY-ONE

'I don't know why he got so angry, Mam,' Hal said morosely. 'He should be proud of what he was.'

It was late afternoon and Hal was helping his mother prepare butterflied chickens to grill over hot coals. This involved cutting the backbone out of the chicken, then flattening it out so that it would cook more quickly and evenly over the direct heat of the coals. His mother was using a heavy cleaver to chop through the ribs along the backbone. Hal was using his saxe. She glanced at it doubtfully.

'You haven't been doing anything unpleasant with that saxe, have you? Not cutting any tarry rope or anything?'

He smiled as he continued chopping. 'No, Mam. And I cleaned the oil off it with boiling water before I started.' To prevent rust, saxe knife blades were kept lightly oiled.

She nodded, satisfied, then addressed his earlier statement.

'It's pride that makes him want people to forget it,' she said. She could see Hal frown as he tried to follow that reasoning and she continued. 'You see, Hal, Thorn can live with people thinking of him as a tramp and a drunk. Although only just,' she added, remembering how close Thorn had come to slipping into a permanent sleep that winter night.

'But what he can't stand is the idea of people comparing him now to what he once was. That would hurt too much. If people were saying, "Look at him. He's a useless cripple but he used to be the mightiest warrior in Skandia," it would be a constant reminder to him of what he's lost. And a constant shame as he had to face how low he's slipped — and how everybody knew about it.'

'I suppose so,' Hal said reluctantly. 'But another thing puzzles me. He's incredibly fast still, and his left hand and arm are amazingly strong. He could still be a capable warrior, even with only one hand.'

Karina smiled sadly. 'I asked Erak about that once. He would have kept Thorn in his crew if he'd asked. But Thorn told him, "There's a big difference between being good and being the best." That difference is just too painful for him to face.'

'I think I see,' Hal said.

They were silent for a while and Karina knew Hal's falling-out with Thorn was still troubling him. She also knew that, in time, their friendship would survive it. Thorn thought too much of the boy to let his anger last indefinitely. But of course, Hal couldn't see that. Young people, she sighed, everything was always so black and white for them. And everything must be put to rights immediately. She tried to get Hal's mind off his troubles.

'Anyway, what have you been up to for the past two days? I've barely seen you, except for meals. You've been locked away in that workshop of yours for hours.'

Hal had the grace to look remorseful. 'Sorry about that,' he said. 'I've been working on something for Thorn — sort of a peace offering.'

She smiled. 'I'm sure he'll love it. Now watch you're not cutting away too much meat with that backbone. I need some left to serve my customers, you know.'

'Yes, Mam,' he said obediently.

After they had split and flattened eight chickens, Hal prepared a bed of charcoal to roast them over, while his mother rubbed oil and aromatic spices into their skins. Once the heat hit them, he knew, the skin would tighten and form a crisp, brown outer layer over the juicy meat beneath.

'Dinner will be in an hour,' his mother told him, as she buried potatoes in the hot, red-glowing coals. They would bake there while the chickens roasted. The first of the chickens went onto the grill with a fragrant, spluttering explosion of juices hitting the fire. Hal's mouth watered instantly at the delicious smell.

'An hour? Fine. I've just got something to do first,' he said.

Karina smiled as her son hurried out of the kitchen. She was willing to bet that it had to do with Thorn and the peace offering Hal had been working on.

He jogged to his workshop at the rear of the large plot of ground where the eating house stood. He slipped the door lock free and stepped inside. It was dim in the workshop. There was a small window high in one wall but the early evening light barely trickled through it. Still, there was no need to light a lamp. The objects he was after lay neatly on the workbench, wrapped in heavy, waxed linen sailcloth.

He tucked them under his arm, let himself out and adjusted the lock again. Then he headed for Thorn's lean-to on the eastern wall of the eating house.

He could see a strip of yellow candle light around the edges of the heavy leather curtain that served as a door closure. Thorn was inside then. Hal hesitated, unwilling to face that cold, unfriendly face he had seen at the Common Green, then gathered his resolve and went forward, knocking on the door post.

'Who is it?' Thorn's voice was peremptory and unwelcoming. Hal swallowed. His mouth was dry all of a sudden. He swallowed again and managed to speak.

'Thorn . . . it's me. Hal. Can I come in?'

There was no reply from inside the lean-to. Then the leather door was abruptly dragged aside. Thorn regarded him coldly for some seconds.

'What do you want?'

Hal could see he was still angry. He gestured to the inside of the lean-to.

'Can I come in? I'll only take a few seconds of your time.' He held up the two linen-wrapped parcels. 'I have something for you.'

Thorn stepped aside and gestured for him to enter. Truth be told, he was angry with Hal. But he had spent the last two days regretting his outburst at the Common

Green. He felt he had been too hard on the boy, but he was too stubborn to come out and apologise. After all, Hal was in the wrong, he thought. He'd had no call to talk about Thorn's past.

On the other hand, he conceded, he hadn't told the boy about how he had been the Maktig. Nor had he sworn him to secrecy. So he couldn't really accuse him of breaking a confidence. It had been some time since Thorn had faced a moral dilemma like this and, inevitably, he acted as he always had done in the past few years. He shut himself away from the problem.

He gestured now to a three-legged stool that was one of the few pieces of furniture in the cramped, slant-ceilinged room — along with a table and Thorn's rope-net bed. Most of the rest of the available space was cluttered with discarded items of clothing and odd pieces of bric-a-brac that had been washed up on the shore and had taken his fancy — bits of fishing net, cork floats and a cane basket with one side beginning to fray and unravel.

Hal sat on the stool. Thorn sat facing him, on the edge of the bed. There was a long silence.

'Thorn, I am so sorry,' Hal said at last.

Thorn said nothing. But he felt a profound sense of relief that the way was now open for a reconciliation with this young boy he had grown to admire and care for. Perversely, he knew he could never have taken that first step, no matter how much he wanted to. He grunted and shifted uncomfortably on the bed.

''S all right,' he said gruffly. 'Nothing to really worry about.'

But Hal had his speech prepared and he went on, barely registering Thorn's reaction.

'I know saying it doesn't mean too much,' he said. 'Saying it is easy. So I made you this as an apology gift.' He held out one of the wrapped packages. 'It's for you,' he added unnecessarily, as Thorn stared at it without moving. Finally, the old sea wolf reached out and took the parcel, placing it in his lap and looking down at it.

'You made this?' he said and Hal nodded.

'I made it for you. Have a look at it.'

Slowly, Thorn unwrapped the oiled linen and found himself looking at a strange contraption.

At one end was a leather cup, about fifteen centimetres deep, reinforced with whalebone stiffening and fitted with two buckled straps passing around it. To this was anchored a piece of polished blackthorn wood, which extended from the closed end of the leather cup. It was a straight piece, but shaped in a half-circle curve at the end. Looking more closely, Thorn saw that it was actually two pieces, with the second piece fitting flush with the first and hinged just in front of the point where it joined the leather socket. He frowned, not quite understanding.

'It fits over the end of your right arm,' Hal explained. He reached forward and took it from Thorn, then slipped the socket over the end of his shortened right arm. The cup fitted snugly, particularly once Hal had tightened and adjusted the two straps. The interior, Thorn could feel, was padded with sheepskin. He moved it experimentally, raising the blackthorn piece before his eyes.

'It's a hook,' he said, understanding.

Hal nodded eagerly. 'But it's better than just a hook,' he said. 'Look.'

He loosened a leather thong on the side of the hook and the free end of the hinged section came away from the main body of the hook.

'You can grip things with it,' he explained. He placed the separated ends either side of a cup on the table, then pulled the cord tight so that the hinged pieces came together, like a set of jaws. The thong had a series of knots tied along it and Hal slipped one into a carved notch to hold the jaws solidly on the cup.

Thorn picked up the cup and moved it around, his face lighting up with a huge smile.

'This is amazing,' he said quietly.

He turned his arm this way and that, admiring its new extension. Then he placed the cup down on the table again, unclipped the knot from its notch and released the jaws. Then he pulled the thong tight again and clipped it off so that the two halves formed a solid hook once more.

'Quite amazing,' he repeated.

Hal touched the curved wood at the end. 'I've shaped this to fit over an oar handle,' he said. 'You'll be able to row again.'

Thorn shook his head in delight. 'Amazing,' he said again. No other word seemed adequate. He looked at Hal, saw the relief in the boy's face that he loved the gift. 'You really made this?'

Hal nodded. 'I actually started on it some time ago but I'd put it aside. I finished it yesterday and today,' he said. He paused, then reached for the other linen-wrapped parcel. He placed it in front of Thorn, who unwrapped it with his left hand, holding it steady with his new blackthorn hook.

The second item had a similar leather and whalebone cuff. But instead of the wooden hook, it was fitted with a thick, straight blackthorn shaft that ended in a heavy wooden ball, reinforced with strips of iron and fitted with brass studs a centimetre long.

'It's a weapon,' Hal explained. 'Put this on instead of the hook and you've got a war club built onto the end of your arm. What do you think?'

Thorn turned the new item over several times, shaking his head in wordless delight. Finally, he found his voice.

'What do I think?' he repeated. 'I've got a new hand I can row with and grip things with. And if anyone annoys me, I've got a new club I can crack their skulls with.'

He paused, shaking his head in wonder, and looked up at Hal, a beaming smile splitting his weather-worn face.

'What more could I ask for?'

CHAPTER THIRTY-TWO

Heron rode easily on a moderate swell, rising and falling as the waves passed under her keel. The sail was lowered and the ship was barely moving. Hal had kept two oars out either side to prevent her drifting over the start line before the race started.

This was their first major sea-going assessment. It was a test of their seamanship, ship handling and ability to work as a crew. They would race the other two brotherbands around a four-sided, diamond-shaped course. Fifty metres away lay *Porpoise*, with Tursgud at the helm. Beyond her was *Lynx*, Rollond's ship. Like *Heron*, they were stationary, with a few oars out to maintain their position short of the line.

Unlike *Heron*, which carried a total of eight oars, the other ships had twelve. In addition, each was equipped with a big square sail. They were former fast coastal traders that had been co-opted as training ships for the brotherband programme. There had been a third ship, intended for the Herons. But Hal had sought, and gained, permission to compete in the *Heron*.

'I don't know,' Erak had said doubtfully, as he studied the little ship. 'She still looks a bit on the flimsy side to me.' But eventually, he gave way, adding cryptically, 'It's your bad luck if things go wrong.'

Nothing's going to go wrong, Hal thought as he studied the *Porpoise*. Her lines were similar to a wolfship, although she was much smaller and wider in the beam. But, like all Skandian ships, even though her primary purpose was trading, she was built so that, in an emergency, she could be used to augment the wolfship fleet as a fighting vessel. *Lynx*, further away, was virtually identical to *Porpoise*. They would be quite fast, Hal judged, particularly with a stern wind. Although to his biased eye, they didn't look as fast as the *Heron*.

'Back water, oars,' he called softly. They had drifted too close to the start line for his liking. If they crossed it before the signal, they would have to turn round, sail back and cross it again — all of which would cost them time. The oarsmen gave one reverse thrust on their oars to check the ship's movement.

He glanced up at the wind telltale, a long pennant that streamed from the stern post, showing the wind's direction. The wind would be coming from over their starboard quarter until they reached the first turning point.

The judges were in a small fishing smack, bobbing up and down in the middle of the course. They were positioned so that they could see if any of the three racers crossed the line early.

Hal glanced forward. The port side yardarm and sail were laid out, ready to hoist. He saw Jarst, in the fishing boat, raise a horn to his lips and heard the mournful tone booming across the water.

'Thirty-second warning!' he called. 'Start counting, Edvin.'

'One jolly goblin, two jolly goblins, three jolly goblins. . .' Edvin counted off the seconds in a flat monotone, using his own formula to time the gaps.

Hal's eyes darted everywhere, taking in the ship's position, the position of the other two ships, the start line and his own crew. Stig and Ingvar were forward, ready to haul the sail and its yard up the mast.

'. . . sixteen jolly goblins . . .' Edvin intoned.

Hal glanced quickly left and right. 'Ulf and Wulf. Get ready to haul the sail tight. Jesper, Stefan, back water two strokes.'

'. . . twenty jolly goblins, twenty-one jolly goblins . . .'

'In oars!'

The two oars were drawn in and stowed with the usual clatter of wood on wood. Stefan and Jesper moved to stand ready to help the twins trim the sail once it was hoisted.

'. . . twenty-six jolly goblins . . .'

'Haul away!' Hal yelled and Ingvar and Stig bent to the halyards, sending the yardarm soaring up the stumpy mast, taking the sail with it. The wind caught the sail and set it flapping. Hal saw Ulf and Wulf reaching for the ropes controlling the sail.

'Wait!' he called. If they hauled in too soon, the ship might gather way and cross the line early.

'. . . thirty jolly goblins, thirty-one jolly goblins . . .'

The signal should have sounded by now, he thought. Edvin must have been counting too fast. Or perhaps the judges' timer was faulty. Either way, they had drifted perilously close to the start line and still there had been no signal to start. In a few more seconds they would be across the line. For a moment, Hal considered ordering the crew back to the oars. But if he did that and the signal sounded while they were moving, the result would be utter confusion. Still . . .

'. . . thirty-four jolly goblins . . .' Edvin's voice was tight with the strain. '. . . thirty-five . . . oh, thank Lorgan for that!'

The last few words were torn from Edvin as the signal horn blared once more.

'Haul in!' Hal yelled and the Herons heaved on the ropes, swinging the long curving yard to the most efficient position to catch the wind, then bringing the sail up taut to form that beautiful curve.

Heron leapt ahead as the harnessed power of the wind hit her sail. She leaned with the wind, the water rushing past beneath her rail, the usual trail of bubbles forming at one of her planks, just below the waterline. She was leaning too far, Hal thought.

'Ease the sail a little!' he ordered. He saw Stig directing the others, letting the sail out so that the ship rode more upright. That allowed her hull to bite more firmly against the water beneath her and reduced her downwind drift. Hal heaved the steering oar to the left and brought her bow slightly upwind. She sliced into a stray wave and sheets of spray flew back over the steering platform.

'Edvin!' he called. Edvin was detailed to watch the other ships and report any significant changes in their position.

'They've both hoisted sails,' he replied. '*Porpoise* was first and she gained a little. But now *Lynx* is matching her.' He paused, leaning forward and peering under his hand to see more clearly. 'They're dropping downwind,' he reported.

Hal nodded in satisfaction. The big square sails of the other two ships would drive them downwind faster than *Heron*'s more efficient triangular sail. That meant that the other ships would have to cover a greater distance to reach the first turning point. He flexed his hands on the steering oar, feeling a surge of pleasure at his ship's superior performance. Too flimsy, Erak, he thought. I'll show you flimsy!

Hal glanced around to see where the other two ships lay. They were well downwind of him, although both of them were moving fast. He looked to the right side — the starboard side — and saw that the judges' boat had moved up the course to observe them rounding the marker, making sure nobody fell short.

The *Heron* would need to turn to the right to round the marker, and as they did so, the wind would shift from just off their stern, till it was coming over their starboard bow. The second marker would then be almost directly upwind. They couldn't head straight for it. They'd have to sail upwind at an angle to the second marker, then judge the right moment to turn to a new course that would take them round it.

The first marker buoy was plunging towards them now, almost upon them. Hal watched it fly past his shoulder, then yelled his orders.

'Haul in! Haul in!' He leaned back against the steering oar, dragging the ship's head around to the right in a turn that left a flurry of white water in their wake. Stig and the others hauled on the ropes controlling the sail and the yardarm. *Heron* was pointing far closer to the wind than either of the other ships could manage. Hal glanced over his shoulder to see what they were up to.

He saw *Porpoise*'s big square sail come sliding down the mast, then caught a flicker of movement either side of her hull.

They've run out the oars, he thought, just as the sunlight gleamed off the oars swinging forward. Then they dipped and dragged backwards into the sea. There was another flash of sunlight on white wood as they rose and swung forward again to take another bite at the ocean.

'*Porpoise* is rowing!' Edvin reported. 'She's heading directly upwind!'

Interesting, thought Hal. Tursgud could row directly into the teeth of the wind, covering a much shorter distance than *Heron* would on her dogleg course. Initially, with all her rowers fresh, *Porpoise* might well move faster than the *Heron*. But how long could they keep that up? The rowers would tire, while the wind driving *Heron* would remain constant.

'What's *Lynx* up to?' he demanded. He couldn't keep looking the wrong way and besides, he had Edvin to keep him informed.

'Still under sail,' Edvin told him. 'But she's falling way behind.'

She would. She couldn't match *Heron*'s performance sailing up into the wind.

'*Porpoise* is gaining on us!' Edvin called. His voice cracked with excitement. Hal glared at him.

'Calm down. They're still fresh,' he said. But he glanced at the Sharks' craft and measured angles and distances with his eye. She was definitely catching them, he thought. He heaved the tiller to the left, trying to head further upwind. He heard Stig's warning shout.

'We're luffing!'

That meant the sail was fluttering, losing power as she came too close to the wind. Instantly, Hal let her fall off a little until the sail came taut again. They'd just have to hope that Tursgud's men would tire before they reached the mark. This was the leg of the race where *Heron* should have an advantage. It was her best chance to gain distance on the other ships. But Tursgud's tactic of going to the oars might well nullify that. For a moment, Hal felt a tingle of doubt up his spine. Then he set his jaw in a determined line. He'd just have to play it out and see what happened, he thought.

Heron sliced into another wave and spray sheeted high on either side of the bow, drenching the sail handlers crouched by the bulwarks. Hal nodded to himself. The waves were getting steeper. That would slow the *Porpoise* down, he thought. The crew would tire more quickly as they hauled the heavy boat into the wind and the waves.

'She's dropping behind!' Edvin yelled triumphantly. He'd been measuring the *Porpoise*'s position relative to their own ship with one eye closed, and using the backstay rope as a reference point. After holding that viewpoint for some twenty seconds, he could see that the other boat was gradually losing ground.

'Where's *Lynx*?' Hal asked.

Edvin pointed to port. 'She's dropped further downwind. She's travelling fast, but she's making too much leeway.'

The wind was blowing the Wolves' ship further and further off course. They might be moving fast through the water, but they were heading away from the turning point.

Hal narrowed his eyes in concentration as he watched the flag that marked the next turning point. It was some distance away and from time to time it was lost from sight as the buoy dipped into the trough of a wave. They wouldn't turn at the buoy this time. He had to judge the moment when to bring the *Heron* onto a new course that would take her to the left of the flag.

He hesitated, estimating angles, drift and distance. Any minute now, he thought.

'Stand by to tack!' he yelled. Ingvar and Stig scuttled forward, the first mate holding Ingvar's arm and leading him over the clutter of oars, ropes and sail. The other boys crouched by the ropes, ready to let go on his command.

'Let go!' Hal yelled and, as the ropes were cast loose and the sail flapped wildly, 'Down port. Up starboard!'

Ingvar and Stig heaved on the port yard's halyards until the spar came free from the stirrup holding it at the masthead. Then as the sail and yard slid down the mast, they hauled the starboard sail up to the masthead. At the same time, Hal swung the tiller to the left, dragging the boat's bow to the right, into the wind, then across it, as the boat cut round in a neat curve.

The port side sail came down. The starboard sail slid up into place. For a moment, it flapped wildly as the wind took it. Then Stig and the others heaved on the controlling ropes and the sail shaped itself into that beautiful swelling curve again and the ship accelerated through the water.

'Haul in!' he heard Stig yelling and the sail handlers fastened the ropes, whipping rapid coils round the belaying pins set along the bulwarks.

He glanced over his shoulder and laughed aloud as he saw they were cutting across *Porpoise*'s path — and leaving her behind. Her oars weren't moving quite as evenly now, as some of the rowers tired and lost their rhythm. By contrast, *Heron* was flying, gaining on her rival with every second.

She cleared the turning point with twenty metres to spare. Hal heaved on the tiller, bringing the bow further to starboard.

Again, Stig and the crew hauled on the ropes to tighten the sail until they were flying down the third leg of the course. By the time the other ships reached the turning point, he'd be more than halfway along this leg. They'd made up the distance . . .

'*Lynx* is in trouble!' Edvin called.

Hal swung round in time to see the big square sail on the other ship crumple, then topple to starboard as the mast snapped.

'What happened?' he asked Edvin. The boy was shaking his head in horror.

'They tried to follow us through the tack,' he said. 'Rollond must have wanted to make up time.'

Hal stared back over his shoulder at the stricken ship. Tacking a square-sailed ship was a dangerous manoeuvre. Compared to *Heron*, the *Lynx* had further to turn across the wind, and she presented that huge square sail area to the wind through the entire manoeuvre. Without enough momentum to carry her through the turn, she'd stalled halfway, so that the wind pressed fully back against her sail. The mast wasn't designed to stand that sort of pressure from straight ahead and it had fractured.

Worse, the mast, sail and cross yard, with all their attached, tangled cordage, had crashed over the starboard side, smashing the bulwark and dragging the ship over in a list. Water would be pouring in despite her crew's desperate attempts to bail her out. Not that there were too many of the crew visible, Hal thought. Some of them must have been injured or trapped by the falling mast and sail.

Porpoise was rounding the second mark now. Her oars came in and her sail was rising up the mast. She seemed oblivious to the other ship's fate as she gathered speed down the third leg. Hal felt the deck planks vibrate beneath his feet as Stig joined him on the steering platform.

'What's happened?' his friend said.

Hal gestured to the stricken ship behind them.

'*Lynx* is sinking,' he said. 'Stand by. We're going back to help her.'

CHAPTER THIRTY-THREE

They came about and headed for the stricken *Lynx*. The *Porpoise,* sail now set and drawing well, maintained her course. The two ships flew towards each other. Thirty metres separated them as they passed. At the helm of the *Porpoise*, Tursgud stared resolutely ahead, ignoring the shouts and gestures of the *Heron*'s crew.

'He's leaving her to sink!' Stig said incredulously.

Hal shrugged. He'd expected no more of Tursgud.

'He wants to win,' he said briefly. Once more, his eyes were slitted as he measured speed and angles. As they came closer to *Lynx*, he could see more detail. The mast, cross yard and sail were dragging alongside, holding the ship over in a steep list. The tangled cordage held the shattered timbers firmly in place. He could see that the starboard side bulwark was smashed for a length of two metres, and water was pouring through the break. Four boys were bailing frantically while Rollond and another three of his crew hacked at the ropes holding the wreckage alongside. There was no sign of the other two crew members.

The *Heron* shot past the stricken ship, and Hal swung her in a rapid one-hundred-and-eighty-degree turn.

'Down sail!' he ordered and the sail and yard slid down into the boat. He judged the turn almost perfectly, washing off speed as they came back alongside the *Lynx*. Stig, ready in the bow, threw a grapnel at the other ship's stern rail. The three-pronged iron hook caught and he and Ingvar hauled the two ships together, bow to stern.

Ingvar might be nearly blind, Hal thought, but he was a godsend when sheer strength and brute force was required. The other crew members didn't need directions. They were poised in the bows behind Stig and Ingvar. As the two ships came together, they poured over the rail onto the *Lynx,* running to the aid of her crew. Ulf, Wulf and Jesper joined the men bailing. Stig, Edvin and Stefan drew their saxes and went to help Rollond cut loose the wreckage. Ingvar remained in *Heron*'s bow, holding the two ships together. With his poor eyesight, he'd be more hindrance than help on board a strange ship. Hal tied off the steering oar and ran forward.

'Keep them close, Ingvar!' he said as he clambered over *Heron*'s bow onto the other ship. Ingvar nodded, saying nothing. His teeth were gritted as he held fast to the rope binding the two ships together. Hal didn't want to tie the rope off. If the *Lynx* went down, he wanted Ingvar ready to cast it loose immediately.

As Hal ran forward, the ship lurched and came a little upright. He could see that Rollond and the others had finally managed to get rid of the shattered yardarm. It drifted astern. Axes and saxe knives rose and fell around the rest of the wreckage. There was no room for Hal to join in so he looked around for something useful to do. An arm was protruding from under the untidy mass of the sail. He cleared the heavy oiled cloth away and revealed the unconscious form of one of the Wolves. He carefully dragged the boy clear of the tangled sail and rope, lying him on the stern deck, out of harm's way — but close to *Heron* in case they needed to abandon the damaged ship. He went back and tossed folds of the sail aside to find the other missing crew member. It was Bjorn, the wrestler. He was conscious, but struggling and trapped in a tangle of rope. Quickly, Hal drew his saxe and cut him free. Bjorn nodded his thanks, went to rise and cried out in pain, reaching for his right shoulder. He grimaced as he met Hal's concerned gaze.

'I've wrenched it again,' he said, between his teeth. Hal helped him to his feet. Of course, he remembered, Bjorn's arm had been injured in his bout with Tursgud.

'Just got it back in shape,' the boy said, his teeth gritted. 'Now it's gone out again.'

Hal helped him move to the stern of the ship, then turned back to see how the others were progressing.

With extra hands at work, the wreckage was almost completely cleared. As Hal watched, Stig heaved a huge, knotted tangle of rope over the side. Rollond, Stefan and Jesper managed to cut loose the shattered mast. The others joined in and shoved it clear, using oars to keep the heavy spar from smashing into the ship's side as it drifted away. *Lynx* lurched back to an almost even keel. But water was still pouring through the break in her bulwarks. Hal looked around for something to plug the gap.

'Use the sail!' he called.

Rollond looked up at him as he gestured towards the hole in the ship's side. Then understanding dawned in his eyes. Together, they bundled up a part of the heavy sail and shoved it into the gap, cutting off the excess with their razor-sharp saxe knives. Stig, seeing what they were doing, grabbed an oar and jammed it against the folds of sailcloth to hold it in position. The flood of water slowed to a trickle and they straightened up, grinning in relief. Several of the *Lynx*'s crew slumped wearily onto the rowing benches. It had been an exhausting ten minutes. Rollond looked around, however, searching for the two crew members who had been caught under the collapsing sail.

'Where are . . .?'

Hal put a reassuring hand on his arm. 'They're aft,' he said. 'One's unconscious, but he's alive. Bjorn has hurt his shoulder again.'

Rollond looked in the direction Hal was pointing and saw his two missing crew members. His shoulders sagged with relief.

'I thought they might have gone overboard,' he said. 'Thanks for your help. I don't think we would have made it without you.'

Hal shrugged. 'Anyone would do the same thing.'

Rollond smiled bitterly. 'Some wouldn't,' he said. Involuntarily, they both turned to gaze towards the finish line. They could see the *Porpoise*'s sail as she crossed.

'I guess he wanted the points,' Hal said. Rollond snorted in disgust.

'He's welcome to them,' he said. 'I don't mind competing hard, but leaving your opponent to drown is another matter entirely. That's not the way Skandians do things.'

'Maybe he didn't see how bad the damage was,' Hal suggested, although he wondered why he was trying to make excuses for Tursgud.

Rollond shook his head. 'He was closer than you,' he said. He glanced over Hal's shoulder and grinned. 'Speaking of which, look who's arrived in the nick of time.'

Hal turned. The small boat with the judges on board was labouring up towards them. The four instructors had manned the oars and it had been a hard pull against the wind and waves to reach them. As they approached, they rested gratefully, slumping over their oars. Sigurd stood and hailed them.

'Do you need any help?' he yelled.

Rollond crossed to the railing and cupped his hands around his mouth to reply.

'Already got all we need!' he called back. 'We're fine. We've got two men slightly injured but we'll make it back to harbour all right.'

'We'll escort them in to make sure,' Hal added.

Sigurd looked at him for a few seconds before he replied.

'That was well done, Hal Mikkelson. And all the rest of you Herons,' he called. Then he and his companions set about the task of raising the small boat's mast and sail. After a few minutes, they were heading away towards the harbour.

'Is everything all right, Hal?' It was Ingvar, and Hal turned towards the big boy. He'd forgotten about him in all the excitement.

'Everything's fine now, Ingvar,' he said.

'Then can I tie this rope off? I'm getting pretty tired here.'

'Just hold on for a few minutes more, Ingvar,' Hal said. He looked at Rollond. 'Can you manage now?'

The Wolves' skirl nodded. 'We'll be fine. We can row back in. Although if you could lend us a couple of men, it'd be easier. I've got two of my crew out of action.'

Hal looked down the length of the damaged ship. Stig was the best oarsman, but if he was going to be short-handed, he wanted him aboard *Heron*.

'Ulf and Wulf!' he called. The twins looked up at him curiously. 'Stay on board and help Rollond and his men row home. The rest of you, back aboard the *Heron*.'

As Stig and the others filed aft and climbed back aboard their own ship, the twins moved towards the rowing benches. Ulf went to climb down onto one of the starboard side seats.

'Where are you going?' Wulf demanded angrily.

His brother looked at him, frowning. 'I always row on this side.'

Wulf nodded several times, still annoyed. 'Did it occur to you that I might like to row that side for a change?' he asked.

Ulf flushed angrily. 'No. It didn't. Because you always row on the other side,' he retorted.

Hal raised his eyebrows at Rollond.

'I'll leave you to sort that out,' he said, grinning.

Rollond watched the bickering twins with a puzzled frown.

'Are they always like this?' he asked.

Hal shrugged. 'Pretty much.'

Back in Hallasholm, there was an inquiry into the accident and its aftermath. Tursgud, of course, claimed that he had no idea how badly the *Lynx* had been damaged.

'But you saw the *Heron* turn back to help us!' Rollond said, disbelief evident in his tone. Tursgud, however, merely shrugged.

'I had no idea why they did that,' he said. 'That was their choice. We were in a race. I chose to continue. If I made a mistake, I'm sorry.'

Since nobody could prove anything to the contrary, no action was taken against him, although Hal sensed a distinct air of disapproval from their instructors — and several townspeople who happened to be standing nearby. Reluctantly, Sigurd awarded the points for the race to the Sharks, although it was noticeable that they showed a certain amount of restraint in their celebration of the win. Hal had the feeling that several of Tursgud's own crew disapproved of his actions.

By contrast, as he and his crew walked back to their quarters after stowing *Heron*'s yards and sails, he found that townspeople were approaching him, slapping him on the back and wishing him well. Word had quickly gone around the town about *Lynx*'s dismasting and the way the Heron brotherband had given up a winning lead to go back and help.

They were halfway back to their camp when they passed a ragged figure sitting on a low wall. Thorn, proudly brandishing his new wooden hook, nodded approvingly at them. Hal left the group and walked over to speak to him.

'Your father would be proud of you today,' Thorn said simply and Hal felt a prickle of tears behind his eyes.

'We lost the race,' he pointed out. Thorn shook his head.

'Maybe. But you won a lot of friends.' He slapped the boy on the shoulder. Thankfully, Hal thought, he used his left hand and not the hook. 'You can always win points,' he said. 'Winning people's respect is a lot more important. Now get back to your camp.'

CHAPTER THIRTY-FOUR

Erak stood watching as the *Raven* slid her prow smoothly onto the shingle of the beach. As her crew set about stowing her gear and setting an anchor firmly into the sand, Zavac dropped over the bulwarks at the bow and strode to where the Oberjarl was waiting.

'Good afternoon, Oberjarl,' he said smoothly. 'Did you want to talk to me, or are you just taking the air?'

'How are the repairs progressing?' Erak said bluntly. He had no use for small talk.

Zavac pursed his lips and turned to study the black ship. Several of the crew were bailing water out of her, tossing the bucketfuls over the side.

'She's still taking in water,' the Magyaran said. 'We've been out on a sea-test for the past four hours and we've been bailing her out the whole time. I think there's a seam close to the keel that's leaking. We'll have to haul her onto her side to find it. It may take a few more days.'

'Then you'd better get on with it,' Erak told him. 'Standing around talking isn't going to get the job done.'

Zavac allowed himself a smile as he tilted his head quizzically to one side.

'Why, Oberjarl, anyone would think you want to be rid of us,' he said.

Erak nodded briefly. 'I do,' he said. 'You've been here long enough. Get a move on.'

With that, the burly Oberjarl turned on his heel and strode away up the beach. As Erak's back turned, the smile disappeared from Zavac's face. He was walking back to his ship when he heard the Oberjarl's voice raised in anger and turned to see what the noise was about.

'Do you spend your whole day lying around drinking?' Erak shouted. He was standing over a shabby, tattered figure who was slumped against a driftwood log. Zavac recalled seeing the man around the harbour several times in the past few days. A beggar, he thought. And obviously a drunk, judging by the Oberjarl's question. Nobody important, he decided, and turned away again.

Thorn grinned up at Erak from his supine position and brandished a stone bottle with his new hand. The bottle was empty. And it had been that way when he'd arrived at the beach around noon.

'What do you think?' Erak said in a quieter voice, jerking his head towards the black ship.

Thorn pursed his lips. 'I think they're foxing. I've been watching them for days now and there's nothing wrong with their ship.'

'He says it's leaking. And they are bailing a lot of water out of her,' Erak pointed out.

'Which they could just as easily have bailed into her while they were at sea,' Thorn replied. 'I think they want an excuse to stay around Hallasholm a few more days.'

'To do what?' Erak asked and Thorn shrugged.

'Nothing honest, I'll be bound.'

Erak pursed his lips, then came to a decision. 'I'll give them another day or two. Keep an eye on them,' he said and, as Thorn nodded, Erak gestured at the polished wood device on his right arm. 'What's that?'

'It's my holding hook. See?' Thorn demonstrated, loosening the hook's clamped hold around the bottle.

Erak shook his head. 'Don't tell me. Hal made it.'

'He's really something, isn't he? He did well yesterday.' The pride in Thorn's voice was obvious and Erak nodded agreement.

'He did. He behaved like a true Skandian.'

'He is a Skandian,' Thorn said, bristling a little.

Erak shrugged. 'He's half Araluan.'

'It's a good mix,' Thorn replied, refusing to give ground, and Erak nodded.

'You could be right. Keep an eye on them.' He jerked his head towards the Magyaran ship, then trudged through the sand and shingle back to his Great Hall.

There were no lessons that afternoon, but a rumour had gone round that Sigurd would be springing a surprise inspection of living quarters and weapons late in the day. The Herons' tent had been a hive of activity as they cleaned and honed weapons, and folded and arranged their bedding and belongings in neat piles.

Hal walked around the tent, looking for any irregularities, any faults in the way items were stacked and displayed. As usual, he had to realign some of Ingvar's handiwork. The big boy had a tendency to just cram his bedding together with loose ends hanging out in all directions. He searched for signs of dirt on the floor or rust on the axes and swords. Finally, he shrugged.

'I can't find anything wrong,' he said.

Stig rolled his eyes. 'I'll bet Sigurd will.'

Hal shrugged resignedly. 'He always does.' He chewed his lip thoughtfully. 'You know, we've had so many drawn contests in the assessments, winning this thing could come down to the points lost and gained in these small items. So everyone check their gear again, then double check it.' He glanced to where Edvin had been totalling the points of each of the three brotherbands.

'How do we stand, Edvin?' he asked.

Edvin looked up. 'We're still in the running. We're not out of the race yet.'

Stefan grinned at the news. 'I'll bet that's surprised a few people.'

Edvin glanced at him then continued. 'After yesterday's result, here's how we stand: the Sharks are on two hundred and twenty points. The Wolves are on two hundred and five, and we've got one hundred and fifty.'

'With two assessments left,' Stig said thoughtfully. 'The night attack and the final navigation trial.'

'So we need to win them both,' Hal said.

Ingvar frowned. 'What's this night attack, Hal?'

'It's simple, Ingvar. There's a small hut on top of a hill. Inside it is a locked box with a slot in the lid. One team is set to defend the cabin. The other has to get past them and place a token — probably a picture of the team symbol — in the box. We take it in turns to be the attackers and the defenders.'

Jesper was frowning as Hal described the event. 'That puts us at a big disadvantage,' he said. 'We're two men short compared to the other teams.'

'Yes,' Hal replied unhappily. 'And knowing Tursgud, he won't be subtle. I'm betting his men will simply try to swamp us with numbers. If they take us one on one, they'll still have two men left over to get into the hut and place their token.'

'So you'll just have to come up with some clever plan to help us win,' Stig said.

'Well, thank you for that show of faith,' Hal said sarcastically. 'Did it occur to you that *you* might come up with some clever plan?'

'I don't do clever,' Stig replied cheerfully. 'I know my limitations.'

'As do we all,' Ingvar put in.

Hal smiled at him. 'More of your wisdom, Ingvar?'

The heavy-set boy nodded, straight-faced. 'I'm renowned for it. What about the other assessment? The navigation one?'

'We have to find a flag planted on an offshore island or a beach. We'll be given a set of cryptic clues on the day and we have to decipher them and follow the course they set us on. If we get it right, we end up where the flag has been planted. We retrieve it and beat the other teams back home.'

'Oh, we'll win that,' Stig said confidently. 'Hal's the best navigator in all the brotherbands.'

'If that's the case, what's to stop the other teams simply following us?' Jesper asked.

But Stig shook his head. 'Each team is given a different set of clues, and a different course to the end point. So really, with Hal as our navigator, we can't lose.'

'Don't be too sure,' Hal warned him. 'Tursgud is a good navigator, and Rollond is better than him.'

Stig waved a dismissive hand. 'Maybe so. But I'm betting on you.'

'Trouble is,' Hal said, 'if we lose the night attack, and the Sharks win it, they'll be so far ahead on points that we won't be able to catch them, even if we win the navigation exercise.'

'Well,' said Edvin philosophically, 'the worst we can do is come second.'

There was a silence in the tent and he looked up, surprised at the suddenly hostile atmosphere.

Stig corrected him. 'No, Edvin, the worst we can do is lose. And we're not prepared to do that.' He looked up at Hal. 'You see? You're just going to have to come up with a clever plan.'

'You keep saying that,' Hal pointed out.

Stig shrugged. 'And I'll keep on saying it until you do.'

CHAPTER THIRTY-FIVE

'Not much here,' said Stig, looking round the interior of the hut.

He and Hal were inspecting the site for the night attack exercise, set for that evening. It was an old shepherd's hut, built of pine logs with a timber shingle roof, and set on a small rise in the middle of open heathland. Clumps of trees and low bushes dotted the surrounding countryside, although an area thirty metres in diameter around the hut was relatively clear.

There was a rickety old table in the centre of the one-room hut, and a bed with a rope frame mattress stood along the wall opposite the doorway. Neither the bedframe nor the rotting mattress looked as if they'd support any weight. Some decaying blankets and pieces of sacking lay on the bed.

The doorway was the only entrance. Hal screwed up his mouth as he looked at it.

'I was hoping there might have been a small window

at the back,' he said. 'Something Jesper could sneak through.'

Stig shook his head. 'Makes it easier to defend. There's only one place an attacker can get in.'

Hal looked at him, an idea beginning to stir in his brain. 'One place. That's right. We can't change that. But we might be able to change the time.'

'The time? The time is tonight. How can we change that?' Stig said. Then he paused and a knowing grin began to spread over his face. 'Don't tell me. You've had that clever idea I've been expecting, haven't you?'

Hal was frowning thoughtfully and didn't answer immediately. Then he glanced up as he heard someone shouting their names. 'Hullo. What's got Stefan so excited?'

Stefan was running up the slope towards them, shouting and waving to get their attention. As he drew level with them, he paused, bending over, hands on his knees to get his breath.

'What's all the fuss?' Stig asked.

Stefan took a few more deep breaths, then spoke, a little breathlessly. 'The Wolves . . . they're out of . . . the competition,' he said.

'WHAT?' Stig and Hal chorused incredulously. Stefan, still breathing heavily, nodded several times to assure them that they'd heard him correctly.

'The *Lynx* is too badly damaged. They can't get her seaworthy in time for the navigation test, and you can't win the overall competition if you don't compete in all the assessments. And Sigurd says he won't have them as spoilers in tonight's contest. He says the winners should win in their own right. So they're out.'

Hal and Stig exchanged a long look. 'So it's down to us and Tursgud,' Hal said.

'And if his team wins tonight, there's no way we can catch them,' Stig said. 'How's that idea coming?' he added, a little anxiously. 'You know I have faith in you, but time is getting short.'

'It should be okay,' Hal said. 'I've just got to make sure that Tursgud's team are the attackers in the first round.'

The last light of the sun was dying away. Sigurd stood between the two brotherbands. Hal and Tursgud were either side of him. He handed each team leader a plaque with a figure drawn on it — a bird for the Herons and a shark for Tursgud's team.

'All right, you know the rules. Just before the start time, we'll place a locked box in the hut. The attacking team has to place its plaque through the slot in the top. We'll toss to see which team attacks first. Tursgud, your team is in the lead so you can call. Axes or bones.'

Hal studied Tursgud carefully. From what he now knew of the big Skandian boy, if he won the toss, he would opt for the more active role. It wasn't in Tursgud's nature to choose to be a defender. And if Hal won, there'd be no problem. He would simply choose the defence role for his team. But there was always the slim chance that Tursgud might not choose to attack. Hal decided that if the other boy won the toss, he'd have to goad him into it.

The coin spun.

'Bones,' Tursgud said.

Sigurd caught it, slapped it onto the back of his wrist, then revealed it.

'Bones it is,' he said.

Before Tursgud could speak, Hal said quickly, 'All right. We'll attack.'

Tursgud reacted instantly – and angrily. 'Just a moment! You lost, remember? It's not your call. If it's so important to you, *we'll* be the attackers. You can defend.'

Hal hid a triumphant smile, doing his best to look confused and embarrassed. 'Oh . . . sorry. I thought –'

'You thought you'd lose the toss and still decide how things were going to be? That's typical. Bad luck. You get to defend first.'

'Hey, don't make such a big thing out if it, all right?' Hal said.

Tursgud took a step towards him, but Sigurd interposed his bulky figure between them.

'That's enough! Get to your positions and deploy your men. You've got thirty minutes before the signal.'

'Come on, boys,' Hal said, and led the Herons away. As they went, he heard Tursgud's mocking voice behind him.

'Find a good hiding place, Hal Who. I'll be looking for you.'

'Don't look too hard for him, Broken-nose,' Stig replied. 'You might not see me coming.'

The Herons chuckled as Tursgud cursed angrily in reply.

The Herons formed a defensive semi-circle, some twenty metres from the hut. Hal settled into concealment behind a log that had fallen across two large boulders. As he peered out into the growing darkness, a hand touched his shoulder. He jumped in alarm, and turned to see that Jesper had appeared beside him.

'How do you do that?' he asked, his nerves still racing.

Jesper grinned. 'I'm a thief. It's my job. Have you got the plaque?'

Hal reached into his jacket and handed him the small plaque. Jesper put it in his own pocket then turned away.

'Give me twenty seconds,' he said, 'then start the diversion.' He began crawling rapidly away on his belly towards the hut. After he'd gone five metres, Hal found it almost impossible to keep track of him. He shook his head, then turned back to face the front. Deciding that twenty seconds had elapsed, he let out a low whistle.

Stig, five metres away behind a bush, rose to his knees and called out loudly. 'Herons! Everyone in position?'

From far out to the right of the line, Wulf's answering cry was heard. 'I'm here, Hal!'

'Me too!' That was Ulf.

'Ready, Hal!' Ingvar waved a hand from his position behind a bush. Hal had originally planned to place him in the doorway of the hut, as a last line of defence, but the rules prevented it.

'Jesper's here!' called Jesper's voice. Curiously, it came from a position well away from where Hal had last seen him. A second or so later, Stefan's voice came from the same direction.

'Stefan! I'm in position.'

Hal grinned. The mimic was living up to his reputation. He looked towards the hut and saw a shadow
slip through the doorway. Jesper was in place, he
thought.

'Edvin! I'm here.' That was close by. Stig had already
called so he didn't call again.

'And me,' muttered Hal. The roll call had probably
given away all their positions. But he hoped it had served
its true purpose — distracting the attention of the attacking Sharks from the direction of the hut while Jesper
slipped inside. He shrugged. It really didn't matter if the
Sharks knew where they all were. They were bound to
overwhelm the defenders anyway.

Although that wouldn't prevent the Herons from doing
their best to stop them.

The horn sounded the signal for the attack to begin.
Hal knelt up behind the log, peering into the blackness for
some sign of their attackers.

After some minutes, he saw shadows moving out on his
left and called Stig's attention to them. By the time Stig
looked, they had gone to ground.

Something rustled the bushes directly in front. Hal
peered in that direction, calling softly to Stig, 'Can you
see anyone?'

Stig shook his head. 'It's a diversion,' he said. Then a
similar rustling sound was heard from a position further to
their left — between the first movement and the figures
he'd originally seen.

'On the right!' Wulf shouted and, as Hal swung
round to look, he saw dark figures on that side going to

ground behind a patch of low undergrowth. His heart pounded. Tursgud's team were doing their job well, keeping the defenders' attention switching back and forth from one side of the line to another as they advanced ever closer. Once they got close enough, Hal knew, they'd break from cover and rush the defenders, knowing they had them outnumbered.

He had a sudden flash of inspiration.

'Look for Tursgud,' he called to Stig. 'He'll have the plaque.'

It would be just like the Sharks' leader to want the glory for himself. He'd taken the lead role for his team in all the contests so far. It didn't matter how many of the other Sharks broke through the Herons' line. If they could stop Tursgud, they'd win.

More rustling in front. Then from the left again. They were edging closer now. Any minute and they'd . . .

A loud whistle sounded across the dark field and suddenly, there were figures up and running at them from three different directions.

Three were running at the right-hand side of the line and he saw Ulf and Wulf rise from cover and sprint out to meet them. The twins grappled two of the attackers to the ground but the third broke through. Stefan came up from behind a bush but the attacker caught him off balance, shoving him backwards. Stefan rolled and came to his feet, setting out in pursuit.

But now two more shadows were sprinting towards them in the middle of the line, choosing their moment as Edvin broke from cover to help Stefan. They came forward, then went to ground again. Two more rose on the left, running like deer through the shadows. One of them lost his footing on the rough ground and went over. But he rolled to his feet and kept coming.

Stig rose to his feet.

'Wait!' Hal yelled. 'Wait till you see Tursgud!'

The two runners on the left had dropped into cover once more. Hal glanced around. His defenders were fully engaged now, except for himself and Stig. And Ingvar, of course, standing now and groping at shadows like a short-sighted bear. This was how he'd thought it would go. But with Jesper in the hut, he was even more short-handed than the enemy expected.

Seven attackers had shown themselves. Three remained hidden. One of them had to be Tursgud.

Hal rose and ran to where Stig was searching the shadows in front of them. Stig was their best chance to stop Tursgud, Hal knew.

'I'm going after those two on the left,' he said. 'Wait till you see Tursgud. He's got to be in the middle somewhere. He's got diversions on the left and right. Ignore everyone else and stop him. Understood?'

Stig's teeth flashed in a grin. 'It'll be my pleasure,' he said. Hal felt a moment of hope then. So far, he'd been hoping for a draw in this event. But if Tursgud ran true to form, they could even manage a win.

He rose from his crouched position and sprinted to his left, angling towards the spot where the two runners had gone into cover again. By deserting his post in this way, he hoped to lure Tursgud from cover. Then Stig could deal with him.

He hoped.

The two concealed runners saw him coming. They rose and started to skirt wide to their right — his left. He changed direction to cut them off, then heard Stig's triumphant shout behind him.

'Tursgud!'

Finally, Tursgud and two other runners had risen from concealment, only a few metres from where Stig was waiting. Hal saw his friend break cover and move towards the Sharks' leader, then saw Tursgud angling back towards Stig and realised he'd miscalculated. Tursgud had out-thought him. He crashed into Stig and the two of them rolled on the ground, grappling with each other. And as they did so, Tursgud's two companions raced for the hut and Hal heard his triumphant laugh.

Hal turned and raced towards them to cut them off. He might have made it, but the front runner suddenly switched direction and charged at Hal, putting his shoulder into his ribs and sending him crashing to the ground, winded and retching for breath.

Lying, groaning in the dust, Hal watched as the second runner, brandishing a white plaque over his head, plunged through the doorway of the hut.

The braying sound of Sigurd's horn signalled the end of the attack.

CHAPTER THIRTY-SIX

Sigurd carried the box out of the hut and placed it on the ground in front of the two assembled brother-bands.

Most of the boys were nursing bruises and scrapes and Sigurd shrugged fatalistically. Technically, they were not supposed to wrestle and punch each other. A simple tag should be enough. But he had never known one of these events where the boys didn't start throwing punches.

He unlocked the box and threw the lid open, revealing the single white plaque bearing the Shark insignia. Tursgud and his team cheered. The Herons shuffled their feet and looked surly.

'Bad luck, Stig,' Tursgud said cheerfully. He had a bruised cheek from his struggle with Stig, but the triumph of their win meant he felt no pain. Stig glowered at him. Hal put a restraining hand on his arm.

'Let it be,' he said quietly.

Sigurd handed the plaque back to Tursgud and re-locked the box, passing it to Viggo to replace it in the hut.

'That's a win for the Sharks,' he said. 'Now change places. Herons are attacking. Sharks defending. Thirty minutes to get into position.'

Hal led his team away into the shadows. About twenty-five metres from the hut, he stopped for a few moments by a pair of low bushes growing close together. He had noticed them earlier and marked them down.

'Bunch up,' he told his team quietly and they grouped closely around him, as if listening to tactics. Instead, he looked at Stefan and pointed to the bushes.

'In you go, Stefan. Wait till you hear me call, "Run, Ingvar, run!" Then start your performance. Don't make a sound until then. You'll be right in the middle of them.'

Concealed by his teammates, Stefan dropped to his hands and knees and crawled under the bushes.

Once he was in position, the rest of the team moved away, dispersing as they went into a long skirmish line. Ingvar, walking close beside Hal, touched his sleeve.

'Hal, I just want to make sure of something. You don't want me to run, do you?'

Hal smiled at him. 'No, Ingvar. I wanted a signal that I normally would never call out.'

Ingvar nodded ponderously. 'That's good thinking.'

'Just stay by me,' Hal said. 'I have other plans for you.'

The Herons dispersed, finding places to conceal themselves. Hal didn't go far. He settled behind a clump of small bushes with Ingvar, only five metres from the point where Stefan was concealed. Stig and the twins fanned out to their left. Edvin went right. Hal grimaced. It was a pretty thin line of attackers, he thought. Then he shrugged. Their real attack was already inside the hut. All he and the others had to do was create as much confusion and disturbance as they could.

'Start moving in, then pull back,' he'd told his team earlier in the night. 'Don't let them get close. Change positions as much as you can. We want them confused when it's all over so they won't know who was where.'

Now, he took off his jacket and draped it over Ingvar's head and shoulders, so that his silhouette would be shapeless and unrecognisable. Then he pulled the other boy's sleeves down to conceal his hands.

'Ready, Ingvar?' he said.

The other boy smiled at him. 'This is going to be fun, Hal.'

Hal nodded. 'Let's hope so. Remember, once you've done your act, I'm going to leave you here. Just sit down and stay quiet. If anyone stumbles over you, belt 'em.'

'What if it's you?' Ingvar sounded concerned.

Hal laughed quietly. 'I'll make sure it's not.'

Then Sigurd's horn blared out, signalling the beginning of the attack, and Hal held his hand up for silence. They were close to the line of defenders and he could hear whispering voices and rustling movement through the bushes as Tursgud's team moved into position.

They sat, hardly daring to breathe, for several minutes. The other Herons did the same, remaining motionless and silent in their various hiding places. More minutes passed.

Then, as Hal had known they would, the waiting defenders grew impatient.

'Anyone see anything?' a voice hissed. It was surprisingly close. Another voice, a little to the left, answered.

'Shut up! They'll hear you!'

He smiled to himself. He looked at the big form beside him, shapeless and indistinct with the jacket pulled up over his head. Any moment now, he thought. He counted to fifty, then reached out, putting his hand under Ingvar's arm and helping him to rise.

Ingvar stood and began to shake the bushes around him violently.

Almost immediately, Hal heard one of the Sharks team call out as he saw the massive form rise out of the bushes.

'There's one of them! Come on!'

He heard running feet crunching in the undergrowth and he yelled at the top of his voice:

'Run, Ingvar! Run!'

But Ingvar kept shaking the branches and swiping angrily at them. As he did, Stefan, concealed close by, let out a shattering roar — a perfect imitation of an angry black bear about to charge. The running feet stopped and there was a cry of alarm as two of the Sharks collided with each other in their haste to stop.

Stefan roared again — sounding even angrier this time.

'Orlog and Gorlog! It's a bear!'

'Let's get out of here!'

The running feet could be heard again, going away this time, as the pair blundered back from the line of defence, shouting in fear. Hal, choking with laughter, pulled Ingvar back down to a sitting position. The big boy beamed at him.

'If I hadn't known that was Stefan, I would have soiled myself,' he said. Then he frowned. 'It *was* Stefan, wasn't it?'

Now Stefan warmed to his task. He shouted out, in a perfect imitation of Tursgud's voice, 'Watch out, everybody! There's a bear on the loose! Pull back! Pull back!'

'Who's that?' the real Tursgud shouted, from off to the left.

'Who's that?' repeated Stefan, still in Tursgud's voice. 'Be careful, everybody. There's a bear loose!'

'There is no bear!' Tursgud screamed.

In response, Stefan let out another shattering roar, then added, in Tursgud's voice, 'What do you think that was? An angry squirrel?'

'Who *is* that?' Tursgud demanded in a fury.

And that was when Stefan had a moment of brilliant inspiration.

'That's you, isn't it, Stefan?' he bellowed. 'You wait till I catch up with you, you lop-eared runt!'

Hal applauded silently. Stefan's ploy was sheer genius. Nobody would expect the real Stefan to mention his own name, and remind all those listening that he was an expert mimic. Now the Sharks were totally confused, not sure which Tursgud to obey. Stefan kept the pressure on.

'They're breaking through on the right!' he yelled. 'Pedra! Knut! Ennit! Get over there now!'

'Stay where you are!'

'Shut up, Stefan!'

'Shut up, Stefan, or I'll kill you!'

'I'll kill *you,* you mean!'

Hal patted Ingvar on the shoulder. 'I'm off to cause more confusion. Stay here. I'll come back for you when it's over.'

He slipped through the trees towards the spot where the real Tursgud's voice was coming from. Stooping, he searched around and found several good-sized rocks. By now, it was becoming difficult to keep track of who was saying what, as Tursgud and the fake Tursgud continued to abuse each other. But he had a good bearing on the real Tursgud's voice. As he drew closer, he threw a rock in the general direction.

A figure rose from the bushes a few metres to the left of his throw. He recognised Tursgud's silhouette, pelted another two rocks at him and ran. Tursgud saw him, yelped with pain as the second rock hit his arm, then yelled.

'It's Hal! Karl, come over here and help me catch him!'

'What do you mean, you fake? Ignore Stefan, Karl! I've already got Hal!' yelled Stefan.

Then Hal's hair stood on end as he heard a voice that sounded exactly like his cry out in pain.

'Owwww! Cut it out, Tursgud! You're breaking my arm!'

Absolute confusion reigned. Then out on the left, Stig made a darting run towards the line and three of the defenders took off after him, yelling directions to each other. Stefan began yelling contradictory directions and Stig went to ground, crawling rapidly back into the bushes. Then the twins began to add their voices to the general confusion.

'Hey! I'm over here!' Wulf yelled.

'No! I'm over here!' replied Ulf, from fifty metres away. But their voices were identical.

Judging that the time was right, Hal put his fingers in his mouth and emitted a piercing whistle. Instantly, the fake Tursgud yelled out.

'Who's that whistling? Shut up or I'll bash you!'

But the whistle was a prearranged signal for the Herons to fade back, move to their right and group together.

They huddled behind the bushes — Stig, Ulf and Wulf, Edvin and Hal. Ingvar and Stefan, of course, remained where they were. Hal was silently counting, using Edvin's method.

'. . . eighty-nine jolly goblins, one hundred jolly goblins.'

Hidden in his bushes, Stefan was doing the same. As he reached one hundred jolly goblins, he rolled out into the open, came to his feet and began running to his left — away from the side where his teammates were assembled.

'They're on our right!' he yelled. 'Everybody this way! Sharks! Follow me!'

Dark shapes rose and headed after him. But only one of them knew he was a fake. The real Tursgud had been waiting for a sight of the person who was mimicking him. In a fury, he took off after the shadowy running figure. He rapidly overtook Stefan and hurled himself on him, driving him to the ground. Stefan curled in a ball, elbows and knees up to protect himself from the wild punches Tursgud was throwing. Then Tursgud, as Hal had done earlier in the evening, realised he'd been tricked. He looked up in horror to his left. There was a group of shadowy figures sprinting towards the hut. Leaving Stefan groaning and bruised, he leapt to his feet and screamed at his team.

'Get back! Get back! They're almost at the hut! Stop them!'

Three of his team heard him and followed at a run to intercept the Herons. The two groups came together a few metres from the hut and dissolved into a rolling, struggling, confused maul of bodies. From time to time, one of the Herons would break free and lunge for the doorway. But each time, he would be dragged down before he could make it inside. Gradually, the Shark team gained the upper hand as more of their numbers arrived to help. Finally, they had all the attackers pinned and restrained. Hal, breathing heavily, looked around his companions, counting heads. His heart leapt as he saw Jesper being held by two of the Sharks. The thief caught his eye and winked slowly. He'd been hiding in the hut the entire time. Once the brawl outside the door began, he had slipped out again and joined the melee without anyone noticing.

Sigurd's horn sounded — unnecessarily, Hal thought — and the contest was over. The four judges strode up to the knot of boys outside the hut. Sigurd gestured for the Herons to be released.

'Let 'em go,' he said. 'It's all over. Looks as if the Sharks have won. None of the Heron team made it inside.'

The Sharks let out a triumphant roar, grinning at each other. The win would put their score out of reach. They began to celebrate the fact that they had won the overall competition. Then Jesper stepped forward and spoke to Sigurd.

'Actually, sir, I did,' he said.

Silence fell as they all looked at him. Tursgud's face worked in a fury of concentration as he tried to remember if he'd seen Jesper when the brawl had erupted outside the hut. But it had all been so confused — rolling, punching, struggling Sharks and Herons mixed together — and he simply couldn't remember. The other Sharks were equally unsure, the smiles on their faces slowly dying as they realised their celebrations might have been premature.

Sigurd gestured to Viggo. 'One way to find out. Get the box.'

No one spoke as the assistant instructor brought the box out and gave it to Sigurd to unlock. As the lid went back, Sigurd tipped the box up. A small white plaque fell out. There was a crude heron shape inscribed on it. The Herons leapt and screamed in victory. Hal and Jesper grinned at each other and Stig slapped a big hand on his best friend's shoulder.

'I told you you'd come up with a clever idea,' he said.

'Shut up,' Hal cautioned him. But he couldn't stop smiling.

Tursgud, his face like a thundercloud, cursed silently as Sigurd declared the contest another draw.

'So it's all down to the navigation test. Day after tomorrow. Get back to your quarters now and get some rest.'

The Herons, in a tight-knit bunch, walked back to their hut, collecting Ingvar and a limping Stefan on the way.

'You all right?' Hal asked the mimic.

Stefan smiled wearily. 'He hit me a few good ones,' he said. 'But it was worthwhile. As for you,' he said to Jesper, 'I'll bet you're glad to be out from under that bed.'

Jesper grinned. 'It was a bit mouldy under there,' he admitted. 'But as you say, it was worthwhile.'

PART FOUR

THE
OUTCASTS

CHAPTER THIRTY-SEVEN

The two brotherbands stood on the beach, watching curiously as the black-hulled Magyaran ship rowed slowly out of the harbour. As she cleared the entrance, *Wolfwind* cast off her moorings and swung out after her with Svengal at the tiller, shadowing the foreign ship as she moved further away from land.

The four brotherband instructors were equally curious. Sigurd turned to a sergeant of the harbour watch.

'What's going on?' he asked, jerking a thumb towards the two ships.

The sergeant grinned. 'Erak's given them their marching orders. Sailing orders, rather. He doesn't want them hanging around Hallasholm any longer.'

Hal, seeing Thorn nearby, had walked over to ask the same question and received similar information.

'I've been watching them all week,' Thorn said. 'They claimed they had a leaking seam but I never saw them doing anything to fix it.'

'So why were they hanging around?' Stig asked.

Thorn shrugged. 'Knowing the Magyarans, they were probably looking for something to steal.' He grinned at the two boys, changing the subject. 'That was good work last night, by the way. I'm guessing that your friend Jesper was in the hut all along?'

Hal nodded, grinning in his turn. 'Yes. But don't go talking about it.'

Thorn raised his wooden hook to his lips. 'My lips are sealed.'

Stig gestured at the hook. 'That's quite a clamp you've got there.'

Thorn brandished his new right 'hand' proudly. 'Yes. I'm rather pleased with this. I'd say it's coming in handy, but that might be too much of a pun.'

'I'm so glad you didn't say that,' Hal said, straight-faced. But Thorn merely gestured to Sigurd a few paces away.

'You'd better get moving. Looks like Sigurd's handing out the navigation notes,' he said. 'Good luck.' He shooed them away, using his hook. Then he looked at it and grinned happily.

'I love being able to do that,' he said. Then he became serious. 'Good luck, Hal. You too, Stig.'

The two friends turned and walked down the beach to where Sigurd was surrounded by the members of the two brotherbands. He glanced up as they arrived.

'How kind of you to join us,' he said. 'I trust you *are* planning to take part in today's exercise?'

Hal and Stig exchanged a quick glance. For a second, Hal was tempted to reply in kind, but it wasn't beyond

Sigurd to hand out demerit points for sarcasm and, if he did, it could put the Sharks' total score out of their reach.

'Yes, Sigurd,' they mumbled together. He harrumphed at them and held out his hand to Jarst, who stood close by.

'Let me have the sailing instructions,' he said. Jarst handed him two rolled scrolls of parchment, sealed with red wax. Sigurd checked the first, then held it out to Tursgud.

'Here's yours,' he said. Then, as Tursgud went to break the wax seal, he hurriedly added, 'Not yet! You wait until you're a kilometre offshore before you read them. Your team instructors will ride along with you to make sure you don't cheat. Since there's just the two teams now, there'll be no points for the loser. It's winner takes all.'

He turned to Hal and handed him the second scroll. Hal regarded it curiously, wondering what he would find inside. He had no idea what form the sailing instructions would take. He had only been told that they would be 'cryptic'. He wondered what that meant, exactly.

He stood uncertainly, waiting for Sigurd to say something further. Or to sound his horn. That was usually the way the contests began, he thought. He glanced at Tursgud and saw that he was hesitating as well, eyes intent on the chief instructor. Sigurd seemed to become aware of their scrutiny. He raised his eyebrows at them.

'Was there something else?' he asked and they both shook their heads. 'Well then,' he continued, 'perhaps you might like to get under way. This is a race as well as a navigation test, you know.'

For a second longer, they stood there. Then Hal was galvanised into action.

'Come on!' he yelled. He shoved the rolled parchment inside his jacket and pelted down the beach to where *Heron* was drawn up at the water's edge. The rest of his team followed him at a run, then he heard Tursgud's startled yell and, glancing back, saw that the Sharks were running as well.

'Edvin! Get the beach anchor!' he yelled. Edvin was the lightest of the group and the best spared from the heavy work of launching the ship. The rest of them took up their positions and began to shove the *Heron* back into the water.

This was where Ingvar was worth his weight in gold, Hal thought. As the rest of them strained to get the ship moving, the big boy spat on his hands, then put his shoulder against the ship's prow, dug his feet into the sand and heaved.

At once, she started to slide, the sand and pebbles grinding under her keel as she moved. And as more of her length was supported by the water, she slid more easily. Judging that he was no longer needed to keep her moving, Hal scrambled up over the bulwark and ran to the steering platform in the stern. He glanced across at the *Porpoise*. She too was afloat. His team came scrambling over the bulwarks and threw themselves onto the benches. Free now of the grip of the sand, *Heron* was swinging gently under the breeze, her stern drifting round to parallel the beach.

'Oars!' Hal yelled, grabbing the tiller. The oars rattled and clattered into the rowlocks, sliding out to poise over the water's surface, ready for the first stroke.

'Hal!' Edvin shouted, pointing back to the beach.

Hal turned and swore as he saw Gort, standing ankle deep, grinning at them. They had forgotten to let the instructor board. He looked across at *Porpoise* and saw Tursgud had made the same mistake. Jarst, their instructor, was on the beach as well.

'Back port!' he yelled and the port side rowers backed their oars, swinging the stern around so that it came back to the beach. Hal leaned over the stern bulwark and yelled at the grinning instructor.

'If you're coming, get aboard!'

Hal's command signalled a subtle change in their relationship. Gort might be their instructor, but once on board *Heron*, Hal was the skirl and he had the authority to give orders to anyone. In addition, Gort could hardly complain about Hal's brusque manner. He was committing a cardinal sin in the Skandians' unwritten rules — he was delaying a ship's sailing.

Grinning still, he splashed forward till he was thigh deep, then leapt up and seized the bulwark to clamber aboard in a shower of sea water. Hal didn't spare him another glance.

'Back port oars, forward starboard oars!' he yelled and the ship pivoted neatly, turning her bow towards the harbour entrance.

'Thought you'd forgotten me,' Gort said mildly.

Hal simply glared at him. 'All oars ahead together!' he ordered and the craft shot forward.

But, fast as she was, *Porpoise* was faster still, with eight oars pulling to their six. And she was closer to the harbour entrance. For a few minutes, the two ran side by side. But *Heron* was slowly falling behind. Tursgud swung *Porpoise*'s bow to starboard, cutting across their path.

'Oars!' Hal called angrily. It was that or risk running into the other ship as she turned across them.

As the rowers paused, the smaller ship's way was checked and the Sharks surged ahead of them towards the entrance. In the grand scheme of a race that would take six or seven hours to complete, it was a small enough thing. But it was a moral victory and Hal and his teammates begrudged it bitterly.

'Pull together!' he ordered, once the other ship was clear. Again, *Heron* surged forward, arrowing down the white water of *Porpoise*'s wake.

They shot out of the harbour entrance into the open sea. Instantly, he felt the deck surge to one of the big rollers sweeping in. He rode the movement easily, looking up to the telltale. The pennant was streaming dead astern. The wind was right in their teeth.

He considered setting the sail. But with only a kilometre to cover, he judged they would reach the start point faster by rowing in a straight line, rather than the zigzag course they would have to follow under sail. He looked at *Porpoise*, now lying slightly off their port bow. She had increased her lead and her oars kicked up white spray as they bit into the sea and heaved her forward. He begrudged the Sharks their two extra rowers, but he had a little extra oar power up his sleeve.

'Edvin! Take an oar!' He glanced to where Ingvar was seated in the second bench port side and added: 'Starboard side!'

As Edvin took his place, Hal waited till he was ready, then called out to Ingvar.

'All right, Ingvar, pull as if Hulde herself was on your heels!'

Hulde was the goddess of the dead, and definitely

not someone you would ever want close behind you. Hal noticed that Gort surreptitiously touched a protective charm he wore round his neck at the mention of her name. Ingvar merely grinned, however, and heaved mightily on his oar. Despite the fact that there was an extra rower on the other side, Hal was startled to feel the *Heron*'s bow veer slightly to starboard under Ingvar's powerful stroke.

Gort raised his eyebrows, noting the slight swing and Hal's compensating adjustment of the tiller.

'What does that boy eat?' he asked.

Hal glanced quickly in his direction. 'Anything he wants to,' he said briefly.

Even with Ingvar's extra power, and Edvin lending his weight to the rowing, the *Porpoise* continued to gain on them. She was two hundred metres away when Hal saw the oars stop their constant beat and she gradually came to a halt, rising and falling on the swell.

'She's reached the one-kilometre mark,' he said.

Gort nodded, then looked around, judging the angles to two prominent headlands behind them.

'Keep going,' he said. 'I'll tell you when you're there.'

Hal drummed his fingers on the steering oar in a fever of impatience.

'Don't suppose you'd care to take an oar?' he suggested to Gort.

The instructor looked at him, pityingly. 'No. I don't suppose I would,' he replied.

'Would you care to steer while I row?' Hal said in his most persuasive tones.

'I don't think I'll even answer that,' Gort told him.

Hal shrugged. 'Ah, well, it was worth a try.'

But Gort remained unmoved. 'No. It wasn't.' Then, barely a few seconds later, he squinted astern, checking the relative positions of his reference points, and announced, 'All right. We're there.'

'Oars!' Hal yelled immediately and the exhausted crew stopped rowing and slumped over the oak shafts. Normally, they could row for hours on end. But that would be at a steady, measured pace. Instead, they had been rowing at top speed for the time it took them to reach the one-kilometre mark.

Gradually, the ship came to a halt. The chuckling sound of ripples along her waterline died away and she rose and fell on the swell.

Hal took the rolled scroll from under his jacket and looked inquiringly at Gort as he went to break the seal. The instructor nodded permission. As Hal broke the seal on the sailing instructions, Stig and Edvin joined him on the steering platform. Hal glanced across to where the *Porpoise* had been stopped. His heart sank as he saw that she was under way again, oars pulling rhythmically. Her stern was towards them, her hull visible only when she rose on the crest of a roller.

'What does it say?' Stig urged.

Hal forced himself to forget about Tursgud and his ship, and unrolled the parchment. Stig and Edvin leaned in on either side of him, peering over his shoulders.

'It's a poem,' he said, his voice betraying his surprise. He frowned at Gort. 'Is it always a poem?' he asked. But the instructor, infuriatingly, merely shrugged his shoulders and raised his eyebrows. No help from that quarter, Hal thought. The he read the short, six-line verse aloud.

'If to win this contest you do wish,
south-west to where the Liar finds a fish
then east-south-east two leagues you are required
to see a fireplace without a fire.
Put it to your back, plus two points nor'
until a V of trees are seen on shore.'

He looked at his companions. Edvin's face was creased with concentration. Stig looked up at Hal, a look of total incomprehension on his face.

'Well, I must say, that's a big help,' he said.

CHAPTER THIRTY-EIGHT

Hal studied the poem again, looking for the meaning behind the words.

'Where does a Liar find a fish?' he asked.

Stig pursed his lips thoughtfully. 'All fishermen are liars.'

Hal glared at him. 'I don't think that gets us very far.'

Stig looked offended. 'I'm only trying to be helpful.'

'Well, you're not succeeding,' Hal told him.

Edvin shook his head, annoyed at his teammates. 'If you'd stop squabbling, we might solve this,' he said, a little sourly. Hal and Stig both had the grace to look contrite.

'All right,' Hal said, 'who's a liar?'

'Not me,' Stig muttered, thinking Hal was criticising him again.

'Loki is a liar,' Edvin said. Loki was the Skandian god of deceit and trickery.

Stig amended Edvin's statement. 'Loki is *the* liar.'

Hal checked the sheet again, excitedly.

'The word "Liar" begins with a capital!' he said. 'That must be it. Now where does Loki catch a fish?'

The answer hit them all simultaneously.

'Loki's Bank,' they chorused. It was a popular cod-fishing site off the coast, where the sea shallowed over a large bank of sand. Many a sailor had, in years past, been deceived by the sudden change in depth — hence the name.

'It's south-west of here!' Hal cried, picturing one of the many charts he had memorised during navigation classes. He glanced at the telltale. The wind was steady from the north-west, streaming the narrow pennant out in a straight line.

'Hands to make sail!' he yelled to the crew. 'Raise the port sail!'

They were well practised now and the yard slid quickly up the mast. *Heron* came alive in the water again, speeding south-west, with the wind from their starboard side, at right angles to their course. They'd be making leeway, with the wind forcing them to the left, Hal realised, and he eased the tiller, bringing her course more to the right.

She plunged on, occasionally carving through a wave and sending sheets of spray cascading back over the crew. But they barely noticed it. The sensation of speed was exhilarating. It was possibly *Heron*'s best point of sailing and the entire hull vibrated under Hal's feet, setting up a deep, almost inaudible, hum. He grinned at Stig, who was standing beside him.

'Can you hear her? She's singing.'

Stig grinned back, his long hair streaming in the wind.

Stefan had the sharpest eyes in the crew. He scrambled up the starboard shrouds to the lookout position at the top of the mast. Forty minutes later, they heard his hail.

'We're coming up on the bank now!'

From his vantage point, he could see where the sea changed from deep blue to a lighter green as the sand bottom of the bank rose up out of the depths. They flew past several fishing boats, trudging slowly along with their nets over the side. Then they were over the bank itself and the waves became shorter and choppier as the shallow water broke up the deep-sea motion of the rollers. *Heron* plunged like a nervous horse.

'Ease the sail,' Hal ordered and Stig went forward to organise the rope handlers. As they eased the pressure on the sail, the ship slowed a little and her motion became easier. Hal checked the poem again.

'. . . *then east-south-east two leagues* . . .' he quoted. He'd need a way to measure distance travelled, he realised. He turned to Edvin. 'Get the reel ready to cast.'

Their new course would mean turning more than ninety degrees to port. Hal gave the order to come about. Stig and the crew carried out the manoeuvre smoothly, sending the starboard sail up to replace the port side one. Gort, who had been silent for some time, nodded approval.

'You've got them well trained,' he said.

Hal barely had time to acknowledge the compliment.

'Thanks,' he said briefly, consulting his sun compass for the correct bearing. Then, as he settled the ship on her new course, with the wind now over their port rear quarter, he nodded to Edvin.

'Let her go!'

Edvin was standing behind him, at the very stern. As Hal gave the order, he tossed a wooden X overboard. A thin cord ran through the crosspiece of the X, connected to a large reel that Edvin now held clear of the sternpost. As the X dragged in the water behind them, the cord began to unreel and Edvin started counting.

'One jolly goblin, two jolly goblins . . .'

There were knots tied at measured intervals along the cord, every fifth one marked with a coloured strip of cloth. As Edvin reached 'thirty jolly goblins', he stopped the cord and checked how many knots had run out.

'A little over six, Hal,' he reported.

Hal nodded as Edvin began to reel in the cord and the wooden X. He did a quick calculation. Unless the wind changed, it should take them just over an hour and a half to reach the spot designated in the instructions.

'Settle down, everyone,' he said. 'We've got almost two hours. So take it easy while you can.' He reached to the hourglass mounted on the bulwark and tipped it over to start the sand running. 'Keep an eye on that,' he told Edvin.

Heron swooped on across the sea, rising to the crest of each roller, then sliding down into the trough, where her bow would part the water like an axe, sending silver plumes of spray flying back either side of the ship. Hal glanced astern from time to time, making sure that the white path of her wake remained straight.

Gort watched approvingly. The boy was not only a good navigator, he was an expert helmsman. He noted the small, almost unconscious movements of the steering oar that Hal made to compensate for continuing variations in wind, wave action and current.

Stig had rejoined his skirl on the steering platform. Edvin stood nearby, watching the hourglass, ready to turn it when the sand ran out. The rest of the crew relaxed on the rowing benches.

'Time!' called Edvin, as the last grains of sand trickled through from the top of the hourglass. Quickly, he turned it so that the sand began running back the other way. Hal glanced at him as he called out.

'Let me know when it's half gone,' he said and Edvin nodded.

Gort leaned back against the lee rail, relaxing in the warm morning sunshine. After watching and instructing this crew of discards for the past few months, he had grown to admire their spirit and ingenuity. Although he was supposed to be impartial, he secretly hoped they would win the overall contest. That might shut up Tursgud's father with his boasting. He might be the Maktig, the Mighty One, but at times he could be a mighty bore.

'Time!'

Edvin's call rang through Gort's consciousness and he realised he'd dozed off, leaning against the bulwark in the sun. He smiled to himself. It was an old campaigner's trick to be able to sleep standing up, he thought.

Hal ordered the sail lowered and brought the ship up into the wind so that the way fell off her. She rocked smoothly on the swell. Gort looked around the horizon, sniffing the air. His seaman's sense told him that the wind had strengthened. He wondered if Hal had noticed.

Hal, Edvin and Stig were grouped together on the steering platform once more, puzzling over the sheet of instructions.

'A fireplace without a fire. What the blazes do they mean?' Hal muttered, not noticing the unintentional pun. He noticed Gort looking at them and said accusingly, 'Who wrote this nonsense?'

Gort shrugged. 'I think Sigurd did it. He rather fancies himself as a bard, you know.'

'I'm glad he does. Because I certainly don't,' Hal said.

Stig, who was methodically searching the horizon, shading his eyes with his right hand, stopped and touched Hal's sleeve.

'What does that look like to you?' he said. He pointed to a spot over their starboard quarter. 'There,' he said. 'That island.'

The island was delineated sharp black against the glistening surface of the ocean. Hal hesitated, but Edvin answered almost immediately. 'A house. A house with a tall chimney at one end,' he said. Then, realising an alternative interpretation of his words, he added thoughtfully, 'A fireplace without a fire, maybe?'

'Exactly,' Stig answered. 'A stone chimney. And where there's a chimney, there must be a fireplace. And this one has no fire in it.'

Hal rubbed his chin thoughtfully. 'Maybe,' he said. 'Maybe . . .' He looked around, searching desperately. But otherwise, the horizon was bare and he could see no other possible feature that might match the line of the poem.

'If we're wrong . . .' he began.

But Stig interrupted impatiently. 'We're not! What else can it be? That's it! The fireplace without a fire!'

Hal came to a decision. Stig was right. There was no other possibility anywhere in sight.

'All right!' he said. 'That must be it!'

He took out his sun compass again. This was an instrument similar to a sundial, which showed the direction of true north. Sun compasses needed constant re-calibration, but he'd adjusted this one only two days before so it should be accurate still. He aligned it now, his back to the distant chimney-shaped island, then took a bearing two compass points north of his line of vision. With only the open sea ahead of them, and no fixed reference point to centre on, he'd have to take constant bearings as they went.

'Make sail!' he ordered. 'Starboard side sail!'

As the crew hauled the starboard yardarm up, the pressure of the wind against the loose sail began turning the ship slowly to starboard. Stig and the crew hauled in on the ropes and once more Hal felt the thrill of the ship coming alive beneath his feet, felt the tremor of power in the steering oar. He swung the bow until the ship was headed along the bearing he had taken. *Heron* heeled over under the freshening wind, water slopping over her leeside gunwale. Stig eased the sail and the ship came a little more upright. He set the twins to bailing out the water that had come onboard.

They were running north of north-east now, with the wind almost on their beam. Hal had noticed that the wind had strengthened. He looked to the north-west and saw a dark line of clouds. He frowned.

'Hope we're finished before that hits us,' he said, to nobody in particular. Then, raising his voice, he called to them all:

'Listen, everyone! We're looking for two trees that form a V shape. My guess is they'll be on an island somewhere. Or maybe back on the mainland. I want everyone on the railings, keeping a lookout. Not you, Ingvar,' he added quickly, as the big boy stumbled to his feet and lurched perilously towards the railing. Ingvar smiled his thanks and sat down again. Hal continued.

'Stefan! Masthead again, please. And keep a lookout all round. We don't know where these trees will be!'

Stefan nodded and swarmed up into the lookout position once more. Stig and Edvin moved to opposite sides of the stern, searching long arcs to either side. Ulf and Wulf did the same in the bow.

An hour passed. Hal checked his direction every fifteen minutes with the sun but there was no sign of any V-shaped trees. Another half hour went by and Hal was beginning to feel the despair of failure in the pit of his stomach. What if he'd made a mistake? What if his bearings were offline? What if the island had been merely an island, and not the fireplace without a fire? But they were committed to this course now and had been for too long. There was nothing they could do now except plunge on like this, searching for the trees, hoping that they hadn't made a terrible mistake somewhere.

He glanced at Gort, hoping to see some sign in the instructor's body language or expression that he was either right or wrong. But there was nothing to learn there. Gort was slumped against the railing, eyes closed again.

'Island!'

It was Stefan, pointing to something off the starboard bow. Shading his eyes, Hal looked in the direction he was pointing. Slowly, the dark mass of an island swam up over the horizon. As they drew closer, he felt Stig's arm gripping his shoulder painfully.

'Look!' his friend cried. 'Look at the pines!'

At the top of a bluff at one end of the island, two massive pines grew side by side. But at some time in the past, probably when it was a young sapling, the left-hand tree had been pushed away from the vertical by a storm. Now it leaned at an angle to its neighbour.

'Two trees that form a V!' Hal yelled triumphantly. And the rest of the crew joined in, leaping, yelling, cheering and waving their hands like madmen. Even Ingvar was cavorting, once he was told that the trees that formed a V were in sight. Hal swung the bow downwind, signalling to Stig to adjust the sail to match their new heading.

As they ran in closer, they could see two small flags fluttering at the foot of the trees. There was a shallow cove with a strip of sandy beach beneath the bluff where the trees stood and he steered for it. He dropped the sail thirty metres from the beach and ran the ship neatly onto the sand, feeling her grate to a halt. He grinned triumphantly at his crew.

'All right. Let's fetch that flag and get out of here.'

'I'll get it!' Stig yelled and vaulted over the rail to the beach. He began to sprint up the sand.

Hal, his face one large grin of relief, slumped against the steering oar as he watched him go. Then Stefan's cry drew his attention.

'Hal!'

Hal swung round to look in the direction Stefan was pointing. Heading into the small bay, oars thrashing the water to foam, was the *Porpoise*.

CHAPTER THIRTY-NINE

Hal looked back to the bluff. Stig was halfway up
the slope now, slowing down as the ground became
steeper. Hal cupped his hands around his mouth and
yelled at the top of his voice.

'Stig! Hurry!'

Off to his right, he heard the grating sound of a ship's
prow sliding ashore. He glanced quickly to see Tursgud
dropping from the bow to the sand, then heading at a run
for the bluff. The Sharks' leader paid no attention to the
Heron and her crew, only a few metres away. The race
was too close now for any time to be wasted on insults. He
reached the foot of the bluff and started to climb. As luck
would have it, he found an easier path than the one Stig
had selected and he sped up the slope.

Hal looked anxiously at Stig again. His friend hadn't
heard Hal's frantic call and had slowed to a walk, out
of breath after his initial burst of enthusiasm. He had
his hands on his hips and his head down. Tursgud was

still running, leaping recklessly from boulder to boulder, gaining ground with every stride. And Stig was oblivious to the fact.

Hal called to the crew. 'Everybody call him! All together. One . . . two . . . three . . .'

'ST-I-I-IG!!!'

The sound of their combined voices echoed around the bay. This time, Stig heard them and he looked down. They saw his start of surprise as he made out the *Porpoise* alongside them on the beach, then a further jolt of alarm when he saw Tursgud, barely forty metres away and moving fast.

Galvanised into action, Stig started running again. He reached their flag and tugged it free, then turned to race back down to the beach. Tursgud passed him, going the other way. But now there were only a few metres separating them.

There was a spontaneous groan from the *Heron*'s crew as Stig slipped and fell, rolling several metres down the slope.

'What happened?' said Ingvar instantly.

Stefan turned to him. 'Stig fell. But he's up again now.'

And he was. But the fall had cost him precious time and Tursgud was breathing down his neck as they plunged down the treacherous slope.

'Careful . . . careful . . .' Hal muttered, in a frenzy of worry. If Stig fell again, it could prove to be a disaster. Even worse, if he fell and injured himself . . .

But he didn't. He kept his feet and emerged at the foot of the bluff, Tursgud close behind him.

'Over the side!' Hal yelled. 'Get ready to shove her off!'

The other six boys tumbled over the rail to the beach. In Ingvar's case, literally. He hit the beach awkwardly and fell heavily to the sand. But he was up in an instant and took his place at the bow.

To their right, the crew of the *Porpoise* were preparing to launch as well.

Stig, hampered by the soft sand, blundered up to the ship's bow. He tossed the flag on board and, exhausted as he was, set his shoulder against the ship's hull.

'Heave!' yelled Jesper, who had the good sense to realise that Stig had no breath for yelling commands. They strained against the hull and she began to move, a few centimetres at a time.

'Heave!' yelled Jesper again, and again they slid her a few centimetres. 'Come on, Ingvar!' he yelled. The big boy set his feet, took a deep breath and shoved with all his might. And suddenly, the ship was floating free. Ulf, Wulf and Stefan all fell as she suddenly moved. But they were up again almost immediately, the two twins blaming each other for the accident.

'Shut up and get aboard!' Hal yelled.

The crew of the *Porpoise* hadn't got their ship moving yet. Then Ingvar lost his grip as he came aboard and fell back to the sand again. Instantly, Wulf and Stefan went over after him, grabbed him and bundled him over the side of the ship.

'Oars!' Hal yelled. The little bay blanketed the wind. They'd have to row her out before they could set the sail. The crew scrambled onto the benches and there was a prolonged rattle and clatter as they ran their oars out.

'Back water! Heave!' Hal yelled. Out of the corner of his eye, he saw *Porpoise* beginning to move, sliding free of the sand. *Heron* began to gather sternway under the force of the oars. Hal waited until he had room to turn her.

'Starboard side back! Port side forward!' he yelled. With the oars working in different directions, the ship pivoted neatly. 'Ahead together!' he yelled and, as the ship began to move ahead, he heaved on the steering oar, bringing her round until she was heading for the open sea.

Jesper, knowing that Stig would still be short of breath, continued to fill in for him, calling the stroke for his shipmates. Hal saw that *Porpoise* was off the beach and had turned her bow to the open water. Her oars were beating like long, white wings.

'Faster, Jesper!' he called and Jesper increased the rate. The seven Herons strained muscle and sinew at the oars. Wavelets chuckled against the hull as she accelerated.

'All you've got, Ingvar!' Hal pleaded. Ingvar closed his eyes and complied, heaving with every ounce of strength he possessed. Hal compensated for the extra thrust on his side and the *Heron* moved faster still.

But, fast as she was moving, she couldn't keep *Porpoise* at bay. Behind him, Hal could hear Tursgud yelling instructions to his crew. Heard the lead oarsman calling an even faster rate to the other rowers. Then he glimpsed movement with his peripheral vision. *Porpoise* was overtaking them. Her bow was alongside *Heron*'s stern. Then it slid forward, creeping past them. He looked across and saw Tursgud's mocking salute as *Porpoise* took the lead.

She was thirty metres ahead when they finally emerged from the shelter of the bay and Hal could feel the strong north-west wind on his right cheek.

'In oars!' he yelled. 'Port side sail up!'

The clatter of oak on pine rang as the oars came in and the rowers threw them carelessly into the bottom of the boat. Then they were clambering over the benches to reach halyards and sheets and the port side yard rose to the masthead, clunked home, and the wind filled the sail.

Heron heeled sharply to port as they tightened the sail. The wind was much stronger now and the grey clouds Hal had seen were closer.

'Ease the sail!' he called and Stig and his sail handlers obeyed. As the pressure on the sail was reduced, *Heron* straightened up and began to fly. The wind was almost directly on their beam – their best point of sailing.

Hal didn't need his compass to set a bearing. He could see the coast of Skandia to starboard and he could see the sun. Their heading was west and he settled her on it.

She plunged into a trough. Spray flew, there was a momentary sensation of her speed checking, then she shook herself free and swooped up the face of the next wave, bursting through in a shower of spray, a third of her hull momentarily out of the water before she sliced back down and then repeated the process.

To port, he could see that *Porpoise* had her sail set. She was a fast sailer with the wind on her beam too. But *Heron* was faster and she was losing less distance downwind. As the small ship crept past her larger rival, the *Heron*'s crew cheered and yelled insults across the water. But the space between them was widening, as their courses slowly diverged, with the *Porpoise* going downwind faster.

For the first time since he had sighted the *Porpoise* entering the bay, Hal breathed easily, leaning on the tiller with relief. Stig climbed up from the rowing benches and they slapped each other's shoulders in congratulation. Stig glanced across the racing waves at the other ship, moving further downwind by the minute.

'She can't beat us now,' he said delightedly. Hal raised a cautionary finger. It never did to boast too soon, he believed.

'Touch wood,' he said, and rapped the tiller bar of the steering oar.

Stig grinned. 'Touch wood indeed,' he replied, and leaned over to rap his knuckles gently on Hal's head.

A gust of stronger wind hit them then, laying *Heron* over so that water sluiced in over the port gunwale. Stig filled his lungs to bellow an order, but already the twins were busy, bailing the water out. He glanced up at the clouds, which were rolling in upon them, racing in from the north-west.

'Wind's getting up,' he said.

A slightly worried frown creased Hal's forehead.

'We should be all right,' he said. 'It's a straight run up the coast, then we'll turn to make harbour. We'll be in shelter by the time it really starts to blow.'

'Touch wood,' Stig said and Hal nodded.

'Touch wood.'

The graceful, curving spar that held the sail suddenly creaked ominously. Two pairs of eyes shot to it.

'Is that yardarm bending more than usual?' Stig asked.

Hal shook his head. 'It's fine,' he said, without a lot of conviction. He sensed a movement from the direction of the lee rail and realised Gort had stepped closer. He too was staring up at the spar, watching how it curved under the pressure of the wind. Another strong gust and another groan.

'You don't think that yard is a little light, do you?' he said. 'Seems to be bending a lot.'

Hal pursed his lips. 'It's fine,' he said shortly.

'Maybe you should reduce sail — take in a reef or two?' Gort suggested.

Hal glanced quickly at him, then looked away. 'I haven't got round to putting in the reef points yet,' he said.

Gort raised his eyebrows. 'You haven't?'

Hal felt Stig's eyes on him as his first mate answered the question.

'It was just a small detail that he overlooked,' he said.

Hal glared at him. 'Maybe we should let the sail out a little,' he suggested.

Stig, still eyeing the yardarm apprehensively, yelled orders to the sail handlers to let out the ropes restraining the big sail. Hal felt the boat's speed drop as they did so. He looked anxiously to port, searching for the *Porpoise*. Even with their speed reduced, they were still gaining distance on her. They soared onto a wave crest and the wind, which had been masked for a few minutes, hit them even harder than before.

And, with a splintering crack, the port yardarm snapped in two.

CHAPTER FORTY

There was instant confusion aboard the *Heron* as the crew amidships scrambled to get clear.

The yard, snapped in the middle, hung drunkenly from the mast, held together only by the sail. The sail, only seconds ago a graceful, powerful curve, collapsed in an untidy shambles. The ropes of the sheets and braces that controlled the sail and yard snaked down in tangles to the deck.

With the sudden loss of power, *Heron* flew up, head to wind, rocking dangerously on the swell that surged under her.

Everyone was yelling at once. Nobody was listening to anybody else. Ingvar, seated on his bench still, looked around myopically, repeatedly asking, 'What happened?'

Nobody seemed in a mood to answer him.

'Quiet!' Hal yelled at the panicking crew. He tried again but his voice was drowned by their excited yelling.

He looked to Stig and made a hopeless gesture with his hands: *See if you can do any better.*

Stig could. He leapt up onto the bulwark, steadying himself with one of the shrouds supporting the mast.

'SHUT UP!' he roared and the crew fell silent immediately. They all looked at him. 'Just settle down while we work out what to do,' he told them. He turned to Hal. 'Your orders, skirl?'

Hal gestured at the sagging yard and tangle of sail and ropes.

'Get the yard down and stow the sail out of the way,' he said. He was grateful that the mast hadn't been damaged, and that the snapped yardarm and collapsed sail hadn't gone over the side. The Herons, with something definite to focus on, moved quickly to follow his orders. Once the snapped yard was lowered and the sail bundled untidily at the base of the mast, Stig looked to him for further orders.

'Out oars?' he suggested. Hal hesitated. He looked to port. *Porpoise* was just visible. She was still behind them and further out to sea. He came to a decision.

'No. Hoist the starboard sail,' he said.

Stig stared at him. 'The *starboard* sail?' he echoed. 'But the wind is from the starboard. The sail will simply blow back against the mast! It won't fill properly!'

Hal nodded. 'I know. It will lose a lot of its shape and power. But the wind is strong and we should be able to keep moving, even with the sail half collapsed. It'll be slow, but it'll be better than nothing.'

Stig shook his head. 'If you say so,' he said and ran forward to supervise the crew as they raised the starboard sail.

The wind took it instantly and Hal felt *Heron*'s bow swing away to port. He steadied the ship on course and, as Stig had predicted, the sail blew back against the mast, flapping and fluttering. He signalled to the crew to haul in as tight as possible. Slowly, awkwardly, as they brought the severely reduced sail under control, *Heron* began to move. Hal wrestled the steering oar to keep her on course. The inefficient sail shape made her difficult to handle. But after a few minutes, he had the hang of it.

She limped along at a vastly reduced rate. Still, he thought, they'd make better time than if they had to row her. He continually looked astern at the *Porpoise*. She was downwind, but she was gradually making up the distance between them.

'She's gaining,' Stig said.

'Not fast enough. We'll have her when we come about for the harbour mouth.'

'Maybe,' Stig said.

Hal grinned tiredly. 'Touch wood,' he said.

Stig rolled his eyes. Last time Hal had said that, the yard had split.

In spite of his assurance to Stig, Hal continued to watch the other ship anxiously as the *Heron* dragged herself along, parallel to the coast.

At least we don't have to worry about reefing this sail, he thought wryly. There wasn't enough power in the deformed shape to put excessive pressure on the mast or yard.

Gort had joined the two friends by the steering oar. Like them, he felt the anxiety that came from watching the *Porpoise* gradually creeping level with them. She was picking up distance laterally, but she was still a long way downwind. When the time came for *Heron* to go about, it would be a race to see if the *Porpoise* could make up that distance before *Heron* reached port.

Off to starboard, they could see the houses of Hallasholm now. Smoke was rising from the chimneys, to be almost instantly whipped away by the steadily freshening wind.

'Now?' Stig asked anxiously.

But Hal shook his head. The wind was almost directly offshore.

'We'll be straight into the wind and we can't tack from side to side. I want to go past so I have room to angle back in one run. Let's just hope we can sail a lot faster than Tursgud's crew can row into the wind.'

They all knew that as soon as the *Porpoise* was directly off the harbour mouth, Tursgud would turn into the wind and row for the finish line — and they'd have the shorter distance to cover. Gort went to say something, then realised that he should keep quiet. It was going to be too close to call, he thought.

'*Porpoise* is turning!'

It was Wulf, who was standing on the port bulwark to get a better view. They all looked and saw the other ship coming up into the wind, her sail disappearing as her crew released the sheets and halyards and lowered the cross yard. Then those twin banks of oars appeared as they ran out from either side of the *Porpoise*'s hull. Ominously, they began their rhythmic rising and falling.

'Now?' said Stig. He was hopping from one foot to the other with anxiety. He had no idea he was doing it.

Hal narrowed his eyes, measuring angles. 'Not yet. We need more room. But get ready.'

Stig nodded and moved into the waist of the ship, speaking to the crew, exhorting them to move at lightning speed when Hal gave the word to come about. He looked up at Wulf, still on the bulwark.

'Where are they?' he asked.

Wulf shaded his eyes and frowned. 'They're coming in fast,' he said. The strain was evident in his voice.

Stig looked pleadingly at Hal but his friend shook his head. They needed more room before they doubled back. He had to do it in one tack. If he miscalculated, they'd have no time to turn and crab back for another go. Tursgud would beat them.

Slowly, he raised his left arm from the steering oar, frowning in concentration as he measured the angle back to the harbour, pictured *Heron* flying in with the wind on her beam. A little more.

A little more. He was saying the words aloud. Like Stig with his dancing from one foot to another, he was unaware of the fact.

'Now!' he shouted, and threw his weight on the steering oar, heaving the bow round to starboard.

The reduced speed made her sluggish and for a moment he feared they would hang in the eye of the wind and be blown backwards. Then he heard a *whoomphing* sound as the sail filled and the bow came round, moving faster and faster as the ship accelerated.

'Haul in!' he yelled but there was no need. Stig and the sail handlers had the sail, now on the proper tack and blowing clear of the mast, hauled in as tight as it would bear. *Heron* slashed through the water, spray from the heavy cross swell bursting over her port bow as she shouldered her way through the rollers.

The feel of the ship was totally different now, like a thoroughbred after a plough horse. The hull vibrated. The rigging hummed in the wind. Hal leaned out over the rail to see where *Porpoise* lay. She was close to the harbour, although still on their starboard bow. Her oars were thrashing white foam from the sea. He measured their relative courses with one eye shut.

Neither ship was gaining on the other. They were heading for a collision at a point about one hundred metres away. Whichever ship was forced to turn away would lose the race — and the entire contest.

He looked at the sail, hoping they might find a few more metres of speed by re-trimming. But he could tell there was nothing left.

Fifty metres. Forty. Still on collision course. Hal swallowed. His throat was dry. Gort had edged closer to him, watching him carefully. Suddenly, he sensed that if a collision was inevitable, the instructor would grab the helm from him and turn the ship downwind, behind the *Porpoise.*

Then it happened. The harbour mouth was barely eighty metres away when a rogue wave, bigger than its predecessors, came at them from the north-west. *Heron*, taking it at an angle, slid gracefully over it, swooping down its back.

A few seconds later, the wave hit *Porpoise* head-on. The bigger ship staggered, checked momentarily by the impact.

On board, one of the crew was hurled backwards from his bench into the rower behind him. The ship crabbed awkwardly with the sudden loss of thrust from two oars. She swung sideways. The rowing crew scrambled desperately to recover and get the ship under way again. Tursgud, at the helm, dragged desperately on the steering oar to bring the ship back on course, but the momentary interruption was all the *Heron* needed. She knifed past the bow of the other ship, angling for the entrance to the harbour.

At the last moment, Hal laid the steering oar over and swung the ship's bow to port, slipping gracefully into the calm waters inside. He could hear the cheers starting from all around, then he looked up in horror and saw that *Wolfwind* was back in her normal position, alongside the wharf and right in his path.

'Get that sail down!' he screamed. As the yard slid down, he hauled the ship's bow further to port, scraping by the moored wolfship with only metres to spare.

He heaved a gigantic sigh of relief, and then the realisation hit him.

They had won. The Herons were the champion brotherband for the year.

Celebrations. Congratulations. Felicitations.

The outcasts, eight boys whom nobody had wanted in their brotherband, had triumphed and Hallasholm was going to celebrate in style, with an enormous feast held on the Common Green. The day became a whirlwind of cheering, back-slapping, and smiling faces. Hal was delighted when a certain blonde-haired girl slipped her arms around his neck and kissed him on the lips. Even more pleasing was the thunderous sight of Tursgud's face when Lotte did so.

Among the thronging, happy crowd, Tursgud was the one stand-out who refused to congratulate them on their success — although all of his crew did so.

The first to offer his congratulations was Gort. He slapped the lightly built skirl on the back and sent him staggering.

'Well done, boys!' he bellowed. 'I knew you had it in you!' Then he paused and added, more truthfully, 'Actually, I didn't. But I hoped you did! And you did!'

Rollond, surprisingly, was the second. He shook hands with each of them.

'You deserve it,' he said. 'You are the champions.'

But the most special moment came when Hal, shoving through the crowd of well-wishers in something of a daze, came face to face with his mother and, just behind her, Thorn.

He hugged his mam as tears streamed down her cheeks. She told him over and over again how proud he had made her. Then she stepped back and made room for Thorn.

For a long moment, Hal and the old seafarer looked at each other. Then Thorn gathered him into a crushing bear hug.

'No words. No words,' Thorn managed to croak, around a large lump in his throat. But the pressure of his hug increased and, when he finally released his young friend, Hal could see there were tears running down his weathered cheeks.

And that was worth more than anything words could say.

Then Erak was upon them, shoving his way through the excited, shouting crowd. He grabbed Hal in a huge hug, crushing the breath out of him. Hal had a moment to wish the Skandians could find another way to express their affection.

'Well done! Well done! You'd have made your father a proud man! You're a true Skandian now, boy, and that's a fact!'

Hal beamed. His heart swelled with pride inside his chest until he thought it might burst with sheer pleasure. All his life, he'd felt like an outsider. Now here was the Oberjarl himself, publicly expressing his total acceptance.

'Mind you,' Erak said, 'I told you those spars were too light.'

'You could be right,' Hal said. After the accident with the port yardarm, he was in no position to argue. But Erak's statement reminded him of something that was on his mind.

'Oberjarl . . .' he began and Erak slammed him on the back with a ham-sized hand.

'What is it, boy? Anything you need! You're the toast of Hallasholm today!'

The people surrounding them cheered and shouted their agreement. A few of them waved ale mugs to show their sincerity, and managed to slop ale over their neighbours.

'The wind's getting up still,' Hal said, 'and I don't like to leave my ship on the beach. It's a little exposed to the north-west. I'd like to get her back round to her mooring in Bearclaw Creek.'

'No problem there!' boomed Erak. He turned and yelled over his shoulder. 'Svengal! Where are you?'

His former first mate appeared at his elbow. 'Here, chief,' he said.

Erak put his massive arm around Hal's shoulders. 'Our champion skirl here is worried about his ship. Take half a dozen men and row her round to Bearclaw Creek. He has a mooring there.'

'Right away, chief,' Svengal replied. He turned away, calling the names of half a dozen of his crew to join him. Erak tilted his head questioningly at Hal.

'Satisfied?' he said and, when Hal nodded, he boomed at the top of his voice. 'Then let's get this party started!'

CHAPTER FORTY-ONE

Before the party really got started, there were certain formalities to be observed.

First, Sigurd declared that the members of all three brotherbands were deemed to have graduated from the training programme. They were now eligible to serve as crew on a wolfship. To mark the fact, each of the twenty-eight newly declared warriors was presented with a horned helmet. They stood in a large group, examining their new headware with pride. A few tried them on, and hurriedly removed them when they felt how heavy they were. Hal looked at his doubtfully.

'Not sure that my head is big enough for this,' he said to Thorn, and instantly regretted his choice of words.

'A few more hours of everyone telling you how wonderful you are and it should be,' the old sea wolf replied innocently.

Hal sighed. 'I walked into that, didn't I?' he said, and Thorn nodded happily.

Then Sigurd read through the scores and declared that the Herons were the winners for that year. The margin, taking into account some demerits that had been applied in the last week, was a mere thirty points. He called upon the winning team to assemble on the podium with him. The eight boys moved forward, deafened by the cheers of the crowd, and stepped up to receive Sigurd's congratulations. Then the chief instructor handed each of them a copper bracelet. These bracelets, engraved with a symbol of a heron, were tangible proof of their status as that year's champion team.

Hal looked at the copper band, his eyes clouding with tears of pride. Stig brandished his to the crowd and was greeted with cheers. Ulf and Wulf promptly began squabbling, each claiming that the other had received the bracelet meant for him, until Jesper told them sharply:

'They're exactly the same, you idiots. Just like you two!'

Then Gort came forward, accompanied by two Skandian warriors carrying a table full of weapons. Each Heron member was presented with a new weapon — corresponding to the one he had trained with. Axes for most of them, and swords for Hal and Edvin. However, unlike the notched, battered weapons they had been issued for training, these were brand new, well made and perfectly balanced — although, in Hal's case, his father's sword was far superior. Still, the presentation sword was a further indication that they were the champion team and he accepted it gratefully.

Then it was Erak's turn to speak. The Heron team was ushered into position either side of him. Hal was on his right hand, Stig on his left.

'What a brotherband!' he declared. 'A thief, a touchy first mate, a short-sighted bear, a joker, twins who can't tell each other apart, a bookworm and a skirl who doesn't know the right shape for a ship's sail.' He beamed at all of them, then added, 'I can't think of better qualities in a wolfship's crew.'

The crowd bellowed their agreement. Mind you, with the number of ale barrels that had been broached already, they would probably have bellowed their agreement if Erak had declared that from now on, the sun would rise in the west and everybody must walk on their hands when it rained.

He held up his hands for silence and the noise slowly died to a low hubbub. No crowd of Skandians would ever be completely silent.

'As you know, each year we have a special honour for the winning brotherband — to show them our admiration and our trust in them as newly initiated warriors.'

The crowd leaned forward and a mutter of anticipation ran through them.

'This year's winners, like all those before them, will be privileged to serve as the honour guard for the Andomal, for one night.'

Hallasholm's most treasured and valuable artefact was kept in a tabernacle inside a small shrine on the hill above the town. It was attended day and night by a rotating honour guard of six warriors, men specially chosen for their courage and prowess in battle. Only the finest warriors could aspire to guard the Andomal.

Hal looked at his companions. Like him, they were overwhelmed by this honour. He shook his head. They had been the outcasts, the unwanted ones, and now they would be guarding Skandia's most precious relic. They had come a long way.

'Your term as the honour guard will begin at midnight,' Erak continued. 'So I suggest that for the next few hours, you busy yourself with feasting.'

At ten minutes to midnight, the Heron brotherband assembled and, to the cheers of the celebrating people of Hallasholm, marched away from the Common Green. Under the direction of Erak and Sigurd, they climbed the steep path to the shrine, bearing the new weapons that had been presented to them. From here, they looked down on the town of Hallasholm, and out to sea. Hal paused, looking around at the spectacular view. He sighed happily. He wondered if life could get any better than this.

Then, he led the Herons to the foot of the earth platform where the shrine was built.

'Who goes there?' a voice boomed out. A large, helmeted figure stepped forward to the edge of the platform. As form dictated, Hal replied.

'The Heron brotherband, champions for this year. Here to relieve you as honour guard until dawn.'

'Then step forward, champions, and take our place,' the sentry called. The Herons began to surge forward in an unruly mob, but Hal's sharp command stopped them in their tracks.

'Stop! We'll do this properly, not like a rabble! Form in pairs. Stig, call the step!'

Hastily, they arranged themselves in two files and marched up the stairs, Stig calling cadence for them. They halted, facing the six guards, now lined up to meet them.

'Warriors, we relieve you,' Hal said. Erak had told him the formula to be exchanged. The guards grounded their axes and inclined their heads. More of a nod than a bow, Hal thought.

'Heron brotherband,' their leader intoned, 'we stand relieved. Keep safe the Andomal.'

'It will be safe with us,' Hal replied and the other brotherband members added a growl of agreement. The guards' leader stepped forward and shook hands with Hal. That was a departure from the usual ceremony, he knew.

'Well done, Hal Mikkelson,' he said. Hal felt his chest swell with pride. Then the warrior gave an order and, with his five companions, strode down the stairs, leaving the Herons with Sigurd and Erak. Erak shook hands with all of them, then bade them goodnight.

'You'll be relieved at dawn,' he told them. 'Enjoy the honour.'

Sigurd echoed the thought, then they were left alone with the Andomal.

'I'll take the first watch,' Hal told his teammates. 'The rest of you may as well get some sleep.'

It had been a long, hard day and the other boys needed no second urging. They settled down on the packed earth in front of the shrine, wrapping themselves in their cloaks or sheepskin jackets. For some minutes, there was a desultory buzz of conversation, then, one by one, they grew silent as sleep claimed them. Hal patrolled the edge of the platform. He was wearing the sword he had been given earlier that night, although he didn't expect to need it. The honour guard at the shrine was more ceremonial than practical. No Skandian would ever attempt to steal the Andomal.

Around him, the wind sang through the branches of the pines, sounding like surf. From far below, the noise of the waves on shore seemed to mimic the sound.

At the end of the first hour, he woke Stig to take over the watch and lay down to get some rest.

Stefan was on watch when Hal awoke suddenly. That told him it must be more than three hours after midnight. The mimic's dark silhouette paced slowly up and down at the front of the mound.

Hal sat up, stretching stiff muscles. He wondered what had woken him.

'Is everything all right?' he called softly to Stefan.

Stefan looked at him and walked closer so he could answer in a quiet tone. 'So far as I know. I was just about to wake Ulf to take over. Did you hear something?'

'No. I don't think so. But something woke me.'

Then he knew what it was. The wind had died. Earlier in the night, it had sung through the branches all around him. Even as he slept, he had been aware of its constant sound. Then it had stopped, and he could hear the sound of the waves more clearly. There was no sound from the town. The citizens had long since taken to their beds.

There was something about this sudden silence that he didn't like. The wind didn't usually just stop like that, he thought. He stood and strode back and forth, searching the darkness below them, his senses buzzing.

Then the first gust from the south hit him.

The wind had veered almost one-hundred-and-eighty degrees. It was now coming from the opposite direction and it was much fiercer than before. The pine branches began their mournful song again, but louder now as the intensity of the wind grew. He looked up. Dark clouds were scudding in from the south, racing to blot out the stars.

The *Heron*! The thought hit him all of a sudden. She was in the creek, at her mooring. But when Svengal had tied her up, the wind had been from the north-west and she'd been well sheltered. Now the wind was from the south-east and a lot stronger than it had been. And the little creek was more exposed to that direction. He wondered if Svengal had moored his ship securely. He should have. He was an old sailor, after all, and an expert seaman. But she was Hal's ship and the worry ate away at him. Perhaps Svengal had already been at the ale, he thought. Or perhaps he'd used single moorings. In this wind, Hal would have doubled the mooring ropes. But the wind hadn't been this strong seven hours ago. And maybe Svengal had been in a hurry to get back to the celebrations. And after all, it wasn't his ship.

Maybe . . .

He paced back and forth in an agony of indecision. It would only take him ten minutes to get down to the creek. Another ten to check the moorings, strengthen them if necessary, then ten more to get back. He'd be back in half an hour.

He knew that, as leader of the honour guard, it would be a serious offence to leave his post. If Erak or Sigurd ever found out he had done so, it would go hard with him. But then, there were seven other boys here to keep watch. And besides, it was a ceremonial guard anyway. Nobody was actually going to *steal* the Andomal.

'I'm going to wake Ulf and turn in,' Stefan said.

'What? Oh . . . all right. Fine. I think I might go and check on the boat.'

'Good idea. The wind has got up quite a bit.'

Stefan's immediate agreement helped to decide Hal. He nodded to the other boy, then plunged down the stairs to the bottom of the earth platform. There were two diverging tracks there. One led back to Hallasholm and the other ran in the direction of Bearclaw Creek. He hurried along it, breaking into a run as he reached level ground.

Heron was plunging and jerking against her mooring ropes when he reached the jetty. He checked the ropes but there was no sign of fraying or wear. Nevertheless, he doubled them, then, satisfied that his boat was safe, he turned and retraced his steps towards the shrine.

The tops of the pines were bending far over under the wind, and the branches were roaring like a heavy surf now. As he reached the uphill section of the track, a sense of urgency overcame him. The sky in the east was starting to lighten and Erak had said they would be relieved at dawn. He had better be back at his post by the time that happened. He started to run, then, reaching the stairs to the mound, he took them two at a time.

There was no challenge from Ulf as he came to the top stair and he frowned angrily. Even if Stefan had told him to expect Hal, he should have given the challenge.

Then he saw Ulf's figure, sprawled against a boulder, his arms pillowing his head.

'Blast you, Ulf,' he muttered. 'Sleeping on watch! What if I'd been Erak?' Then he realised he had no right to be angry. Asleep or not, Ulf at least had stayed at his post. Hal had deserted his.

He crossed quickly to the sleeping figure and leaned down to shake him. Ulf stirred, waving an annoyed hand, trying to knock away the intrusive hand that was shaking him.

'Get away!' he said, still half asleep. Then he raised his head and stared, bleary-eyed, at Hal. For a second, he didn't know where he was. Then realisation dawned and his eyes filled with guilt.

'Hal! I just closed my eyes for second! Honest!' he began.

But Hal was staring past him, to the shrine, and his face was a mask of horror. The door to the shrine was ajar, swinging slightly in the wind. It had been locked when he left. He knew that it had.

Forgetting Ulf for the moment, he pelted up the few stairs to the door, shoving it aside, his heart in his mouth.

It took a few seconds for his eyes to adjust to the dimness inside. When they did, he could see that the door to the polished timber tabernacle was gaping open, hanging drunkenly on a shattered hinge.

And the Andomal was gone.

CHAPTER FORTY-TWO

'**I** can't believe you could let this happen! How could you do it?' Erak's voice mixed scorn and fury in equal proportions as he faced the eight members of the Heron brotherband. The boys kept their eyes lowered and shifted their feet awkwardly. Erak let his glare travel along the line, but none of them was willing to meet his eyes.

'The Andomal!' he shouted at them. 'Are you aware that it's Skandia's most treasured relic?'

Again, no eyes would meet his. No voice answered his question.

'Do you have any idea how long it has stayed safe in that shrine? Any idea at all?'

The repetition of the question seemed to indicate that this time he expected an answer. Hal glanced to either side, saw his friends were still standing, heads bowed in shame. It was up to him to answer, he guessed. He was the skirl.

'Two hundred years?' he ventured.

Erak's blazing eyes trained on him. The other senior jarls present — members of his inner council — stayed silent. But waves of disapproval, and even hatred, emanated from them.

'Two hundred years? I should have known you wouldn't have bothered to study Skandian history. You're a high and mighty Araluan, after all, aren't you?'

Hal flushed, feeling his cheeks flaming. His anger welled up and he opened his mouth to reply indignantly, then closed it. He had no right to object to the Oberjarl's accusations. Anything Erak said, he deserved.

'We've kept the Andomal safe for three hundred and twenty years. Three hundred and twenty years! And you pathetic lot couldn't look after it for one night! I should have you flogged! All of you! And if I thought that would bring the Andomal back, I would do it — without a second's hesitation.'

The Great Hall, solid as it was, shook with a sudden gust of wind. The weather had worsened since the Herons had come running down to report the loss of the Andomal. There was now a full storm blowing from the south-west.

'Did you see or hear anything? Do you have any idea who might have done this? Any clue at all?'

The eight boys shook their heads. Erak took a deep breath and began to stride up and down in front of them. The main door opened, admitting the shrieking wind, which set the torches and candles in the room flaring. Gort and Sigurd, summoned the moment Hal had confessed the loss of the Andomal to Erak, entered. Another figure slipped in behind them. Hal, half turned, recognised Thorn. The old warrior remained in the shadows at the rear of the hall. Gort and Sigurd hurried to the front, where Erak and the six members of the council faced the boys.

'What's happened?' Sigurd asked. He had already been told by the messenger sent to fetch him but he simply couldn't believe it. Erak looked at him balefully, jerking a thumb at the line of boys.

'Your precious champion brotherband has let someone walk off with the Andomal.'

Gort turned away, a curse erupting from his lips. Sigurd, infuriated, took a pace towards the boys.

'Who? Who did it?'

Hal faced him. 'We don't know, sir,' he said. He had been through all of this with Erak. But Sigurd had a new question, one that Hal had been dreading.

'Who was on watch? Were you all awake?'

'No,' Hal said, fearing the questions that would follow. 'I set a watch roster so that one man was on duty for an hour while the others slept.'

'You SLEPT!' Sigurd shouted, his face only a few centimetres from Hal's. 'You slept while someone stole the Andomal? Who was on watch?'

There was a long silence. Then Ulf stepped forward, his head still bent in shame.

'I was on watch. I fell asleep,' he said wretchedly. There was an intake of breath from the members of the council and Sigurd rounded on Ulf in fury. But before he could say anything, Wulf spoke up.

'It wasn't him. It was me,' he said.

Ulf's head snapped up and he stared at his twin in shock. 'No,' he said, 'it was —'

'Me. I was on watch,' Stig declared. Then Jesper, Ingvar, Stefan and Edvin all chorused the same.

'I was on watch.'

'Orlog curse the lot of you!' Sigurd snarled. 'If you think this sort of clever nonsense is going to lessen your punishment, you've got another think coming!' He glared in fury at Hal as he stepped forward, out of the line, with his hand raised to gain his instructor's attention. 'What is it?'

'Sir,' Hal said, 'it doesn't matter who was supposed to be on watch. I was in command. The responsibility is mine.'

'You can bet your life it is!' Sigurd shouted at him. 'But that won't let these other slackers off the hook! They should have —'

He stopped as the door opened, emitting another huge gust of wind and a flurry of rain. Again, the torches and candles flared briefly.

All eyes turned as Svengal shoved the door firmly closed behind him. He was rugged up against the wild weather, in a heavy sheepskin coat, with a thick woollen watch cap on his head. Water dripped from him onto the floor as he strode down the length of the Great Hall to report.

'It was Zavac,' he said flatly. A murmur of anger ran round the council of jarls. Erak held up a hand for silence. Zavac had been the first person he had suspected, but until now, there had been nothing to support his suspicion.

'How do you know?' he asked quietly. Svengal moved closer to the fire, loosening his sheepskin coat. Steam began to rise from it as the heat of the fire hit him.

'We searched along the foreshore either side of town, as you ordered,' Svengal said. 'He must have turned back last night after we'd seen him on his way. We found the spot where he beached his ship. The mark was still in the sand.'

'How do you know it was Zavac? It could have been any ship.' Borsa, Erak's Hilfmann, put the question, although two or three others had the same thought.

Svengal regarded him and nodded. It was a fair question. But it was easily answered.

'The ram on the bow,' he said. 'It gouged a deep groove in the sand when they beached her. Much larger than the narrow mark that would be made by keel of a wolfship or a trader.'

That was the signal for excited discussion among the jarls, everyone talking at once. But Svengal raised his voice to get their attention.

'There was something else . . .'

From the tone of his voice, Erak sensed he had something unpleasant to add. Erak, his eyes narrowed, nodded for him to continue. Somehow, he knew what his old second in command was going to say. Svengal waited till the others had stopped talking.

'They killed two of the Town Watch,' he said quietly. 'We found their bodies close by the spot where Zavac beached his ship. Their throats had been cut.'

Another outburst of muttering greeted this news. Erak held up his hand for silence again.

'Who were they?' he asked.

'Keese Malletson and Pern Bighand,' Svengal replied.

Erak shook his head sadly. He had known both men well. 'They were good men.'

Svengal nodded. There was nothing more to say.

The sound of footsteps approaching from the rear of the hall distracted them all and they looked as Thorn emerged into the circle of light where the investigation was taking place.

'Then it's as well that the boys were all asleep,' he said.

Erak regarded him suspiciously. 'How do you figure that, Thorn?'

Thorn shrugged. 'If their sentry had been awake, Zavac and his men would have cut his throat as well. So at least we have that to be thankful for.'

Borsa was frowning. 'I can't help but wonder why they didn't kill them as they slept anyway,' he said.

Thorn looked at him. The Hilfmann had never seen action of any kind. He was an accounts keeper.

'It wouldn't be easy to kill eight people, sleeping or not, without making some noise and raising the alarm. There'd always be the chance that one or two would get away in all the confusion. Safer to let them sleep while the thieves got into the tabernacle and stole the Andomal. The wind would have covered any noise they might have made.'

Erak regarded his old crew member thoughtfully. 'You may be right, Thorn. And it's a good thing that we don't have more deaths on our hands. But even so, this doesn't excuse the Heron brotherband for what was the worst possible negligence. The fact remains, the Andomal was stolen on their watch and they have to bear the responsibility for it.'

Thorn sighed deeply and his head dropped. 'I suppose so,' he conceded sadly.

Erak looked at him for some time, then nodded, seeing that Thorn was not going to try to sway his opinion in the Herons' favour. He turned to Svengal.

'Get the crew of *Wolfwind* together. We'll leave at first light and go after Zavac.'

But Svengal was already shaking his head. 'We'll never make it out of the harbour mouth, chief,' he said. 'The wind will be dead against us and there are two-metre waves coming through the entrance. I've already had to shift *Wolfwind*'s moorings to get her out of the way.'

Erak smacked his fist into his palm in anger. 'All right,' he said. 'But get the crew aboard anyway. If the weather eases, we're going out at once.'

'I'll do it,' Svengal said. 'But don't hold your breath waiting for this storm to ease. It's going to be with us for at least two days.'

'Just do it,' Erak said, and his second in command turned and left the Great Hall. Erak watched him go, then turned back to the line of boys standing before him.

'All right,' he said. 'Let's see what else we know. Do you have any idea what time Zavac and his men stole the Andomal?'

The question was addressed to Hal. He considered for a few seconds, then replied.

'Let's see . . . Stefan was on watch when I left. I came back before the storm blew up and —'

'Just a minute!' Erak stopped him, his eyes narrowing. 'You came back? You came back from where?'

Hal swallowed nervously. He had known this information was bound to come out sooner or later. There was no point in trying to avoid it. His eyes dropped and he said, in a low voice, 'I went down to the creek to double *Heron*'s moorings.'

'You *what*?' Erak demanded, his voice rising in pitch. Sigurd and Gort stared in disbelief at Hal. He heard Thorn utter a groan of despair.

'I swear I was only gone for ten minutes,' he said. 'Twenty minutes at the outside. I was back . . .'

'You left your post?' Sigurd said incredulously.

Hal made an apologetic gesture with his hands. 'Just for a few minutes. Stefan was on watch. There was no need for me to be there.'

Gort looked at him coldly. Earlier, there might have been a trace of compassion or understanding from their instructor. Now there was nothing but condemnation.

'There was *every* need for you to be there,' he said.

Hal looked around for some sign of understanding. The faces of Borsa and the other jarls were stiff and unyielding. Erak's jaw was set in a grim line. Thorn wouldn't meet his gaze.

Hal sighed. His world was crumbling around him. He had enjoyed such high hopes the previous night, finally accepted as an equal by the Skandians. Now, he was a pariah — even more than before.

'You're all to blame for this,' Erak said. His voice was cold, his expression bleak. 'You, more than any of the others, Hal, because you left your post. And because you were the responsible one.'

'Yes, Oberjarl,' Hal said miserably. He wondered what their punishment was to be. He didn't have long to find out.

'Hand back those armbands,' Erak ordered. 'Do it now!'

The final three words snapped like a whip. Hal flinched, then looked down at the copper armband around his wrist — symbol of their victory, the symbol that marked them as the champion brotherband. Slowly, he worked his off his arm and stepped forward. Erak pointed to a table beside the dais where he stood. Hal dropped the armband onto it with a dull clang. The other seven followed suit.

'From now on,' Erak said, 'there is no Heron brotherband. Sigurd and Gort, remove all references to them from your records. The winning team will be declared to be the Sharks.'

'But . . .' Hal began. Then he stopped. It was right, he thought. It was just. And it was fair. Erak glared at him, waiting to see if he had more to say.

'Yes?' he prompted.

Hal dropped his head again and muttered, 'Nothing, Oberjarl.'

'Nothing indeed. Where are the weapons you were presented with? And the helmets?'

'They're at the shrine, Oberjarl,' Hal told him. Once they had realised the Andomal was gone, they had run immediately to the Great Hall. None of them had thought to pick up their weapons.

'Have them here by ten o'clock,' Erak said. 'Hand them in. They're the weapons of honourable Skandians and you have no right to them. Your helmets too.'

Several of the boys groaned aloud. The helmets were the sign that they had passed brotherband training. Now they were to return them.

'Everything,' Erak said coldly. 'They're all forfeit. All your property is forfeit.' He paused, then added meaningfully, 'Including your ship.'

'My ship?' Hal's head jerked up. 'The *Heron*?'

'Do you have another one?' Erak asked sarcastically. 'Yes, the *Heron*. I'm taking it.'

Hal's voice choked in his throat. Not his ship! Not the beautiful, graceful *Heron*? Erak couldn't do that! He heard a low groan from the side and turned towards it. Thorn was slowly shaking his head, his eyes fixed on his young friend. Then, as Hal watched, he turned away and walked out of the Great Hall, his boots ringing in the silence.

'Please, Oberjarl . . .' Hal began in a small voice.

But Erak ignored him. He turned to Sigurd and Gort. 'Adjust your records. The winning team was the Sharks. The Herons don't exist. As far as I'm concerned, they never did.'

The two instructors nodded grimly. Hal, looking around for some sign of hope, saw agreement written on the faces of all the jarls present.

'Now get out of here,' Erak said, his voice full of scorn. 'I don't want to look at you for a second longer. Not any of you. Go!'

Silently, the dejected Herons filed out of the Great Hall. Not a word was spoken as they followed Hal and Stig out of the town to the path leading up to the shrine. Hal was grateful that the early hour — it was just after dawn — and the wild weather had combined to keep the residents of Hallasholm indoors. He couldn't have borne to face the accusing looks of the townspeople as the news of their criminal negligence ran round the town.

Then he had a terrible moment of foresight as he realised that he would be facing those accusing looks for the rest of his life. He would be known forever as the person who abandoned his post and lost the Andomal. If he had been an outcast before this, things would be ten times worse in the future.

The taste of abject despair was bitter in his mouth as he led the silent procession up the steps to the shrine, to reclaim their weapons.

CHAPTER FORTY-THREE

Thorn walked blindly away from the Great Hall, oblivious to the massive wind that buffeted him and pierced through his threadbare coat, chilling him to the bone.

His heart was a lump of lead in his chest. Like Hal, he could foresee the future that lay before the members of the now-defunct Herons. They would be shunned, hated, reviled — Hal more than any of the others, because he was their leader, and an outsider.

Thorn loved the boy. Loved his enthusiasm and ingenuity and energy. And he could see how those qualities would be crushed out of him by an unending atmosphere of hatred and bitterness. The wind and rain whipped at his face and there were tears mixed in with the rain running down his cheeks. He couldn't bear to see that happen to the boy. He knew he wouldn't be able to stand idly by, unable to help, while he watched that vibrant young person ground into the dirt and destroyed.

For the first time in many years, Thorn wanted a drink. Not just a drink. A succession of drinks. He wanted to drink himself into oblivion so that he didn't have to think any more about the boy he loved and the fate that was in store for him.

Without consciously planning to, he had stumbled along the path to Karina's eating house, bent double at times by the wind. His dark little lean-to shuddered in the gusts, the heavy leather curtain that served as a door billowing inwards. He lurched inside and reached under his cot for a haversack.

Inside the canvas sack was a bottle of strong brandy. He had kept it here for years, ever since he had stopped drinking. At first, he hadn't been completely sure that he could stop, and so he had kept it because the thought of not having a drink readily available was terrifying for him. Then he had almost forgotten it was there. But this morning, he remembered. He took the dark bottle from the sack and unstoppered it. His senses reeled with the pungent smell of the alcohol and he raised it to his lips.

And stopped.

When Karina heard the news, she would come looking for him. He couldn't bear the thought that she would see him drunk once again. She would have enough sadness in her life when she heard what had happened to Hal. Carefully, he re-corked the bottle, placed it in his haversack again and plunged out into the wind and rain. He'd go to a quiet spot, free of prying eyes. He knew just the place. There would be nobody there today. He clambered up a steep path through the trees, then down the other side until he eventually found a secluded place, sheltered by a stand of pines.

He settled down on the ground and pulled his jacket closer around his shoulders. The wind moaned through the pine branches above him, sounding a counterpoint to his misery. Once again, he took the cork from the bottle and raised it. He hesitated, the powerful smell of it filling his nostrils.

Then, before he could change his mind, he hurled it away from him, through the trees. He heard it thump on the soft ground, then shatter as it struck against a rock. Brandy wasn't the answer, he realised. If he drank himself insensible, he would eventually wake up. And the situation would not have changed. There was only one solution he could see. He would leave Hallasholm. He could strike out over the mountains and find one of the passes through to Gallica or Teutlandt. Chances were good he'd die in the snow on the mountains, but he didn't really care too much. If he managed to make it, he'd make a living somehow. He had money — a lot of it. It was stored in his chest in Erak's treasure room. There was enough there to buy a small farm in Gallica. Or a fishing boat, perhaps. With the new hand Hal had made for him, he'd be able to handle a tiller.

Hal. The name struck a sword into his heart.

'A fine job I did keeping an eye on him,' he said. He looked up. Through the gaps in the pines, he could see the wind-driven clouds, racing across the sky, grey and melancholy.

'I'm sorry, Mikkel,' he said softly. 'I did my best. But I guess it wasn't good enough.'

As if in answer, he heard voices. Young voices. He frowned. They were coming from behind him, at the top of the hill he had just climbed. But they were too far away for him to make out the words. Staying low to remain concealed, he crept up the slope to get closer.

It was a sad and silent group that began collecting the weapons where they had left them by their sleeping places. Out of habit, the Herons rolled their blankets and stacked them neatly. Hal glanced up at the shrine. The door was still open and he walked up the steps and closed it. The tabernacle door was broken and there was nothing he could do about that. But the open swinging door of the shrine, banging in the wind, was a constant accusation to him.

He came back down the stairs to find the other seven boys standing in a loose half circle, waiting for him. He realised, with a sense of surprise, that they were still looking to him to tell them what to do next. He gestured to the weapons at their feet.

'I suppose we'd better hand these in,' he said quietly.

Edvin raised the sword he had received the night before and looked at it sadly.

'I was getting used to this,' he said. 'It's so much better than the drill sword they issued me.'

There was a murmur of agreement from the others. The new, well-crafted weapons and the helmets were the final remainders of their life as the Heron brotherband. Once they handed them in, that phase of their life, that wonderful, triumphant phase of their life, would be over forever. It would be as if it never happened.

Ulf looked round at his companions and said, shame-faced, 'I'm sorry, fellows. This is all my fault.'

For once, his twin didn't seize on an opportunity to upbraid him. The others shifted their feet, not making eye contact. Finally, Hal broke the awkward silence. The temptation was to scream abuse at Ulf for bringing them to this pass. But in his heart, he knew that would serve no purpose. From now on, the only friends this group had would be each other. They couldn't afford to alienate one of their number. And deep down he knew that he, ultimately, was the one to blame. That was the burden of leadership.

'Forget it, Ulf. Thorn was right. If you'd been awake, Zavac's men would have killed you.'

There was a mumble of agreement from the others. Maybe it wasn't wholehearted, but it was there, nonetheless.

'I guess it's really all over,' said Stefan miserably. 'What are we going to do?'

'We'll never get a place in a wolfship crew,' Stig said. 'They'll never forgive us.'

'I liked being a Heron,' Ingvar put in sadly. 'For the first time in my life, I felt people actually respected me.'

Wulf looked at him and laughed bitterly. 'Better get over that. From now on, being a Heron will make you a target. Everyone hates us. And they won't stop hating us.'

'We should stick together,' Jesper said. 'After all, we're all we've got.'

'But what can we do? Nobody will hire us, at least, not for anything worthwhile.'

'Maybe in time, they'll forget,' Edvin said hopefully.

But Stig shook his head. 'Not in our lifetimes. This was the Andomal, remember? They won't forget that we were the ones who lost it. Wulf is right. There will be nothing for us. No jobs. No respect. Nobody here will want anything to do with us.'

'We don't have to stay here. We could become traders,' Stefan suggested.

Ulf looked at him scornfully. 'Traders need a ship,' he said.

'We've got the *Heron* . . .' Stefan began, then he remembered. 'Oh . . . yes. They're confiscating that, aren't they?'

Hal had listened to them without a word. The picture they painted was a bleak one. But it was accurate. There would be no future for any of them in Hallasholm. So that left them only one alternative.

'I'm not going to let that happen,' he said quietly. They all turned to look at him.

'You plan to fight them?' Stig asked. His tone said he thought that idea was crazy. But Hal shook his head.

'Hardly. The way they feel about us, they'd be queuing up to kill us. I plan to take the *Heron* and sail away — if enough of you will come with me to form a crew.'

Now the idea was out in the open. It was a definite proposal and not just wild talk. They all fell silent, thinking about it.

'But this is our home,' Edvin said uncertainly, breaking the silence.

Hal nodded. 'It is. But it's not going to be much of a home for us from now on.'

'I'll go with you, Hal,' Ingvar declared suddenly. He ran his short-sighted gaze around the blurred group of figures. 'Who else is with us?'

Hal looked at the big boy in surprise. He had honestly expected that Stig might be the first to volunteer to go with him. He looked now at his best friend, a note of appeal in his voice.

'Stig?' he said. 'How about you?' He hated the fact that he had to ask. But he knew that, without Stig, he couldn't do it.

Stig shuffled his feet awkwardly. His face flushed.

'I don't know. I hate the idea of just running away. It's kind of cowardly, I guess,' he said apologetically.

Hal nodded. He should have known better. Stig's first instinct always would be to face up to a problem and try to batter it down. Stig preferred positive action to simply slinking away. But he had misinterpreted Hal's intention.

'I'm not planning on just running away,' Hal said. 'I plan to go after Zavac and get the Andomal back.'

That got their attention. Now there was a glimmer of interest in their eyes.

'Don't you see?' He pressed his advantage. 'This is the only way we can ever put things right! This is the only way we can ever live normal lives here. We won't be remembered as the people who lost the Andomal. We'll be the people who got it back!'

Stig's face was split by a huge grin. He moved towards Hal and gripped his hand, pumping it furiously.

'Now you're talking!' he said enthusiastically. 'Count me in!'

'Me too!' said Ulf and Wulf in a chorus. Then they turned on each other.

'I said it first!' said Wulf.

'The heck you did!' Ulf told him. 'I was always going to —'

'Stop!' Hal yelled at them. But in spite of the situation, he couldn't help laughing. These two would never change. They looked up at him, confused, then they smiled.

'Sorry, Hal,' they chorused.

'I suppose you could use a good thief on your journey,' Jesper said. 'I'll come.'

'Me too,' Stefan said, grinning. That left only Edvin. They all turned to look at him. He was frowning.

'Catch Zavac and get the Andomal back?' he said thoughtfully. 'It's a big ask. Do you really think we have the slightest chance?'

Hal went to answer, but Ingvar forestalled him.

'Put it this way, Edvin. We never had *any* chance of beating the Wolves and the Sharks. But we did. Because we're the Heron brotherband. And we can do anything we set our minds to.'

Slowly Edvin began to smile. 'Thanks for reminding me of that, Ingvar,' he said.

The big boy sniffed derisively. 'I've told you before. I'm short-sighted, not stupid.'

'All right,' Edvin said, addressing Hal. 'I'm in too. But there are practical matters we should consider.'

Stig groaned. 'Do we *have* to?' he asked. 'I hate practical matters.'

'So I've noticed,' Edvin told him. But then he went on. 'We're going to need supplies and tools and money and stores for the ship.'

'Stores and tools are fine. I've got plenty at the work site at Bearclaw Creek. Supplies I can get from my mother's storehouse. I'm sure she'll forgive me.' Hal added the last a little guiltily. He hated the idea of stealing from his mam, but he could see no other way.

The others nodded. They were eager now to get moving.

'We've got our weapons, and all the other kit we'll need is at our barracks,' Hal said. Then he held up a warning hand. 'One thing,' he said. 'You can't tell anybody. If word gets out, Erak will stop us. Leave notes for your families if you have to. But don't tell them what we're doing.'

He glanced at the sun. 'I figure we have about three hours before Erak expects us to hand in our weapons. We need that time to load the ship. If anyone gets wind of what we're up to, it's all over.'

'What about money?' Edvin asked. 'Whatever supplies you can get won't last forever. We'll need to buy more.'

Hal hesitated. 'Maybe we can become traders, as Stefan suggested. Carry passengers or cargo. We'll manage somehow.'

'I've got money,' said a new voice. 'I've got all we'll need.'

They turned, startled, as Thorn emerged from behind the shrine, where he had been listening.

'Thorn!' said Hal, with a delighted grin. 'Where did you spring from? And what do you mean, "all we'll need"?'

'I've been listening back there since you got here,' Thorn told them. 'And I have to say, I think this is the only thing you can do. Unless you want to spend the rest of your lives as outcasts. And believe me, that's no life. I know.'

The Herons exchanged excited grins. Somehow, it bolstered their confidence to have an outsider confirm that they were doing the right thing.

'As for "all we'll need", I'm coming with you, if you'll have me. I was planning on leaving anyway, and this will save me a long, cold walk over the mountains.'

Impulsively, Hal darted forward and threw his arms around the old sea wolf's neck.

'You're welcome on my ship any time!' he declared, and the other boys chorused their agreement.

When Hal released Thorn, Stig stepped forward and shook his hand firmly.

'It'll be great to have you along, Thorn,' he said and their eyes met for a few seconds. Thorn nodded meaningfully. Any problems they might have had in the past were behind them. He turned back to Hal.

'One thing. You're not going to rob your mother's storeroom. Take what you need, but I'll give you gold to pay for it.'

'Yes, Thorn,' Hal replied. He felt a weight rise from his shoulders.

But now Jesper had a question. 'Hal, how are we going to get *Heron* to sea? I heard Svengal say it'd be two days before this storm blew out.'

Hal nodded. 'The harbour entrance faces south-west — right into the storm. Bearclaw Creek faces the same way, but in the last hundred metres, it takes a sharp turn to the left. So we'll be coming out with the wind directly on our starboard beam. We'll manage it easily.'

'If the wind's from starboard,' Stig pointed out, 'we'll need to use the port yard. And we haven't repaired it. Do we have time to do that?'

Hal considered briefly, then came a decision. 'Transfer the starboard yard to the port side,' he said. 'We'll repair the port yard when we're down the coast. We need to get away from here first.'

He looked around the group.

'Stefan, Ingvar, you come with me and we'll get the supplies. Thorn, you go fetch your money from Erak's treasure room and meet us back at Mam's storehouse. The rest of you, pick up your kit from the barracks tent — sleeping gear, clothes, tools, extra weapons, any personal items you've got. Get ours as well — and don't forget my crossbow. Then get to the boat. Stig, shift the starboard yard and sail to the port side.'

He paused, wondering if there was anything he'd left out. He couldn't think of anything, but he'd probably remember something once they were under way. He looked at Stig, grinning.

'Any "small details" I might have forgotten?' he asked and his friend grinned in return.

'You mean aside from how we're going to find Zavac?' he said. 'I don't think so.'

CHAPTER FORTY-FOUR

E rak was supervising the loading of stores into *Wolfwind* when Tursgud approached him.

'Oberjarl? I wonder if I could have a word with you?'

Erak regarded him. At the best of times, he had a strong dislike for Tursgud. And this was far from the best of times.

'You appear to be doing that already,' he pointed out coldly and Tursgud smiled, determined to maintain a feeling of good fellowship.

'Well, yes. But I just wanted to take the opportunity to thank you.'

'For what?' Erak asked, then turned away to berate a seaman lifting a net of clay jars onto the ship. 'Careful there! Those things are breakable, you hamfisted idiot!' He turned back to Tursgud. 'For what?' he repeated.

'For reinstating my team as the champion brother-band,' Tursgud told him. 'We're all grateful to you.'

'Reinstating you? I don't recall that we reinstated you. I recall that you lost and then the team that beat you was disbanded.'

Tursgud shrugged. 'Yes, well, same thing really. Everyone knows they fluked the win — that we were the rightful winners.'

'Everyone knows that, do they? Not there, you fool! Further astern to distribute the weight!'

'Sorry, Oberjarl!' came the cry from another offending sailor.

'I mean, I can't say I'm surprised that they let you down so badly. To have the Andomal stolen like that, right from under their noses . . .' Tursgud stopped, as if words had failed him.

Erak turned an unfriendly eye on him. 'Try not to be too thrilled about that, would you?'

Tursgud hurriedly composed his face and said, in a more serious manner, 'Anyway, we wanted to volunteer to join you when you go after the Magyaran ship.'

'Who wanted to volunteer?'

'My men. The Sharks brotherband. The champions.' Tursgud drew himself up proudly as he said the name. But Erak was already shaking his head.

'I've got a crew,' he said flatly.

Tursgud hesitated, taking that in. Then he tried another tack.

'Well then, perhaps I could join your crew?' he said.

'No. I don't think so,' Erak told him. But then he was distracted by the sound of someone calling his name. He looked up to see one of the Town Watch running along the beach towards him.

'Oberjarl! Oberjarl!'

As the man came closer, he slowed to a trot, then pulled up in front of Erak, sucking in lungfuls of the frigid air. His breath came in clouds of steam as he panted.

'Something wrong?' Erak asked.

'They've gone!' the man said. 'All of them!'

'All of who?' Erak asked and the man, still panting heavily, waved a vague hand in the general direction of the brotherband training ground, high in the hills above the town.

'The team . . . the brotherband. The Herons,' he said.

Tursgud stepped forward and gripped the man's jacket.

'Gone? Gone where?' he demanded. The man looked at him, an expression of distaste on his face, then reached up and detached Tursgud's hand from his lapel.

'Keep your hands to yourself, boy,' he said. Then he turned back to Erak.

'I checked the shrine, and then their barracks. Their bedding and equipment is all gone. They're gone.'

'Stop saying that!' Tursgud shouted, his voice cracking. 'Where have they gone?'

'They've gone to get the Andomal back,' said a new voice. They turned to see Karina standing a few metres away. She had a sheet of paper in her hand. She held it up now.

'Hal left me a note. Said there was nothing here for them now so they were going to get the Andomal back to make things right.'

'Hah!' The derisive sound exploded from Tursgud. 'As if they could!'

Karina turned a withering glare upon him and Erak placed a heavy hand on his shoulders, gripping the muscles and tendons there until Tursgud winced and shifted with the pain.

'One day,' Erak told him, 'you'll learn to keep your mouth shut. Let me know when that happens, will you?' He shoved Tursgud away from him. For a moment the boy debated whether to try to regain Erak's favour. Then he decided against it and walked away.

Karina waited till he was gone, then said in a low voice, 'You were too hard on them, Erak. You left them no hope.'

'They let down the whole town, Karina. The whole country, in fact.'

But she wouldn't have it. 'They made a mistake, that's all. They're only boys.'

Now Erak was shaking his head at her. 'They're not boys any more, Karina. That's the whole point of the brotherband programme. They're qualified now as warriors.'

'All the same . . .' she began, but a cry from the watch tower interrupted her.

'Sail! Sail to the east!'

They looked in the direction he was pointing. They could just make out a tiny, triangular sail, emerging from behind Bearclaw Headland and speeding south-east, away from the coast.

'It's the *Heron*!' the lookout cried in surprise. There was no mistaking that sail shape. Most of those present surged up onto the harbour mole for a better view. Erak and Karina followed more slowly.

Erak stopped, shading his eyes and looking after the rapidly receding white triangle.

'Well done, boys,' he said in a low voice. 'May Ullr guide you.' Ullr was the god of hunters. He looked back at Karina now and said, not unkindly, 'This was their only chance for any sort of life.'

She frowned at him. 'You knew they'd do this?'

He smiled sadly at her. 'Why do you think I gave them until ten o'clock to hand in their weapons?'

He turned to look back to the south-east, but a large squall was sweeping across the sea and the *Heron* was lost from sight.

READ ON FOR A PREVIEW OF BOOK 2

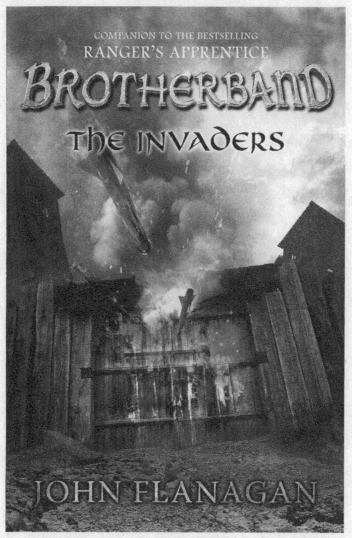

COMPANION TO THE BESTSELLING
RANGER'S APPRENTICE

BROTHERBAND
THE INVADERS

JOHN FLANAGAN

CHAPTER ONE

'We can't keep this up,' Stig said.

Hal looked at him, eyes red-rimmed from salt water and exhaustion. He'd been at the tiller of the *Heron* for the best part of ten days now. The storm winds had continued to sweep out of the south-west throughout that time, keeping them on a constant starboard tack – which was all to the good, as there had been no opportunity to repair the yardarm broken in the final brotherband race.

As first mate, Stig had tried to give Hal short breaks whenever he could. But the wind-driven waves had grown so high and steep that they were regularly breaking over the small ship and flooding her. Everyone on the crew was forced to bail continuously. They worked in teams of four, an hour on, an hour off. When a team's shift was over, the boys would fall, soaked and exhausted, to the deck, trying to snatch a few minutes' sleep, heedless of the freezing seawater constantly smashing over them. So Stig hadn't had much time to help Hal – not that Hal liked to hand over control. He felt the responsibility for the safety of his ship and crew deeply.

Stig glanced doubtfully back over the wake the *Heron* was carving. There was no pursuit in sight. But they'd be there somewhere.

'D'you think we're far enough away from Hallasholm now?' he asked.

In the hope of recovering the Andomal, Skandia's most sacred artefact, the boys had left the Skandian capital against the orders of the Oberjarl, Erak Starfollower. And they'd taken Hal's ship, *Heron*, which Erak had planned to confiscate. The boys were in no doubt that Erak would order a pursuit and, if they were caught, Stig didn't like to think what their punishment might be.

'I don't want to risk them catching us,' Hal said.

Stig shrugged, and looked at the angry seas around them.

'They won't catch us if we sink,' he said. 'But that won't do us a lot of good.'

'True,' Hal said. 'They may not have even left harbour yet. This storm's been blowing nonstop since we got away.'

Whether they were being pursued or not, it was definitely time to look for a safe anchorage. Hal sensed that the wind had increased in force in the past half hour. There was white spray being blown from the top of the waves. He gestured for the bigger boy to take the tiller, then ducked under the canvas screen into the small sheltered nook in the stern of the ship where he kept his navigation equipment and notes — notes he had assiduously collected during the brotherband training period.

He studied the chart for the eastern coast of the Stormwhite for some minutes before he found what he wanted. The majority of bays and coves along this coast faced south-west — almost directly into the wind and sea. But then he spotted a small, almost insignificant gap that cut into the coastline, with its entrance facing north and with high ground on the south-western side to provide shelter from the wind and sea. It looked an ideal place to set up a camp until the weather improved.

He carefully wrapped the notes in their waterproof oilcloth cover and ducked out into the open again. A breaking wave drenched him and set him spluttering. Then he grabbed hold of the backstay and climbed onto the stern bulwark, balancing easily against the ship's plunging motion, studying the coastline a few kilometres away.

There! He could make out one of the landmarks noted on the chart, a high headland, cliffs on either side, and denuded of trees. The dark granite rock was obvious against the grey-green of the pines that covered most of the coastline.

He dropped lightly to the deck and took the tiller once more. Thorn, sitting huddled in his soaked sheepskin jacket with his back to the mast, had noticed his movements. He came aft now to join the two boys.

'Thinking of putting in to shore?' he asked.

'There's a little sheltered bay about three kilometres south,' Hal said. 'I'm heading for that.'

Thorn nodded. Not that Hal, as skirl of the *Heron*, needed his approval in any way. A skirl, even a young one, had absolute authority on his own ship. But Hal was glad that Thorn agreed. It would be foolish to ignore his opinion. The old sea wolf had seen a lot more storms at sea than either Hal or Stig.

In the event, they very nearly missed the entrance to the bay. Visibility was bad, with the air full of flying spray and rain, and the small gap between the headlands guarding the entrance had a high, timbered hill directly behind it, making it look as if the coastline was uninterrupted. At the last moment, Thorn's keen eyesight noticed a flash of sandy beach in the gap as *Heron* rose on a wave. He threw out his shortened right arm, pointing with the wooden hook Hal had fashioned for him.

'There it is!'

Stig and Hal exchanged a quick glance. There was no need to give Stig orders. He scrambled forward, beckoning Stefan and Jesper to join him at the ropes holding the reefed sail taut against the wind. As Hal brought the ship round to port, so that the wind was coming from astern, the three crew members eased the sail so that it stood out almost at right angles to the hull.

Heron, with the wind and sea now behind her, began to swoop over the rollers like a gull. It was an exhilarating sensation but Hal kept a watchful eye astern for rogue waves. If one came at them harder and faster than the others, the ship could easily be swamped from behind. There was no relaxing in this sort of weather.

After several minutes, he saw Thorn glance at him in an unspoken question and he nodded. They'd come close enough to the coast now to swing back to a course that would take them into the bay. As he heaved on the tiller and brought the bow round to starboard, Stig and the other two hauled in on the sail, setting it taut to the wind. The motion of the ship changed again, going from surging and swooping ahead of the wind back to the rolling, shuddering impacts of the waves coming from the beam. Hal glanced ahead and gauged his leeway — the amount the wind was setting the ship downwind and off course. He adjusted the ship's heading until he could see that he'd clear the entrance to the bay easily.

They glided into the bay. As the high surrounding cliffs masked the wind and waves, the *Heron* rode more upright, cutting smoothly through the calm waters. The boys relaxed as the motion eased. They sprawled on the rowing benches, setting aside the buckets they had been using to bail the water out. Only now, looking at them, did Hal realise how close they had been to utter exhaustion. He'd decided to look for shelter not a minute too soon, he reflected.

At the bottom of the bay was a strip of sandy beach, with wooded hills rising behind it. Hal pointed the bow towards it and the *Heron* responded, the bow wave chuckling down the hull, audible now that the noise of the storm had abated.

'Welcome to Shelter Bay,' he said to Stig.

'Is that what it's called?'

Hal gave him a tired grin. 'It is now.'

Initially, they slept aboard the beached ship, with its heavy tarpaulin cover rigged as a tent to protect them from the weather. They had spent the previous ten days bracing themselves against the wild movements of the *Heron*, even when they slept. It was a welcome change to be able to relax completely, without having to subconsciously guard against a sudden lurch or roll that might pitch them against the hard timbers of the hull. But by the second morning, they set to work constructing a more permanent shelter, similar to the framed tent they had built for their brotherband training.

When they had retrieved their weapons and personal belongings from their brotherband camp site, Stig had experienced a flash of inspiration. He had stripped the canvas cover they had used as a roof and bundled it up, stowing it aboard the *Heron*.

'Never know when it might come in handy,' he'd said.

Now, Hal and the others appreciated his foresight. They cut and trimmed saplings from the forest to make wall and roof frames, then stretched the canvas tightly over the top to make a snug roof. The walls were lower than their original tent but the pitched roof gave them ample headroom inside. Mud-daubed woven side walls did a reasonable job keeping out the worst of the weather, although invariably there were chinks that let in the keening wind when it hit full power. But they were young and a few draughts weren't enough to dampen their spirits.

Thorn chose to sleep on the boat. With the others quartered in their tent, he had plenty of room to himself. The others respected his desire for privacy. He had spent many years alone and he had become accustomed to keeping his own company. Besides, even though he liked the *Heron* crew, they were teenage boys, with the usual tendencies of that breed to squabble, talk loudly and tell jokes they thought were brand new, unaware that generations of boys before them had told the very same tales.

Once their sleeping quarters were organised, Hal, assisted by the ever-helpful Ingvar, built a small shelter to use as a workshop. Then he and Ingvar and Stig went into the forest to select a sapling to replace the broken yardarm. After several hours, Hal found one to his liking and gestured to Stig.

'Cut it down.'

Ingvar carried the sapling back to the camp, where they stripped off the bark and left the sapling to dry for a few days, removing the surface sap. Then Hal cut and trimmed it to shape and they attached the port sail. Only then did Hal feel a sense of relief. Being ashore with a half-crippled ship had been preying on his mind, he realised. Now the *Heron* was fully ready for sea in case of any emergency.

He set up a roster for camp chores, with each boy taking a turn at cooking. This didn't last long. After successive meals prepared by Stig, Ulf and Wulf, Edvin had put his foot down.

'I didn't come on this quest to die of food poisoning,' he said acerbically. 'I'll do the cooking from now on.'

And since he had already demonstrated some skill in this area, the others were glad to leave the task to him. In turn, Hal relieved him of other camp duties, such as wood and water gathering. After a few days, Edvin sought Hal out with a further request.

'We've got plenty of dried foods and provisions,' he said. 'But we could use fresh meat and fish.'

The bay was teeming with fish and Stig and Stefan were both keen anglers. They undertook to keep a steady supply of bream and flounder coming. Hal and Jesper went into the woods in search of small game. Once again, Ingvar went along as Hal's faithful shadow. Unfortunately, he was a good bit noisier than a shadow, blundering through and into the trees, stepping carelessly on deadfalls. So while the two hunters saw plenty of evidence of small game — rabbits, hares and game birds — they saw none of the actual creatures themselves. Eventually, Hal had to put his hand on the huge boy's arm and stop him.

'I'm sorry, Ingvar, but you're making too much noise.'

'I'm not doing it on purpose,' Ingvar said.

The young skirl nodded. 'I know. But you're scaring all the game away. I want you to sit here and wait for us, all right?'

Ingvar was disappointed. Since he had joined Hal's crew, he had felt a new sense of worth and purpose. In his short life before this, nobody had ever looked to him to contribute, or expected much of him. But as a member of the Heron brotherband, he had participated in their success and their victory over the other teams. Hal had been the first person to expect anything of Ingvar and Ingvar hated to feel that he was letting his skirl down — although, deep down, he knew Hal was right. He was too clumsy and noisy to help with the hunting. But now that all the heavy work of building was finished, he had nothing to do.

'All right, Hal. If you say so.' He lowered himself to the ground, leaning back against the bole of a tree. Hal saw the disappointment on his face.

'Ingvar, don't worry. I've got a job in mind for you. And you'll be the only one who can do it. Just be patient.'

Leaving Ingvar a little mollified, Hal and Jesper continued further into the woods. Almost immediately, Ingvar's absence bore fruit. They hadn't gone fifty metres before they saw a plump rabbit, nibbling at the moss on the base of a fallen log on the far side of a large clearing.

Jesper put his hand on Hal's arm and pointed. Carefully, Hal unslung his crossbow. Putting his foot in the stirrup, he drew the heavy cord back with both hands until the retaining latch clicked into place.

The rabbit looked up warily at the sound and both boys froze. The fat little animal's nose quivered as it tested the air, and its long ears swivelled back and forth, searching for any further foreign sound. By sheer chance, they had come upon it from a downwind direction. They waited, holding their breaths, until the animal satisfied itself that it was safe to continue grazing.

Hal slowly raised the crossbow to his shoulder. He flipped up the rear sight. They were less than twenty metres from the rabbit, so it would be a flat shot, with no elevation necessary. He set the bottom mark on the sight against the foresight pin, let out his breath, took in half a breath and held it.

Then squeezed the release.

There was the usual ugly CRACK as the bow's limbs snapped forward and the bolt streaked away across the clearing.

'I got him!' Hal said triumphantly. He dashed across the clearing, Jesper following a little more slowly.

'You certainly did,' Jesper said dryly as he caught up with the triumphant shooter. 'The question is, where is he?'

The heavy, iron-tipped crossbow bolt, designed to penetrate chain mail, had totally demolished the rabbit. The crossbow might be a useful weapon in a battle. But for hunting small game, it was sadly deficient.

'Maybe we should build some snares,' Jesper said.